Praise for

APRIL ON PARIS STREET

A lush, gripping and satisfying read, full of humour, with a mystery as shadowy and twisty as someone at a masked ball packing heat. The scrumptious mise en scene creates so lush a feel of Montreal and Paris that it is positively edible, and the utterly winning Ashley negotiates her way through this geography like a combination of razor sharp, clear thinking Wonder Woman and slightly vulnerable millennial who can knock the socks off an unexpected little black dress, but can't quite read her boyfriends and hasn't figured out boundaries around her family and friends—or fostering cats.
 —IONA WHISHAW, award-winning author of the
  Lane Winslow mystery series

Exuberant, idiosyncratic, and smartly irreverent, *April on Paris Street* —from the deft pen of Ms. Dowdall—is a delectable romp you won't be able to put down.
 —GUGLIELMO D'IZZIA, award-winning author of *The Transaction*

This clever and inviting novel by Anna Dowdall, third in the Ashley Smeeton series, is brimming with mystery and intrigue. With its vivid characters, evocative setting, and numerous twists and turns, *April on Paris Street* is a captivating read from start to finish. A great book to curl up with on a cold winter's eve.
 —SHARON HART-GREEN, author of *Come Back for Me: A Novel*

A rollicking cross-genre mystery, featuring smart and irreverent private investigator Ashley Smeeton, as she unwinds a bird's nest of a case. Bubbling with quirky, funny and dangerous characters ...
  —DENIS COUPAL, Arthur Ellis Prize finalist and author of *Blindshot*

A mad romp through the streets of Paris and unrelenting tension are controlled by a deft and confident hand. Humour and a bittersweet grasp of humanity produce a gripping tale of survival and forgiveness.
  —SHEILA KINDELLAN-SHEEHAN, author of *The Gang of Four*

Praise for
ANNA DOWDALL'S PREVIOUS NOVELS

A nicely complicated, sinister plot, a gothic setting, romantic entanglements and some ambiguous characters ...
— JOAN BARFOOT, Giller Prize and Man Booker Prize nominee,
   on *After the Winter*

[*The Au Pair*] ... offers a resourceful heroine, atmospheric settings, and well-plotted suspense. First introduced in *After the Winter*, Ashley is a likable heroine whose inquisitive nature helps her navigate the complicated dynamics of the Sampson family ... The storytelling is strong and confident. This instalment should appeal to fans of Louise Penny. A well-drafted Gothic suspense story with an engaging heroine ...
— KIRKUS REVIEWS, on *The Au Pair*

A welcome dash of simmering noir in [these] well-received books ... The sharply drawn scenes of Montreal and the surrounding Quebec countryside and detailed attention to the weather (the author is Canadian after all) are a refreshing change ...
— THE THRILLING DETECTIVE WEBSITE

MIROLAND IMPRINT 31

ONTARIO ARTS COUNCIL
CONSEIL DES ARTS DE L'ONTARIO

an Ontario government agency
un organisme du gouvernement de l'Ontario

Canada

Guernica Editions Inc. acknowledges the support of the Canada Council
for the Arts and the Ontario Arts Council. The Ontario Arts Council
is an agency of the Government of Ontario.

We acknowledge the financial support of the Government of Canada.

a mystery in two cities

APRIL ON PARIS STREET

Anna Dowdall

GUERNICA
EDITIONS
TORONTO • CHICAGO • BUFFALO • LANCASTER (U.K.)
2021

Please note: While there is an actual *rue de Paris* in the Montreal district of
Pointe-Saint-Charles, everything else in this novel is fiction.

Connie McParland, series editor
Julie Roorda, editor
David Moratto, cover and interior design
Guernica Editions Inc.
287 Templemead Drive, Hamilton, ON L8W 2W4
2250 Military Road, Tonawanda, N.Y. 14150-6000 U.S.A.
www.guernicaeditions.com

Distributors:
Independent Publishers Group (IPG)
600 North Pulaski Road, Chicago IL 60624
University of Toronto Press Distribution (UTP)
5201 Dufferin Street, Toronto (ON), Canada M3H 5T8
Gazelle Book Services, White Cross Mills
High Town, Lancaster LA1 4XS U.K.

First edition.
Printed in Canada.

Legal Deposit—Third Quarter
Library of Congress Catalog Card Number: 2021933083
Library and Archives Canada Cataloguing in Publication
Title: April on Paris Street / Anna Dowdall.
Names: Dowdall, Anna, author.
Identifiers: Canadiana (print) 20210141492 |
Canadiana (ebook) 20210141522 | ISBN 9781771836234 (softcover) |
ISBN 9781771836241 (EPUB) | ISBN 9781771836258 (Kindle)
Classification: LCC PS8607.O98738 A77 2021 | DDC C813/.6—dc23

For my dear cousin Robert,
who insists on reading my books

CONTENTS

PROLOGUE 1

1 FAULTLINES 5
2 THE PLACES IN BETWEEN 20
3 SHE ALWAYS KNEW YOUR NAME 35
4 THE CITY OF LIGHTS 53
5 WELL-MADE PLAY 70
6 FIRE AND ICE 83
7 BETWEEN DOG AND WOLF 94
8 MASQUERADE 108
9 GIRL ON FIRE 125
10 STORM 139
11 LA BÊTE HUMAINE 149
12 LADIES ON A TRAIN 164
13 SHOW ME A SIGN 180
14 BEAU DOMMAGE 191
15 DIVERSIONS 207
16 HARBINGER 229
17 DARK UNFAMILIAR STREETS 245
18 THE NIGHT IN QUESTION 259
19 THE CHILDREN OF LUCIFER 276
20 IF THEY SAY I NEVER LOVED YOU . . . 297

EPILOGUE 305

ACKNOWLEDGEMENTS 317
ABOUT THE AUTHOR 319

PROLOGUE

F OR A DARK day in late October, Ashley admitted, Pointe-Saint-
Charles was satisfactorily eerie.

Hemmed in by elevated expressways, obsolete canals and
the Saint Lawrence, bisected by tracks and maintenance yards, the
Point was a silent maze of streets. Little of its ancient New France
past survived. The factory shells, workers' cottages and two-storey
flats were from the nineteenth century. And still time kept pace
with the river, bringing gentrification and its discontents. Ashley
couldn't help but admire the bijou renovations, with their lilac paint
and curated jack-o-lanterns. At the moment, though, she was preoccupied with rents.

Unless you counted oxidizing aluminum windows or a *faux*
stone front circa 1960, modest rue de Paris had resisted gentrification. Stoops sagged, the municipal plantings were stunted, and iron
stairs squeezed up against the narrow sidewalk. In the blurred
atmosphere and dim light, the street had a charm of its own.

In the five minutes during which Ashley had been cooling her
heels on the pavement, the only sign of life was an old man cycling
by on a one-speed delivery bicycle.

Aram, when he emerged from the house next door, looked
about twenty. A community college student, he explained he'd been

asked by his working parents to show Ashley the *logement à louer*. It was a great flat, he said. They'd painted it, put in new copper wiring, and with the owners next door she wouldn't want for anything. It had been vacant for a few months, he conceded, leading her up the circular stair to the second floor. It was just that the layout didn't work for everyone.

Once she was through the front door, Ashley could see why. You stepped into either a too large foyer or an inadequately private living room. But the visibility was just right for an office. Its two tall windows struck a refined yet business-like note, and there was plenty of room for her needs. Draughty in Montreal's brutal winters? All the better to send clients promptly on their way.

Aram led her across a passage to an elongated boxcar room.

"If you ever need a secret way into the kitchen," he said, opening a two-foot wide wallpapered door in a corner.

Ashley laughed. "That's handy."

The appeal of the sly second exit was undeniable. Another tall window here overlooked the street. The narrowness made this room snug, den-like, something she liked in a living room.

The kitchen and bathroom were roomy, old-fashioned. The main bedroom, which took up the back width of the flat, was another pleasant surprise. It had its own balcony, as Perez had said when he'd told her about this rental, with another iron staircase leading down. A weed tree's yellowing canopy leaned near and the spiral stair seemed to descend into the heart of the tree. It was like being in a tree house.

They talked terms. There was dedicated parking out back for her Crown Victoria Interceptor and the subway was close. The rent Aram mentioned hadn't unduly shocked. Its potential was obvious. Honestly, why hesitate?

She wandered back to the bedroom, Aram in tow. For the briefest moment she imagined herself and Jon—sometimes she remembered him that way, sometimes as the Perez guy—entwined on a king mattress on the floor. Perhaps looking out over the moving leaves that gave the room its fitful ochre light.

Jon Perez. She'd met him last summer, during that strange job in the Laurentians. She hadn't seen him since and she didn't expect to: He was probably back in Colombia now. But Ashley had no regrets. It was what people more romantically versed than her, more in the know, called an interlude. That he'd mentioned this vacant flat in a stray comment about shacking up was neither here nor there. Pure coincidence to find herself here, now that she needed new digs.

She and Aram chitchatted some more. He liked computers but was studying political science, to the despair of his parents who didn't think this was practical. He was enthralled when she offered her card: *Ashley Arabella Smeeton, Licensed Private Investigator.* This was a career he'd never thought of, maybe he should. They agreed, all smiles, that renting the apartment looked promising. She would ring this evening.

While they'd been inside, the weather had changed. A wind had risen abruptly and the sky was now stormy.

"How did you hear about the rental?" Aram zipped his hoody as he followed Ashley down the winding stair. A fierce gust loosed volleys of dead leaves along the street and threw dust and grit into Ashley's eyes. Her good mood sagged a little.

"Oh, I saw the ad," she said. "Rue de Paris. I wonder how it got its name."

Aram said he didn't have a clue. Maybe it pointed towards Paris. For himself, he'd never been out of Canada.

"Have you ever been to Paris?" he inquired.

"Never, no." Ashley pursued the departing dust devil with frowning gaze.

Now she felt only restlessness. Perhaps, she thought, the time had come to do something about that.

1

FAULTLINES

"WE WERE TWO against the world. And then we weren't." Chantale Barry carried her ashtray around with her. So she had no problem lighting up in Ashley's kitchen. How she'd got past the office to the kitchen was more of the same. Did she have a case? Did she ever have a case, she assured Ashley, removing a shred of tobacco from her lip. But she threw herself into a lurid description of the situation as befits next-door neighbours.

"Where's Marie Ambre?" Ashley spoke in what she hoped was a neutral tone. The tea sloshed as she placed the cup in front of Chantale.

A passing gratitude illuminated Chantale's face, but had no effect on the full spate of her speech. *"Parfait, merci! T'es tellement gentille, Ashley."* Ashley felt a twinge of guilt. "Marie Ambre? She's over at Ibrahim's house."

The Idrises were Ashley Smeeton's neighbours on the other side, as well as her landlords. Chantale sounded a little vague, considering Marie Ambre was five. But it was that kind of neighbourhood, and quiet rue de Paris was that kind of street. Marie Ambre and Ibrahim, an older gentleman of six, had been going steady lately, and were invariably together somewhere.

"When I said case, Chantale," Ashley said, "I meant the kind of case a private investigator like me would pick up. When you need to know something. So Dominique Taillon owes you money for rent and bills, a loan. You know where she is now?"

"Sure." Chantale shrugged. "She moved out to the east end."

"Like where?" Ashley offered a few districts at random. "Hochelaga? Rosemont? Anjou?" Just names—places practically unknown to her as an English-speaking Montrealer.

"No, the *east* east end." Chantale's voice dipped as she named this mythical place. A member of the Pointe-Saint-Charles Barry clan going back generations, despite her French mother she could probably count on the fingers of one hand the times she'd been east of rue Saint Denis. With fingers left over.

"You know where—good. Because you'd have to serve her papers. Your logical next step would be to sue her in small claims court."

Chantale looked distinctly shocked at this wild sort of talk.

"Well, I'm just saying. A private eye finds evidence but, from what you're saying, you already have the evidence. There's nothing, really, for me to do."

Ashley knew that Dominique had been Chantale's roommate, friend. And possibly her lover—it was hard to say otherwise where the sense of acute betrayal was coming from. Perhaps from the depths of Chantale's hard life. Ashley placed a package of Whippets on the table, shoving aside a venerable Montreal daily now offered free at her morning coffee spot.

Chantale's attention strayed to the newspaper headline and she changed tack. "I don't even know what's happening anymore in Montreal." She was reaching for another cigarette when Ashley said quickly: "Could you hold off, Chantale? The fan isn't working." But she could see why Chantale had reached for a smoke.

"CITY THREAT LEVEL: HIGH!" the headline shouted, quoting some law enforcement bigwig. With a surfeit of work on her plate, Ashley had only skimmed the article. Threats from radical Islam, threats from white supremacists and their organized crime bedfellows, or was it from some kind of born-again lunatic fringe nationalist underground—she hadn't honestly taken it in. Complicated even further by ideological game-playing among the levels of government. The pundits in the story contradicted each other as well.

Chantale was reading the article aloud. Citizens must remain vigilant—but calm. At all times you were supposed to exercise caution—but reasonably. She gave melodramatic conviction to phrases like "known intentions," "potential attacks" and "imminent danger." The words did linger in the imagination. Especially after last month's deadly car bombing in Saint Léonard. Followed by those police raids farther east.

"We live in troubled times," Ashley murmured. Fatuous words, although useful to trot out in the current climate. She finished her tea thoughtfully. Montreal had been stirred up lately. It was a mood, not a tangible thing you could put your finger on. This kind of news story didn't help. It all seemed unreal, though. Immensely remote from the sleepy Point. Like a story about another Montreal —the mythical east end maybe.

Chantale's fearful credulous face, as she muttered about "*les Musulmans*," somehow increased Ashley's scepticism. She remembered her friend Nico's cynical joke about the terrorist threat level going up when politicians needed more money. Nicolas Latendresse was a highly-placed Montreal cop, surely he would know. Of course, he and his police officer wife happened to be down in Washington DC at the moment, on some urban terrorism task force thing—but didn't even that sound like an exercise in bureaucracy?

Ashley heaved a sigh. She had work to do. "Let me think about it, Chantale—but honestly, maybe you should forget about Dominique." She gathered the mugs.

"I'll never forget Dominique," the other said. The words were so calm, so final, that Ashley was taken aback.

"Hi! The door was open."

Aram Idris appeared in the kitchen doorway with his characteristic smile. His little brother Ibrahim trailed after him, engaged in conversation with Marie Ambre who, encumbered by an occupied bird cage, brought up the rear.

"Marie Ambre was looking for her mom," Aram said.

Ashley thought this was likely somewhat true—although Aram had been hinting about working for Ashley and found excuses to interface as one future colleague to another.

Chantale was looking alarmed. "Marie Ambre! Why are you out with Stanley? He needs to stay indoors until his wing is healed. He can't get excited." Everyone stared at the starling, and the starling stared alertly back.

"He wanted to go for a walk," the little girl said. "With me and Ibrahim." A pause. "Ibrahim asked me to marry him." She developed a conscious look. "I said yes." Into the silence, Ashley cautiously tendered congratulations. Ibrahim licked his lips.

"That's nice," Chantale said in an absent-minded way. "But Ashley's about to blow a fuse so let's get out of her hair. You guys can feed Stanley while you tell me about your wedding plans. And we can look at Ralph the squirrel."

The Barry household had a rotating collection of strays and rescue animals, that all did surprisingly well under the care of Chantale, known by name at the urban wildlife rescue centre.

Ashley went ahead with the Whippets box to entice the visitors in the right direction.

"Sure, thanks Ashley," Chantale said, "but you know what they're like with those cookies. They'll just eat the chocolate from the outside and then leave the half-chewed bits of marshmallow on the furniture somewhere ..." A metallic clatter. "Marie—you give me that thing!"

Marie Ambre had very nearly dropped the cage. Ibrahim offered husbandly advice and Stanley contributed his thoughts in Barry-like tones.

Aram was disposed to linger. "You want me to look at your computer, install that software?"

"Yes—no. I do. Later. I've got calls to return."

Ashley finally got the lot of them out the door, but not before a blast of frosty late November air flooded the room. She took the precaution of bolting the door, and went in search of her phone.

* * *

This walk-in arrangement she had, with a discreet brass plaque by the door, encouraged its share of frivolous custom, Ashley reflected as she sat back in her desk chair and surveyed the office with approval. She'd moved to her new digs in the Point a little over a year ago, and had never regretted the change. A lot of her PI work involved electronic communication on the fly with clients while driving around the city in her police auction Interceptor, but she still thought of the office as the spiritual base of her operations. This old-fashioned front room, with its bookcases, desk and seating area, its tall stained glass windows, felt just right. The rest of the flat suited her too. She'd even come to think of the mint green wringer washer, a non-working fixture in the kitchen because Aram's mother was fond of it, as a conversation piece.

Ashley stretched her long legs and put her booted feet up on her desk as she checked the weather. Big surprise—snow was on the way. She wondered whether she'd be able to take time off during the approaching holidays, beyond a quick trip to Waverley to see her mother and brother. Her workload was heavy. She was still building her practice and never felt she could turn down jobs, as a flood of work could dry up in a flash. Aram, a computer junkie, had helped her once or twice as a friend, and she'd been thinking about carving out a steady role for him. IT support, for instance. The job she'd handled last month for an investigative journalist had brought her to the limits of her technological capabilities. As had the substantial fraud research Maritime Insurance had recently thrown her way.

She settled back comfortably. It was surely a testament to her growing reputation that this technically exacting work was coming to her already, and she not out of her twenties. It was hard not to feel even a teensy bit smug. And these jobs were right up her alley. She got her share of heartbreak cases too, suspicious Party A of the first part wanting the dirt on cheating Party B of the second part. The dirt that would bring them to their knees when they got it. This messy work was lucrative and Ashley accepted it, but she accepted it cautiously, almost with unease. That these cases seemed to pursue her was just one of those things.

She made her way briskly through her messages. All predictable and easily dealt with, until she came to a message from an individual who identified himself as Robert Aird, private secretary—how posh—to the poshly named Monsieur Charles Saint Cyr. He was calling on Saint Cyr's behalf. Monsieur Saint Cyr wanted to speak to Ms. Smeeton on a confidential matter. She was to call his confidential line—number provided—at her earliest convenience. However, he would be available to speak with her at two pm today if convenient. The matter, Aird reiterated, was delicate—confidential.

It was now twenty minutes past two. Ashley decided she'd better *carpe diem*, although really she'd have liked to mumble around in her brain for a bit the vibe of all those confidentials.

Charles Saint Cyr's voice at the other end was neutral, cultivated. Mrs. Marigold Dreyfus had given her a glowing recommendation for discretion, he began by saying. Ashley remembered last spring's client, and where wildly indiscreet Marigold's strange hobby of luxury car smuggling had taken them. He was interested in retaining Ashley's services. It was about his wife—he said "young wife"—and the matter was sensitive. He seemed no more willing than Robert Aird to come right out with the thing. Just as she was opening her mouth to propose a face to face meeting, he said: "Ms. Smeeton,

I've sprained my ankle and I'm temporarily incapacitated. Would you drop by my home?"

While Ashley hesitated, he said: "I have offices here, I conduct some business at home. Robert and other staff are here." He gave an address that Ashley realized was an exclusive circle amid the upper crags of Westmount. "The matter is better discussed in person."

Ashley's curiosity had by then bloomed into sturdy life. "Yes, it sounds like it." *From the number of confidentials. And the young wife.*

They arranged a date for the following morning and disconnected. Ashley retrieved the box of Whippets and plunged zestfully into an online quest for information on this Charles Saint Cyr. She wasn't disappointed. Although she'd never heard of him, Charles Saint Cyr was a big noise around the city. He was the head of the Montreal-based Holopherne Incorporée, that seemed to manufacture and sell women's clothes all over the world. He was socially prominent as well, judging from the number of high society photos he appeared in, at events like the museum Arts and Crafts Ball. He was a dark-haired man with a soigné beard, with tall good looks to spare. Middle-aged, but, as her Gran used to say, well-preserved. She imagined how his prominence would lead to a preoccupation with confidentiality.

She had a harder time finding out about the youthful Madame Saint Cyr, but then came across a two-year-old photograph of a small wedding group on the snow-crusted steps of Saint Patrick's Basilica. It was an impromptu distance shot—as if there weren't supposed to be photographers there at all—and it wasn't easy to make out the bride. But the elegant set, under a filmy scarf, of a coiffed blonde head on graceful shoulders gave Ashley the impression of a very attractive woman. Mirabel *née* Duval, the caption read. She had a modest online presence: a few society photographs, a reference to that name in a list of graduates from somewhere called Collège Marie des Anges in Lausanne, a private Facebook page.

Ashley returned to the wedding picture. It didn't look like any wedding photograph she'd seen. Maybe it was the leafless branches of the trees, or the steepness of the steps up to the Gothic Revival church marooned on its hillock. Or maybe it was the way those graceful shoulders were lifted, as if the photographer had caught Mirabel in the act of ducking, captured an instinctive urge to hide, or to escape.

* * *

Ashley parked at the Westmount lookout, planning to walk the rest of the way to the Saint Cyr residence. Google Maps hadn't prepared her for the wildness of the very top of Westmount, where Montreal's richest citizens dwelled in seclusion and splendour. The road twisted and turned vertiginously, and the single file sidewalk was squeezed against exposed rock, retaining walls and tangled undergrowth. Amid the bare treetops Ashley could see big old houses, that would have been hidden by leaves in summer. It was a cold and sunny morning, and the air was sharp and fresh, a mix of soil, dying vegetation and coming winter.

Number 12, Belgrave Heights was a sprawling grey stone house that was too old and much too well-designed to be a McMansion. It was also beautifully situated, in an artful clearing on a relatively modest treed lot. From the pavement, Ashley was able to see beyond the house to another version of the lookout view, only higher, rarer, better. Beyond the broad sweep of the island city, the faraway river lay flat as a knife blade. She could see all the way to the two extinct volcanoes that marked the southern horizon. The house itself, freshly trimmed in white and with sparkling windows, preened in the sunshine.

Ashley caught a glimpse of herself in the glass as she pressed the bell. She'd taken longer than usual over her appearance, and hoped that the plain belted coat, open over dark jeans, struck the right note. Her luxuriant wavy black hair was tied into a low pony tail and, holding nothing back, she'd applied some of her now rare because tragically discontinued Bonne Bell Treacle Tart lip gloss. For Ashley, this was going all out. She'd never been much of an eye makeup person, but then very few people had Ashley's wide tilted sloe eyes, inherited from her Abenaki father.

Robert Aird, a neutral-looking man in his late thirties, opened the door right away. Ashley repressed the thought that he'd been lurking behind the curtain. His thin smile held scrutiny. He led her through an impressive foyer and along a broad shaded passage that went on and on. The house was bigger than it appeared. It was all hushed space and measured elegance, priceless furnishings, with a whiff of beeswax and hothouse flowers.

Charles Saint Cyr's at-home office was a magnificent modern room with a southern view. Limping slightly, Saint Cyr led her to an arrangement of armchairs, offering her coffee, which she declined. Ashley gave him a quick once-over. He was very like his picture, tall, darkly saturnine, beautifully turned out. In person she got an additional sense of the man: his dominant personality, a calculating intelligence. This upped his attractiveness, undoubtedly. Your basic one percenter, she decided, with maybe more of an artistic flair than most, due no doubt to his work. She commented briefly on the view as she got out her notebook. He smiled acquiescence and said: "I know you'd like to get down to business. Let me be candid."

His young wife—Belle, he called her—was in Paris, and showed no sign of coming home any time soon. This was the problem. She'd gone there to take in the fall fashion shows, with the idea that it would help with an anticipated role at Holopherne. A meandering and allusive explanation followed: Belle had only recently become his bride, the challenge of taking on the quasi-public role as his wife couldn't be overestimated, she was, of course, young and there was an absence of *formation professionelle*. "They" were exploring the possibility of a role for her in the organization; evidently "they" would have to see what could be done. What was suitable for now. Ashley, parsing this as well as the arrogant body language, speculated that he hadn't managed to knock her up yet and in the meantime he was humouring her "aspirations." And yet, there was always more. For instance, Saint Cyr seemed genuinely anxious, and was making a visible effort to hide it.

The fall shows were long over, he said. And still she stayed on, giving her husband no clear picture of her plans.

By this stage Ashley had caught sight out of a framed photograph on the desk of a woman she recognized as Mirabel. She derived an impression of a finely modelled face and a vague, almost faraway, air. Yet there was a vividness there too.

"Do you know Madame Saint Cyr's current location?"

"I do." Saint Cyr named a Parisian street that meant nothing to Ashley. "It's near the medieval quarter, by the Seine. She's taken an *appartement* on a short lease."

"Are you in touch with her by phone?"

He took longer to answer this. "Yes—yes. But she's asked me not to call her, or not to call her often."

"Have you asked her point blank when she's coming home?"

"Oh, yes. But she won't say."

Ashley frowned. "Hm. But I'm getting ahead of myself. I should really have started by asking you exactly what you want from me."

"To go to Paris and come back with Belle." He cleared his throat. "But first, to report back to me, on what she's doing. And with whom."

Off with the gloves at last.

"You think she's seeing someone in Paris?"

"Without doubt."

"Why don't you go over there and see for yourself?"

He hesitated. "She's told me to stay away. Belle can be—for a very agreeable young woman, Belle can be very stubborn. I could go to Paris any time, but it might make matters worse."

Ashley pondered this. "And Madame Saint Cyr wouldn't mind me showing up as your representative?"

"To begin with, I'd want a covert report." Saint Cyr spoke calmly, although there was a cold glitter in his eye. "Bringing Belle home would be the next stage."

Ashley's eyebrows rose. "So you said. With her agreement, evidently."

"Evidently. Look—I'm trying to understand what's happened to Belle. This isn't at all like her. It can't simply be boredom, there's a wealth of things to occupy her time." Saint Cyr looked vaguely at a bowl of roses on a cabinet, as if doing the flowers had been part of these *très riches heures*. "I want her to be all right. I want her back with me. I want everything as it was before."

Saint Cyr's voice was carefully modulated, like an actor's. He was deliberately presenting himself as the reasonable husband. Now he became philosophical, almost sentimental, perhaps also for Ashley's sake. He spoke of love, quoted a poet.

To move off poetry, she brought up terms. They discussed the business end of things for the next five minutes. Saint Cyr wanted her to go to Paris as soon as possible, certainly before Christmas, and his highly satisfactory offer to treble her rate, with every conceivable expense allowed, was nothing if not generous.

But there was more than that to think about. On the face of things, this was a Party A wanting the goods on Party B kind of job, in Paris, with Party A being a rich and powerful man. On another level, Ashley wasn't at all sure. The reporting stage, if occasionally sordid, was predictable. It was Saint Cyr's nebulous stage two that raised a flag. If a grown woman didn't want to leave Paris and return to her husband, Ashley didn't see where she as a private eye had a role to play.

She gathered her things. Now that she knew the scope of the job, she said, she needed to review her schedule. She would be in touch first thing tomorrow. His nod as he handed her over to Aird was aloof. Ashley couldn't help but admire the poker face, all the more so because she sensed what it concealed. Not that she doubted for a moment that the man was sincerely in love with his wife, this new young wife of his who was already leading him a merry dance in Paris.

What fools these mortals be, Ashley thought to herself on the street once more, not at all sure she was getting the quotation right and where the heck it came from anyway. Far above the factories and the various sprawling *arrondissements* where people waged the battle of life at its most basic, Westmount's air was pure and clean. And very welcome after that airless interview.

Ashley had a cautious little script prepared when she called Charles Saint Cyr the next day to turn down the job. It was a scheduling issue, she said. She just didn't have the time at the moment to take off for Europe for an indeterminate period. This was true, so far as it went. She need not have worried. Saint Cyr sounded unsurprised. What he wanted Ashley to do wasn't everyday. It was just that he was worried about Belle. And Marigold Dreyfus had said Ashley could make unusual problems go away. Ashley made modestly appreciative and regretful noises.

She'd thought about the job offer all evening. It wasn't just the bounty hunter impersonation she didn't like. She realized even the investigative component rubbed her the wrong way. Who knew what use Saint Cyr would make of the information? This wasn't a question she normally pondered, but then Saint Cyr wasn't your typical jealous husband.

"Let's at least stay in touch," he said at the end of the call. Her agreement was ready and casual. But it was several weeks before Ashley even thought again about Charles Saint Cyr, or of his dreaming vivid bride.

***

Ashley liked the holidays as much as the next person, and she had to admit rue de Paris celebrated the season with a homey verve. Around December first, as the snow tumbled obligingly down, residents put up lights. By some unspoken agreement, they were of the multi-coloured kind, and snow-clad spiral stairs and window frames sprang to life with old-fashioned cheer. The snow continued to fall. Marie Ambre, Ibrahim and a flock of other children appeared with toboggans and erected forts with even less regard than usual for the scant traffic.

The snow caused the inevitable problems for Ashley as she drove around, but, as a relentless reminder of Christmas, it may have been why she picked up a modest balsam fir at the Atwater Market. She plunked it in her office window. The naked tree was an excuse for Chantale to drop by and inquire into Ashley's decor plans, offering her surplus decorations. Thus the tree got its start, and one thing led to another. It was her official first tree. And it made her feel she was keeping her end up when an ancient festoon of lights appeared in the window of the older couple, the Plourdes, who lived downstairs.

She called her mother in Waverley to confirm that she'd be down no later than the twenty-fourth. Roy, his wife Lucie and their preschooler Lilou would be there as well, along with a pair of cousins of Lucie's visiting the big city from Alma. Ashley's mother Marlene had moved into her Gran's large house a little over a year ago, and there was plenty of room for everyone. This would be the second Christmas since her grandmother's death, and the memories had softened. It would be nice to see the old house on Elm Street so full.

A few evening trips downtown took care of Ashley's holiday shopping: books all round for Roy and his family, a luxurious sweater for her mother, that Marlene might or might not wear, some techy gadgets for the cousins-in-law she'd never met, and a miscellany of candy, fancy tea and the like to deal with eventualities.

She also bought half a dozen Beanie Babies since you never knew when they would come in handy. At least they were called Beanie Babies like the ones she'd had, although with their gigantic pupils they looked like they were on crack. As an afterthought she had a look at dresses. She'd been invited to a few parties. Nothing appealed and she ended up buying a finespun pullover with three-quarter sleeves, and a fitted black skirt that came down to the top of her knee. She supposed it was an outfit for the over-forty crowd, but the sweater tucked nicely into the stylish high waistband.

She put on a gruelling spurt of work and got two jobs out the door. One involved busting, in a stroke of accidental genius, a small Siamese theft ring and returning a few irate cats to their owners. Such cases, combined with Women's Lacrosse for Fun Week, where Ashley's recreational team played every comer every evening in a wild week designed to interest girls and women in the game of lacrosse, absorbed her attention and energy. If the city was still on edge, she was too busy to connect the dots. A headline here, a scare word there, but they didn't sink in. It was easy to tune out the bigger picture.

Chantale Barry had an open house for the neighbours one Saturday evening, attended by Aram and Ashley and some Paris Street residents she knew to say hi to. Also a lively crush of other guests, reminding Ashley of Chantale's deep roots in the Point. She brought wine, her new outfit attracted compliments, and she enjoyed feeling socially normal.

It was nice to see Chantale bedecked in silver sequins and looking happy, while Marie Ambre ran around with an assortment of children. Aram's mother and father, Québécoise Delphine and Kurdish Birkan, stopped in and they chatted for a time. Any party was of course appealing to Ashley for the opportunities it provided to people watch. A lot of the faces she saw still bore the signs of their Celtic heritage and Ashley marvelled at the ability of the Point to hang onto its identity.

Her attention was drawn in particular to a stranger who spoke from time to time with Chantale. A heavy-set young woman with a certain dash, with short sandy hair and restless, bright green eyes. It was only towards the end of the party that Aram whispered that the green-eyed woman was the notorious Dominique Taillon. By then Dominique had left, presumably to undertake her odyssey back to the east end. Her attendance was food for thought. The manner of the two women together—hardly warm, and yet deeply palsy-walsy—was also curious. Were Dominique's debts being discharged? Were they once more two against the world?

"She has remarkable eyes," Ashley commented to Aram.

"Ashley, come on, they're contact lenses. You really are above all that, aren't you?"

She was puzzled. "Above all what?"

Aram laughed genially. "Never mind. You look so nice tonight! Even France said so." France was Aram's fashionable fourteen-year-old sister, who had made a brief appearance.

Gatherings such as this, a party at the home of her old friends Tom and Sally Munro, and a jolly secular dinner *chez les Idris*, filled Ashley with unexpected seasonal cheer. More bling made its way onto her tree, and she went out and got her mother a supplementary gift of a huge basket of luxury bath products, the kind that mimicked other things—champagne, cake, cream, tropical fruit. Judging from the type of presents aimed at women, Ashley thought, you'd conclude they were the scruffiest people in the world. Or the hungriest.

2

THE PLACES IN BETWEEN

THE DISTRIBUTION of a few last minute Beanie Babies around the neighbourhood marked the completion of Ashley's to-do list. On December twenty-third she set out for Waverley, the back seat piled high with presents. She'd invested some of her recent earnings in her cherished classic Crown Victoria Interceptor, and the powerful motor purred as the car effortlessly ate up the miles through picture postcard countryside. Big dainty flakes began to sweep across the windshield and she speeded up slightly while looking for a radio station playing seasonal music, which was all of them.

Waverley, on the Abenaki River in the Eastern Townships of Quebec, was Ashley's childhood home. It had a regenerated downtown area, thanks to a recent massive ski resort development only an hour away. The town even had "suburbs" now—if tracts of jerry-built, chalet-like bungalows a short drive out of town could be called suburbs. The old core of Waverley had hung on to its period charm. As she drove through slush along Railway Street, Ashley recognized the Redbird Cafe, where her mother had once waited tables. Then she and the owner, Benny Tam, had gone into business together. Now Marlene Smeeton owned and managed the Seaton Valley Ski Resort's most celebrated restaurant. Ashley's father had died when she was a baby, but Marlene had worked hard and made a success of her life.

Her Gran's brick three-storey house was on the periphery of the Victorian town centre, and just down from the public library where Ashley, reading all the Nancy Drews she could lay her hands on, had made up her mind to become a detective years ago. The house looked spruce, thanks to some exterior work, and picturesque in its treed lot. Greetings were celebratory and effusive. Roy, Lucie and Lilou had just arrived from Fabienville, and Marlene had managed to steal a few hours from work. She'd put on a spread, and a chicken pot pie and several side dishes were arranged on the dining table. They all had a pleasant and noisy lunch together—the noise mainly contributed by Lilou, wired to snapping point with pre-Christmas excitement.

"You've done wonders with the downstairs, Ma," Ashley said. Marlene had renovated the kitchen and living room.

Lucie nodded vigorously. "When are you getting around to the top floors?" The second and third floors contained several bed-rooms and Marlene's widowed mother had once used these floors as an intermittent bed and breakfast. The attractive plaster mould-ing and wood trim were obscured under layers of paint and the floors sloped. The bathrooms were ancient. There was plenty of work to do upstairs.

"This room first," Marlene said, indicating the old-fashioned dining room. "I'll focus on restoring its period charm. Separate dining rooms are fashionable again."

Marlene kept looking at her watch, and Ashley knew she would have to hurry back to work soon. It was odd in a way that Marlene, a busy career woman in her fifties, had wanted to live in what had been her childhood home. The place was far too big for one person, and Waverley was an hour's drive from the Seaton Valley. With the kind of hours that Marlene worked, she'd be much better off with a sleek new condo in the resort village. It was unlikely that Roy and Lucie, who lived in the regional town of Fabienville down the highway, where Roy worked as a licensed mechanic and Lucie was training to be a teacher, would ever want to live here. Ashley certainly didn't. Marlene would make a nice bundle when and if she put the restored house on the market. But Ashley didn't think this was the reason her mother had decided to live in the house.

They discussed renovations, over Lilou's shrill interjections. Groans met the Vachon *bûche de Noël*, but wills proved feeble. Marlene had her coat on when she placed the coffee pot on the table and told everyone she had to head out. But they should kick back.

It was good to be home. And yet.

"Can I come with you, Ma?" Ashley suddenly felt that the afternoon would be a long one.

"And do what?" Her mother smiled. "Fill the salt cellars like you did at Benny's? You should take it easy." That had been one of Ashley's jobs, when she was little and hanging out at the restaurant under the nose of patient Benny.

While Lilou napped and Lucie studied, Roy and Ashley went for a meandering walk around town. Eventually their feet led them out of town along Route 9, and they turned on a whim up Old Route 9, crossed the bridge over the Etang des Abenakis, and followed the county road all the way to Midwinter. Midwinter was a striking old Second Empire house of yellow stone, standing on its own on a slope above the road. It marked the boundary beyond which none of the town's children, no matter how relaxed their mothers, were allowed to go. It had once been a private house on extensive lands. Now it was a corporate retreat, surrounded by a newish cedar hedge through which the rows of encircling chalets could hardly be seen.

"Remember when Ma worked here as a housekeeper?" Ashley asked. Roy had been a toddler and barely did.

There had been a few brief snow showers but now big flakes began to fall steadily. They made their way back along the secondary road, which was not nearly so traffic free as it had once been, and which actually had a sidewalk now.

"Remember when I found the body of Madame DuBois in the

lake right under here?" Ashley asked, when they stood on the bridge over the Etang des Abenakis. In a misty hollow and encircled by black trees, the bridge contrived to look as haunted as ever. Roy certainly didn't remember that.

"This was where Ignace Bérubé hung out, wasn't it?" He looked at his sister sideways.

"Well sure. I remember Ignace. Out among the trees. He's never going anyplace."

Roy shrugged mildly. "Why would he?" The comings and goings of the local ghost, a twelve-year-old Abenaki boy who had drowned in the lake in the nineteenth century, were inevitably subject to uncertainty.

Ashley had a brief thought about her dead father, and said: "Have you seen your dad?"

It was a relevant question. Roy's charismatic father had done hard time in a federal penitentiary, been repeatedly denied early release, but had recently been paroled.

Roy shook his head equably. "Nope."

"How come?"

"Well—for a start, he's my father in name only. But I guess the practical reason is he violated the terms of his parole after a week of freedom, and he's back in jail already."

Ashley pursed her lips. "Convenient?"

"Yeah, you could say that. Especially for Ma."

"I don't think she cares."

"No, you're right. Just the nuisance factor. Not like Leo." Leo Francis had been Ashley's father, dead in an oil field accident out west years ago.

"They'd already broken up, but Ma was wrecked when Leo died," Ashley said.

They lingered in silence on the bridge. Ashley put out her mittened hands to catch snowflakes, and then Roy did too. "Stop copying me."

Her brother smiled down at her. "Leo has some family around here—in the Abenaki village." It was the way everyone local referred to the Abenaki reserve, at the outskirts of Fabienville.

"A brother, yes."

"Last I heard, the mother was still alive too. You'd think—strange how ..."

Ashley turned to Roy. "Don't you know? Gran managed to offend everyone at Leo's funeral. You know Gran. Ma told me all about it, you must know. It wasn't pretty. We all used to make allowances for her. I guess the Francis family didn't feel like making allowances. Anyhow, it caused a rift between Leo's family and us. That's why no one's in touch with anyone."

Roy frowned. Barely out of his teens, he was a devoted husband and father of a preschooler—the complete family man. "I can't see how it could have dragged on so long. Must have been a real feud."

"That's just the thing. It wasn't such a big deal. It just dragged on, as you say, the way these things do. It can seem at the time like a small thing, I guess. Somebody ruffles some feathers at a funeral, someone else gets in a huff. Everyone figures it will probably blow over. But it doesn't. Time sneaks by, decade after decade ..."

"Whoa. Six out of ten family feuds begin at funerals."

She jostled his arm. "You made that up. But I wouldn't be surprised."

"Do you think Ma cares?"

"I don't think so. Leo's long gone, for a start. And in spite of everything, her loyalty was with Gran. Plus she's got no time to care. Anyway, she's got you and me. What in-laws could compete with us?"

Roy thought about this. "We have Francis cousins too, I think. Leastways, you do ..."

This topic had taken Ashley by surprise, and now she didn't want to talk about it anymore. "Maybe, I don't know. Lilou will be awake, Lucie will be feeling abandoned. Let's go back."

The snow was heavy now, and in no time obliterated their footprints as they trudged back to town.

* * *

Lucie's cousins, a live-wire pair just turned twenty-one, showed up from Montreal on Christmas Eve. Yves and Yvette were staying over as guests on Elm Street until Boxing Day and then everyone minus Ashley and her mother would head down the highway to Lucie's family home in Félicien, a speck on a map beyond Fabienville. The Boisvins were an old French family and focused their traditions, including gift giving, on *le jour de l'an,* so Lilou and the others could look forward to a second celebration.

Marlene spent most of Christmas Eve at work, inevitably, but the hours passed quickly for the others in outings to the skating rink and the sledding hill, visits to old neighbours, and last minute gift wrapping. Everyone was ecumenically inclined and up for the picturesque seven o'clock mass at Sainte Cécile in town. Supper was late, leisurely and languorous after they got home.

Roy and Ashley had chased their mother out of the kitchen, and the menu consisted of Saint Hubert spinach quiche, frozen curly fries, and the opening of every chocolate box in the house. Yves and Yvette poured from the three bottles of wine they had brought and someone put on Christmas music. People soon migrated to the big oak-floored living room to admire the tree. Lilou, dressed in the regulation glittery frock, checked the night sky continually for signs. She was inclined to explode with nerves and kept Roy and Lucie on their toes. But the young couple looked content as they clinked glasses on the couch. Ashley's brother looked like a tall thin version of John-Boy Walton. For the holidays he'd done himself proud in a forest green chamois shirt and Waltonesque corduroy suspender pants. Lucie was an effervescent brunette who made her own clothes. Tonight, this meant a purple velvet dress that Ashley suspected had started life as curtains. Yves and Yvette, fraternal twins, sported matching black and white penguin outfits, although they didn't resemble each other that much and Yves was a head taller. Even Ashley had dressed up in her new clothes and been duly complimented. Marlene, curled up in an armchair and looking sleepy, was wearing a holiday sweatshirt that even *Village des Valeurs* would have rejected.

The seven-foot tree towered and twinkled in the background. Christmas oranges, candy canes and fudge made their way onto the coffee table next to the chocolates. Maybe it was the Crozes Hermitage—where did college kids get their money from, Ashley thought, feeling old—or maybe it was the hour, but the scene, shot through with the pixie dust of anticipation, was undeniably idyllic. They were like a picture: "At Home on Christmas Eve."

In contrast, December twenty-fifth was not without its bumps. Because some of the Seaton Valley lifts were still running on Christmas day, the restaurant was open too, on reduced hours. Marlene had made plans to take the day off, but a supervisor's last minute personal emergency found her hurrying to dig up her car keys by mid-morning. Ashley and Roy promised they would take care of Christmas dinner, and there'd be a plate of hot food and a glass of wine waiting for her when she got home. But neither of them knew much about roasting a turkey, and the bird was overdone and dry in places, while a suspicious faint pink inside. They might have done something about that, except that Waverley's antiquated power system experienced its traditional two pm outage, the result of everyone in town having their ovens on at once. So they ate by chilly candlelight, from the outside of the turkey. The conversation couldn't seem to get off the topic of the differences between salmonella and botulism, as a freak snow squall clobbered the house and an emergency siren howled in the distance.

"You hear that? Someone set fire to their house with candles or something," Ashley explained in a dead-pan tone to Yves and Yvette, who were drinking a good deal.

Roy and Lucie, so blissful yesterday, had been kept up half the night by Lilou, and were inclined to spar. Yves and Yvette brought out a bottle of vodka that had been stashed, apparently, in their luggage. When the food was cleared away, Lilou's new computerized Pickles the Panda toy showed a tendency to lapse into a coma, and Roy, trying to fix the problem, made it worse. Yves and Yvette were discussing the purchase of a funeral plot for Pickles, over the acrimonious tears of Lilou, when Marlene walked through the door.

Evening fell and eventually the lights came back on, the house warmed up, and Marlene did something with the wreckage of the turkey that involved walking a bin bag outside. The rest of Christmas was calm, without mishap. Roy felt impelled to pull out old family photo albums to show the Alma branch of the family. Whether Yves and Yvette appreciated it, Ashley wasn't ready for this trip down memory lane. There was a handful of snapshots taken just after she'd been born, that she hadn't looked at in years. She didn't really want to see them now either, badly composed pre-digital pictures whose blurriness couldn't conceal Marlene's happiness, as she stood there smiling into the camera and holding the bundle of white blankets that was Ashley. Leo Francis was in a few photos as well, a tall handsome man standing not quite alongside Marlene, his expression hard to read.

Ashley developed a sugar headache and began to feel a certain despondency. She found herself thinking of a few cases from work, with longing. Lilou finally sobbed herself to sleep on the floor and Roy carried her up the stairs. Over the objections of her mother Ashley cleaned up in the kitchen, and followed Lilou soon after, hoping she had aspirin in her purse and counting the blessings of childlessness.

***

"Ma, when was the last time you had any contact with my dad's family in the village?"

It was the day after Christmas and the others had just left for Félicien. Ashley and her mother were relaxing in the living room with their feet up. There was a tea tray nearby, some plain sandwiches, the ever-present chocolate boxes. They were passing between them an open bag of chips that Ashley had found tucked behind the quinoa on the highest shelf. Famine chips, as she liked to think of them.

"It depends what you mean by contact," Marlene said, brushing crumbs.

"Well, whatever *you* mean by contact."

Marlene took her time responding. "A bit over a year ago. Eric came by here, the day after your Gran's funeral. When you'd already gone back to Montreal."

"Who's Eric?"

"Eric Francis. Your father's brother."

"What did he want?"

"To offer condolences on the death of my mother."

"I didn't know that. That was nice, wasn't it?"

Marlene tilted her head. "He wasn't what you'd call warm and friendly. Formal—courteous, I guess."

Ashley made a face. "Why did he bother coming?"

A slight smile. "I think his mother made him."

"His mother?"

"Your grandmother."

Ashley realized, with a slight falling away like in a dream, that Marlene wasn't referring to Gran. "My grandmother." She said tried the words on her tongue. "I see ..." Not that she did, really. "Do you think she wanted to make friendly overtures to you?"

"I'm not sure." Marlene sighed. "I don't really think so. Odette"—*so it's Odette, is it*—"always stood on ceremony. I mean ceremony was important to her. What's owed to a situation. Like sending Eric around after the funeral."

"Why not send this Eric to the actual funeral? Why not attend herself?"

Marlene put out her hand for the chips. "She's old now. I think her health is poor. And maybe she thought it would have been disruptive if a Francis just showed up, in the middle of everything."

"Waverley likes its gossip."

"That kind of thing, as well."

Ashley was tired, in that moody untethered way of the day after Christmas. Now she felt afloat in a sea of her own wonderings. She cast her mind back in time. She retained only vague memories of Leo's funeral, that she, Gran and Marlene had attended. As a little girl growing up, she knew there'd been a rift, but it had felt unconnected to her. Her mother had chosen never to repeat Gran's words. This only added to the mystery. The separation had become almost mythic in Ashley's mind, as if the break between the Smeetons and the Francises was fate, part of the march of history. Not something that she, Ashley Smeeton, private individual, could ever influence.

Marlene was looking at her quizzically. "Why the questions now, pet?" she asked in a mild tone.

But Ashley couldn't answer that. If there was a trigger for such reflections, it wasn't an obvious one. Lots of people were more or less fatherless nowadays—Marie Ambre Barry, her brother. Even her mother's workaholism was by now a customary part of life. Was it something to do with Christmas, or with Ashley's stage of life? As her mind continued to drift, for no obvious reason she remembered words that she'd heard more than a month ago. Words uttered by Charles Saint Cyr, of all people.

"I don't know what this thing is that has come between us," he'd said to Ashley. "Belle and I, we were—are—terribly in love." The words he'd used had been "*éperdument amoureux*." His elegant hands had reached into space, as if trying to grasp and remove some invisible barrier. He'd quoted someone called Rilke, and the words came back to Ashley with eerie clarity: "It was as the German poet says—'the love that consists in this: that two solitudes protect and border and greet each other ...' That was Belle and I."

Charles's attitude at the time had struck Ashley as pretentious and insincere. Now the words all of a sudden seemed to be chock full of portent—as if they had a darker application, and were about every rift, every loss and every barrier in the whole tear-sodden world.

She accepted the chip bag from her mother and solemnly inspected the last of the crumbs. "I don't know, Ma. I'm glad we're, you know, friends ... And Roy too, and Lucie and Lilou. All of us."

"Me too."

"It's so difficult, more difficult that you'd think, to have a Christmas as nice as ours."

Marlene's smile was casual as she stacked the tray. "Did we have a nice Christmas? I guess we did. It was better than that family's, the one that had the fire."

Marlene's natural limit for serious conversation had been reached. Her next words were bone-dry, their tone verging on callous: "Sometimes, sweetie, I think people like their feuds, more than they like their connections. There's something—comfortable?—in a falling out. Like giving up. Feuds are easier." A pause. "They're like those terror risk security warnings."

"What?"

Her mother laughed. "You know. They make us feel safe."

* * *

The house was big and quiet and empty, with Marlene at work and the others in Félicien. Ashley tried to do things around the house she thought her mother would appreciate, and then took to driving the countryside around Waverley, along the fast-flowing Abenaki River, as far as the spectacular Seaton Valley. One day she went in the other direction, ostensibly in search of Boxing Week bargains in Fabienville. She picked up a six-pack of white athletic socks at Giant Tiger, and a cat calendar at the indie bookstore, but wasn't otherwise inspired. She dallied over a fancy coffee in the

Café Choco-Paradis. The Collège des Cantons de l'Est, where Lucie had just finished up, was across the street and Ashley wondered idly if she'd ever go back to university herself and get something on top of her Bachelor's in social work. Criminology, maybe? Nicolas Latendresse had a Master's in that.

She began to check Google Maps on her phone, in case there was some place she'd missed on her shopping quest. In scrolling around, she came across an area of yellow, that called itself, depending on whether you zoomed in or out, Oxford Township, Saint-Marc and Réserve Indienne des Abénaquis. The reserve was no more than a couple of kilometres away. With an inner quickening she thought there was nothing stopping her from going there now, to say a casual hi to Eric Francis. If he was around, obviously. Or Odette—although Odette wasn't well, according to her mother. Perhaps Eric then.

It was mid-afternoon when she pulled into a gas bar on the reserve and, after filling her tank, asked the teenager in a Canadiens sweater where she could find Eric Francis. He recognized the name at once and told her how to get to the band office. "Maybe it's closed for the holidays," he added in an afterthought.

"Does Eric work there?"

"He's the deputy chief," the boy said. Now he was taking her in more carefully.

"He's my uncle." Ashley felt she should explain. "I never visited him here before." *Or anywhere else.*

The boy considered a little, sizing her up and then the car. He was not unimpressed by the gleaming police Interceptor. "You got that car around here?" he asked.

"At a police auction in Montreal. You can see the bull bar. It's great ride. Modular V8, big 4.6 litre engine." She handed him a wad of bills. "What I like especially is the body-on-frame." They stared at the car, its sleekness, its lower-middle-class thuggish lines. "The look, too. The grill, for instance? I just replaced that."

Ashley left with exact instructions for how to get to Eric's house through the reserve's unnamed meandering streets. The empty streets resembled those of any other small Quebec town, modest houses covered in pastel vinyl siding, an old-looking white clapboard church, a corner store, a community hall with a few kids going in and out. Maybe more space between the houses. More fields, more trees. It was a misty grey day, the distances smudged—as if the community was prepared to reveal only so much of itself to visitors.

Eric's house was a blue vinyl split-level at the end of a dirt road. It was nicely built into a slope down to a creek lined with willow and alder. A truck and a boat on a trailer were parked by a stand of trees, but a parking space close to the house was empty. Ashley knocked a few times, her heart beating out a small *chamade,* but no one was home. She should have asked the attendant where Odette Francis lived.

She drove around some more. She passed only one person, a little girl, who was standing in a ditch waving a stick around in the company of a wolf-like dog. It made Ashley think of divination. From the road, only the child's upper torso and head were visible, which made her calm-eyed stare somehow more disconcerting.

Eventually Ashley stopped into the convenience store and got directions to the band office. It was beside the school and shared space with the health centre. There were a few people milling around in the main lobby. Ashley got into a conversation with someone called Martha, at a reception desk under an attractive wood ceiling canopy intended to suggest a long canoe. Beyond Martha's head was a wall directory and Ashley saw Eric's name on the board. Besides being deputy chief, he was director of consultation services.

She'd honed her approach by now. "Hi. I'm Ashley, Eric Francis's niece from Montreal. I went by his place and he's not home. I was just wondering—is he maybe around here …?"

But Martha could only shake her head. "He's away, out of

town. The offices are closed until January 13." She looked down the hall for a moment and then back at Ashley. Wrote something on a pad. "Ashley ... There's just no one around. You can call his cell?" By then Ashley had memorized the telephone number on the wall and she nodded.

She felt slightly disappointed, but also slightly relieved, as she pulled onto the highway. The thickness in the air had created a premature twilight and she drove with her lights on. She was anxious to get back to her mother's house. At least she had Eric's number, that was something. But she wasn't going to use it right away. Marlene's birthday was in mid-January and she'd be heading back to Waverley for a quick visit. She'd arrange things ahead, and pay a visit to her uncle then. Maybe even to her grandmother. It sounded like a sensible plan.

But Ashley was feeling jittery and unsettled. The half-light was tricky to drive in, especially with Quebec drivers zipping by at special Quebec driver speeds. But it wasn't that.

If it was a sensible plan, why was she feeling tense—tense and unloved? Also, now when it was over, afraid.

* * *

Ashley arrived back in Montreal on the afternoon of New Year's Eve. The day was bright and sharply cold. Montreal was its usual bustling and lively self, filled with people in a holiday mood, children in their bright snowsuits everywhere. How she liked cities and crowds. As she drove through the downtown streets she couldn't help but notice the heightened police presence. Had something happened while she was away in Sleepy Hollow? She decided to pick up a free newspaper, and stopped for groceries as well. When she came out of the store, the December day was already closing fast and the city's streets were blue canyons filled with red-gold light.

She had no plans for New Year's Eve, but that was all right. She

3

SHE ALWAYS KNEW YOUR NAME

THIS JANUARY IN Montreal was like any other January in Montreal: eternal, gulag-like, but with more slush this year. Ashley's life resumed: too many cases, with intervals of killer lacrosse. She took down the tree after people started commenting. Aram did some work for her, and she even paid him once.

Then, a quick visit to Waverley, for her mother's birthday. Roy and his family couldn't make it—Lilou had picked up something from day care and the whole family was laid low. Benny Tam, Marlene's old boss from the Redbird Cafe, paid a surprise visit, but it was otherwise a low-key weekend. It was just as overcast and mild in Waverley as in Montreal, and Ashley recognized the intrinsic mournfulness of slush.

She'd told her mother that she'd arranged a visit with Eric Francis, and perhaps her grandmother, although Eric had been unclear about that. Marlene advised bringing a gift of food. Thus Ashley raced down the highway with freshly-baked muffins, heavily wrapped so they'd hold some residual warmth when she hit the reserve. A little time was lost explaining to the tribal police what the hurry was but she still made good time to Eric's house.

One thing Eric wasn't was effusive. He was a tall, sturdily built, dark-haired man in his late fifties or thereabouts, with a pleasant manner that could have meant anything. He welcomed her into his home as he wrapped up a business call on his cell phone, and invited her to sit. The living room, whose decor Ashley would have described as a work in progress, in the style of men everywhere, smelled of smoke from a woodstove in the corner. Marlene thought he must be either a widower or divorced. There were a few plastic toys under the coffee table.

"My grandchildren were here for a visit over the holidays," he said. "From Calgary."

Ashley looked at the insulated food carrier on her lap. "I feel like the pizza delivery guy. I made these for Odette"—she'd made up her mind to use names—"but I'll give them to you, while they're still technically fresh from the oven."

Eric nodded gravely, with an additional shade of warmth unless Ashley was imagining it. "I'll make us some tea," he said, as he carried them into the kitchen.

So this is my uncle. Ashley tried to relax. She could detect the resemblance to Leo. He didn't seem friendly or unfriendly.

When she'd telephoned Eric after the holidays, he'd been calmly interested in meeting. He hadn't sounded surprised to hear from her. Ashley belatedly realized that her December visit to the reserve hadn't passed unnoticed, and more people than Martha with her notepad and observant eyes must have conveyed the news to her uncle. Even the tribal police hadn't seemed surprised. They asked her what kind of muffins she was carrying.

"How's your mother?" he asked when he came back from the kitchen. "I was sorry about her mother's passing."

"She's well. She runs the restaurant at the Seaton Valley resort, she's always busy. My mother appreciated your visit when Gran died." Ashley toed the carpet. "How is my grandmother?"

Eric thought about this. "She's old enough now. She has some problems. Arthritis. Her heart isn't good. But she's still in her own house up by the church." A slight sideways motion of the head.

Ashley took the bull by the horns. "I thought it was time I met you. You and Odette. Can I see her today?"

"We'll go there in a little," he replied. He brought out mugs and a plate with Ashley's muffins on them. "You live in Montreal now, Ashley?"

She told him about herself, feeling as if she was at an interview. Her childhood, her brother and his family, her university years in Montreal, her decision to become a private investigator.

Eric nodded. He might or might not have known some of this. "Why did you decide to contact us now?"

Ashley knew she'd be asked this question. "I think I must just have been too young to think about it before. Later, I began to think I should. We were looking at old photographs at Christmas. There were pictures of me when I was a baby, with my mother and Leo. It made me think about things. Like my background."

Eric was now looking a mixture of things: a little kind, a little sympathetic, a little mocking. "You came to discover your Abenaki roots?"

"I'm not planning to sell a book by calling myself First Nation, if that's what you're wondering about."

He twisted his lips in what might have been a smile at this smart alec comment. His nod suggested qualified approval.

"Also," she said, "I was curious."

"Did you ever think about being Abenaki, the time when you were growing up?" He sounded curious himself.

"Think about it?" She was ready to protest. "I thought about it all the time. There were Abenaki kids in my school, two in my grade. We knew who we were. My mother always was clear about that, who I was." But in reality it had been a word. Abenaki. A potent word, filled with the kind of childish meaning that no child can ever explain.

He was thinking of something else. "Your mother cut herself off from Leo, did you know?"

37

ANNA DOWDALL

"Did she?" Ashley felt a little helpless. "I don't know too much about that. I do know she missed Leo. She really loved him, I think. Wasn't my father kind of into partying back then?"

Eric considered. "You could say that. He was a bad little brother for a while. He straightened out though. We were all pretty surprised when he went out to Fort Mac."

"How so?"

He smiled slightly. "He was a real homebody."

He offered the plate and Ashley accepted a muffin she didn't want. Thank God, they weren't too bad. "If he hadn't gone away, and then died, I'm sure I would have known him. My mother would have wanted it and I would have wanted it."

Another brief smile. "Could be. When he went to Fort Mc-Murray he lost touch with us as well. That's the way, sometimes, when people move away.

Ashley seized on this. "One of your kids is in Alberta?"

"Danielle. In Calgary. She and her husband are the lucky ones, they still have jobs. She's got two little boys. My boy, Nathan, he's even farther—Vancouver."

"You have another girl?"

Eric nodded. "Antoinette. She's my youngest. About your age."

"Where is she?"

He didn't answer immediately. "Montreal."

Ashley blinked. "What does she do there?"

"She's studying. Math and Science. Pre-engineering."

"Wow." There was a silence, as Ashley realized she had come to the very end of what she had to say.

"I have something for you." Eric left the room and returned holding a small chunky notebook with a battered cover.

"Leo was in a twelve steps programme for a while, some nice lady thought he should write a journal. Now if you knew my brother you'd know he had many skills, especially with his hands, and he liked to think about things too. But the idea that Leo would write

38

his innermost thoughts in a notebook, well that would be a surprise. Anyway, you'll see when you look at it, it's not much of a journal. Like one day, he writes, 'Feeling pretty good today, yep,' and then he's got two rows of stars like he was trying to think of something else to say." Eric thumbed through the book. "He makes lists. Here's a packing list for a hunting trip. Here's one with some car parts, he was always rebuilding a car. Another entry, he writes: 'It was a fine sunny day in June on the reserve,' like he was going to tell a story and ran out of steam. He gets to telling jokes, he made some of them up." Some more rifling of pages. "Here's one: 'How did the ancestors discipline their children?'"

"I don't know."

"'They sent them to stand in the corner of the wigwam.'" Ashley laughed, but Eric said: "Well he didn't make that up, that's an old joke." So Ashley laughed again, at herself. "Anyway—here it is. If you want it?"

Ashley took it awkwardly.

"It's not radioactive."

"I do want it, thanks a lot."

"Now let's go see my mother."

They took their cars separately and pulled in behind the church where a few cabin-like houses surrounded by shrubbery stood in a small gravel circle. These little dwellings were different from the rest of the houses Ashley had seen, as if they predated the reserve, had a secret life of their own. Odette's was of rust-red asbestos siding, with a listing front porch and windowboxes filled with what would have been a cheerful summer display.

"Mom, I've got Ashley with me," Eric called, as she followed him inside. The house was dark and warm, full of knick-knacks and displays of handiwork—in that regard like her grandmother Smeeton's. The old lady under a shawl in the corner armchair didn't get up to greet Ashley, but extended her hand. "Bring her here," she said.

When Ashley was in front of her, sitting on a hard chair that Eric had placed, she saw a compact little person with grey hair in a modish pixie cut, looking at her out of a pair of chilly black eyes.

"She's like Leo all right," Odette said, continuing to look.

"Hello Odette," Ashley said, her heart almost failing her. They shook hands. "And I can see my father in you."

Eric put the rest of the muffins on a table near Odette. "Ashley made these."

Odette's gaze swung to the muffins and back to Ashley. She inclined her head in appreciation. *Like a freaking queen*, Ashley thought, mesmerized.

Eric poured them all some juice and sat down. Odette expressed her condolences on the death of her grandmother and then exchanged a little chitchat with her son about people Ashley didn't know. Every so often she'd look over at Ashley, taking in some new feature or element.

"You're old now, you're what?" she asked. Ashley replied, while grasping that what her grandmother really wanted to know was: "Why did you take so long to visit us?" She could have asked a similar question of them, but she wasn't ready to hear the answer.

By now Ashley's inner ear had become attuned to the special timbre of these conversations, their pace, their small silences, their circumlocutions. She thought she was even getting into the gentle swing of the thing. They discussed who resembled whom, including Eric's three children. Odette gave her an update on the cousins, and Danielle's little boys. Mentioned other grandchildren, asked her about Marlene, her brother and his family. Out of the blue she said: "Eric and Leo both took after me, I had two girls too, who looked more like their father."

"My sisters, Rita and June. They passed some time ago," Eric said.

"Are you thinking of getting married?" Odette asked.

"God no." The words popped out of Ashley's mouth before she realized. "Well, not in the foreseeable future anyway."

"She's too smart, women are just too smart nowadays," Odette said, with a laugh like the crackling of burning thorns.

"So you keep telling me, Mom."

The conversation languished, or so Ashley thought. She interjected into the silence her little speech about wanting to discover her roots. She thought it had gone down all right with Eric, but she wished almost immediately that she hadn't repeated it to Odette. The old woman looked at her without word or expression, although you could tell that thoughts were being thought.

"What does that mean to you, that you're Abenaki—through your father?" Odette eventually asked.

Ashley could only say that she didn't know but wanted to find out.

"Is that what you want?" Odette said, after a pause. "What it means, though ..." A little shrug. "Because nowadays none of us are always sure." The temperature in the room had dropped a little.

After more chitchat about Eric's job, and a lengthy exchange in the Abenaki language, in which Ashley's uninformed ears traced a meandering vein of sorrow, Odette said: "I'm tired." And she did look tired, tired and old. A middle-aged woman who must have been hovering in the kitchen appeared in the doorway. It was time to leave.

As they exited the front door, Odette said something final to Eric in Abenaki. When they stood outside by their cars, Eric lit a cigarette. "That wasn't a big mystery, what my mother was saying to me just now. She just said that I should invite you to come back and visit another time."

Ashley nodded. "Did she? I feel like I've gone from F to D conditional."

Eric laughed. "No, not D conditional." *C minus then.*

He took a deep and satisfying lungful of smoke. "My mother won't let me smoke inside."

Ashley nodded, half listening. The conversation in Abenaki had been unexpected. She knew that few of the young still spoke the traditional tongue. "My grandmother seems fluent in Abenaki."

"She is. We're trying to bring the language back to the youth. We've got an immersion programme. We want to make the school an Abenaki language first school, the whole curriculum."

"What was the other thing she said to you in Abenaki?"

Eric took another puff, then laughed. "She was just talking about my job. I'm the director of consultation services. I work on land claims, resource development agreements. She just said that the next time that truck of mining surveyors shows up uninvited on the traditional territory, I should chase them off the way she and my father and the others did, the times before." His smile was easy, his eyes opaque. "Long ago now, that was. She likes to remember all the times when stuff like that happened." The smile continued. "The way she tells it, you picture pitchforks …"

Ashley weighed this. "I had the impression she was telling some sad story, when I heard, I don't know, the repetition …"

"No, that was her enumerating. 'And then there was that time back in '69 when we got them good, and then we got them good that other time … and that other time …' Even if you couldn't understand, that history was intended for you."

He stubbed out the cigarette and put the butt in his pocket. "She sends Muriel out to count the butts. My sister June died of lung cancer." He turned to Ashley abruptly. "You're heading to Montreal now?"

"No, to my mother's. I'll head back after supper." She hesitated. "I didn't know I had a cousin in Montreal. Where exactly in Montreal is she?"

"Antoinette? She lives out by the Collège Morgan, where she's studying. Maisonneuve, I think, Hochelaga? You can see the Olympic stadium."

"Could I—I thought I might look her up. Do you think I could contact her?"

Eric gave her a level stare. "I'll tell her about your visit," he said eventually. "I have your number, so ... If she wants to get in touch with you, she will." And with that Ashley had to be content.

As they said goodbye, Eric, after a brief hesitation, offered some parting words. "My mother—she was glad to see you. I know that. You're Leo's only kid. She counts her grandchildren, her great grandchildren. She always knew your name." Another pause. "She's old now. Well, she's not really that old, but sometimes, you know, she likes to pass for about two hundred."

Over dinner, Marlene was all ears as Ashley recounted her afternoon. "Are you glad you went?" Ashley said that she was.

Driving back to Montreal on the dark highway, Ashley took stock of the visit. Glad was just a little part of what she felt. And it would take a while, maybe quite a while, to unpack the rest of it. She'd committed various blunders, but at least her feet were in the river now.

She was weary by the time she arrived at rue de Paris, just as snow began to fall. The silent snowbound street asked no questions when she pulled up, and the flat welcomed her in the same discreet way. She switched on lamps, turned up the heat and, as she always did on a Sunday night, checked her voice messages. The usual hand-ful of calls from clients wanting to know the status of their cases. And a call from a voice that she recognized, even before the caller identified himself.

Charles Saint Cyr hadn't gone through his secretary this time. He said it was about the situation they'd discussed before the holi-days. Now the circumstances had changed. He had another pro-posal to put before her. There was an urgency to the matter that hadn't arisen in December. He hoped she would contact him with-out delay. And he left two numbers.

Ashley settled herself on her couch with a couple of cushions. She could only wonder what the captain of industry and his lovely Belle had gotten up to in the intervening weeks. And, considering

43

she'd turned him down before, what kind of job Saint Cyr wanted to put before her now. From where she reclined, she could see the streetlamp, one of those gentrified pseudo-antique ones, shining through the window. Snowflakes, slanting picturesquely across the pane, filtered the glow. She felt relaxed, but energized and intrigued as well. Since it was now too late to telephone, however, she'd just have to stay intrigued until morning.

* * *

"The circumstances have changed, Ms. Smeeton."

Ashley and Charles Saint Cyr were in the same elegant office with the same million dollar view, this time under an overcast sky. The bowl on the cabinet was filled with masses of small fragrant irises, although where you got irises in late January was a mystery to Ashley. Saint Cyr had lost his limp but not his soulfulness. He seemed to Ashley just as picturesquely unreal as ever.

"Belle called me herself two days ago. She's afraid. Things have happened. I know she wants to come home." He took a breath. "She ... when she gets like this, though, she finds it hard to make up her mind, to act. She wants her sister to come to Paris and extricate her from the situation she's in. The trouble is, Isabel can't go to Paris. She's in the middle of her teaching term and can't get away. And Belle doesn't want *me* to come. She's made that blisteringly clear. I was almost decided to go anyway—and then I thought of you."

Ashley was having trouble understanding this. "Hang on, I need to make sense of this. Madame Saint Cyr wants to come home. She wants her sister to come and collect her?" He nodded. "This sister of hers isn't able do this. But your wife can't just—buy a plane ticket?"

"This may seem strange to you, but Belle has odd reactions to things. She had a complicated childhood ... Sometimes she gets ... paralyzed. But you have to understand that the situation in Paris

44

has become a difficult one. Anyone might hesitate, not know what to do. I should explain. There's been an accident and a disappearance, the police have become involved."

His voice became flat, dry. "I can't quite come to terms with it myself, but this is what she told me. The man she was friends with —we can assume she's been having an affair with him—has disappeared. I think he may have been the kind of man who disappears from time to time anyway. The police are involved because recently he and Belle were on the highway and were, according to her, deliberately driven off the road. There were no injuries, but they ended up in the ditch and the car received significant damage. It could have been much worse. The police are treating the man's disappearance as suspicious. The two things may be linked. This individual may have been involved in certain business dealings of a questionable nature. I can't tell how much of this the police know ..."

Ashley realized she was staring. "I see. At least I think I do. She's not being prevented from leaving, is she? By the police, I mean."

"No." He shook his head. "I don't think it's like that at all. She wanted Isabel to come so she wouldn't be alone, dealing with the police, for instance. She's worried; she's afraid; she needs someone to help her decide. Before her marriage, she always relied on Isabel in this way. She's evidently torn because of the disappearance of her—this man, but I think she wants to leave."

"You're not sure?"

He weighed his words. "I'm fairly sure."

"And you want me to go to Paris and, as you put it, 'extricate' her from the situation and bring her back to Montreal?"

"Yes."

Ashley sat back on the couch, picking her words. "The thing is, Monsieur Saint Cyr, I could go to Paris on your dime, but what makes you think I could help your wife in any way?"

"You're a trained and licensed private investigator. You are reputed to be a very resourceful person."

"Well, okay. But number one, I'm not licensed to work in France. And number two, your wife wants her sister and I'm not her sister."

He directed a calm gaze at her. "I wouldn't be hiring you to act as an investigator in a straightforward sense. Although your experience will be beneficial, your role would be more—discreet. As for you turning up, there'd be no problem. I've spoken to Belle. She wants you to come to Paris. She was plain. She'd like you there as soon as possible. Very soon, I'm sure, she would agree to return home with you."

Ashley's mind was now jumping all over the place. "Under my statutory code of conduct, there are requirements for cooperation with the police, in the event I come across evidence of something illegal, for example ..."

His manner didn't alter. "Of course. And I have no evidence about anything illegal, you understand, and the idea that Belle would be involved herself in anything illegal is farcical. But surely your code of conduct doesn't apply in France anyway—as you say."

She blinked. *Touché.* "True. And you don't want me to find this friend of hers either?"

"He can remain out of the picture." Preferably in the pit of hell, his expression conveyed.

Ashley gathered her thoughts. "In summary, go to Paris, help Madame Saint Cyr deal with whatever arises, as a sort of hired friend. And you'd like me to try and convince her to leave?"

"That summarizes things, yes."

"I certainly wouldn't be in a position to put pressure on her."

"All I would want is for you to suggest the wisdom of a return to Montreal and, when she agrees, help her wrap up her affairs there. The lease, for instance, it's a problem. If you could commit to two or three weeks, and if she was unwilling to return with you at the end of that time, then that would be the end of the job as far as I'm concerned."

Ashley mulled this over. "I'm inclined to accept the commission," she said finally. "On the previously discussed terms." She adopted a detached tone. "However, there are a couple of conditions. I'd like to confirm all this with Madame Saint Cyr. And I'd like to have a conversation with the sister as well. It's not that I doubt your account. It's that in matters as sensitive as this, the chance of success will increase if I reach out to your wife and establish rapport first. And anything the sister can tell me will only help." Ashley smiled pleasantly. *Touché back on you.*

But Saint Cyr was apparently unperturbed. He readily scribbled contact information on a sheet of paper.

Ashley felt very alert. The job, no longer bounty hunter but rescuer of a damsel in distress, was more palatable although as weird as ever. She was eager to speak to these two women, to see what light they could shed. But she already knew she wanted the case.

* * *

Ashley had two jobs she needed to put on extended life support so that she could take the Paris gig. Aram received his instructions, which rendered him slightly euphoric. On the phone, he was inclined to issue messages in code, like "the package is in transit, boss" and "your cousin Jock is getting impatient." In the absence of packages and a cousin named Jock, Ashley was frequently mystified, but she didn't mind. Aram was a careful worker, and anyway she could see how much he loved this sort of thing.

She called Isabel first. Isabel Jadois, Saint Cyr had written. There was traffic noise in the background when she connected with a rapid fire and unsurprised voice.

"I'm in your neck of the woods," Isabel said. "Why don't we meet at the Atwater Market coffee shop, La Grenouille?"

Twenty minutes later, Ashley was facing Isabel Jadois ("call me Isa") across a couple of Americanos. She was a haggardly attractive woman with keen brownish-green eyes and multi-coloured hair that made her look like she'd run into an early Holi festival. She exuded Montreal bohemianism, with artistically shredded clothes and a small septum piercing. The look suited her. In her mid-thirties, by Ashley's estimation, she had a husky voice, laugh lines. A committed smoker, at a guess.

"I have to head back to the college, so let's cut to the chase. No wonder you want to talk to me, and to Mira too. Trust me, I'd go myself, but I took some time off last term, more than they liked, and I can't take anymore." She had a teaching contract at the Collège Morgan, she said, which triggered a faint ping in Ashley's brain, and she was angling for a permanent post. "If Charles wants to pay you to go to Paris and ease my sister back to Montreal, I'd say go for it. Mira had a thing with a guy over there, to be candid. Raymond Boissier. Some sexy fashion exec or freelancer or something. Now though, with him having disappeared, plus that road rage incident, she's in over her head. She just needs some big sisterly help, that's all."

Ashley nodded cautiously. Saint Cyr had told her Mirabel was thirty, older than Ashley by a few years. But then, she supposed the big sisterly role need not be age dependent. "You said road rage? Aren't the police treating it as more than random road rage?"

"I guess. Regardless, the best thing for Mira now is to come home. I don't always see eye to eye with Charles, but we agree on this. And Mira certainly wants you over there." Isabel smiled. An intelligent smile. "Mira's always been a little—lost? She's unique. You'll like her though. When all's said and done, I think she loves Charles. This Raymond episode, it was probably just an impulse. She can be a little child-like sometimes? I love my sister, but really, they'd been married two years. Of course, Charles can be—well, he's Charles. They're suited though. Their plan was to have kids right away, but things don't always go according to plan. It's left Mira a little unclear about her role."

The phrases came across as rehearsed. Ashley sensed tension underneath them. "Hm. She's beginning to find herself, is that it?"

"Find herself? Mira? Maybe." Isabel seemed privately amused at the idea. She took a quick look at her watch, said "*Merde,*" and fished a pack of cigarettes from her bag. Her stare was direct. "Ask me any other questions you want, but this is a legit job and you should take it."

Ashley stared back. "Point taken. Here's my question then. What are you afraid of?"

Isabel's expression dissolved, replaced by mild shock and something furtive. She didn't say anything for a moment. "It's not what you think," she said at last.

"I'm not thinking anything."

"All right." Isabel searched for words. "To be completely honest, I'm always worried about Mira. It's complicated. Our parents died when we were kids. It affected her more than me, who knows why. She had the best of everything growing up. It was like she won the adoption lottery. But there's more to life than that, I guess. Charles is good for her in a way, but he's an old school husband."

Ashley frowned. "Domineering?"

"You noticed? Charles and I keep trying to put her in a safe box, square her away. Maybe that just isn't possible. It's not just the Paris situation. It's Mira herself. For example, she told me last week she didn't think she could break the lease, and I told her she should look at the agreement, and she said what agreement. And so on and so forth. Antiques. She can't leave before she checks out some antiques. But it comes back to the same thing though. It's time she returned to Montreal. Talk to her, you'll see for yourself."

At length, Ashley nodded. She knew Isabel was still holding out on her. But she didn't doubt for a moment the sincerity of the woman's words. Isabel was worried. She wanted her little sister home.

* * *

Ashley would have liked to see Mirabel as they spoke. She was struck by how different she sounded from Isabel. There was the accent, for a start—a lilting, mid-Atlantic French, in contrast to Isabel's pure Québécoise tones. Her voice was high, light, liquid, but saved from childishness by its poised and cultured qualities. Marilyn Monroe meets Catherine Deneuve. Ashley could picture the vague yet vivid features as the voice assured her that, *mais oui,* she wanted to come home, she would find Ashley's help invaluable, but she was really worried about Raymond, whom she hoped would surface soon. And she did feel she should stay until then, apart from the fact that she just needed to wrap up a few other little things ...

Listening to Mirabel was like listening to crystalline water circling but never quite flowing into a drain. It was musical, but it made Ashley dizzy.

"Are there legal questions I need to know about at the outset?" she asked, trying to pin Mirabel down to something.

The other woman sounded a little shocked. "For me? Oh no, Ash*lee*, not at all. The *police judiciaire,* they're really nice. All those questions, of course. But—I find you can't always tell the police absolutely everything. Have you found that?"

Ashley had definitely found that, but she issued a *pro forma* cluck of disapproval. "What about Raymond?" she said bluntly.

"Raymond? But he had no way of knowing ... I don't think he did anything deliberately wrong, not for a moment!" There was a brief silence on the line. "I'd like to talk to you about that. Charles tells me you're a private investigator?"

"Yes, but I wouldn't be accepting the job as such."

"Oh, I understand, at least I think I do. It's just that you would know so much! It would be good to talk to you, once you were here ..." There was more of this back and forth, but Ashley could get nothing definite. "Please come," Mirabel said. "Can you come tomorrow?"

Ashley rolled her eyes and said she had a business to run. *Also a big fancy spinner suitcase to buy.* She could be there in a week.

***

Another good thing about the gig, she told Aram afterwards, was that it would dispel the troublesome feelings that lingered from her visit to Eric and Odette.

"Well, that's good. Um—what feelings?" His voice was muffled because he was under her desk doing something with her electronics cords.

"Just bothered, I guess. I finally met my grandmother, and my uncle, and what did it amount to? I don't know what it all means." How to explain something that had got inside her, was acting on her like a virus?

His head appeared. Ashley swallowed a laugh. "Oops, brush your hair off. I'd better Swiffer under there."

"Everything should be up and running now." He sat back on his heels. "What did you want it to mean?"

"I thought the visit would be more ... definitive. I thought I'd see myself differently."

"That might take more time."

"Aren't you wise? Back when I was a little kid and being Abenaki was mainly a thing in my head, it was easier. A part of me wants to go back to the village, force myself into some kind of immersion so I'll figure it out. Not that they'd appreciate that. And I wouldn't know what I was trying to achieve anyway."

This was an unusual mood for Ashley, who wasn't much for spilling the beans about feelings. She remembered something now. "That must have been what Odette meant when she told me Abenaki people feel that way sometimes. Like even they don't know what it means always."

Aram just nodded gently.

"Anyway, I don't like it." Ashley flung herself into her chair and abruptly pushed away her keyboard. "It's like now I'm neither one thing nor another."

"Yes, I get that. Neither one thing or another."

Ashley looked up, startled at his tone. Her conscience smote her then, because olive-skinned, blue-eyed Aram, despite the irony in his voice, seemed a little sad.

"Hey, thanks a lot. This is great. What do you want me to bring you back from Paris?"

"The Mona Lisa. But you should get a dress or something. Haute couture."

"The way you say that. I can't believe I'm going to Paris. It must have been fate, living on rue de Paris. Of course it's incredibly exciting." She shrugged. She knew she sounded ambivalent, as divided as she felt.

She shuffled the keyboard again, trying to get it back to where it belonged. She told herself she'd feel differently when she got there.

4

THE CITY OF LIGHTS

ASHLEY SMEETON ON the Champs Elysées said to herself: *I think I should turn back*. She'd walked a long way, wanting to shake off the fatigue of the plane trip. It was an overcast day, with a low sky pressing down on the rooftops—darker grey on grey. The passers-by in their subtly chic clothes were in a hurry. Early February dusk couldn't be far away. And while Paris in winter didn't seem to have the brutal cold of Montreal, the damp had stolen into her bones. Room service? It sounded inviting.

She'd checked into the Hotel Beauséjour, a quiet little place according to Saint Cyr, and the lap of luxury from Ashley's perspective. It was near the Seine, and not far from where she'd found Mirabel's *appartement* on Google Maps. The streetlamps had shimmering haloes in the twilight and her feet ached by the time she got back to the hotel.

She had a low-ceilinged room under the eaves, with a captivating view of the city against an indigo sky. She made lavish use of the hotel's fancy Violettes de Grasse toiletries in the shower, and ordered up an *entrée* and a *plat principal*. She turned down a suggestion from the soothing voice on the line for *amuses-gueules*. The voice then came back a smidgeon more insistent with: "*Certainement, Madame, je vous proposerais alors les fromages.*" And who could refuse proposed cheeses? Ashley was philosophical when a carafe of wine she didn't remember ordering appeared with the dinner. The enormous brass and wood tray itself was a marvel; the glasses and silverware twinkled; there were quantities of white linen. And the food, consumed as she leaned against a brocade bolster while thumbing a tourist brochure, was delectable.

The plan was to have a business call with Mirabel before going to bed. Ashley hadn't reckoned on the effects of wine on top of a sleepless flight. When she'd eaten all she could and suspected she was about to lapse into a pleasant coma, she made a last effort and hunted up her phone.

Mirabel Saint Cyr had been waiting for her call. She expressed surprise that Ashley had checked into a hotel. "But I have so much room in the *appart,* you must stay with me. There's everything here. Three bathrooms. It includes maid service." Ashley mumbled something, wondering how she could refuse.

They exchanged a few cautious pleasantries by way of overture. Mirabel had so much she wanted to tell Ashley face to face. She was sure Ashley could help in so many ways, a sentiment that alarmed Ashley slightly, especially as Mirabel didn't elaborate. As before, she sounded eager and unfocused all at once. And return journeys certainly didn't seem to be on Madame Saint Cyr's mind. "Charles tells me you've never been to Paris? We can do things together, I hope?" Ashley couldn't think of anything to say to this either, while doubting Saint Cyr wanted her to play tourist—if that's what Mirabel meant—with his errant wife.

There was a brief silence on the line. "Oh, Ashley, I'm so glad you've come!" Mirabel's words were almost childish, and would have come across as gushing but for their total sincerity.

They agreed to meet at Mirabel's the next day and rang off. Ashley brushed her teeth with a sense that she'd have to exert some control over things. She fell asleep almost before her head touched the pillow, and didn't hear the little wind that blew across the mansard roofs of Paris all night long.

* * *

Breakfast appeared on a smaller version of the same ornate tray, complete with the smiles of a little server who opened Ashley's curtains like a housemaid in a novel. As she ate, Ashley decided that black coffee, steaming milk in another silver pot and a basket of warm *brioche* had North American breakfasts beat. Another grey day seemed in the offing but that didn't bother her. She was looking forward to getting on with the job.

The thing about Paris, she realized as she walked to Mirabel's place, was that it could change quickly from one street and neighbourhood to the next. The Beauséjour was on a quietly bourgeois *place* tucked away behind a chic shopping thoroughfare, but soon Ashley was making her way through crooked narrow streets bordered by age-stained walls. There was an otherworldliness to these dark and echoing streets. A block or two from her destination, she left this pocket of medievalism behind and found herself among newer buildings, all in the prevailing Second Empire style but very grand. Everything now exuded wealth. Old ladies in ropes of pearls, that looked like they were from Ardene's but obviously weren't, passed on the sidewalk with nasty small dogs, and smart delivery trucks took the corners on two wheels. Florists, apothecaries and "*drogueries*" all made deliveries here apparently, of what Ashley wasn't always sure. Occasionally she caught glimpses of cloistered courtyards encircled by multiple storeys of ornate balconies. The noise of frenetic Parisian traffic was deferentially muted. Google hadn't captured every last *ruelle*, but Number 37, rue des Arabes seemed near the river.

The address came as a surprise. It was a pair of tall black double doors with a gargoyle bell pull. Just as Ashley was making up her mind to pull the thing, one of the doors swung open and an aproned woman appeared. Yes, Madame Saint Cyr lived here and had mentioned that she was expecting a visitor. She, Madame Caron, could take Mademoiselle there. Madame Caron led Ashley through a cobbled courtyard to the actual building entrance, up a wide flight of polished stairs and along an elegant hallway with only a few doors.

In her slouchy duffle coat and scuffed motorcycle boots, Ashley felt like an intruder. *I'm delivering detective services,* she thought. Although she had no clear idea, really, what it was she was supposed to be delivering.

The woman who stood in the open doorway, against a receding vista of luxurious rooms, took Ashley's breath away. Mirabel Saint Cyr was a fair blonde with blue-grey eyes. She had a well-proportioned figure, seemed tall but wasn't really. It was how the various elements were assembled that made the difference. Her naturally ash blonde hair was in a thick chopped wavy style, like a grown-out fifties Italian boy cut. It suited the shape of her head perfectly, and framed features whose purity verged on the angelic. These included a pair of remarkable eyes that changed colour and moved like restless water under the impulse of thoughts and emotions. When she took in the presence of Ashley, the effect was of light striking sombre water, sideways. On top of everything else, the woman looked far younger than thirty.

There was a lot of talk out there about your trophy wives. If there was even such a thing, Ashley decided now, Charles Saint Cyr had snagged himself the original and superlative trophy wife.

Mirabel showed Ashley into a grandiose *salon* and they sat across from each other on chairs that for all Ashley knew might once have supported royal derrieres. The place looked like a cross between an apartment and a luxury hotel suite. She was determined to take control of this interview. She'd prepared. She got out her notebook and pencil.

"May I call you Mirabel? All right, Mirabel. You know I've been hired by your husband to bring you back to Montreal. Also, he's indicated that you're in a difficult situation and I want to help you with that—to facilitate your return."

Ashley was on the lookout for emotion as she spoke. Mirabel seemed calm on the whole, nodding meekly as she rearranged the folds of her elegantly asymmetrical lounge outfit.

"Before we talk practical steps, please explain your situation to me in your own words. I need to know what you're afraid of, and the barriers to your return."

Once more Mirabel nodded demurely.

"So why don't you start with that."

The other woman hardly hesitated. "I won't tell you why Raymond Boissier and I became lovers, at least not now, because that is my business." She picked up a silver letter opener from the coffee table. "Raymond is a fashion designer. He also imports and exports, buys and sells—in other words, he works as a freelance retailer too." Ashley had no idea what this meant.

Mirabel assumed a mildly disdainful air. "He's not part of the fashion establishment, the world of mass manufacture and decadent haute couture. He's part of the fashion underground." Mirabel might as well have progressed to Swahili now, but Ashley kept an agreeable look pasted on her face.

"They hold unFashion Week shows. It's a very exciting scene, not just fashion but theatre, live-action happenings all over the city. Mainly, he supplies luxury fabrics to new designers who can't afford them." A slight reluctance. "And labour. Skilled labour ... Models, sometimes. Now that there are so many legal restrictions, you know, all those body mass index laws ..."

Mirabel pulled her phone from an exquisite leather satchel at her feet. "I have a picture of him somewhere," she said, as if this would explain everything. She made a pretty *moue* as she scrolled. "The police think he's a crook."

By now Ashley had formed this conclusion herself. He sounded like a con man who worked various angles. A mental picture arose of someone unrolling a blanket of fake Rolexes on a sidewalk. The scale had to be very different. Contraband, maybe knock-offs, and she even caught a whiff of human trafficking.

"Here he is, here's Raymond." Mira extended her phone. The picture was of a dark and dazzlingly handsome man who looked like a youthful Alain Delon, although with more sex appeal and less morality.

"Very nice," Ashley said. "So what's the problem?"

"It's the truck. The truck he found. The whole thing was a fluke. He was supposed to meet someone outside Paris, to do with a shipment of materials, but his contact didn't show. And he found this truck instead. Abandoned on the edge of a side road. He looked inside, as anyone would. It was full of designer clothes and accessories. Chanel, Dior, Hermès."

"Stolen?"

The reply was perfect in its obliqueness. "He just treated it as a lucky find. I mean, he didn't see any reason to believe that anyone would know he found it. So—he took it. But, well, he was wrong. Now we think he was terribly wrong." Mirabel sounded mournfully reasonable. Ashley wanted to reach over and slap her. "He found out later that his contact had run into trouble, bad trouble, with this shipment and they were on to him—onto the contact, I mean—and then they were somehow onto Raymond as well."

"They?"

Mirabel wrung her hands. "Raymond didn't tell me much. Some brothers, Bortnik, I think. The Bortnik brothers? There's a lot of black market activity involving fashion. Lots of people want knock-offs. But not everyone. In Russia, the oligarchs, you know, they want the real thing. They have their contacts, their suppliers here."

Yawning vistas opened before Ashley. She had to search for words. "You mean to tell me that your boyfriend helped himself to a truck of contraband designer duds destined for Russia, and now the Russian mob is after him?"

Mirabel nodded.

"And you're sure of this—because?"

"Well, that time we were driven off the road. I know Charles told you about that. Raymond says the Parisian Russian mob always drives around in those giant SUVs with blackened windows—and that's what drove us off the road. But also people have warned Raymond the Bortniks are after him." Mirabel was now looking apprehensive for the first time. "The police have their own ideas."

"Can't oligarchs pay full price?" Ashley asked.

"They could," Mira replied seriously. "But Ashley, you must know *no one* ever wants to pay full price."

Ashley was keen to cut through all this. "If your description of the situation is accurate, you're crazy not to leave Paris as soon as possible."

"Yes, I know. But Raymond ... What if he tries to contact me? Of course, I want to leave, but his disappearance does change things. For a start, the police."

Ah yes, the police. "There are such things as phones. Unless they think you're implicated?"

"No. They don't think that because I asked them. They might think—that I know more than I'm saying. Because I am, evidently. I don't want to get Raymond in more trouble than he already is."

"Has Raymond tried to get in touch with you?" An important question. One Ashley should have thought of sooner.

"No—not yet." Mirabel's face was perfectly blank.

"Do you think he deliberately disappeared?"

"I don't know."

"The police. They've come here? What did they want to know?"

"Inspector Jaubert, yes, and there was a captain too. They keep wanting me to go over things again. They want details. It's a different system here. There's something called the *police judiciaire*. I might have to provide testimony to an examining magistrate. They have my statement but the magistrate might have questions. It's how it's done."

"I need to talk to the police," Ashley muttered. They obviously suspected foul play.

"Well, they're coming back tomorrow, so you can," Mirabel said brightly.

Ashley wanted to yell at Mirabel: "I'm buying us tickets to leave today!" But she knew that wouldn't work.

She jotted a few words in her notebook. Mirabel seemed reluctant to leave Paris, but the reason wasn't completely clear. Order and method, Smeeton … "One, you'd like to know that Raymond is all right. Two, you're not sure if the police have any more questions. Is that it?"

"Yes."

She slipped in a trick question. "You think Raymond may try to contact you?"

Mirabel looked at her hands. "I have no idea, but obviously I hope so."

Ashley sighed. "Are you planning to return to your husband eventually?"

"Oh—yes." Madame Saint Cyr sounded oddly sure.

"Do you love Charles?

"He's my husband." Mirabel's large eyes, half shaded by black lashes, had a drowned look now. That blue-grey made Ashley think of rain, tears.

"Do you love Raymond?"

"It's very close to love. But I'm Charles's wife."

Cashed out, this meant that Raymond was a sex bomb Mirabel might not be quite finished with, but she had something with her husband that no one else could provide. Like money, maybe. How the hell did she manage to look so innocent when she said those things?

Ashley realized she was curious about money. "You don't have to answer this, Mira, but what's the financial situation between you and Charles?"

Mirabel's smile made her look every one of her thirty years now. "You're wise to ask that. I was adopted and raised by a very wealthy family, and I had everything. Private education, finishing school in Switzerland. They wanted me to train for a profession too, but I'm not like Isa. I'm not a brainy type. They gave me an allowance through my twenties. When I married Charles, the allowance ended. Which makes sense. The Duvals have other children. But for now, yes, I'm dependent on my husband. We had been thinking of starting a family right away, as Charles is older than me." She added, with specious virtue: "Meanwhile though, I've been discussing with him a role in Holopherne."

Which you were training for with Raymond and his unFashion happenings.

"And Charles has been supporting me while I'm here. He's really been very good that way."

Ashley had nothing diplomatic to say to this. Fortunately, she thought of something else. "Not relevant maybe, but you and your sister weren't adopted together?"

"No. We were separated. I was adopted by the Duvals, Isa was adopted by a different family, the Jadois, and—yes ..." A ghostly sigh hovered in the air between them. "We're quite different, as you might have noticed."

There was certainly a family resemblance, uncannily strong at moments, but with obvious differences as well. If Isabel and Mirabel had been paint-by-number outlines, two completely different artists had gone to work on them.

"I was just wondering." Ashley tapped her notebook with her pencil and gave Mirabel a keen look. "When we sort out Raymond's safety and square the police, are you willing to return with me to Montreal?"

"Oh, absolutely, Ashley!" The eyes were wide and of a cloudless blue. "This will take some days though, I know. But now, let me take you around the apartment and you can see for yourself why you should stay with me."

Ashley had no reason to refuse this offer, once she got the tour. Elegant balconied room followed room, with tall windows everywhere letting in a muted light. The bedrooms were suites in their own right. It was a hushed and luxurious place that made the Beauséjour look ordinary in comparison. They passed a very modern kitchen where someone called Béatrice was introduced to Ashley.

"Béatrice takes care of me, and she cooks too when we need it," Mira explained. "But the restaurants around here are wonderful."

Ashley felt she couldn't justify staying at a hotel when there was an offer of a room on rue des Arabes. Also, being around Mirabel would surely help her bring an end to this bizarre situation. She said she's come back with her suitcase later that day.

At the door, Mirabel offered effusive thanks, as if Ashley had somehow agreed to do her a favour. "I feel so much better already, Ashley! I know you'll help me. But Ash*lee*"—a tiny note of wheedling—"I do want you to get something out of your visit to Paris as well. I want to show you places, take you to restaurants. I really do need someone like you to go with to the Paris Flea Market, and other places like that. You saw our house in Montreal. It has some antique furniture, but it needs some European pieces. And something else, Ashley, I couldn't help but notice, but you would look *fantastique* in a designer outfit. Oh, not Dior and that predictable sort of thing. I'd like to see you in something by a new designer. Would you let me do that for you?"

She thought for a moment, during which her eyes avoided Ashley's. "There are *arrondissements* you really need to see, I mean the ones off the beaten track. It's wonderful right here, but there are parts of Paris where the tourists never go. I'd like to take you there. Have you heard of the district called the Goutte-d'Or? It's notorious in its way, but they say the food makes you think you have been transported to Marrakesh. Will you let me repay you? Will you let me do that for you?"

The door was shutting slowly as Mirabel, in a buoyant rush, offered these observations and sentiments. Ashley somehow couldn't avoid a reluctant nod.

On the way back to the hotel, through a light drizzle, she was thoughtful. She'd made some headway, if finding out about that awful Raymond and the bloody Bortniks could be called progress. On the subject of who had controlled the conversation, however, it was a tie at best.

*　*　*

Inspector Claude Jaubert's gaze was dismissive and shrewd at once when he understood that Ashley was a private detective. Even after she assured him she was in Paris in an informal capacity, his manner remained cold. She hadn't planned on letting the police know. It was Mirabel who blurted it out artlessly.

Jaubert and a side-kick had shown up first thing that morning. Still jetlagged, Ashley had scrambled to make herself presentable. Now they were all in the living room, the hollow-eyed Jaubert in a disreputable *imperméable* a distinct contrast to his baby-faced subordinate. Pierre Bourque, whose hand-knitted V-neck jersey made him look like a schoolboy from another era, sat off to the side. Jaubert wandered the room, until he perched restlessly on a chair facing Mirabel and Ashley on the couch. The questions came casually, but Ashley wasn't fooled. She planned to say as little as possible.

Béatrice appeared with espresso. Bourque's eyes followed Mirabel, in cerise angora, when she handed the cups around with the incongruous air of a *châtelaine*. Ashley's sartorial efforts were sadly frumpish in comparison. She'd refused Mirabel's offer to take her shopping, but now the pale Parisian sunshine splashing the carpet hinted at *grands magasins* and overpriced *boutiques insolites*. In their brief email exchange last night, Saint Cyr had said: "Take what time you need."

Jaubert downed his coffee in two Parisian gulps. "Please tell me again, Madame Saint Cyr," he said, "about the incident on the A28. We are confirming details."

Mirabel's eyes became dreamy. Her account was anything but vague.

"It was four days after Raymond told me his contact didn't show up for their meeting." Some back and forth on dates and times followed, as Bourque busily scribbled. "It was just before Alençon. It was dark, raining, some fog. Raymond told me fog is common in that low-lying area. It's the sea." An unexpected reference, until Ashley remembered how near the Atlantic was.

"One of those big SUVs came up behind us, then fell back, then drove up again. I didn't notice at first, but suddenly the car was filled with glare from its high beams. Raymond couldn't speed up—but he was trying to change lane when the SUV swung out as if it was going to pass us, just much too close to us. But it didn't pass. It just kept coming up and then dropping back, with screeches of brakes and then acceleration. And then it swung into our lane and hit us on the side. Raymond accelerated and the SUV dropped behind us again. But then it rammed us from the rear. Twice. Raymond is a good driver but we were now swerving all over our lane. Then came that curve, the one I told you about, with the industrial park on the left. We might have stayed on the road, but the SUV came up on our side again and rammed us hard. We went careening off into the other lane. Thank goodness there was no traffic, and Raymond didn't oversteer. But he could barely control the vehicle and we ended up on the shoulder—and then we were suddenly driving at high speed in the ditch."

She reflected for a moment, shrugged. "It was amazing that we didn't hit one of the sides of the ditch. Raymond just drove us to a horribly bumpy stop."

She lifted her hands in a graceful gesture. "And then I called 112, since Raymond didn't seem to be able to take his hands off the wheel. What else? The SUV just kept on going after it hit us the last time. It didn't slow down. Like I said last time, I wasn't able to see the licence plate or the occupants."

Ashley, hearing all this for the first time, was shocked. The attack had been very violent. She supposed the gangsters had been issuing a warning—signalling they wanted their contraband back. But it could so easily have ended in death, and how would that have helped them? Mirabel's composure was also odd.

Bourque now scooted in between them and began to show Mirabel pictures of SUVs on his smartphone. "This one, the Escalade, it's favoured by American gangsters, you may have seen it in musical videos?" Mirabel just smiled apologetically. "But do you recognize the grille, Madame?"

Mirabel shook her head. "Sorry."

He shuffled up more images and Mirabel continued to shake her head. Then she leaned forward, pointed. "It was a big grille, I can picture it—higher than that one, for example."

Bourque looked pleased. *"Très bien, Madame*—this one?"

"I ... think so, yes."

"Mercedes G-Class," he said to Jaubert, and they exchanged a look.

Ashley had been conducting a parallel search on her own phone. She had just come across images of the brutish and unique-looking vehicle, in a link entitled "Cars Driven by the Russian Mob in Paris and Other Major European Cities: a Compilation." Truly you could find everything on the web nowadays. She watched on mute a hair-raising video of what purported to be mobbish stunt driving on unnamed European motorways.

She felt impelled to speak. "Why do you think this incident is connected to Monsieur Boissier's disappearance?"

"Wouldn't it be logical?" Jaubert's expression was wooden.

Then followed an exchange on Raymond's movements. He'd planned to meet with his business contact somewhere outside the city, Mirabel said—she didn't know where and Raymond had only told her it was about some materials for a fashion event—but the contact hadn't shown up.

When the police brought up the truck, Mirabel had little to say. "A truck?" A pretty frown. "Hmm ... he might have talked about a missing shipment. But maybe that was later?" She shrugged apologetically. "He didn't talk to me very much about his work."

Raymond changed, however, after the Alençon incident. He'd spent a lot of time at Mirabel's but she didn't see him as much afterwards. During this period he told her that his business contact might have done something he shouldn't have—her angelic gaze swivelled to Jaubert when she said this—and it was perhaps then a missing truck came up? Anyhow, Raymond thought he was being targeted. "I'm not sure *why*," she said with a manufactured guilelessness that was impressive.

"But you believe he deliberately disappeared due to this missing shipment?" Bourque asked. He was back in his chair in the corner.

The question was a delicate trap but Mirabel evaded it. "Oh, I don't know anything about that. He just became unreachable suddenly."

Ashley now strongly suspected the two had been in contact subsequently. Mirabel knew an awful lot. That whole Bortnik brothers rigmarole, for instance. And how else to explain the composure?

"You could have died that night." Bourque was insistent. "It's dangerous to withhold information from the police."

The defenseless look appeared in Mirabel's eyes but she didn't drop her gaze. "But you're the police. You should know where he is."

"Madame, he didn't confide in us."

The police next wanted to discuss Raymond's assets. Mirabel said she knew little about these. Also, what assets? Didn't they realize Raymond was an artist and had they seen his modest studio apartment? At the mention of the studio, Jaubert and Bourque shared a brief conscious look. Ashley gleaned that the apartment was on Ile Saint-Louis, Raymond would have spent about half his nights there and, no, Mirabel had never stayed over. Ashley wasn't sure what interest it held for the police.

She started to think the conversation had gone on long enough and Mirabel seemed to think so too. She was asking Béatrice to bring them pastries when Jaubert dropped a bombshell. He announced they had found a body.

"In the river, as we often do."

It wasn't Raymond Boissier, of that the police were certain. They were seeking confirmation that it was the business contact Raymond had set out to meet. A man by the name of Langelier. They were already moving towards the door as Jaubert said to Mirabel: "This is why, Madame, you shouldn't keep anything from us."

Ashley couldn't believe they had held back this vital piece until now. "Hang on a second!" she protested. "This is important. Is Madame Saint Cyr in danger? What are you advising? Should she leave Paris?"

Jaubert's eyes narrowed. Disconcerted, Ashley suddenly realized that with his slanted brows and high cheekbones he resembled Vladimir Putin.

"We believe Boissier to be in danger," he said. "Which is why we're interviewing Madame Saint Cyr. She may be in danger. It depends on how much others think she knows. The men responsible for this would stop at nothing. Langelier didn't die of drowning. He was beaten to death."

Mirabel made a faint sound. Ashley felt a surge of fear.

"Maître Tellier, the examining magistrate, is likely to have questions. It would therefore be convenient if Madame stayed in Paris a little longer. As for whether she should return to Montreal, that isn't a police matter."

They were all at the door. Jaubert briefly examined the lock. "You could have the security here checked. Don't go outside unnecessarily." The two men offered formal salutations and decamped.

When Ashley turned to Mirabel, the latter was bouncing back with a speed that was out of place.

"It's how the police here gather information," she explained, as if it were incumbent upon her to offer this sort of cultural clarification to visiting private detectives. "They leave you with a need to find out more from *them*. It sets the stage for the next interview."

Mirabel could be ingenious, sometimes. But her puzzling calm was beginning to tick Ashley off. "Or it could be revenge for the lies you fed them. I don't get why you're not more afraid! Dead bodies in the river? Not to mention that incident on the highway—if they really just wanted their truck back."

Mirabel seemed genuinely interested in the latter point. "Maybe revenge?"

"Revenge? That's a reason out of the movies."

"Why do you think we were rammed then?"

"Sending a message, what else? Money, ultimately."

"Well yes, of course money. But there is always room for revenge."

This was the sententious loopiness Ashley was coming to expect, but she had a sudden thought. "You mean if they already *had* their truck back ..." The air in the big apartment seemed cold. She shivered.

Mirabel put her arm around Ashley's shoulders. "Let's not think about it anymore. It's lunchtime. Béatrice is making us a meal, and then we can go out for the afternoon. No, listen, we'll take cabs! We can't stay holed up always, especially as we'll be here for a while. You heard the police, they want me to stay." Ashley hadn't heard that at all, of course. "With you beside me, I'll be very safe!" She smiled a dazzling smile. "You're in Paris, Ashley, and my guest. Have you ever eaten *cassoulet?*"

Ashley shook her head, hoping it wasn't snails.

5

WELL-MADE PLAY

THE AFTERNOON, COOL, gently brooding and very un-winter-like by Ashley's standards, passed in something of a blur. Jet lag was interspersed with periods of espresso-fuelled elation that she, Ashley Arabella Smeeton from insignificant Waverley, Quebec, was swanning around Paris.

Mirabel seemed to have forgotten her scorn of mainstream fashion as she ushered Ashley around the exclusive seventh *arrondissement*'s Le Bon Marché. ("It's the oldest department store in Paris, you must look inside.") Elegant purchases just happened around the lovely Madame Saint Cyr, who was evidently known to the staff. Ashley didn't think she had ever seen anyone shop so casually, or so fast.

Mirabel was also determined to give Ashley a good time. When she pounced on a black dress of low-sheen taffeta, stiff but ethereal, declaring it perfect for Ashley—and entreated Ashley to try it on for fun as Mirabel would love nothing more than to buy her a little present, Ashley absolutely drew the line. This didn't somehow prevent her from walking out of the store in the fullness of time carrying a fancy box stuffed with tissue paper and the dress.

She had tried it on to quell Mirabel's wheedling; at least that was the reason she gave herself. The fitting in itself was a ceremony, in a big chandeliered change room with lounge chairs and discreetly murmuring staff, one of whom pulled out a needle and thread and made a microscopic adjustment while Ashley was actually in the dress. Not that Ashley could see the purpose of it: Mirabel's choice has been flawless. The dress, fitted but with small ingenious tucks and folds here and there, and with a deep square neckline, was stunning. And Ashley was stunning in it.

"With my black hair, I don't think black ..." she said.

"Oh yes, *with* your black hair," Mirabel insisted, gathering up Ashley's wavy locks with gentle hands into a loose chignon. Ashley hardly recognized herself in the vast tilted mirror. She'd once read a book that described the capable heroine as agreeably "handsome," and had thought that was probably the word for her, on a good day. But with her hair off her neck and in the coal-black dress she looked like another person—like a widow on the cover of a vintage pulp novel. A young and stylish black widow, dressed to kill.

"I'd have no reason to wear it."

"Don't be silly, Ash*lee,* the dress can be worn everywhere, it's so simple ..." And it was simple. Simple like a work of art. The leading Madame in the change room did not press or gush, but one lifted docent eyebrow indicated her satisfaction. Realizing this would go on until she accepted some sort of gift from Mirabel, or at least that was the reason she gave herself, Ashley surrendered. She pretended she didn't hear Mirabel murmuring something about "a Guerlain lipstick" and "the right shoes."

On the street again, Ashley was aware of an unreliable euphoria. If the whole thing had been a little like an out-of-body experience, now it seemed to affect the way her body moved physically through the air, the way her feet touched the pavement. Perhaps this was the reason for the discreet stares. Parisians were of course a good-looking bunch, and suave up the eyebrows. Nevertheless, men and women both seemed to find the exquisite blonde and her striking dark-haired companion worth a curious second look.

These things, Ashley told herself, with a slight toss of her hair, must be endured.

She'd telephoned Charles while they waited for their *cassoulet*. He'd been understandably alarmed by the news about Langelier, even with Ashley's deliberately cautious language, but quick to say that she should humour Belle. Though she was biddable in some ways (he'd actually said that), pressure on Belle was like trying to hold water in your fingers. Her job was unchanged: to watch over Belle, deal with the lease situation whatever the cost (Ashley had already begun to work on this) and get her out of Paris. During lunch, Ashley had tried some strategies of persuasion, but between Béatrice popping in and Mirabel's slipperiness she made little progress. And Mirabel had begged, although with a glint in her eye, that they must put aside the topic for the afternoon—she'd insisted.

When they picked up a taxi near the department store, Ashley wasn't sure at first where they were going.

Les Puces de Saint-Ouen at the Porte de Clingancourt was a shock, after the sleek, rich and slightly dull *septième*. They came to Paris's main flea market after a long time on increasingly dingy and windswept *grands boulevards*, populated by a different sort of Parisian, and over which the darkening sky shed an appropriate pall. The Porte de Clingancourt area was a hellish jumble of traffic circles, a multi-lane overpass and a hub *ferrovienne*. When the taxi approached the elevated *Périphérique* she thought they were about to plunge down a black tunnel along with other cars. But the driver darted into another lane and led them abruptly into a totally unexpected scene. Instead of elegant nineteenth century boulevards and atmospheric medieval passages, or even the gritty carscape they'd just escaped, here was a sort of jerry-built souk.

An un-souk-like northern wind greeted them when Mirabel dismissed the cab, having given the driver their parcels to deliver to rue des Arabes. "That wind's come out of nowhere," Ashley commented, seeking to discourage.

"But walking gives you the real feel of *les Puces*," Mirabel said.

They were on rue des Rosiers, the flea market's main drag, a straight narrow roadway tapering into the charmless distance. On either side, improvisational one-storey structures huddled. Coffee, plastic washpans, priceless antiques and who knows what else were for sale. Mirabel soon led Ashley into a series of serpentine lanes off des Rosiers, that were narrower, more medina-like. The buildings here were practically shacks, suggesting to Ashley a world free of building codes. The place seemed huge, although perhaps they were going around in circles. And the mood, to Ashley, was off.

"Watch your bag, there are pickpockets here." Mirabel spoke casually. "On the weekend, when all the shops and booths are open, the crowds are awful. Only some are open today."

Ashley could see shuttered buildings. She realized that was what she'd been missing about the market: people. There were some pedestrians, mostly men. They seemed alternately too few and too many. There was an air of shifty desolation about the place, although there was a playfulness too. Half-deserted and under a discordant grey sky, the market gave Ashley a mixed feeling of having stepped into a folkloric time warp, charged with something mournful, quirky, ominous.

Far beneath the racing clouds, the rising wind rushed around corners and down the alleyways, picking up debris as it blew. A young man was sitting alone outside a tin-roofed eatery impassively drinking tea in a little glass. A picturesque scene, but the wind changed everything: great gusts as they flew by whipped his robes and flung volleys of dust around him. If it hadn't been weighted down, the plastic table would have blown away.

Mirabel wanted to explore the antique shops, whose open doors suggested treasure-filled caves. Ashley gratefully ducked in after her, and hovered near. She didn't pay much attention as Mirabel scrutinized ponderous old chests and sideboards, lost in her own uneasy thoughts against the noise of the wind.

"Let's get out of here," she said when they were outside. It was now distinctly colder. "What did the weather report say anyway?"

"I don't know. Sometimes we get cyclone winds from the Atlantic." With an air of satisfaction Mirabel tucked a few business cards into her bag. "Certainly, we can leave now."

The larger antique shops had been in a classier area. Now Mirabel led them away from there, through tiny crooked lanes that petered out. They arrived at a long narrow alley slicing through blank walls, barbed wire and graffiti. Mirabel was trying not to look puzzled. "I think we'd better keep going this way."

The end only revealed another wall and a suggestion of industrial activity beyond. Here the shops were all shuttered, but there was plenty of ersatz life thanks to the boisterous wind. They were both looking at their phones, while Ashley realized yet again that Google Maps was not so useful in Paris, when a prolonged and howling gust charged out of nowhere. It ripped a panel off a tin roof and hurled it at them. The projectile missed them by an arm's length, and came to rest impaled on a yellow plastic awning featuring palm trees.

"That was close," Mirabel said, very reasonably, after a moment. But Ashley had had enough. She hustled Mirabel back the way they'd come and in a surprisingly brief time they were at the exit.

In a taxi once more, Mirabel said it was too early to return to the apartment and since they were up here anyway why didn't they head a little east to the Goutte-d'Or. The taxi driver had provided his meteorological insights—a cold front moving through—and weather alone didn't seem sufficient reason to curtail the afternoon's adventures. "You can't ever only be serious about things, Ashley," Mirabel said. She spoke as though this was a gobbet of the purest wisdom, and her mantra, which perhaps it was. When she suggested a coffee pick-me-up, Ashley resignedly agreed.

The Goutte-d'Or was a relief to Ashley after *les Puces*. It seemed like a normal enough working class neighbourhood in comparison, shabby five-storey buildings mixing with a medieval-looking church or two, and occasional vast sunken yards of train tracks. A busy indoor market spilled out into a few adjacent streets. Their cab passed scenes, feral in their energy, of cry and bustle, of high-pitched bargaining and muscular young women stylishly manhandling big crates of lettuces. That these young women were wearing hijabs didn't prevent a vague yet vivid image from forming in her mind's eye of other brawny-armed market girls—museum paintings of street scenes?—slinging crates of vegetables and baskets of flowers in just such a way. Impressions competed in Ashley's tired brain. Present-day Paris, she sensed, held onto its past beneath the surface—held on and recreated it. Waverley's nice Victorian houses with their stained glass windows dissolved as a reference point in Ashley's world view. They just weren't in the running.

On a nondescript street corner where the wind seemed to blow from all directions at once, Mirabel ushered them into an apparently squalid hole in the wall. They sat down in plastic chairs at an unsqualid zinc table and drank tiny coffees of an exceptionally concentrated nature—half sugar and half grounds from what Ashley could judge. With each sip she felt the blood vessels in her head dilating. Mirabel asked if they had their special dessert—she waved her hands and mentioned rosewater syrup—and the server, his face alight, hastened to bring them two ugly Styrofoam boxes of what looked like Timbits in syrup.

"What are they?" Ashley asked the man. He offered a few different names, none of which Ashley retained.

And they were indeed fried dough balls, although the syrup which bathed them had never seen the inside of a Tim Hortons. Mirabel and the man scrutinized Ashley with amusement as she speared one warily with a plastic fork and took a bite. They continued to watch in satisfaction as her eyes half shut. She could only nod, slowly. Unctuous, dreamy, heady with gentle rose—this had to be one of the best desserts she'd ever tasted.

Mirabel signalled for more coffee. "I knew you'd like it. Some-times," she said, "Raymond and I would pick up a couple of helpings and then we would go back to the *appart*, to this place on the roof which I must show you. And we would drink a nice wine from the Garonne, and eat them under the stars, and make sticky yet tem-pestuous love."

Ashley was speechless.

"It's a North African, maybe Middle Eastern, dessert?" Mirabel said. "Anyhow Nabil is Moroccan ..."

"You come here a lot?"

"I did, in the evening, with Raymond." She gestured to a pas-sage leading to the back. "It's bigger there, they do special dinners, there's music. It's strictly by invitation though ..." Mirabel didn't elaborate.

This left Ashley with a slightly delirious picture of unspecified raciness, possibly the African variation on an opium den, the plangent strains of a mandolin or some such in the background, a take-it-or-leave-it *plat du jour* and of course an abundance of these superlative dough balls laid on. Her overheated imagination had drifted on to the kind of dancing never practised by lay mortals when she caught sight of Nabil's peaceable face as he scrolled through his phone behind the counter. Still, she could readily conceive how Mirabel would find all this more exhilarating than arranging flowers back in Montreal.

"Let's walk to work off that dessert," Mirabel said on the side-walk, reapplying lipstick as to the French manner born—Ashley noticed it was Guerlain. They came out once more alongside the market, now wrapping up for the day. The magical vegetable girls had vanished. Ashley didn't much like the look of the groups of men clustering and loitering at various corners. They were a universe away from Le Bon Marché, where being run down by a Mercedes Benz felt like your biggest risk. If the wind was no longer battering strength, the day was darker.

"Let's walk a little faster."

They carried on through a confusing maze of shabby and winding streets, bounded by a broad tangential thoroughfare or two.

Just how confusing became evident when Ashley recognized the same display of flapping plaid shirts and African robes they had passed fifteen minutes earlier. "Oh no, we're going in circles!"

A man brushed by them and Ashley felt for the first time the sting of fear. She took Mirabel's arm and marched them forward like she knew where they were going. They arrived quickly at a congested intersection, with a diagonal street bisecting a boulevard, and a few small sidestreets adding to the madness of car and foot traffic.

"At least we can see where we are now on Google Maps," Ashley said as they waited for the light to change. She got no response from her companion. An odd slackness in Mirabel's posture drew her attention. Mirabel was looking behind them and she wasn't moving. She didn't respond to a little poke from Ashley.

"Ah ... Ashley." She pointed back the way they had come, a street as narrow as an arm span and crookedly dark within walls of five-storey buildings. "That car ..."

Ashley saw something in the gloom. Not the vehicle itself, it was too dark for that, but headlamps on high beam, high off the ground, shining in their direction.

Mirabel's eyes were wide and still. She was looking like the proverbial petrified deer. "That's exactly what I saw behind us on the A28."

They continued to stare. And then, from the obscurity, they heard a big engine rev. The vehicle slowly accelerated, revealing its heavy lines, its tinted glass windshield like the aperture in a turret, through which more than one large silhouette was visible. The passenger door now opened very slightly.

Ashley grabbed Mirabel's arm. "I'm sure it's nothing. But let's run."

They plunged onto the boulevard, along which for a lucky

moment no traffic raced, and now Ashley found she didn't have to pull Mirabel anymore. By the time they were on the median, the SUV was at the corner where they'd been seconds ago. But they were stuck in a chaos of roadwork barriers, along which a temporary pathway was funnelling pedestrians, nothing but a strip of wire mesh and an orange cone or two separating traffic from pedestrian flesh. The light changed. They hurried along this exposed chicken run of doom.

Mirabel stumbled. Two old ladies with gigantic purses blocked their way. Then, out of the blue, they were at another crosswalk. Mirabel uttered a squeak as they winged across amid horns and Gallic curses. Ashley expected to feel at any second the shattering impact on delicate femur and sacrum of two thousand pounds of hurtling metal. But they made it. And there, before them, a blocked-off pedestrianized street beckoned. Never had cement barriers looked so good to Ashley as the two of them bolted down rue des Filles Martyres, turning again and again onto sidestreets until they could run no longer for lack of breath.

They leaned against a wall.

"Were we in danger, Ashley?"

"Better safe than sorry."

Mirabel scrolled through her smart phone. "Let me find us the nearest taxi stand." She sounded calmer than Ashley felt. "It's close! We can go through this *passage couvert*, it's just out the other side."

They were in front of a shop that seemed devoted entirely to the sale of pashminas and every description of brass knick-knack. Mirabel lifted a shawl with a pleasing pattern of cream and flame-coloured logarithmic spirals. "Oh, how unusual. Unless you'd like to look at pashminas? Some of these have a surprisingly high percentage of cashmere, not like those cheap ones you get in Montreal."

"Can we just go back to the apartment?"

Mirabel slipped her arm almost tenderly into Ashley's. Now it was Mirabel's turn to lead the way.

* * *

That their escape onto rue des Filles Martyres was from an imminent threat, Ashley had little doubt in the moment. Back in the familiar surroundings of rue des Arabes, this conviction fell apart somewhat as they explained everything by phone to the police. It wasn't that Captain Bourque wasn't interested. But there was a dearth of hard evidence. He gave Mirabel some credit for her identification—probable identification—of the Mercedes G-Class. And even for Mirabel and Ashley's instincts. But no attempt had been made, neither a hit and run (chilling) nor an abduction (even more chilling). No faces or weapons had been seen. And—here Ashley wanted to kick herself—they couldn't tell police the licence number of the SUV. It was second nature to Ashley to scan plates, but they looked distractingly different here.

All Bourque could tell them (they were on speaker phone) was that they should be careful. "Also, Mesdames, why you were visiting the Goutte-d'Or ?"

"This is Ashley's first time in Paris and I wanted her to see some local colour," Mirabel said in her silliest voice. There was a suggestion of a sigh on the line.

"Is the neighbourhood supposed to be a dangerous one?" Ashley asked. "Also what about *les Puces*? We were there too."

"*Les Puces*? I see. These neighbourhoods have been designated as sensitive urban zones." Bourque's tone was diplomatic. "As to danger, it depends what you mean. They are not no-go zones, that is ridiculous. But your cell phone stolen by a pickpocket in the Goutte-d'Or can show up for sale an hour later at *les Puces*."

Annoyed on a few fronts, Ashley was silent. Mirabel said sweetly: "Oh, but Captain Bourque, if someone was really after me, the neighbourhood would make no difference surely?"

Another sigh. "*Madame, franchement ...*"

The conversation went on a little longer. Ashley resolved at the end of it to consider their security from now on from a more professional point of view. Never mind that she wasn't in France in an official capacity—or that she couldn't be sure what had happened that afternoon. There was more they could do, including improve the locks in the apartment. As for how they went out and about, the trick would be convincing Mirabel. The endgame was to get Mirabel back to Montreal. An even bigger trick was likely to be required there.

Mirabel's *appart* seemed extra luxurious, warm and safe, after the day's adventures. The temperature in Paris was still dropping, Béatrice told them as she knotted her scarf. She had prepared some light dishes they could graze on when they felt like it. Even Mirabel had no interest in going out to dinner that evening.

During a hot shower, Ashley incubated a plan to get Mirabel relaxed enough to spill some of the things she must be hiding. It seemed even more urgent now to understand what was going on. Mirabel's shower had been quicker. She greeted Ashley with a goblet of wine. As the excellent Merlot began to perform its magic, Mirabel suddenly said: "Ashley, your dress! You must try on your dress for me again."

Ashley took a long swig. "I'm in sweats, for pete's sake."

Mirabel refilled Ashley's glass. "I want to see it again! Please, Ashley, bring it out here."

So Ashley retrieved the dress from where Béatrice had hung it in her bedroom under a careful tent of pinned tissue paper, and, stripping to her cotton Hanes under the living room chandelier, slid into its crisp black folds. Mirabel helped her with the zipper and tweaked it here and there with clever fingers and eagle eyes.

"It's perfect, Ashley. Look at yourself." She pointed to the ornate mirror over the fireplace. She lifted Ashley's pony tail thoughtfully. "Let me just—Ashley, I want to do something with your hair. Stay here and have some more wine. Also I have some shoes that just might work. This is fun!"

Mirabel returned with a variety of tools of the trade. Her hands with brush and comb were deft. A lulled Ashley acknowledged to herself that the techniques that soon produced a pretty chignon *dégagée*, with a few damp black tendrils escaping her and there, the whole held in place by a heavy amber clip, were hopelessly beyond her. The shoes were slender mid-heeled pumps, black suede and absolutely plain. They pinched, but the look, proclaimed Mirabel, was perfect.

With narrowed eyes she next considered Ashley's scrubbed face. "Those eyebrows, those dark eyes, they need nothing. And your pores—they're tiny. The completely bare face is very in right now in Paris, but few except teenage models can risk it."

"I think I've heard of the no makeup look."

"No, that's different, the no makeup look requires extra make-up. But you do need one thing—lipstick." She carefully applied a red stain, dull and lush, to Ashley's shapely lips.

"This is it, this is your look," Mirabel said and ushered her towards the mirror. What Ashley, on a footstool, could see from the hipbones up looked mighty fine, if scarcely recognizable. Something like the day's earlier elation returned, but this was less a matter of nerves than singing blood.

And then the doorbell rang. Mirabel and Ashley looked at one another in befuddlement. It was after nine pm and no one was expected. Mira was in pyjamas and mink bunny slippers.

"Oh, I wonder ... I'm not even dressed. Should we buzz the person up? But wait, that's the bell from right outside the door. Ashley, what should—could you—"

"Let me look," Ashley said, and walked across to the peephole, attributing the teetering swing of her steps to the unfamiliar shoes.

Someone slender, dark, female, stood in the corridor. Mirabel had a peek too and nodded uncertainly. "I'll get my dressing gown."

Ashley was therefore alone at the door when she opened it. The woman sized her up. The expression on her face was many things—conflicted, with an overlay of uncertainty. Complicated.

"So you are Mira," she said. "That's funny—oh well." Her voice was aggressive now. "I decided it was time we met."

Ashley was taken aback. "No, I'm not—hold on. Who are you if it comes to that?"

"Since you ask—I'm Mira. Yes, that is who I am. I am Mira." The accent now seemed vaguely French Caribbean. Ashley also noticed the stranger was young and good-looking—very pretty, in fact, in an androgynous way.

"That's very unusual," came a mild voice behind them. "Because I'm Mira." Mirabel came into view, tying the belt of her robe, and peered at the woman in the doorway. "Would you like to come in?" she offered politely.

The Mira in the hallway stared for a moment. "All right, yes."

"Come in here. Ashley and I were just having wine. I'll get another glass. This is a little confusing to us, in part because we are slightly drunk probably. Although of course it's very interesting too. I mean, three Miras would have been too much, but even two needs an explanation."

"Well, here's your explanation." The newcomer stood in the middle of the ornate room looking like a tall attractive adolescent. An adolescent about to fly into a rage. She tossed her coat onto a chair. "I learned about you from the police, after Raymond disappeared. It was a surprise, I promise you. I decided to visit."

She took a deep breath. "I'm Mireille Borel, and I'm Raymond Boissier's girlfriend."

6

FIRE AND ICE

THE EVENING PROVIDED Ashley with a deeper understanding of the French term *de trop*. Mirabel (the Saint Cyr Mira) insisted she remain with them. So she was in the living room while the other Mira (Mireille Borel) dove into a dramatic and succinct account of her prior claim on Raymond Boissier's heart.

It boiled down to this. They'd been together some years; they had an "understanding"; they were devoted in their way, which did not include the bourgeois convention of marriage. He spent a good chunk of time with her at her *"appartement grand et chic"* (these words uttered defensively) in the Montsouris district—while keeping his studio on Ile Saint-Louis, but strictly for business purposes. Although the studio's versatility wasn't lost on any of them.

Mireille's tone was one of simmering anger, as if she wanted to blame Mirabel for Raymond's two-timing ways, yet couldn't quite bring herself to. Complicated. She wound herself down eventually, with a reiteration of the theme of "you can imagine my surprise when *les maudits flics* ..."

During this recital, Mirabel had been silent, assiduously plying the visitor with wine. "I had no idea," she said at length. Her tone was low, sober. Meek. "I hope you believe me, Mireille. May I call

you Mireille? To avoid confusion? And you can call me Mirabel."
She took a sip of Merlot, let out a sighing breath. "He never said."

The grey-blue eyes were thoughtful and Mirabel's voice contained wonder, but Ashley couldn't detect deep disappointment, let alone hurt. "Myself, I'm in another relationship. In fact, I'm only in Paris temporarily. I have a husband in Montreal. My feelings for Raymond have been—very sincere, but he always knew I'd return." Was she offering these words to mollify the other?

Mireille flung herself back in her armchair now. She had been guzzling the wine as if rants were thirsty work. Her eyes roved over Mirabel, the lavish room, took in Ashley briefly, then back to Mirabel, where she dwelled for a moment on the mink bunny slippers. "Raymond not in an intimate relationship? How could you be so simple!"

Mirabel said nothing, just pulled out her phone and scrolled to the picture of Raymond Ashley had looked at before. Mireille bounded onto the couch beside Mirabel. "Did you take pictures of him?"

"Well, just one or two, but this is his professional head shot. I was just wondering if I could see dishonesty in his face." Mirabel sounded genuinely curious, and Mireille leaned forward with evident curiosity as well. Ashley herself couldn't resist peeking. In the modishly black and white photograph, Raymond had one elbow leaning against a bridge railing and a cigarette dangled rakishly from a lip. A lip formed, it now seemed glaringly obvious, to utter tissues of lies. It was an insufferable pose, but no less effective for that. He smiled back at them, all dark and throbbing soul, like the handsomest devil in the nine circles of hell.

"He does look just like a serial cheater," Mirabel murmured.

Mireille roughly angled the phone towards her. "He looks like a *sale con*. I could stomp all over that face now." Her tone and shrug were quintessentially French, and contained a hint of finality.

"Well, could you use your own phone?" Mirabel said politely.

"Anyhow, *je m'en fous*. It wasn't like there wasn't someone else for me too. I knew François before I met Raymond, from my job in *les relations médiatiques*, and we still sometimes see each other." Mireille's face was a battleground of cynicism and encroaching depression.

Mirabel studied her sympathetically. She touched her arm. "I've found it useless in life to brood over tragedy." Ashley thought the words ridiculous on these over-privileged lips, until she remembered Mirabel's early loss.

"Would you like tea?" Mirabel was saying.

Ashley jumped up. "I'll make some for everyone." She escaped to the kitchen, but not soon enough to avoid hearing Mireille says something about *"ta belle amie"* and Mirabel launching into a candidly humorously account of the reason for Ashley's presence in Paris, in which she used the words *"elle est bien originale"* and *"mon pauvre Charles."* The latter words seemed to provoke snorts of laughter.

Ashley filled the kettle to the top to buy herself time. As she waited she leaned against the counter and rubbed her eyes. She noticed her new dress had a few creases—Béatrice would know how to remedy that. She breathed deeply. This was a bizarre turn of events, although completely banal from another perspective. She hoped, anyway, it would make it easier to pry Mirabel from rue des Arabes and get her on a plane.

When she reappeared with the tea and a plate of biscuits, the women's heads were together and the atmosphere was less tense.

"Merci, Ash*lee*," Mirabel said. She sounded in better spirits, bordering on perky. There was a new bottle open on the table. "We're trying to come to terms with all this. We've decided that Raymond did have his uses, mainly of the bedroom kind. This we can judge and on this wholeheartedly agree." Mireille knit her brows and pursed her lips at these sentiments—*like a judge at a thoroughbred show maybe*, Ashley thought. The shift in mood was palpable. Mirabel's wineglass-half-full strategy seemed to be working.

Mireille actually looked uninterested now. "Yes, *le sexe. Toujours le sexe.* I love these Bonne Maman *galettes au caramel.* Everybody's favourite, like your Oreos." She sounded about fourteen. She had the body type of a tall boy, and the look she went in for—beige corduroy pants, an orange shirt buttoned to the throat and a head of short curls poised on a delicate neck—added to the misleading impression of adolescence.

"More like Peak Freens in Canada," Ashley said.

"Peak Freen? What a funny name!" They all agreed and had a barely coherent conversation about Peak Freens and then Dare Whippets. Meanwhile Mirabel had uncorked a third bottle, and brought out the cookie package, dinner leftovers, and a bowl of fruit.

"Your dress is chic. Also, you have a very interesting job," Mireille said to Ashley.

In keeping with the lightened mood, Ashley chronicled her case involving Marigold Dreyfus and the luxury car theft ring. They laughed appreciatively at the outrageous details. "It was like I was paid for nothing," Ashley said, before realizing the words were less than diplomatic in the circumstances. Refreshments were briskly circulating, however, and no one seemed to have noticed.

Then Mirabel recounted a version of the afternoon's drama, and Mireille, who had learned of the A28 incident from Jaubert, assured them hotly that she believed their account and, yes, she knew *all* about the Bortnik brothers. Also, all about Raymond ... She made a seemingly random comment about how easy it was— did they know?—to move large amounts of cash you didn't care to declare out of the country on gift cards. So simple. Mirabel nodded politely, while Ashley wondered if she'd really gotten the point.

"I'm puzzled why—" Mirabel cleared her throat. "Why the police told you about me, but didn't tell me about you?"

Mireille shrugged. "Perhaps because they thought Raymond's real relationship was with me." Triumph flared briefly in her eyes, and died.

"If they were looking for a way to find Raymond," Ashley said, "why would the Bortniks send someone after you, Mirabel, and not Mireille? Have you been followed, Mireille?"

"Not that I know of. But you can't expect those Bortnik thugs to be that thorough in their research. Some of them work for tips." Mireille looked out of countenance, however, whereas it was Mirabel's turn to look proud. Ashley wanted to shake them both.

Mirabel sighed. "But, in matters of the heart, who can say what is real?" Her tone was diffident, as she refilled the other's glass.

"Well, there's that," Mireille said, and now it was her turn to pat Mirabel. "Love is dignified madness."

The conversation was assuming an absurd character, and Ashley seemed alone in her awareness of the lateness of the hour. She picked up the teapot. "I'm going to refill this one last time—whoa, look at the time." Mireille was showing Mirabel photos of Raymond on her phone and they ignored her.

Waiting in the kitchen, Ashley was startled by a stealthy thump at the window. It was snow—snowflake clusters were floating and tumbling through the blackness and some were sticking to the pane. Snow was unusual for Paris, their cabdriver had told them: It wasn't like in "the old days." Whatever those were: A picture of medieval-walled Paris snowed in and encircled by wolves was all Ashley could summon. Her mind loosened, and she imagined snow falling over the Point, over the sleeping hills of her childhood. Roy and Aram had texted her a couple of times, but she'd felt increasingly disengaged from things back home. It was the Saint Cyr world that now held her—and Paris.

She lingered in the kitchen, wool-gathering. When she returned to the living room, Mirabel and Mireille's conscious look made her think something was up. The level in the third bottle had dropped significantly. They seemed fired by an idea.

"I never told you, Ashley," Mirabel said, "that Raymond did communicate with me after his disappearance. But it wasn't much, just a text that said he was changing to a burner phone and would be in touch. And I was to tell no one. He sent the same text to Mireille."

Ashley bit her lip and poured tea.

"Four days after he disappeared," Mireille said. "So we know that he was all right then. But if the Bortniks are hunting him, maybe he can't reach out to us now. He must have heard about Langelier. He must be afraid." She paused judiciously. "We know more about Raymond than the police, about places he goes, his friends, business acquaintances. We think we could find him ourselves."

Ashley was silent, waiting. Cooking this up would have been impossible without wine. "We should at least try." Mirabel emptied the bottle. "We may be able to offer Raymond help. I guess we owe him that."

A sullen gleam in Mireille's eye made Ashley think the two Miras were working somewhat different emotional angles. She also sensed that they were unlikely to take her advice if it didn't mesh with their own hare-brained scheme. "I see. It's nice of you to worry about him." She addressed Mirabel. "But you *owe* him? Raymond has put you in harm's way. Looking for him could increase your danger. How exactly would you go about it, if it comes to that?"

Mirabel beamed. "Why, just like you as an investigator—we'd ask around. But we'd be very discreet, naturally."

"That could so easily attract the wrong kind of attention." She struck a formal note. "I'm being well paid to bring you back to Montreal in one piece, and I'm contractually obliged to try my best." Mirabel looked ethereally pained while Mireille appeared impressed. "Which is why I can't recommend it. If I tell Charles about this, which I may have to, my instructions could change."

Mirabel's smile was obliging, reasonable. "Well, even if Charles's instructions change, it's not like you or he can do anything about this. You can't kidnap me!" She let out a light-hearted laugh. "So let's not worry too much about that. Besides, Ash*lee,* we won't do anything you advise against."

Ashley gritted her teeth. "Paris is big. He won't be hanging out in his usual places."

"Maybe not," Mirabel said with a note of triumph, "but he had specific plans for *le Carnaval de Paris,* with a lot of money on the line. He's supplying clothes and models to another unFashion event—at night, in the Bois de Boulogne. Even if he has to lie low, he can't cancel his obligations. He'll have to find a way to carry on business, communicate with his partners."

It sounded thin to Ashley. Surely this was Mirabel at her most scatter-brained. "Do you even know who his business partners are?"

"You need not worry about that," Mireille said, "because I do."

The conversation went on. But Ashley knew she had lost the round. She'd better ring Charles before she went to bed. The whole situation was out of hand. Why didn't the two Miras just pull each other's hair for a bit like in a movie and move on? This must be a different movie. The two of them seemed absurdly satisfied with themselves.

"It's snowing heavily—in case that matters to you, Mireille," Ashley said.

Mirabel jumped up, happy like a little girl. "Oh, snow falling over Paris! I know what we should do! Get your coats. We'll go up to the roof." Mireille looked like she was up for it and Ashley didn't see the point in protesting.

They took the elevator to an attic of sorts, and followed a passageway narrower and plainer than the elegant halls below. They came to a metal door.

"This one locks automatically from inside, but we can wedge it," Mirabel explained as she opened it. A cold blast met them. Dingy iron steps went straight up. Then they were stepping onto the slope of zinc roof tiles, and into another world.

It was a world of rooftops blanketed with snow, line after crouching line of chimney pots, and a higgledy-piggledy of wires, satellite dishes and crooked antennae. Out of the giant cup of the sky snow floated by in waves and Ashley felt she was floating too, like a bird. The Parisian panorama stretched in all directions: the glimmering web of roof lines punctuated by stately domes and spires, scored with the long burning lines of the *grands boulevards*.

Mirabel pointed. "Look Ashley, over there—it's the best cliché in the world."

The illuminated Eiffel Tower glowed on the western horizon. Ashley, who had once watched a trestle bridge burn, thought that it was like that—all on fire, the snowy coppery air around it like smoke.

Mireille tossed her head in the wind, looking positively feral, and lit a cigarette. Mirabel hugged herself in the skins of dead animals. Ashley tried to take it all in, this living midnight world of roofs and snow and veiled radiance, also the two women standing beside her, lost each in her own thoughts, but still in some way joined.

They shuffled back indoors eventually, after Mireille said her *putain de manteau* was useless in this weather and she had better hurry up and find a cab.

"Tell me about the *Carnaval* anyway," Ashley said, but Mirabel and Mireille were sending each other their phone numbers and didn't hear her.

* * *

Back in her bedroom, Ashley was having no luck reaching Charles Saint Cyr. Eventually she left a detailed message. Her phone rang an hour later. She was surprised to hear the voice of Isabel Jadois, wanting to know what was going on with her sister. The two Miras' cracked sleuthing plan was unwelcome news to Isabel, and she peppered Ashley with impatient and alarmed questions. She'd been in contact with Charles earlier and he'd told her about the afternoon's scare. She had questions and many opinions. Ashley did her best. But since Isabel's lively spewing echoed her own thoughts and feelings, she was fresh out of brilliant ideas. "Maybe you could talk to her directly—or Charles could, he *is* her husband," she said.

Isabel made an impatient noise. "I can try. And I think Charles is trying to call her. But he's dealing with some kind of labour unrest, smashed machines. I don't know. It's quite an emergency."

"Yikes." Ashley had scanned the Montreal news online, and had only seen something about a major holdup in the city's financial district. "I didn't read anything about that."

"Not in Montreal—in Bangladesh." Isabel's laugh was cynical. "It won't surprise you to learn that Mira sometimes screens and even blocks her calls. Ashley, you're there on the ground with her. Figure something out, okay?"

There was a good deal of this, while Isabel's voice cut in and out, competing with static and badgering public announcements of some sort. The whole conversation was frustrating and felt useless to Ashley. She didn't need more nagging.

"*Bon bien*, I have to go," Isabel said after an explosion of interference. "But the specific reason I'm calling is to tell you that Charles is on his way to Paris, as soon as he can, maybe even tomorrow. You freaked him out with your news. You'll have that to deal with soon. He didn't want to tell Mira ahead of time, but I thought you should know. You might want to prepare her." Isabel could give no more precise details to Ashley and the call ended.

Ashley tried Charles again and sat back against her pillow to think. A singularly useless exercise. The only result was a spike of acute annoyance that everyone she was dealing with was so uncooperative and also so damn shifty. Charles Saint Cyr was a throwback, but surely even he couldn't believe all the things that came out of his own mouth. And coming to Paris now, after he'd paid Ashley so he could stay away. Boissier was a cad and a petty crook, who might have opened up a very deep end for them all to fall into. Jaubert and Bourque were a bureaucratic nuisance. Isabel was full of opinions but she wasn't helping. Mirabel herself was nothing more than a case of arrested development, who didn't seem able to distinguish spoiled little-rich-girl whimsy from the wildly inappropriate and imprudent. And as for that Mireille Borel—she had basically egged Mirabel on. A sudden unpleasant thought came to Ashley: Why had Mireille really come to rue des Arabes that evening? Could she be working some dodge of her own?

Ashley had had a general plan of wearing Mirabel down, dealing efficiently and tactfully with the alleged barriers like the apartment lease. But with these various characters popping out from behind columns, or about to pop out, the stage was getting much too crowded. The city itself, vast and lovely, densely populated by millions of strangers, now seemed almost claustrophobically tight around Ashley.

Her phone pinged. Bloody hell. This was Mirabel, in her suite, deciding that it was a good time to send Ashley additional photos of Raymond. There were several. Mirabel had taken more pictures than she'd admitted to Mireille. Some were just of Raymond, but a third person had taken a few of Mirabel and Raymond together. Ashley found herself returning to one in particular. She couldn't take her eyes off it. Raymond was staring straight into the camera, his sultry gaze throwing out a lazy challenge. He had his arm around Mirabel, who was leaning against him with her head tilted back, a drugged expression on her face. There was something almost indecent in such feeling displayed, but beautiful in a way too—or maybe it was sordid, but the couple, the dark-haired man and the fair sylph, were beautiful together.

Mirabel's apparently muted reaction to the news of Raymond's infidelity was surprising, Ashley thought. Did this kind of love just wither as quickly as it bloomed? Now Mirabel was helpfully texting her: "'Love is like a fever which comes and goes quite independently of the will.' That's Stendhal."

Something close to rage flared in Ashley, and she tossed her phone on the bed. But wasn't that ephemeral moment captured by the unknown photographer what so many people longed for all their lives? The thing that bothered her most, Ashley was honest enough to admit, was that underneath all her common sense a part of her honoured such feelings. If only with suspicion and fear.

She moved to the window and there brooded for a while. The snow was still falling. Eventually, deciding she might as well get the bad news over with, she made her way quietly to Mirabel's suite at the other end of the apartment. The door was ajar and Ashley looked in. Mirabel was sitting cross-legged amid a billowing heap of designer linen, her lovely blonde head tousled like a child's, as she leaned into her small pink cell phone. She was speaking to someone in a low voice. Ashley hesitated in the doorway, undecided, watching Mirabel. But the conversation, which seemed an intense one, continued. Eventually she padded back to her room. The news was going to have to wait.

7

BETWEEN DOG AND WOLF

THE NEXT MORNING Ashley woke to brilliant sunshine and a very cold room. The view from her windows, of narrow snowy streets and sunshine glittering off windows, was almost like a Christmas scene. All it lacked was the French version of holly and ivy. Ashley fiddled with the thermostat, which had been turned down. A sullen hum and a trickle of lukewarm air from a vent reminded her that Parisians were unused to very cold winters.

Mirabel confirmed this over breakfast. She'd practically frozen with that useless comforter, she said. In the end they agreed that Ashley, who was going out to investigate door hardware (on the principle that a DIY upgrade was something you could apologize for later) would pick up a couple of down comforters. Mirabel's instructions for the highest quality German white goose down and the right places to shop were very precise. It was minus fifteen Celsius, exceptional for Paris, Béatrice told them. Mirabel said that she for one was happy to stay indoors today, not just because of the cold but also—Béatrice was nearby—to "rest" after yesterday. Ashley was glad she didn't have to nag.

Mirabel tried to convince Ashley to borrow her fur coat. Ashley demurred, but said she might look at coats. Her duffel had seen a few winters and the down parka she'd left in Montreal was also old.

Mirabel's instructions on where to look for coats that combined the right quality and style with the right warmth were equally precise. And if Ashley was going out, she really should do a little sightseeing.

After breakfast, Ashley drew Mirabel aside and broke the news that Charles was apparently on his way to Paris. Mirabel didn't seem unduly amazed by this information, or even particularly dismayed. "Oh, Charles," was all she said. Ashley wondered if her hushed conversation of the previous night had been with Isabel, or even with her husband. Ashley herself had had a business-like text from Charles: "I'm on my way, after I deal with a business matter here, will update you." The Bangladesh matter, Ashley assumed.

The cold was biting, but Ashley's step was lively as she walked down towards the Seine. She'd slept well, the sun was shining, and today Mirabel was being "biddable," to use that awful word of her husband's. Anyway, Charles's arrival, she'd decided, might have its upside.

Paris in the grips of a real winter day was lovely, charming and comical. There was something almost carnival-like about the sights and sounds of Parisians, kitted out in their idea of winter clothes, skidding and floundering through snow, swearing dramatically as they greeted each other with what Ashley thought was even more kissing than usual. There were abandoned vehicles, gendarmes directing traffic at busy intersections, and snow clearing underway.

People were making the best of it. Amid the workday rush, an elegant man in a camel hair coat was pulling two charming small children on a toboggan. Parisians were staring, but at the toboggan, as if toboggans were a rare winter fashion accessory. There were even a few jolly groups of people clustered on the balconies, their extravagant outfits suggesting they were continuing a party from the night before. And the cafés were bursting. Apparently cappuccino was the answer, to this as to so many other things.

As she was nearest to rue de Rivoli, Ashley started there, and dutifully picked up two enormous comforters at the Galeries Lafayette for the staggering number of euros she'd been instructed to consider.

Although Paris prices now officially horrified her, she decided she'd better go to rue Saint Antoine anyway to look at coats. The Monsieur who'd served her in the bedding department had said the mercury was still dropping.

Whatever Parisian designers made of down, and for all she knew they adored it, Ashley in fact settled for a Korean coat. It was long, dramatically full, with a dashingly wide shawl collar that somehow turned into a hood, indescribably cunning stitching, the fastenings off to one side, the hem subtly asymmetrical. It was made of expensively coarse grey cloth, waterproofed, gushed the sales assistant, and was positively stuffed with luxurious wadding. In no world could this be called a mere parka, and it had a price tag to match. But with the money she was making from this gig Ashley figured she could splurge. It was warmer than her old parka, she was pleased to note when she stepped outside, her old coat bundled in a bag. For the next little while, Ashley just enjoyed swanning around fashionable rue Saint Antoine, with a side trip to the exquisite Place des Vosges—like she belonged.

Hunger intervened. She found a cab, dropped her shopping off at rue des Arabes and continued west to le Petit Palais, where they had a nice lunch place according to Mirabel. The museum also had wonderful exhibits, she'd said, and Ashley could see the Place de la Concorde and other famous places on the way. This was grand public Paris. They drove along shining black boulevards, past breathtaking feats of architecture amid lavish grounds, made all the more spectacular by several inches of dazzling snow that wasn't melting. Perhaps it was the coat, but she was led to a very good table in the Petit Palais restaurant, and dined on an omelette and a carafe of wine, the view of a snow-laden courtyard supplying a melancholy enchantment. Then Ashley delivered herself to the artistic offerings of the Petit Palais, which included two special exhibits on the Art of *Carnaval* and, more unexpectedly, the Art of the Plague.

Carnaval had been a very big deal in Paris for several hundred years, according to the exhibits. There were winter carnivals every-where, from Quebec City to Rio, but in Paris it seemed to have been a unique mix of the medieval and theatrical, of myth, fantasy and release, with costumes and masks, grand balls and fancy dress par-ties. And things much more unpredictable, like the procession of a massive bull through the streets and dances for the laundresses of the city and their chosen queen. Judging from the crowd scenes, Parisians of all social levels took to the street, to savour the diver-sions of the day, and the pleasures of the night. Nowadays it was a lesser affair, but some events were making a comeback.

The Art of the Plague exhibit was educational if not for the faint of heart, and after a while it didn't even seem much different to Ashley. She'd disregarded the ground plan and she wandered back and forth between the two exhibits at random. Eventually she couldn't have said in which exhibit she'd seen the various pictures: creatures in sinister white and malicious black masks, hysterical crowds under lurid skies, flames, whether celebratory bonfires or plague pits, semi-phantasmagorical packs of nighttime creatures, wolf-like, rat-like, goat-like, swarming across broad bleak squares and pouring down narrow alleyways. Was the line between un-inhibited celebration and the panic of disease so fine?

She was back in the restaurant, reflecting that Europe was a bit weird as she refreshed herself with an espresso, when Mirabel called.

"Oh Ashley," she said. She was slightly breathless. "I just want-ed to let you know. He's here."

"Already? That was fast."

"Not Charles." A silence. "It's Raymond. Raymond is here. But it's safe, don't worry. He's not staying. He came over the roofs." The last bit was offered as a perfectly ordinary way to visit.

Ashley felt a surge of mingled irritation and alarm. "I still haven't made it to the hardware store, but I'm coming back right now."

"Of course, Ashley. Whatever you like. I'm sending Béatrice home early, by the way—on account of the weather."

Collecting her thoughts during the taxi ride back was an unproductive exercise. If Mirabel's flower-arranging life was devolving into French farce, at least she had the advantage over Ashley of knowing her role in it. Her own job for the most part was about getting at the facts. This had been a peculiar assignment to begin with, more to do with persuasion than detection. Now she didn't feel very useful at all. She was worried Charles Saint Cyr might feel the same way. He was about to erupt, the vengeful husband, into Mirabel's subsidized love nest. And how was Ashley to play the scene? She felt like one of those pillars on an increasingly crowded stage, from behind which some people eavesdropped, others plotted, and still others met in illicit, if straitened, assignations.

She caught a glimpse of herself in the big mirror on the shadowy landing as she hurried upstairs. In her snazzy new coat, she didn't look like herself. She suddenly wished she hadn't bought it, and hadn't gone to le Petit Palais, hadn't swigged a carafe of wine during the day and looked at creepy art exhibits on someone else's dime. This was guilt and proved, she told herself, that she was an honest person. When Saint Cyr turned up she'd get clarification about expectations. But she was left with a faint sense of moral panic, compounded by a headache—the first symptom of plague as she had learned today. Bortnik thugs on the horizon were adding to her stress. But it was personal too and, unlike her aching brow, couldn't be dealt with by an aspirin.

The lights were out in the *appart* and all was quiet. Mirabel's bedroom door was shut. Ashley eventually heard faint noises. Rustles, whispers. Etcetera. Mentally giving up, she beat a retreat to her room to dig up the aspirin. When, some time later, she heard the click of a latch and low voices, she emerged from her end.

"Oh Ash*lee!* I'm so glad you're back." Mirabel seemed innocently happy to see her. "I want you to meet Raymond Boissier."

At least *he* was fully dressed. Mirabel had changed into a pair of brown satin pyjamas and the mink bunny slippers. Her loose top was carelessly misbuttoned and sweat had created angelic tendrils around her glowing face. Ashley, with the skills of the semi-repressed, assumed her most wooden expression.

Raymond shook her hand with amused self-possession. He was pretty much what she had expected from the photo gallery. He was a tall confident specimen, elegant as all get-out. His attractively slouchy sweater was in the Frenchman-does-snow theme, and Ashley supposed the snug gabardine slacks he wore were also a French fashion statement. The whole dark and dazzling effect was, of course, expected. But his eyes surprised her. She had imagined them a lustrous matinee-idol chocolate, whereas they were actually light hazel—shrewd or dreamy or restless, depending on the moment.

Mirabel draped herself in a cashmere throw and brought them tea. "Raymond loves Twinings English Breakfast," she explained to Ashley, as if this were a delightful affectation.

"So you came over the roofs," Ashley said.

Raymond smiled. "Not exactly. Did Mira say that? There's another entrance to the building, from a street over. The buildings join."

"Like in *The Magician's Nephew*," Mirabel said.

The literary allusion irritated Ashley. She cut to the chase. "You're in some danger, Monsieur Boissier, and Mirabel may be in danger as well—because of you. Your contact is dead and the *police judiciaire* are looking for you. Also, Monsieur Saint Cyr is on his way from Montreal. My goal is to ensure Mirabel returns there quickly. I'm sure it's her husband's goal. And I'd be very surprised if it wasn't Mireille Borel's goal. Now that Mirabel's been able to see that you're well, I hope we can agree that she should leave as soon as possible."

Raymond nodded noncommittally at this little speech. He didn't seem embarrassed by the mention of Charles and Mireille, but Ashley could see he didn't like it when she brought up the police. His suave expression was now a little hard.

"When Ashley gets like that, it's best to agree," Mirabel said in a meek voice.

"It is entirely up to Mirabel, Mademoiselle." Raymond's tone was indifferent. "She's not my captive—not entirely." His smouldering look passed over Mirabel, kindling in her an unconscious response of appeasement and animal hunger. This made him smile coolly. Ashley looked away.

Mirabel stretched on the couch like a pretty cat. "Don't worry, Ashley," she said. "I know what I have to do. I'm just glad I've been able to talk to Raymond, that's all." *So that's what you were up to in there.* A cool giggle from Mirabel, who had read her expression.

"But there is just one thing. I got a call from that Inspector Jaubert earlier. The examining magistrate wants to interview me after all, and I have an appointment at the quai des Orfèvres tomorrow. It's really about poor Langelier."

Raymond looked suitably, if insincerely, mournful.

"But the judge also wants to talk to me about what happened on the A28." Ashley frowned, and Mirabel said: "Naturally I'll be discreet but it's not something I can easily refuse."

There was more talk about this. Mirabel was apologetic and Raymond slightly bored. He should, Ashley thought, be in the grips of fear. She was getting a sense of something very hard-boiled, very cold-blooded, beneath the smooth surface.

"It must be done," Mirabel said, picking up a macaron.

She and Raymond took alternate bites of it in that lovers' manner most grating to the out of love, as they chatted about his plans for the unFashion Event in the Bois de Boulogne. Ashley had trouble grasping the essence of this function. She gathered that many people would be cavorting among the trees and shrubbery. They would be in costume, fashion would be displayed or dramatically presented, and much money would, somehow, be made. Raymond would also be presenting his own designs.

Mirabel pulled a portfolio from his Bleu de Chauffe satchel and invited Ashley to look. It was hard to say whether the sketches were of clothing models and or of well-dressed supernatural beings. A blonde in a Pierrette-themed coat and a pert hat resembling a spider reminded Ashley of Mirabel, except that the figure's eyes were all black, as if the pupils had exploded with shock. She saw a look of Mireille Borel in a lanky winged gamine dressed as a female Harlequin, holding a machete behind her back. Ashley looked at the other sketches with interest. Were they all based on girlfriends? They were disturbing, anyhow. But Ashley—fresh from a crash course in French cocktail dresses and Korean coats—couldn't deny the designs were fine. There was substantial talent here.

"You can see how good he is, can't you?" Mirabel said. "Raymond is the real thing." Ashley glanced unwillingly at Raymond and saw faint amusement on his face.

To Ashley's relief and Mirabel's relatively muted sorrow, he left soon after. Ashley was in the living room and didn't intend to see the clinch at the door. Raymond was looking extra piratical in a greatcoat. Mirabel had entwined herself around him, and his hands were everywhere while he covered her face with kisses.

Mirabel was rebuttoning her top as she came back into the living room. She looked flushed and dazed.

"Did you give him money?" Ashley asked. "Was that why he came to see you?"

Mirabel didn't look put out. "I gave him quite a lot of money, actually." There was a pause. "But, Ashley, tell me, did you have a nice time? The duvets are perfect—I want to ship them home. But did you enjoy yourself today? I hope I sent you to the right places." She seemed very artless as she said this—young and wanting to please.

Ashley closed her eyes. Time passed, but nothing changed and she opened them again. "I am an expert on the plague. Also, do you want to see my new coat?"

**

The next day Charles Saint Cyr still hadn't left Montreal. Ashley caught Mirabel in one or two hushed phone calls before breakfast. They could have been late night calls in Montreal time—so Ashley hoped.

At breakfast, for which Béatrice had been keen to make American pancakes and syrup, which, however, emerged as lacy French crepes with delicate poached fruit, Mirabel said she wanted to go to le quai des Orfèvres alone. She would look unreliable if accompanied by Ashley.

"You're not my keeper," Mirabel said—mournfully, since that was pretty much what Ashley was. "I *am* capable of telling what happened."

Remembering Mirabel's lucid account of the highway incident, Ashley had to agree. Mirabel said she would take taxis and surely nothing bad could happen to her at the prefecture, which was simply rotten with police and judges. She was at her most demure this morning, with a white shirt buttoned to the neck and a neat grey flannel skirt. Raymond Boissier seemed to be a forgotten topic.

Ashley herself was off to the rental company to sign papers and arrange for Charles to e-transfer pots of euros so they could break the lease. He had delegated proxy signing authority to Ashley for the altered contract. Agence Immobilière du Faubourg Saint Honoré liked to do things in person and in triplicate.

She was still on edge, and she decided to walk. It was a day of fugitive sunshine and stealthy cloud masses that moved broodingly over the city, quenching it periodically of light. The cold was holding. Ashley was glad of her fine new coat.

The Faubourg Saint Honoré, with its dignified squares and shops catering to the ultra-rich, was another memorable experience. The well-dressed Madame who conducted the business with Ashley was courtesy itself. They sat on velour banquettes in the hushed ambience of the agency, where the aura of wealth was so thick—a lesser Mademoiselle offered her coffee with what amounted to a small bow—that she found herself breaking into a sweat. The thing was done eventually. There was a fixed move-out date for the end of the following week, for bureaucratic reasons that Ashley believed were related to maximum cash extraction. Still, tangible progress at last.

She'd been planning to head over to the hardware store for those door and window bolts. However, she changed her mind once she'd read in the contract that if residents made alterations of any "fixed" kind to the *immeuble,* they were liable for punitive damages and other sinister additional consequences. They thought of every-thing, didn't they?

With time on her hands, Ashley decided she'd have a look at a mouldering old church or two. She'd been intrigued by several as she'd crisscrossed the city. She told her driver to bring her to the oldest church in Paris. To her surprise the taxi came to a stop in the Goutte-d'Or neighbourhood once more. When she remonstrated, he gestured to a stone building across the street that did indeed exude hoary decrepitude. "Saint-Denys de la Chapelle," he said with an irritable flourish. "The oldest church in Paris!"

"The guide book says it's on the left bank," Ashley said.

"Mais non! It's what tourists think, but they are completely wrong. The foundations of this church date from 475 AD, and pre-date the other by seventy-two years. This street is on an ancient pilgrimage route!" Since she'd recognized various landmarks along the way, including the huge sunken railyard, Ashley would hazard a peek while she was there.

Another of those heavy clouds blotted out the sun the moment she was alone. The neighbourhood really wasn't a very good one. The buildings were shabby and graffiti-adorned, the little shops mysterious in purpose, and refuse blew fitfully down the wide road once travelled, according to the cabby, by early medieval pilgrims. It was also discouragingly empty on this very cold day, barring in-determinate lone men shuffling along the cracked pavement.

The church was open, empty and frigid. A rickety sign pointed down winding stairs to a crypt. Ashley was happy to skip that part of the tourist experience—and she was the only one. The church itself, small and humble compared to the grand cathedrals, was crypt-like enough. And authentically old, a thousand years old even by the time teenaged Joan of Arc reputedly prayed in it, one long and lonely night, before things went from bad to worse. A few votives burned at the back and Ashley, on an impulse, dropped some coins in a slot and lit one for her Smeeton grandmother. Funny how we make offerings for the dead, she thought—and yet the living were so often in danger.

It was an atmospheric place, and Ashley lingered a while. The vastness of the Parisian past once more rose up before her. When she stepped out onto the street again, the day had darkened further. She headed south. Without incident, she came to the shop where they'd stopped after running away from the SUV. She decided on an impulse to look at the allegedly authentic bargain-priced pashminas. The cream and red one with logarithmic spirals was still there and she paid for it—a token present when this was all over for Mirabel, surely the queen of precise circumnavigation.

The relaxed mood deserted her moments later. She passed a threesome of staring men, who barely made room for her as she went by. Moments later, she was abruptly accosted by one of them, a big jittery specimen. The muttered words were incomprehensible, but the drug-fuelled aggression was clear. She picked up her pace. The two other men melted away but the big one followed her, talking either to the air or his favourite demons. Thinking to get away, she turned into a narrow street with shuttered doorways, realizing too late this wasn't a good place to be. She was deciding to run when, to her relief, a little shop rolled up its metal screen with a clatter and a man in an apron appeared with a crate of apples. She found the courage to look behind her. Her follower had disappeared. She bought an apple from the shopkeeper, who exuded brusque Parisian normality.

Ahead was a busy street with pedestrians and she crossed it. She took a deep breath. She was all right—as long as a jigging pulse and a metallic taste in her mouth didn't count. Really, she was okay. Why hadn't she just taken to her heels, she wondered.

She took one of those forks you so often find at Paris intersections. She now saw that this wasn't much of a street either. Residential and commercial at first, it made a couple of bends and became alley-like. She was now in a sordid area of blank-faced walls and snow-filled courtyards with stacks of packing cases and a few vehicles. The odd car bucketed by and she had to jump onto the narrow sidewalk, which had not seen foot traffic or snow removal.

Ahead of her, a vehicle seemed to be having trouble with the snow as well. At least, it was proceeding her way very slowly. Its headlights were bright in the gloom, and shone annoying in her eyes. The lamps were high off the ground—familiar. As was the distinctive grille. Ashley was looking at a black Mercedes G-Class, and it was moving steadily towards her.

She lost her nerve in a flash. She turned and ran—back to the intersection. But there she was blocked by a snarl of traffic. She took a panicked look behind her. The angle of the street obstructed her view, but she thought she heard an engine. Paris was full of noise, that composite breathing of a city: machinery, humming ventilators, big internal combustion engines, throbbing and revving. What was wrong with the red light? The light changed and she was off. Half running and half walking, her feet like stones in the snow, a stitch in her side. Ahead of her, a *place* and a taxi rank. She threw herself into a cab.

***

She was still putting the experience behind her a few hours later, when Mirabel breezed through the door. She was carrying a huge bunch of dark red roses ("Madame Caron accepted delivery for me, look!") and had a lot to say about her experience at the prefecture. It had all gone well. Maître Tellier had even complimented her on her recall.

"From what he said they might be closing in on a suspect. For the Langelier murder."

"Was it a Bortnik hoodlum?"

"He wouldn't tell me that."

"Who are the roses from?" Although Ashley thought she could guess.

Mirabel peered at the card. "Charles." If she was disappointed, she didn't convey it.

Ashley recounted her own adventures. Mirabel had little reaction to the news that Ashley had resolved the lease issue but stared when she heard about the sighting of the black Mercedes G-Class.

"I don't know if I overreacted. I'd just been followed by that creep, and then I saw it. There must be thousands of these SUVs in Paris. Anyway, I've become good at running through Parisian streets, like a fleeing heroine."

"Oh, I don't think you overreacted at all," Mirabel said. "Although—why would it be following *you?*"

"Well, exactly."

"Still."

"I *was* rattled."

"I'd have been terrified."

"But it's weird. Real fear is so ... physical. Not smart, not even that emotional. Say a bullet comes your way, you turn and stagger off like you could outrun it, or you put up your hand. Also, it's strange the way you feel like you're watching yourself ..." This was abnormally confidential for Ashley.

Mirabel's eyes widened. She hurried to the kitchen to summon something with sugar "for shock." Béatrice came into the living room with a tray. "That's a nice new purse, Madame," she said, pointing to a washed leather bag with a well-known designer name on it beside Mirabel on the couch.

The truth dawned on Ashley after Béatrice had left the room. "Raymond gave you that, didn't he?"

"Yes, Ashley, he did. Have a madeleine."

Ashley said nothing. She could easily imagine the price tag, judging by what she'd seen in the Faubourg Saint Honoré windows. It was no doubt from the missing truck—stolen, in other words. If so, Mirabel was in possession of sizeable stolen property. A Criminal Code offense, if they were in Canada—and France was bound to have something similar on the books. She'd have to talk about this with Mirabel. But just not now. She took a madeleine.

"The whole thing might have been my sorry imagination. Mirabel, I like my tea without sugar."

Mirabel kept spooning. "If it was just your imagination working overtime, then you have nothing to worry about."

But to Ashley, whose reasoning powers were her pride and solace, the idea that she had begun to imagine things was like a cold exhalation from a cave.

8

MASQUERADE

THE FOLLOWING DAY Charles arrived in Paris. Ashley assumed that he'd want to stay in the rue des Arabes *appart,* but Mirabel said he was checking into his usual luxury hotel near the Place de la Concorde. "He's not that ungracious," she said, to Ashley's amusement.

Charles did come by in the afternoon. Ashley had been burningly eager to vacate the premises, but Mirabel wouldn't have it. Apart from needing her for support, Charles might have questions to ask.

By the time he'd returned to the Hôtel de Crillon, Ashley thought she'd have willingly faced another Mercedes G-Class episode rather than more of the Charles and Mirabel show. Charles was self-assured and calm when he came through the door. Even if he didn't have Raymond's spectacular cheekbones, Ashley was struck all over again by his austere good looks. Also his air of command. The Saint Cyrs greeted each other like a husband and wife who hadn't seen each other in three or four days and wanted to get that part over with.

Béatrice left them lunch before heading home. Charles ate with a slight frown, as if the food was suspect, or uninteresting. In a manner suggesting she was the only other real adult at the table, he made cursory conversation with Ashley. He had questions to ask about the lease. Now embarrassed, Ashley was silent about the latest hypothetical Mercedes G-Class episode. Charles professed himself satisfied with the leasing outcome. Thank God for that.

He was patient, in a mildly hectoring way, with Mirabel. She, for her part, was demure and diffident. Her high-necked dark blue blouse matched her eyes but robbed her creamy skin of warmth. And just a little *Handmaid's Tale*-ish, to Ashley's way of thinking. The big diamond drop earrings gripping Mirabel's earlobes didn't help. When Charles pointed to the meat on her plate and said in a bossy voice: "Belle, finish that, you know protein will help you conceive," Mirabel made an effort to obey. A trapped Ashley emptied her wine glass and excused herself at last.

She went to her bedroom on the pretext of needing to discuss some things with Aram back in Montreal. Since Charles and Mirabel remained in the living room, a shut bedroom door was useless against the big fight that followed. She might have tried harder to avoid eavesdropping, but she couldn't help herself.

Ashley heard the tone of the voices going on and on: Charles's as he badgered and browbeat Mirabel gently and thoroughly, and Mirabel's as it wavered across the register, evasive, defensive. Ashley couldn't even understand why they were fighting. Barring one more possible meeting with the examining magistrate, which she would find out about soon, Mirabel had run out of barriers, real or imaginary, to her departure. On that score, she wasn't even putting up a fight. Nor was she making an issue of Charles's arrival in Paris. As for Raymond, when Charles brought him up, in a voice that dropped ominously, Ashley was clearly able to hear Mirabel's words: *"Mais là, c'est fini!"* She repeated this plaintively.

Perhaps he was over his fright, or perhaps it was the fright speaking, but he treated everything to do with Mercedes G-Class SUVs as a regrettable lapse on Mirabel's part, the result of her childish unwillingless to seek guidance from him. The tone of wounded reproach here was impeccable. Just when Ashley was meditating some grimly awkward diversion, silence fell. It was an unsettling silence that dragged on. Had Charles left? She hadn't heard any doors. Maybe they'd taken it to the bedroom? Eventually she felt she had to investigate.

Charles and Mirabel hadn't taken it to the bedroom, but they were taking it. The blouse and skirt were on the floor. Charles was holding Mira's arm as he led her from the living room. She was leaning her exquisite blonde head against his shoulder. It was, Ashley could have sworn, the surrender of love. Charles, on the other hand, held her arm like an arresting officer, and seemed most focused on getting her to navigate the area rugs in the most expeditious manner.

Paralyzed in the hallway, Ashley stared at the retiring couple. Was there something she should be doing here? Should she intervene? Should she remind herself that the man was a client and mind her own business?

When they were at Mirabel's bedroom door, Charles pulled down the shoulder straps of Mirabel's teddy, commenting in a weary tone on the quality of the silk. Ashley beat a retreat.

Time passed, and the apartment began to feel cold. Ashley played around with the thermostat in her bedroom, then dug out another sweater. She'd have liked to chat with Roy or Aram but neither of them was available. She read the Wikipedia articles on Saint Denis and Joan of Arc. If Saint Denis was the patron saint of France, he'd certainly been eclipsed in the popular imagination by youthful Joan. Saint Denis, called Dionysius back in his day, had been decapitated by the Romans. The pro-English Burgundian faction during the Hundred Years' War had burned nineteen-year-old Joan at the stake. Both martyrs, Joan on technical grounds of dressing like a man. At her show trial, she'd tried to tell them it was to avoid being raped during her long captivity, but the ecclesiastical court was having none of it. Dressing like someone else can be a freeing experience, Ashley mused, remembering her new dress, her Korean Hwarang warrior coat. But not without its complications.

Ashley finally heard voices and the shutting of the apartment door.

"Ashley?"

Mirabel was fastening her dressing gown in the kitchen. Her hair was tousled, there were small mauve marks under her eyes that, for all Ashley knew, might have been there under makeup all along. But her mood was matter-of-fact, as if the afternoon had been all in a day's work for the wife of Charles Saint Cyr.

"I could use a snack, what about you, Ashley?" she said, as she took milk from the fridge.

They leaned against the granite island counter while sliding a box of biscuits back and forth.

"So that was Charles. Although you've met him of course. My other man." She drank milk, bit with youthful relish into a biscuit. "You were probably shocked by some of that, Ashley. Then again, you're not married." She smiled enigmatically. Now she didn't seem young at all. "When you think about it, it wasn't too much of a scene for a betrayed husband. He had to let off steam. It was bound to end in the bedroom. Charles is not as confident as you might suppose, and when we have a fight he asserts himself afterwards with sex." She took another bite. "I'm sure he's not the only husband like that."

Ashley had trouble imagining autocratic Charles Saint Cyr as lacking in confidence. She still said nothing and Mirabel leaned forward confidentially. "With Raymond in bed, it's all drama. Charles isn't Raymond. But he knows what he's doing. The things I could tell you—" Ashley raised her hand in alarm and Mira said: "Don't worry, I won't. The point I'm making is that he has his own unique way of doing things and it's erotic in its way. If you know what I mean."

Mirabel said this without blushing. Not so Ashley. Also, she hadn't a clue what Mirabel meant. Was the glint in Mirabel's eye mockery?

"Charles never misses a chance to try and get me pregnant. Although, I'm sorry to say, that won't happen." In the silence that followed Ashley played with crumbs, but didn't miss the sadness on Mirabel's face as she looked out the window. "Look, more snow. A little anyway. Snow in Paris is so charming, I think." She finished her milk. She bore no resemblance to the browbeaten wife of earlier.

A phone call for Mirabel ended this perplexing yet informative conversation, leaving Ashley alone in the kitchen to contemplate the snow and how out of her depth she was feeling.

* * *

Mireille Borel's call to Mirabel the next day had two purposes: to find out how Mirabel's interview with Maître Tellier had gone, and to ask her and Ashley out for drinks that night.

The conversation was long and chatty—Ashley could only marvel—and Mirabel told Mireille, as Ashley frowned, that she'd check with her "flatmate," but that she herself thought a night out was overdue and well-deserved.

"Aren't you planning on spending the time with Charles?" Ashley asked.

"Not today. I told him I needed my space today, as I found yesterday *bouleversant*. He was very understanding. Anyway, he has Holopherne business to conduct, including a dreary business dinner. He sometimes works with Parisian designers, although even his most expensive lines are made in Asian special industrial zones. I'd hoped he might be interested in working with Raymond, but Charles isn't like that—he's too conventional." There was no end to the interesting things that could come out of Mirabel's mouth.

"Also, *le Carnaval de Paris* begins this evening, did you know?

There'll be a parade, not the big one. This one's for adults only. This is the best night for us to go out if you want to experience the authentic *Carnaval*. A once in a lifetime experience." After her visit to *le Petit Palais*, Ashley could not deny she was intrigued.

They went for an afternoon walk along the Seine. Ashley was aware of an excited vibe in the city, a tingle of anticipation in the brisk air. There were already people about in costume. Under pale winter sunshine, it was far from Halloweenish, as those dressed up were all adult and behaved very much in character. In many cases the costumes were highly elaborate or sinister. Ashley surreptitiously kept her eyes on the traffic. She dismissed an uncomfortable feeling of being watched.

"This will be so much fun!" Mirabel exclaimed. She dragged the semi-willing Ashley into shops as well. It was Béatrice's role to buy groceries but they'd been running low on gourmet *pralines*, apparently. Mirabel insisted on buying Ashley her own Guerlain lip stain, and was keen to look at winter boots now that there was snow. Mirabel didn't like any for herself, but she did buy Ashley a pair of stylish boots that she said would look just right with the new dress that evening. They were made of waterproofed felt and didn't go up much above the ankle. They had a fleece lining, looked unexpectedly chic when they were on and were an astronomical price. Ashley refused. Then Mirabel said she was buying them anyway and Ashley might as well try them on or they'd end up with the wrong size. And that would just be a waste. Ashley would still have held out, but Mirabel had just got for herself a pair of exquisite Belle Epoque pink sapphire earrings—because Charles had told her she should get herself a little something—and the scale of this purchase was so eclipsing of everything Ashley knew about cheap and dear that she acquiesced.

The three women met that evening at a resto-bar on a sidestreet in the fashionable Marais district. Mireille said they would go elsewhere later but first she wanted to talk. The place hadn't filled up yet, and they were alone but for a late espresso drinker or two and a dining foursome across the room. The latter were in 1890s costume, playful but grave in black eye masks with unnervingly small eye slots.

Over *apéros,* Mireille launched into an enthusiastic diatribe against Maître Tellier, *les flics* and Raymond, who, she freely admitted, had paid her a visit. Mirabel had already admitted the same. Mireille was in green lamé, with an outlandish patchwork Harlequin coat in ratty black, grey and white fur that she told an impressed Mirabel she saved especially for *Carnaval* every year. This was *the* evening to dress up, Mirabel had told a doubtful Ashley, and Ashley had on her new dress. Béatrice's unsuspected hairdressing skills had been called upon and Ashley's hair was in an attractive updo. To her surprise, Mirabel had donned an actual costume. She was a famous Gaul warrior queen who fought the Romans, she explained to Ashley. This didn't ring any bells for Ashley, and the long smoke-coloured dress, heavy cloak and faux fur wolf draperies around her head and shoulders didn't either. But the effect was arresting: Mirabel's dark-ringed grey-blue eyes picked up on the wolf's button eyes, the total impact far from campy.

Mireille was suitably impressed. Her hot brown eyes dallied over Mirabel and Ashley, and she pronounced them perfectly turned out for the people they would meet later. François would be there, and he was bringing friends. They would be a party of six or eight. It would be *drolatique,* whatever that meant.

She gestured to the waiter for more drinks and shoved the tray of small bites their way. "There is life after Raymond. Here, have some of these, they're delicious."

"Are you breaking up then with Raymond?" Mirabel asked.

An indescribably French shrug. "Do you ever break up with Raymond?"

"Very true," Mirabel said. "It's more like non-breaking up." She looked at Ashley. "Did you ever non-break up with someone, Ashley?"

Ashley thought of her brief and ambiguously concluded summer dalliance with Jon Perez, that now seemed half a lifetime ago. She took a swig of her drink. "Yes, absolutely," she said. Mirabel and Mireille seemed inordinately pleased with these words. They all clinked glasses and Ashley felt like one of the gals.

"But I really want to talk about is the situation with the Bortniks and the missing truck," Mireille said. "Tell me if you have any news."

Mirabel shook her head. Ashley volunteered an account of her unpleasant latest sighting of a Mercedes G-Class, complete with disclaimers of uncertainty. Mireille frowned. She said she hadn't been followed herself. Then again, she wrote ad copy from home and she practically never went out in winter—and when she did there was a Métro station right there and a cab rank next to it.

"Look, I know we talked about finding Raymond, but now we've found him, or he's found us, so *bof.*" She directed a fierce but impersonal stare at Mirabel. "Anyhow, I've lost interest in rescuing him—or even listening to his excuses. Raymond, he's a big boy."

She sat back in her chair, very business-like. "I've been thinking. It's the truck I'm interested in. Well, the truck is probably a burned-out hulk in the Forêt de Retz, but the contents must be somewhere. I could do a lot with the contents of that truck. I do freelance fashion work, you know."

To Ashley, this sounded like she had a client or clients willing to buy. From wanting to wipe the floor with Raymond to relieve her feelings, Mireille seemed to have progressed rapidly to more practical forms of redress.

"If you're right, you have to wonder where Raymond stashed the contents," Ashley said. If no one else was pretending, then why should she?

"Exactly. Raymond rents various spaces and there are two or three small storage sheds he uses. It wouldn't be hard to find out if the goods ended up in one of them."

"And this has something to do with me?" Mirabel asked politely.

Mireille lifted an eyebrow. "There you go! I knew you were smarter than you pretend to be. Well, I have an idea." She tapped the side of her head with a finger and leaned forward. "I think I could find the goods, but I need a way to move them. To Marseille. And that costs money. I need a business partner. Someone to front the cost of a truck—preferably one that says something completely misleading like *Déménagements Barthélemy et fils* on it. And for gas and things like that—Marseille is far." She studied Mirabel. "If you were my business partner, there'd be a cut in it for you."

Ashley could hardly believe her ears. Before she could protest, Mirabel, in a much too reasonable voice, said: "But how could we do this without alerting the Bortnik brothers? How could we get away with it?"

Ashley didn't like the "we." Nor any other part of this zany idea.

"But don't you see?" Mireille said. Her gaze swivelled towards the foursome across the room. "Disguise. The simplest way in the world to avoid the Bortniks. Look at those people. Do you have any idea who they are? None." The people in the corner took this moment to stare in their direction, through peculiar pea-sized eyes. The Miras and Ashley hurriedly looked away.

"I'm not looking for anything more than financial backing," Mireille said. "And the bank would get a very fair return, I promise you. I could easily be the driver, down to Marseille. I'd be the *fils* in *Barthélemy et fils*." Her expression was falsely modest. "I've been praised for my adolescent male roles in community theatre productions."

Mirabel looked intrigued, the way a Gallic rebel queen with time on her hands would look intrigued. "The tricky part would be getting the goods out of the city, everything to do with that. Once you were safely on the A6, it would be plain sailing. What about once you were in Marseille?"

"Don't worry about Marseille. I know my way around. It's

where I'm from. I have four brothers there. The interest there is strong. And Marseille is controlled by two rival gangs. The Bortniks are big in Paris but Marseille is off their patch. They'd hesitate to start something in Marseille." Mireille sounded disreputably confident. Ashley could well believe she hailed from that tough southern city. There'd always been something fishy about her.

The rebel queen smiled thoughtfully. "Clever."

"I think you mean dangerous," Ashley cut in. "*Déménagements Barthélemy et fils?* That's crazy talk. Remember Langelier, who was beaten to death? It's *Bortnik et frère* we should be thinking about." The others were enraptured at this sally, although impervious to the message.

As their drinks were refreshed, Mireille insisted they should have more food, for it would be a long night. The conversation moved onto technical details. How to acquire the getaway truck, how to disguise the truck, how to investigate the storage sheds without being followed, how to load the truck, how to get out of the city unseen. Ashley, torn between disbelief and professional interest in details, put up several practical objections along the way. Mireille had an answer for everything. Mirabel conceded the required sum named by the other was "feasible," and she suggested a separate conversation on her cut.

"Because everyone is so steamed up about the missing truck," Mireille said, "we have to hurry."

Mirabel nodded sagely. "Of course. Do you know where the storage sheds are?"

The question put Mireille a little out of countenance. "With some digging, inquiring around ..."

"But what if word got out?"

"Well, how would we find them then? Believe me, I've put some thought into this."

"Why don't we ask Raymond himself?"

Mireille's eyes positively glittered. "But why would he tell us?"

"We'd tell him we wanted to help him. We have his burner number now. Don't you think that would work?"

Mireille said nothing. Her eyes roved the restaurant. "Well— yes. I mean, perhaps. Since Langelier turned up in the river, everyone is avoiding Raymond like the plague. They're scared, they don't want to be on the bad side of the Bortniks and end up like Langelier. So, yes, he might accept my help."

"Our help." A tiny emphasis. "Why don't we say we want to meet him, somewhere crowded, to talk. All we need are the shed locations, the keys or security codes, yes? We'll say we're doing it for him, I mean we *aren't,* but he won't know ..."

It was now crystal clear—Ashley hadn't been one hundred percent sure until this moment—that Raymond was out of the picture. A curious apathy stole over her. She felt like a swimmer who'd lost sight of land. In a sea of gelatine. She made an effort. Reasoning with the Borel woman would be a waste of time, so she turned to Mirabel.

"Why would you do this? You don't need the money. You have so much money you buy seven thousand euro earrings, you buy me presents for no reason. Mireille could ask anyone else to help her." She leaned forward. "Do you hate Raymond so much?"

Mirabel's wide eyes were calm. "Hate Raymond? No. But all that money, Ashley, it's not *my* money. Don't you understand what a difference that makes? Also"—now she looked like a hurt child— "I really like giving you presents. It makes me happy. The dress is so beautiful on you and the *bottillons,* they're perfect. You know how if you don't have the right boots in winter it can just spoil an outfit. I didn't know you minded ..."

"That's not what I meant, I don't mind presents at all," Ashley said in protest.

Mireille cut in. "I was with that creep for three years, I thought we had something. So I'm doing this for revenge *and* for the money —which I happen to need." Mireille's tone was frankness itself. You couldn't go wrong, it seemed to say, in trusting someone whose motives were so transparent.

"Of course," Mirabel said, "I do understand that." She turned to Ashley again. "You don't have to take everything in life so seriously, Ashley. We're just having a conversation. Just talking about possibilities. Tomorrow or the day after, we may do something else, or something else will happen, we can never be really sure what." Her voice was soft, patient. "Something like this, it's a game."

Ashley snatched at a straw. "Well, if it's just a game and you don't mean—"

The resto-bar had been filling up. Mirabel waved to the *garçon* for the bill. "Mireille has made an interesting suggestion. Why wouldn't we at least consider it? You keep bringing up reasons, good and bad. Don't judge money as a reason. Are your reasons for doing things any better?"

Ashley was unprepared for a discussion on moral philosophy. "How about danger then? Is that a sufficient reason? Honestly, Mira, I don't understand. You were scared enough when I first met you. Why aren't you thinking about the danger now?"

This seemed to give Mirabel pause. She emptied her glass and replaced it on the table with delicate care. "But I've always been scared, Ashley, of everything. I was scared when I was growing up, without my parents. I was scared thinking I would never find my— find Isabel again. When Charles asked me to marry him, I was really scared." Ashley could clearly read the unspoken words in her eyes: *Charles scares me.*

Mirabel rearranged her wolf furs. "The world is a terrible place. Our ideas of safety are often just illusions. You can't always run from danger either, and you don't always want to. Sometimes, danger is something to play with." She smiled at Ashley, pleased to have provided her deepest philosophical insights in a drunken nutshell.

"So you won't meet up with Raymond then?"

The two Miras exchanged a glance. "Oh no, we'll need to meet with him."

On their way out the door, Mireille turned to Ashley. "You asked earlier why it had to be Mirabel I asked for help. The thing about you"—a throaty chuckle—"is that you ask the right questions, but you don't always see the answers when they're there in front of you. *Cette charmante Madame.* She's rich, of course, and she might enjoy fleecing Raymond, whatever she says. But the real reason I chose her? It's because Mirabel is the kind of person who doesn't back away from risks. Mirabel would do anything!"

And she skipped out ahead of Ashley like a demented Tinker Bell, leaving a trail of chartreuse glitter in her wake.

* * *

The night that followed was one of the more unusual that Ashley had experienced.

Their cab took them deeper into the secluded medieval corners of the city. The streets grew narrow and maze-like. They were dropped at a gate and went through more gates and a metal door, down long passages, until they came to their destination. A scene of bedlam.

They were in a spacious old-fashioned, high-roofed hall, bursting at the seams with noisy revellers. In the lurid light of flares and lanterns, which created a cave-like atmosphere, hundreds of people in fancy dress drank and played. There was constant motion but no single focus to it. Many things were happening at once. Above the roar of voices, music reached them from all sides, fiddles, drums, competing boomboxes. And there was dancing everywhere, on the floor, on makeshift tables and on the raised areas at the base of columns. It was a mainly adult crowd, but there were family groups too, picnicking circles with pint-sized Pierrots and diminutive

Pierrettes running around their elders. Long sinuous conga lines twined through the mob, wine bottles in one hand and streamers whirling around them. And everyone was wearing a face mask.

Mireille had come prepared. She passed eye masks to Ashley and Mirabel and put one on herself. And she handed out streamers.

"Take care of these, don't lose them," she shouted. "These are retractable and I had such a hard time finding them!" She demonstrated by sending a bright silver and gold spiral exploding into the air and drawing it back with a snap of the wrist. A woman shrieked and a couple of people applauded.

"Oh they're wonderful!" In her mask Mirabel looked even more arresting, flickering mask eyes staring out beneath dead wolf eyes. They were attracting attention. Someone stroked Mirabel's wolf fur with a lascivious gesture, and a being in cardinal robes kissed Mireille before seizing Ashley by the elbow, pirouetting her around, bowing deeply, and disappearing before she could react.

"Follow me!" Mireille yelled. Single file and hand in hand, they made their way among the noisy throng, sticking as close as they could to the wall. Ashley was startled when they came to a couple of big stone vats or troughs that held water and saw wild souls throwing themselves in with abandon.

"Is this a public bath house?"

"One of the old Parisian communal laundry houses." Mireille turned from time to time to play guide, making herself heard with difficulty above the din. She thought the place had been in use hundreds of years ago. It was no longer a wash house, and there was a plan to restore it. The *blanchisseuses* had held their famous dances here, during *Carnaval* long ago. Someone had had the bright idea of throwing a party in the spirit of the wild old days. It was wholly unofficial—there was no official permission at all. Who knew how long before it was raided. Meanwhile, here they were, and wasn't it *fantastique!*

They were suddenly engulfed in a group of seven or eight people in fancy dress, a couple of women and the rest men. Masked, good-looking to the extent you could tell, distinctly louche and overjoyed to greet Mireille. Their eyes raked Mirabel and Ashley like these two were prizes, as they handed round drinks.

The group had staked out an area and there were some folding chairs, a circle of bottles on the floor. Coats were dumped. The cardinal returned and was introduced as François Brault. He lifted his mask and Ashley saw intense eyes bent on mischief. He kissed Mireille again and lifted her away onto the dance floor.

The two women in the group looked like sisters, red-haired and dressed in *piquant* variations of Columbine. They were assiduous hostesses and Ashley and Mirabel's glasses were never unfilled. Conversation was yelled fragments augmented by gales of laughter. Bags of French junk food snacks—Ashley hadn't known this kind of thing existed—were passed around. They wanted to talk about Montreal. When was Quebec going to separate—wasn't it time for another referendum on independence? Had she ever met the famous Quebec writer Esmerelda LaFlamme? Ashley could only shake her head. She was accused of bringing the cold weather. Mirabel's wolf theme was acknowledged with playful howls interspersed with rational criticism of the Canadian wolf cull. Then Mirabel was whisked away by the redheads to dance a punk version of the revolutionary Carmagnole that had taken hold in their vicinity. Yanis, a member of their party, put an arm around Ashley's waist. He wore a formal top hat and tails, rendered sly by a frightening-looking long-nosed white mask. He pulled her into the tail end of the human snake writhing by and they went circling around the room. Ashley's hair came partly undone and people reached out as she passed and tugged the black tendrils, stroked her shoulders and arms, in a way she found unnerving.

More bottles had appeared by the time she and Yanis made it

back to the table. Time to curtail her drinking, but Ashley was hot and thirsty.

And so it went, at the notorious *Bal macabre de la buanderie*. They were out of there before it really degenerated, and well before the *gendarmerie* raided the old wash house.

There were other stages to the evening, but these were less clear to Ashley. They went to other venues, also filled with disguised revellers. They ate, they drank. There was music, more dancing, plenty of running around with streamers and sparklers. The children had long disappeared from among the crowds, and the adults were taking it to the limit. Wild love triangles seemed to be the theme, and who could say how genuine the emotion was. People were behaving like depraved children. Ashley was not immune, and there was a little light necking with Yanis in some passage to a bathroom.

At one point Ashley and the two Miras, with a few of the original group and some new hangers-on, joined a human procession through the streets. To the beat of drums, they poured eventually into a wide square filled with many hundreds of revellers. The crush of the crowd was great, and suddenly Ashley recognized no one around her. A gang of men dressed as wolves surrounded her and she was afraid, but when they laughed she saw that they were women, the followers of a mighty woman carrying a flaming torch and decked out, so said her banner, as the Great She-Wolf. Then they were gone and she was surrounded by another group in costume, this time women in black robes with life-like and disturbing goat masks. But these turned out to be men, and flowed by her on either side like a silent wolf pack, all but the last one, who tilted his mask slightly and kissed Ashley on the lips before racing on. She flailed in his direction, but unavailingly—he was gone. She was on the edge of panic when the two Miras hove into sight, talking over each other about their own adventures.

The three of them sought refuge on the steps to a church facing the square. Just then there were soft popping sounds and fireworks exploded in the black sky. From where they stood, they could see an illuminated human swarm, but humanity transformed—nothing familiar in any face among the nocturnal horde. In the distance, sirens wailed. More and more sirens, getting closer and closer.

"*Les flics,*" Mireille said. "It was bound to happen. Try that door."

To their dazed surprise, one of the church's side doors was open, and they entered. They huddled in an empty pew, while Ashley tried to make sense of what she was doing there. Time passed. Mirabel seemed to nod off. When they finally ventured outside, the square was garbage-strewn but mostly empty again. François Brault and the others were nowhere to be found.

They had to walk through nighttime Paris for what seemed forever before they could catch a taxi. And then they took a long and meandering drive through the sleeping streets of southern Paris to drop Mireille off in Montsouris, during which they checked their belongings on Mireille's instructions and found to their drunken delight that no one's wallet had been stolen. The ride back across the Seine was even longer, and this time Ashley might have napped. When they were finally back at rue des Arabes and Ashley was on the edge of her bed pulling off her tights, she told herself she'd never be able to sleep after the night's wild adventures.

But it was late morning before Ashley had another conscious thought, and that was to wonder whether Mirabel or Béatrice had come in at some point and thrown the luxurious duvet over her semi-clad form as she slept.

9

GIRL ON FIRE

THEY LAY LOW in the apartment that day. Mirabel stayed in the kitchen with Béatrice, under the pretext of learning how to make some of Béatrice's signatures dishes. Ashley knew Mirabel was avoiding her. She tried to come up with a strategy for dealing with the two Miras' madcap scheme—if it was a scheme, as opposed to a carnivalesque flight of fancy. Then Mirabel went out to dinner with Charles, and didn't come home until late.

It hadn't been a success, she reported to Ashley. They'd had an argument about whether Charles would accompany her to her next interview with Tellier. "You would think he didn't trust me." *Imagine that*, Ashley thought.

The call from Mireille came the next day, early. She'd been in touch with Raymond Boissier. He was willing to meet them. He'd suggested the Forum des Halles, a large and very busy shopping precinct built over Paris's old central market. Its soulless indoor and outdoor stores sprawled over a few blocks, and there were always crowds of a mixed sort. Les Halles was widely recognized by Parisians as an eruption of something alien in the middle of its Second Empire core. But this in no way diminished its popularity, especially among bored adolescents from the outer *arrondissements,* and the city's entire tribe, sooner or later, of petty crooks, touts and rogues.

"A clever choice, don't you think?" Mirabel said. They were picking at the remains of breakfast in the kitchen. Béatrice was vacuuming elsewhere.

"Hmm. I was wondering how you were going to get the money from your husband to front the costs, like that truck, all the etceteras."

"You don't need to worry about that, Ashley. Charles is very generous with spending money. I just need to account for it eventually. By the time he asks any questions, I'll have the return on my investment. I'll just tell him I was moving some money around ..."

Ashley went over to the brass cappuccino machine for a refill. "I'm not familiar with French law, but what you'd be doing can't be legal," she said casually. "Stolen property—being in possession of it, proceeds from, that kind of thing."

"Was anything reported stolen?" Mirabel's blue eyes were wide and guileless. "Jaubert and Bourque are from the major crimes against the person unit. They don't even seem that interested in any actual theft. Maître Tellier is building a murder case. He didn't either. Anyway, they'd need the property itself to charge someone with theft. *Habeas corpus*, I think it's called?"

"That has nothing to do with *habeas corpus*."

"Well anyway, a truck can be missing, but there may not be theft involved. Also, Mireille and I know nothing about that."

There was a shrewdness to this equivocation. In Canada at least, if you didn't know property was stolen you were unlikely to be indicted. And even if the Miras were ever charged in connection with a theft, these charges—directed against a pair of emotionally fraught ex-girlfriends with a grievance—were of the sort to be dropped well before trial.

Ashley sighed. "Do you actually trust Mireille?"

"Why not? We both have an equal stake, something to gain, something to lose."

Ashley scowled. "Is that trust?"

"Yes, isn't it? I think she's trustworthy. In some ways"—an

oblique look in Ashley's direction—"her motives are very pure. She was a good friend to us the other night. She could have dumped us. Everyone else did. Who knows what could have happened? She stayed with us all night, like when the *gendarmes* came, remember?"

This seemed a weirdly cogent argument to Ashley. "But you paid for everything."

"Why wouldn't I?"

"How does she have those connections in Marseille?"

"The brothers, obviously. She's never done anything like this be-. fore, she said. All kinds of people decide out of the blue to take a risk."

"Do they?" But to this too Ashley could attest, from her work. She heaved a sigh. "How much do you think you'd make from this —business venture?"

"Mireille is guaranteeing me a minimum cut. But let's not discuss this anymore. I meant to tell you that Yanis called me. He asked for your number. I didn't give it to him, but I have his for you. He'd like you to call him." The top-hatted gentleman was looking for another inning. Ashley had a picture of next bases. She shook her head impatiently.

Mirabel left soon after, promising she'd take taxis.

It was another unnaturally cold day in the city, but after staying indoors the day before Ashley wanted air. Charles Saint Cyr was off somewhere and had no requests of her. She decided to get souvenirs for family and friends. Nothing much could happen to her amid the crowds of rue de Rivoli, she told herself. And she wanted to explore further its continuation, the non-touristy rue Saint Antoine, with its hulking churches and purely Parisian shops.

But Ashley's mood was off. The cloud cover and the dirty snow made the city look dingy. *Carnaval* was working itself up to the big concluding weekend parade, and the appearance on the streets of Parisians in costume affected her nerves. It gave her the impression of seeing things out of the corner of her eye. She must have had her fill the other night.

After dipping into numerous shops and buying an overpriced leather wallet for Lucie, and for Roy some hand-hemmed linen handkerchiefs which were his latest affectation, Ashley stopped for coffee. She was cradling a cup at a café window when she realized someone was staring at her through the pane.

Like men all over the world, Parisian men had their own unique and culturally distinct ways of making women uncomfortable. But she'd never encountered this. The man was very tall, waistcoated and caped all in black, and wore a revolting white vinyl full-face mask in the style of chainsaw horror movies. He was motionless before the window, unpleasantly near. Through the glass, the eye holes of the mask bored into Ashley's eyes. As if his stillness commanded hers, she was unable to move. While she watched in numb fascination, he raised a gloved hand to his face, and removed the mask. Horror lay beneath it: another visage, all red dangling flesh and lipless teeth, eyes like oily pits. Ashley shoved her chair back in shock—and then realized that this too was a mask. A mask beneath a mask. With an exaggerated gesture he raised his high-crowned homburg to her, the gentleman's hat crowning the travesty of a face, but she was already over at the counter to make a complaint.

But there was nothing to complain about. When she looked back at the window, the creature had vanished.

This experience set Ashley to walking again. Without thinking about it, she headed in an easterly direction, away from the winter tourists and chi-chi shoppers. Soon she entered another type of district. It had the omnipresent five- and six-storey Second Empire buildings, here interspersed with different ones, of ochre brick with striking dark red accents. She could have been in some European mystery city. There were small unassuming parks and the shops were of the kind the lower middle class everywhere frequented: modest chains, local businesses and neighbourhood restaurants. This must be where the average Parisian lived, if there was such a thing. The streets were narrow but sidewalks were moderately busy, with neatly-dressed women carrying shopping bags, delivery men darting in and out of buildings, the odd *lycée* student or *flâneur*. She had no idea where she was.

Under a bright sun, the area might have felt different. But the iron-grey day had robbed the quiet scene of any low-key charm it might have possessed. It was not without its own mood, however. In the thick cold air the edges of things were slightly blurred, and this gave the streets a dreamlike feel. Were they getting near the Seine, she wondered. It looked like mist—but mist on so cold a day? A single large snowflake pirouetted lazily before her eyes.

She had come to a building on the far side of the street, whose Art Deco doors framed in pale green tile were like nothing else in the neighbourhood. A woman was exiting just then, a chic woman in a deep red coat that leapt out against the tile background. As she continued to look, a dreadful coldness seized Ashley's heart. She recognized the woman: far from les Halles, and looking unlike herself yet unmistakable, Mirabel Saint Cyr was tripping along the sidewalk, her ankle boots making a tap-tapping sound on the pavement. Ashley stared open-mouthed. The street, rue des Capucins, was especially narrow here and she could see Mirabel clearly in every detail. The coat was a belted style, and the collar was up. On her coiffed fair hair, a pale green velvet cap was tilted at an angle. It had a veil that dropped down over the top part of Mirabel's face —until Ashley realized she was in fact looking at clever *Carnaval* makeup to resemble a lace veil. Mirabel looked like she'd stepped out of some old movie; but as she stopped with a familiar look of mild annoyance to adjust one two-toned boot, she fairly burned with three-dimensional life.

Ashley was paralyzed. What on earth would Mirabel be doing here? She had just exited this anonymous apartment building. What business could she possibly have in this neighbourhood? But even more disturbing, *how* could Mirabel even be here? It made no sense. It was in fact impossible. Mirabel had just texted Ashley, saying she and Mireille were at les Halles, staked out in a coffee shop of a bookstore—she even named it, *Au Bonheur des Livres*—and awaiting Raymond.

"Mirabel!" Ashley yelled as loudly as she could. Across the street, the woman turned—and gave Ashley an empty look. If this was Mirabel Saint Cyr, then it was Mirabel in a trance or a dream. The gaze was that of an indifferent stranger passing over Ashley. She took a step off the sidewalk, and provoked a blare of sound from an oncoming delivery truck. It swept by inches away, amid gesticulations of the driver. And was followed immediately by another truck that hit the brakes with massive inconvenience right in front of her. Ashley could now see nothing.

She ran along the sidewalk, as the truck aggravatingly kept pace, and it was long moments before her view cleared. She was just able to catch sight of the flame-bright coat, the little bobbing hat, disappearing around a corner. Provoking more driver ire, she dodged among cars—how had the traffic become so busy?—and made it to the other sidewalk. She raced to the corner and looked down rue de la Charette, one of those dim alley-like sidestreets, where Mirabel had turned. The air was filled suddenly with snow. In the white blur of tumbling snowflakes, there wasn't a soul to be seen.

How could that be? Mirabel had come this way less than a minute ago. Ashley hurried up the street. There were the usual double doors and gated courtyards of a Paris sidestreet—but they were all closed. After a few minutes she came to another intersection. Here there were people passing and plenty of traffic. And five different streets angling off in a variety of directions. As for the woman in red—Mirabel Saint Cyr, for heaven's sake, because that's who it was—Ashley was prepared to swear, she had disappeared.

She sat down on a cement traffic barrier to catch her breath and think. The snowflakes continued to dance indifferently around her. All at once she was furious. She felt sure she was being played.

She texted Mirabel: "Where are you?"

Mirabel would have to account for herself. Since she'd come to Paris, no, even before, Ashley had been surrounded by Saint Cyr half-truths and perhaps downright lies. What really went on between Charles and Mirabel? She had no idea. But she knew one thing: Neither of them, nor Isabel Jadois or Mireille Borel, had been telling her the whole truth about anything. She'd actually come to a point where she was taking everyone's chronic evasions for granted. Was there a bigger picture? Were there dots she should be connecting? All she could see were parallel tracks of evasion, games and lies.

A memory surfaced—of Mirabel's private calls in her bedroom. Who was on the other end? Never mind that—something else flashed like a light in a dark corridor, and made her stomach tighten. During these calls Mirabel had, she remembered clearly, used a pink cellular phone. But that wasn't the phone she used most of the time. Why hadn't Ashley picked up on that sooner? Who was Mirabel communicating with? And why did she need a second phone to do it?

Ashley checked her screen: Her text to Mirabel was unread. She found her own location on Google Maps. She had travelled in an arc, and now she was near something called the Bassin de l'Arsenal, that flowed down into the Seine. How had she ended up here? Her nearest Métro stop was Ledru-Rollin. When she got to it, it was nothing like the other stops she'd seen with their lovely Art Nouveau signage. Here only a big yellow M lit up the snowy gloom. What better time to try the Paris underground for the first time?

Half an hour later, after sampling three different-coloured Métro lines and recognizing there might have been a more direct route back to rue des Arabes, Ashley had calmed down somewhat. She was still off balance. She craved an explanation. But as she waited in the Strasbourg-Saint Denis station, not much liking her surroundings, she was forced to acknowledge that Mirabel might not be able to provide one.

It was because of the way the woman in red had looked right through her. The flat coldness in the woman's briefly lingering glance had been unmistakable. Ashley could remember times when she'd been thinking of someone, often someone she wanted to avoid, and then they would suddenly appear in front of her. A second glance at the empty gaze of a stranger would dispel the impression. The mind played all kinds of tricks. The woman's eyes had been disguised and her coat collar had been up, in a sort of Mata Hari way—part of why Ashley had looked twice. Had she really seen enough of the face to be sure? Anyway, why the elaborate and complicated hoax? Practically impossible to pull off, in fact, since Ashley hadn't been planning on visiting this neighbourhood.

In her work, everyone was always trying to hide things from her, including clients. It seemed to be part of human nature to want to conceal things, to hold your pettiest secrets near. Ashley had learned that lies didn't equate to guilt, and she also knew that people's deceptions, their sensitivities, were strange, and often pointless. There didn't need to be a conspiracy.

Mirabel had eventually texted back: "We're still waiting for Raymond. Will wait a little longer." It sounded like she was still with the Borel woman at the Forum des Halles, and that could be checked.

Her anger had focused on Mirabel. Perhaps for that reason, it was now dissipating. Mirabel Saint Cyr was by any standard a victim: a victim of her husband, of her own emotions and weaknesses, and long before that a victim of the fate that had more or less eradicated her family. If she was maddeningly hard to predict, opaque in her motivations, questionable in her judgement, wasn't that something that lay, like a big irritating speck of dust, in the eye of the beholder?

An announcement proclaimed delays on the line. *Veuillez patienter* and more of the same. Just like Montreal, Ashley grumbled to herself. The station was cold, but she wasn't. She stared down broodingly at her elegant feet. That habit of Mirabel's, for instance, of trying to shower Ashley with presents. She'd wanted to buy Ashley an absurd pin the other day, a Hello Kitty Sherlock Holmes pin. Solid gold, of course. Ashley had refused point blank.

"Yes, you wouldn't like that, I understand." Mirabel had looked crushed and Ashley had felt guilty.

Mirabel had only been trying to please, in her own way. You often lied your head off when you received a gift you didn't want. Her grandmother Smeeton had always been knitting her horrible sweaters, for example. Ashley had never told her to stop. She still had those sweaters, in a bottom drawer, unwearable in salmon pink and No Frills yellow. Now they sandwiched the old journal of Leo's that her uncle had given her—just as purposeless, just as unsettling. Ashley gritted her teeth. She hadn't wanted to think about the failed sweaters, her father's halting thoughts. Her father, whom no visit to the reserve would ever bring back, his little life erased by time, just as her little life would be one day. She was far from home, and her heart ached.

A pair of heavyset types with flattened faces passed on the Métro platform. They didn't give her a second look, but she had a wild moment of wondering if they could be envoys of the Bortnik brothers. That sent her mind off on thoughts of those unnerving, confusing SUV sightings. And then she wasn't confused anymore. Why hadn't she seen the glaringly obvious? She and Mirabel were just under surveillance. Although her work was more prosaic than most people thought, Ashley herself had tailed people from time to time. First, of course, came online stalking. But if that didn't yield what you needed, you had to do things the old-fashioned way. Sometimes it took weeks of patient watching. The Bortniks wanted their contraband back, and what better way than to send minions to watch the people who could lead them to Boissier? Mireille too was being watched, whether she realized it or not. And there was no great mystery to Ashley being included in their tail. They'd naturally suppose she was somehow involved as a private investigator—because what would they know about her actual job, about the Saint Cyrs' private troubles?

She and Mirabel probably weren't even in much danger. Unless and until they put themselves in a position to lead the Bortniks to the contraband. Then everything would change. She needed to talk to Mirabel.

She arrived back at rue des Arabes just after the Miras. It was patently obvious that the two women had been thoroughly spooked.

"He never showed up at all." Mirabel shook her head. "How long did we wait—was it two hours? More! We told him exactly where we were. He said he was coming and then he never came. If something came up last minute, why not text us …"

"Did you go anywhere, leave your spot, separate, during that time?" Ashley asked.

"No!" They both spoke at once, protest mingling with sincerity in their voices.

"Were you followed?"

"It's les Halles. How could you tell? And he isn't answering his phone." Mireille was looking pissed off as well as alarmed.

Ashley could see the upside of this. If they failed to reach him, maybe they'd be forced to abandon their lunatic plan.

Mirabel shrugged. "Anyway, there's nothing we can do now."

"I might have an idea or two of my own," Mireille mumbled.

Mirabel just looked discouraged and said: "It was a good plan." She checked her watch. "Stay for lunch, will you, Mireille?"

Ashley was somewhat reassured. There was nothing here to suggest they were lying. Now, if only Mirabel would lose interest. She bit her lip and crossed her fingers that the thing wouldn't pan out.

Béatrice had held lunch and they were sitting down in twenty minutes. When they'd finished the Dauphine ravioli, Ashley pushed back her plate and crossed her arms. "Well, I had a weird experience earlier today." She gave them each a hard look in turn. "I need you both to be very honest with me when I tell you."

This got the Miras sitting up and interested. And Ashley told them, with suitable detail, about her sighting on the rue des Capucins.

"I was *so* sure it was you that I called out your name," she said to a wide-eyed Mirabel. "Now, obviously, I don't know what to think." A pause. "You guys wouldn't be lying to me about going to les Halles or anything, would you?"

They stared at her, mouths open.

"But what are you saying? You think that was really Mirabel?" Mireille finally burst out. She began to laugh. "It couldn't have been, she was with me the whole time!" She didn't seem in the least insulted. In fact she appeared to be entertained. "*Mais c'est fou, c'est rigolo!*"

"I was a few metres away," Ashley said impassively. "If it wasn't Mirabel, then she has a double in Paris."

"Well, that must be it then!" Mireille seemed even more thrilled. "A double, a *doppelgänger* ..."

This had to be explained to Mirabel. Then they wanted Ashley to tell it all again. She described the woman's clothes, the makeup that looked like an eye veil, the remoteness of the woman's gaze, her rapid disappearance into the snow squall.

"That's the Arsenal area ... or maybe the Quinze-Vingts." Mireille screwed up her face. "You walked far."

"Ashley, I promise you, I was with Mireille all the time." Mirabel's voice had gone high. "I don't know what you think you saw, but it wasn't me." She squeezed her hands. "This is turning into a very complicated day. First Raymond doesn't show up, and now this. But that wasn't me." She looked completely sincere. And nervous.

When Mireille left, Ashley cornered Mirabel. She didn't mince words. She told a cowed Mirabel that it was a stroke of luck that Raymond had pulled a no-show. As if she'd been sure all along, she explained they were under surveillance and would remain so until they either led the goons to Raymond or found the stolen goods themselves. Finding the stuff themselves would be worst of all. It would make them targets, whereas now they were only the means to an end. No matter how clever Mireille thought she was being with cunning disguises and painted trucks, it wasn't worth the risk. Didn't Mirabel see this?

Mirabel looked wretched. "You have no idea, *no* idea, Ashley, how I would like that money," she said.

Ashley was having none of this. "Really, Mirabel. You could do what other people do, get a job."

Mirabel studied the floor, but Ashley caught the mulish look in her eyes. "I have a job, a hard one, in case you hadn't noticed."

"Well, get Charles to settle some money on you," Ashley said.

This wholly random suggestion perked Mirabel up. "It might be possible," she murmured. "I could ask him. It would be a start."

A start to what? But Ashley was losing interest in Mirabel's alleged money woes. "Raymond not showing up should tell you how dangerous the situation is," she said. "It's very odd he didn't call or text." Odd and ominous. "Are you taking this in, Mira?"

Mirabel sank further into the sofa and dipped her chin in a gesture of submission. Ashley's experience with Mirabel's slipperiness left her sceptical. She took a weary breath. "At least promise me, will you, that before you do anything with the Borel woman you'll talk to me first?"

Mirabel's limpid eyes met hers. "Very well."

Ashley had to leave it there. The pot was off the boil anyway, at least for now. Best to hold off getting Charles or the police involved, she decided. It was premature, on balance, it might backfire. Besides which, cops often caused otherwise avoidable complications. All this left her uneasy.

That evening, Charles Saint Cyr came to collect Madame Saint Cyr for dinner. They had coveted reservations at an exclusive restaurant, positively *le dernier cri*. Mirabel was an apparition in a form-fitting dress of bronze sequins with a slit up the side, accented with heavy platinum jewellery. Ashley shouldn't wait up, they might go by his hotel afterwards, she said without emotion, as Charles slid a proprietary arm around her waist.

Ashley's first task after they left was to pour herself a glass of something called Thunevin-Calvet, encouragingly described on the label as a *"vin doux naturel."* Her second was to ransack Mirabel's closet for the clothing she'd seen on rue des Capucins. She found the wolf costume, and an array of beautiful clothes. Also a couple of boxes with men's stuff she supposed must belong to Boissier. But there was no sign of the red coat, or of the unique cocktail hat or two-toned boots. She wasn't especially surprised. It had been an outside chance.

Searching through Mirabel's things didn't make her feel any better. Alone in the big empty apartment, her uneasiness amplified. This had been an odd and emotion-packed day, one way and other. There'd been that nasty face in the window ... and then ending up who knew where and seeing who knew whom ... and then the news of the Miras' adventure, which was far from encouraging if you were Raymond. And even watching the good-looking Charles just now, his eyes dallying over his beautiful wife, had been unsettling.

This was Charles's wine she was polishing off. What a delicious punch it packed. She squinted into its ruby depths. Would he disapprove if he found out? Speak to her in that dehumanizing tone he took with Mirabel? Ashley felt ashamed of her impatience with Mirabel. Mirabel had looked tense earlier. What had that been all about?

The apartment was cold as well as quiet. What was it with the French and sub-standard central heating? The empty fireplace in the living room gave off a bleak, almost a baleful, air. Why couldn't they have a log fire? There was nothing worse than staring into a cold and empty hearth on a winter night.

She was being forced to accept that the woman in red hadn't

been Mirabel. Not that this was particularly reassuring, since it led to worries about her imagination running amok. From there she got to scrutinizing her earlier insights, about Mirabel's second cellphone and the possibility they were under long-term Bortnik surveillance. She didn't feel so sure about anything anymore. People had multiple devices nowadays. The city was full of Mercedes G-Class SUVs. How could she trust any of her suppositions, since she was so far out of her element?

After consuming three quarters of the bottle, she shoved the rest back in the fridge and went to bed. She fell asleep quickly and didn't hear Mirabel come in. But even her dreams, in which Jon Perez returned from some distant limbo and made deft sardonic love to her, were unsettling.

10

STORM

THE NEXT MORNING Béatrice arrived with a handsome brown-eyed urchin in tow. She was full of apologies to Mirabel for having to bring her grandson to work. It was just that her daughter had been faced with a sudden emergency. If this wasn't *convenable,* she'd take the boy home with her. To Ashley's surprise, this didn't faze Mirabel in the least. She said she would like nothing better than to keep little Jules amused. As the day wore on, she demonstrated a real knack for handling small children.

Béatrice was also full of new weather warnings that Ashley didn't quite take on board, since Parisians talked nonstop about the weather anyway.

There was still no word from Raymond Boissier. The two Miras texted briskly back and forth. Ashley was unsure whether Mirabel understood just how ominous his silence was.

Charles, she told Ashley, was putting renewed pressure on her to return to Montreal with him.

"Well, why don't you? Maître Tellier can talk to you on the phone if he needs to, can't he? And the same goes for Raymond."

"It's not that, Ashley. It's Isa. She says she's coming to Paris too. She's leaving tonight."

"What—why?"

"It's because of Raymond, because of the way he didn't show up. I can't stop her. She thinks she can do more if she's in Paris with me."

"Well, why not? I might as well not even be here for all the good I'm doing." Ashley hadn't meant to sound so sore about the thing.

Mirabel reacted with surprise. "I don't see it that way, Ashley." Her tone held a trace of austerity. "After all, it was Charles who hired you, not me. I'm glad you're here. Don't be discouraged."

Ashley almost laughed out loud. Mirabel's words didn't help. She disliked not getting a result when she was being paid, especially this much. She texted Isabel Jadois herself and was surprised when the other replied promptly, considering it was the middle of the night in Montreal.

"Yes, on my way," Isabel wrote. "Things just too crazy. Why are you going outside at all?"

While Ashley was poring over this text, trying to sort the panic from the latent criticism, Charles Saint Cyr phoned. He seemed divided between worry and gloating that Raymond hadn't surfaced. He wasn't excessively bothered that Isabel was on her way, and like her held the view that Ashley should keep Mirabel in the apartment.

It began to snow soon after, a heavy driving snow. Béatrice had the radio on in the kitchen and it finally percolated through to Ashley that a major storm was coming.

A little after lunch, the housekeeper reappeared in the living room looking even more apologetic than earlier. "If I don't leave now I won't get home before the storm." She mentioned a distant eastern suburb. "Manon lives closer to the centre and can come by at dinner time. Would it be a terrible imposition, Madame, if Jules stayed here for another few hours?"

Ashley thought this was a bit much. Not so Mirabel, apparently.

"We'd love to have Jules for the rest of the afternoon." She sounded genuinely enthusiastic. Jules, beside her on the couch, smiled up at her like a mini-Raymond in training.

Then Mireille Borel called Mirabel to say she was in the neigh-bourhood and would be over soon. It seemed like a social call, de-spite the odd timing, but Ashley began to suspect otherwise. This time Mirabel made no effort to keep Ashley in the living room and in fact asked her to take Jules somewhere else. Ashley got the little boy distracted with the Pickles the Panda website in her bedroom while she lay on her bed. She was aware of intense low-voiced con-versation, interspersed with silences during which Ashley thought they might have gone into the far bedroom.

When Mireille left, Ashley rounded on Mirabel. "What were you plotting?"

Mirabel looked absurdly furtive. "I shouldn't be telling you. Mireille thinks she has a lead on where the stash is. She's not sure exactly where, so don't ask me! Also, I didn't give her money, or anything—or make any promises."

"Why didn't she phone? Why did she have to come over?"

Mirabel dropped her gaze. "Just for the reason she said, Ashley. She was in the neighbourhood. Anyway, look, I'm staying here. She's not going to do anything today, with the bad weather."

"Speaking of which, when is Jules's mother coming over?"

"In two hours." Mirabel fiddled with the remote. "Béatrice said we should keep the television on." Ashley figured something was up, but could get nothing further from Mirabel.

Ashley hadn't been interested in weather reports, but the stead-ily intensifying Météo-France warnings finally changed that. The snowstorm was to continue, with whiteout conditions. Already ac-cidents were being reported on all the major highways of France. The heavy snow would lessen around midnight, with intermittent squalls thereafter. Then a major Atlantic warm front would sweep in. It would create a big mess, with snow turning into mixed snow and freezing rain. But the worst was still to come. A deep depres-sion had formed out in the ocean beyond it, with a barometric pressure almost unheard of at this time of year, and it was moving fast towards Europe. Long before morning, it would bring a massive cold front into collision with the slow-moving warm front ahead of it, creating powerful winds and mixed precipitation when it hit land.

The warnings were dire. The French meteorological map was alight with orange and red. The expected winds would gather strength over the land. The television announcer first talked of gale force winds, which evolved into a Beaufort scale "violent storm."

Jules seemed to be taking in more of this than a little boy should. They didn't tell him when his mother texted again to say she'd be further delayed. A call from a desperately apologetic Béatrice gave them the impression that Manon could be a feckless mother. Around dinnertime, Charles phoned with the weather on his mind. He made noises about coming to rue des Arabes but Mirabel put him off. Ashley started to get worried texts, one after the other, from Montreal. Isabel updated them periodically on her flight, which was looking less and less likely. Manon texted that the Métro was now "impossible" and she would try to get a cab.

Soon Madame Caron appeared at the door with a custodian, whom she introduced as her husband, to ask them if they wanted help closing their shutters. There was a hand crank behind the draperies, to wind the heavy exterior panels shut and lock them down. They should do this at the very latest before they went to bed. It wouldn't hurt either to fill available containers with water. She told them where candles, matches and a flashlight with fresh batteries were stored in the utility room. Did they have enough heavy clothing, blankets?

They first heard the term *bombe météorologique* at eight o'clock that night, right around the time Béatrice called to say Manon was not going to be able to get over to rue des Arabes. For Ashley, *le Nuit du Grand Vent,* as it was afterwards called, was all about the sound. She fell asleep to a background of thudding wet snow and rattling ice pellets against the shutters. Some time later she woke to violent shaking of the shutters themselves and the whistling wind in the chimney. It was as if something was trying to get into the apartment.

She got up to check on Mirabel and Jules, who were fast asleep together, their arms flung above their heads and their faces equally childish in repose. She padded through the dark shuddering house, checking windows. The shutters, at least, were holding. Far too alert for sleep, she curled up on the couch. The worst of the storm, according to the muted television, was just coming up on Paris. All around her she could feel shaking—the racketing of the heavy wooden shudders, the window glass flexing horribly like sheet plastic, the whole building rocking as it took the gusts. Beyond this cocoon of turbulence, out in the black night, the sleepless city boomed and cried. Although it wasn't the tumult of the human city she was listening to, it dawned on Ashley as the sound rose. It was the wind itself, howling over the rooftops of Paris.

Time passed and Ashley fell asleep at last under an inadequate throw. She woke to a cold and silent morning, in an apartment still dark behind closed shutters. She could do something about the darkness, but not the cold: the electricity was out. Before its charge expired, her phone informed her the power was out in half the country. Major damage to one transmission system in particular meant that most of Paris was included in the outage.

They were drinking lukewarm cocoa in their coats and trying to convince Jules it was an adventure when Monsieur Caron came to the door to check the windows and shutters. The building had sustained some roof damage, he told them, nothing too serious. The big bundle of firewood in his arms was a joyful sight. Soon they had a fire crackling in the fireplace and Ashley had set up a sort of trivet affair and was heating water in a pot.

But the city was at a standstill. When Charles called and told them they should come to his hotel, which had generators, it sounded like a wonderful idea. But they soon found out, on Mirabel's weakening cell phone, that there were major disruptions in public transit—and finding a taxi would be like finding the Holy Grail. In fact, an official state of emergency had been declared, and the French emergency measures organization had ordered everyone to stay home, to stay in place.

More texts from Manon and Béatrice, more excuses, more apologies. Mirabel was a pleasant companion during the long hours, optimistic, calm, matter-of-fact. Monsieur Caron brought more wood, and Madame Caron, having some privileged relation-ship to a small generator somewhere in the building, produced a tureen of *bonne soupe*. They ransacked the kitchen for anything to heat or toast. Mirabel stacked blankets and quilts in front of the fireplace and said it was like camping. By which she meant camping after lights out in the dorm of her select Lausanne finishing school for young ladies. Their devices died. They played children's card games with Jules and exchanged stories of other power failures they had survived. Ashley found herself telling Mirabel quite a lot about her life. Mirabel listened with an almost unsettling attentiveness.

Just before midnight, when Jules was asleep once more in Mirabel's bed and they were reconciling themselves to another night of the same, the lights came back on with that anti-climactic abrupt-ness you were always ready to forgive. How welcome the thrill of jacking up the thermostat, plugging in phones and computers, turn-ing on the radio and television to get the latest news. Not that this was pretty—millions of homes outside Paris were still without power, most planes were still grounded, storm surges on the coast had cre-ated local flooding, the Seine had flooded in parts too, and there was extensive damage to trees and property due to near hurricane-force winds. Twenty-nine confirmed deaths were attributed to the storm, which had gone off to wreak lesser havoc in Germany and Poland.

By morning the death count had gone up to thirty-one but Paris was slowly making its way back to normal. Some planes were flying.

Many workplaces and all schools were still closed but at least the Métro was running. It was Béatrice who finally came to take a belatedly tearful Jules off their hands. Mirabel's goodbyes were tender. Her sharp resentment of Manon's possible lackadaisical tendencies, expressed once the door was shut, seemed out of character and exaggerated to Ashley.

There was a tragic temporary shortage of baguettes and croissants, but Paris rose to that challenge. Mirabel surprised Ashley by coming up with a very passable *pain perdu* for breakfast. Their phones pinged briskly as they ate. People from Canada, including her mother and brother, wanted to make sure Ashley was all right and to hear her adventures. Isabel was still looking for a flight. Charles said Mirabel should come over to his hotel and then announced he would visit rue des Arabes instead. Mireille Borel called Mirabel, but Ashley couldn't make sense of the conversation from her end. The Borel woman seemed to be exercised about something— the impassibility of the city, local damage, Ashley wasn't sure. It was all a jumble as far as she was concerned, tired after two nights of broken sleep and an absence of coffee. God, she needed a cup.

They went out together to scout for supplies. It was a milder day than they'd had in a while and there were people on the sidewalks pursuing similar missions. The big job of clearing wet snow was underway. The Naturalia a few streets away had run out of several basics including milk. The youth behind the counter was getting an earful from customers. When they stepped out onto the pavement, triumphantly clutching the last bag of coffee beans, Ashley was struck by the freshness of the air.

"It took Elvire"—the name they were giving the storm, from some character in an opera apparently—"to clear the pollution," she remarked.

"I can't believe people are hoarding coffee," Mirabel was saying with mild disapproval. "That's not very civic-minded."

Ashley kept her eye on the passing vehicles—she couldn't help it. Traffic was light. In contrast, there were knots of people on the pavement seeing what they could find in shops and chatting with one another. A pair of smokers loitering in front of a greengrocer's blocked their way. Their Gitane smoke bothered Ashley, and distracted her from something another part of her brain was trying to process. It wasn't until they got to the corner that it came to her.

She experienced the familiar adrenaline surge, but also the thought, *this is getting tiresome.* She took Mirabel by the arm. "Don't look back, but I think I saw those two men before."

They were the pair that had passed her on the Strasbourg-Saint Denis platform—or she could have sworn they were. As they turned the corner Ashley took a rapid glance behind her. Someone else partly blocked her view, but what she saw—the barrel-like bodies, the shaved heads, the general thuggishness—wasn't nice.

"Don't squeeze," Mirabel said in protest. Are you sure?"

"Pretty sure. Let's move."

Mirabel pulled a silver compact from her bag and checked her makeup artlessly. "Two hefty men—one has a Bluetooth—they've turned the corner anyway and are coming along behind us."

They were trying not to run now. They were still at least a long block from rue des Arabes and the apartment. "Turn in here," Mirabel said suddenly, indicating a doorway flush with the sidewalk.

Ashley was surprised when Mirabel pushed the gate with confidence. The men were picking up their pace. "Wait, we can't get backed into a corner!"

"We can get home this way." Mirabel spoke calmly as she hurried Ashley through a small courtyard. She produced a fob and opened a door in a corner. Before it locked shut behind them, Ashley just managed to catch sight of the men in front of the gate, which seemed to interest them more than a little.

They were in a service corridor with muted lighting. Mirabel led the way to the end of this, to a set of stairs. "We're going to the fifth floor."

The stairs looked like service stairs. Small windows in each landing dimly lit the worn steps, the old metalwork and paint. They were breathing heavily by the time they reached the top. Another door took them into a narrow passage under the eaves, that snaked off into the dim distance.

"Come Ashley, I know my way," Mirabel said. "This floor is remarkable because it connects three different buildings." She adopted the tones of a tour guide. "It's where the servants used to sleep. It goes back to the time when bourgeois families occupied the big flats downstairs. The servants sometimes worked for more than one employer and had to access more than one building."

This was hardly the time for history. Ashley couldn't help being curious though. The passage was cramped, with a steeply sloped ceiling, but airy too with several dormers that framed the jumble of Paris rooftops. Along the other wall, closely-spaced doors receded from view. Some were just doors, old, needing paint. But others were kitted out, almost like cottage doors, with doormats and elaborate little mailboxes and spiffy paint jobs.

"There might still be a few servants up here. But other people live here now. I think some of the walls have been knocked down to make bigger suites."

They passed a varnished door with frosted glass, through which frilly calico curtains peaked.

"Who lives here?" Ashley wondered aloud. "Little Bo Peep?"

"Well, this one, rich people. It's chi-chi to have a place up here. They get their mail downstairs like everyone else, Raymond said the mailboxes are just for show." Ashley ducked a cornerpiece as they turned off onto another branching corridor. "I suppose it helps to be short. Now we're coming into our building on the rue des Arabes. Watch your step."

The floor dropped down a centimetre or two. The lino was different and so was the paint job. Another door opened to Mirabel's key card and Ashley was surprised to step directly into the rue des

Arabes elevator.

"Now we can just get off at our floor," Mirabel said with a smile. "I'm still tingly inside, aren't you?" Ashley was.

Mirabel's smile altered a little when Charles Saint Cyr met them outside the apartment door.

"Let me make coffee for everyone," Ashley said when they were inside, keen to get away.

"Don't tell him we were just followed," Mirabel whispered.

They all sat and drank coffee, and politely discussed the storm. It had been life as usual at Hôtel de Crillon, apparently: just fewer staff, as some hadn't been able to make it in from their *banlieu* boltholes. Charles had his arm around Mirabel, who now didn't seem loath. Ashley cleared the cups and stayed in the kitchen to let them talk. She caught a peek of Charles kissing his wife, and then the two of them exiting, Ashley was sure, to finish things in the bedroom. Although the apartment was huge, once more Ashley felt she was far too close to the connubial action. It was partly the way Charles, and Mirabel too for that matter, did it, she thought. They didn't bother to conceal what they were up to at all. The bedroom had a door, but it might as well have been a viewfinder.

To hell with being on the job, she said to herself, *and to hell with the Bortnik brothers*. She put on her coat and went for a long walk through the storm-battered city and along the Seine. She stubbornly trudged through wet snow that had already begun to refreeze, eventually arriving at the pont d'Austerlitz. There'd been no sign of surveillance at any point. Trying to compose herself, she lingered by the bridge in the fading light. The river was a mournful sight, the moored boats and barges huddling forlorn in chaotic ice formations. The water level was high against the piers and there were treacherous open pools everywhere, that gleamed with a metallic light under the westering sky.

11

LA BÊTE HUMAINE

"I PROMISE YOU, Ashley, I've thought it through. If we find something tonight, we take pictures and send them to ourselves so we'll have times and dates. Then I finalize the investment side of things with Mireille. No, Ashley, no"—Mirabel gently wagged her finger—"this is safe also, because she knows that if I don't get my share I will have no problem going to the police, and then she'll be a wanted woman instead of making a bundle which is what *she* wants. And that's the end of my involvement. Until I collect my return. All the risk is Mireille's after that." Mirabel had the grace to hesitate after these outrageous words.

"Maybe there will be a difficulty if Mireille can't move the *péniche* to a place where she and her brothers can unload it. But we won't worry about that. Anyway, time is running out, you have to see that. The Bortniks are becoming a real nuisance."

Thus did Mirabel chide Ashley, who couldn't justify for two seconds being on this dangerous fool's errand to recuperate Raymond's stolen goods, but could have justified even less letting Mirabel go alone. If things went to hell, there was always Charles. And the police. As long as it wasn't too late.

It was after dark, two days later. A clear evening on the south bank of the Seine, just opposite the hulking walls of the Sorbonne's celebrated Pierre and Marie Curie college of sciences. This area of the riverbank had been refurbished in recent history, and upper and lower pedestrian paths, stairs, trees and sculptures vied with the feel of a working river. There were the usual apartment buildings above them and they passed a dog walker or two, but the place seemed otherwise to have settled down for the night.

Mirabel had imitated Ashley by dressing all in dark clothes, pants and a puffer jacket with a hood, and, unusual for her, sturdy boots. She was chipper, full of beans—and chatty.

"You can't have expected me just to hand over the keys to Mireille. I think I was very clever, looking through his boxes with her when I knew they were in my jewel case. I don't know why I didn't think about Raymond's houseboat. The fact that he kept a set of keys at my place should have made me realize."

Also: "Isabel was always the brainier one, but I am calmer under fire. Do you think, Ashley, we're like those 'black' operatives?"

"I feel like Marge Simpson in that black ops episode where things go very wrong," Ashley said.

"That was just a cartoon. You know, Charles really loves me, I do believe, but he doesn't understand me at all." Mirabel's voice held a private amusement.

Ashley made a face in the dark. Like so much Mirabel said, this only half made sense. Engaging in sneak-thief wrongdoing seemed to agree with her, however.

They'd taken a chance by hopping a cab at the rue des Arabes exit. They'd had to choose, and figured the goons would now be camped out on the next street. So far so crazy.

At least someone had done a semi-decent job of clearing the snow. A man with a little girl in tow and holding a gigantic dog on a leash bid them good evening with Parisian politeness. Maybe so far so good. Ashley just wanted to get the thing over with.

There was river mist down here and the path was feebly lit with widely spaced mercury vapour lamps. The darkness lying in wait for them between islands of pearlescent light had a strangely inviting effect. Mirabel was scrutinizing the line of moored houseboats and small barges. "It's called la Capricieuse. Isn't that a good name? Raymond said he wanted to bring me here and make love to me. We never did though. I think it's a bit of a dump, honestly." She pulled the flat's emergency flashlight from her backpack. "I should use this. Look for red paint. Raymond said he'd painted the ledge around the boat so it should be easy to see."

But nothing jumped out. They walked and walked, while Ashley began to hope they wouldn't find it. She eventually recognized the familiar arches of the pont d'Austerlitz ahead of them. "We've gone too far. We should turn back. It's not good here."

They'd had to choose between going up a level or staying on the river's edge, where they could access the boats. Down here they were hardly on a path anymore. Ashley could see trees in unculti-vated clumps, lines of dumpsters that said *Propriété de Paris* and a mysterious riverine structure that might have been a shed unless the parts that stuck out were winches. Ashley knew nothing about boats but she knew this was a different kind of area, without people or apartment buildings.

Mirabel was suddenly jubilant. "Here it is, I think. Yes! La Capricieuse."

The strong beam of the flashlight revealed a shabby vessel, a houseboat or barge. There was a pilot cabin, and a sizeable raised structure in front that might have been living quarters or a storage hold. If that was where you slept, no wonder Raymond never got around to taking Mirabel here. Most discouragingly, the vessel listed to one side a few feet from the quay, gripped apparently in a frame of ice. An anchor line disappeared into the ice, and another line was attached to a bollard. At the moment they seemed com-pletely unnecessary.

The solidifying ice must have pushed the vessel away from shore. There was no walkway. It wasn't all ice in the gap. Dark smooth areas indicated open water. For all Ashley could tell, the white surfaces were just floating there, ready to tilt horribly beneath feet. "Sorry I didn't bring my portable gangplank," she muttered.

Mirabel disregarded the sarcasm as she let her flashlight play over the gap. "I think we just jump? The ledge is wide enough."

Ashley wanted to say many things, but she settled on, "Let's look around for something."

To Ashley's surprise, they found a serviceable length of plywood behind the row of dumpsters. The boat sagged a little as they stepped onto the plywood. The panel wobbled as they crossed it, but it could have splintered. They were aboard.

"I don't know what the various keys are for. Here, Ashley, would you hold the flashlight?" Mirabel peered at the new industrial-looking padlock on the cabin door. She found the right key and they both squeezed inside. The cabin was freezing and smelled of fuel and damp.

"Why are we in here?" Ashley said. "You're not planning to take us for a spin, are you?"

"I could. Look, here's the key to the ignition, probably. I guess you don't access the hatch through here. Let's go outside."

They found the hatch entrance on the river-facing side. Between a porthole and a big sliding shutter, it was a low door with another shiny padlock. It took some squeezing and wriggling to get inside and they half-tumbled down the ladder-like stairs. The place was as cold as the cabin but the smell here was of recent carpentry, with a musty accent of cardboard box and a whiff of air sanitizer.

"He was renovating the inside," Mirabel said, as she fished out the flashlight once more and turned it on. What they could see of the interior was lined with new wood panelling. There were other signs of recent work: a heavy-duty metal grille over the porthole, a raw pine workbench and a sort of murphy bed, folded up. A ceiling light bumped against Ashley's head.

Foto from Ikea, a small part of Ashley's brain numbly observed, as Mirabel's flashlight played over the interior. The rest of her brain was taking in the view.

Every inch of floor space, but for a couple of narrow passages, was filled with big corrugated boxes, bales and plastic crates on heavy-duty blue polyethylene pallets. The boxes were taped and flex-tied, and lavish use had been made of the kind of wrapping plastic that looked like the work of Shelob in *The Lord of the Rings*. The hold was stacked to the ceiling.

Mirabel took Ashley's arm. "We've found it!" She sounded excited. "Or some of it, don't you think?"

Ashley tried to take it all in. "How would we know?"

The Foto lamp didn't work but the flashlight revealed plenty. "This is retaped with duct tape here," Mirabel said. "I think someone already looked inside. We need a knife."

"Here." Ashley produced her Swiss Army knife, a complicated-looking affair geared towards the upper-range user.

"That's a very business-like knife," Mirabel said admiringly. "Since when do you carry that around?"

"Since I kept getting stopped going through security with my Leatherman. Shine some light here."

Ashley carefully peeled the layers of tape and plastic back one by one. She was glad she didn't have to cut the cardboard, which had already been cut into two door-like flaps. She took a bundle out, carefully unwrapping the layers of protective non-woven breathable fabric.

Ashley held in her hands at last her first ever Kelly bag, in deep pink. Not that she recognized it. "A purse, right?" She turned it over. "I had a pink purse when I was five. It says Hermès here, so we're on the right track. How much would this kind of thing set you back?"

"About thirty thousand Canadian, I would guess."

"What? Well, I won't be buying one any time soon."

"Oh, Ashley, I won't either, no matter how much money

Charles makes. These are for the A list. You can't just be a regular person and walk into a store. I wonder who this one was made for? Somebody's not getting their purse."

"You mean Mrs. Oligarch?"

"No, I mean the person it was supposed to go to as a special order, before Mr. Oligarch decided he wanted one for Mrs. Oligarch."

This was all a little too much for Ashley. "It's not that special. You could live on the price of this for a year."

"I know, and people do," Mirabel said with surprising intensity. "I like beautiful things, but I'm not a slave to labels."

They pulled out more small packages swathed in the same breathable fabric. Soon there was an array of deluxe belts, beautiful scarves and showy *bijouterie*, all saying Hermès, lined up in front of them.

They stared at it all. "I hope there's enough light to take decent pictures," Ashley said.

"Wait." Mirabel brought over a high-intensity LED lantern from the workbench. She fiddled with the switch and the hatch was flooded with bright white light. She worked the dimmer. "How about this?"

The pictures were very clear. They went about systematically photographing the scene, focusing on the bills of lading stuck to the containers. The pictures they sent into the protective ether would mean they'd never have to return, Ashley consoled herself. Mirabel was inclined to linger and marvel but it was time to leave. Ashley had to chivvy her up the ladder.

As they came around to the shore side, a police siren wailed in the distance. After the silence of the hold, the night was full of small noises—nearby branches rustling in the wind, a scraping sound on the path. In the dark, something shifted. At the foot of the ganglank, a hulking human form emerged into the silver bubble of light.

"Good evening, *Mesdames*," said Bortnik Thug One, because who else could it be. He advanced towards the gangplank. "Time to come down." He spoke in a Slavic accent, and with the relaxation of someone who had no worries about what would happen next. He held a big handgun loose at his side.

Ahead of Ashley, Mirabel stopped dead in her tracks. Ashley began to edge around her. The man took another easy step forward. Everybody stared at the plywood sheet, as if it had the next move.

"We're not coming across—so you should just go away," Mirabel said in a shrill voice.

Ashley looked up and down the shore. Thug Two was nowhere visible. A comment, she sensed, on how easy they thought this was going to be. Dull anger bloomed in her all at once. Was she going to be like those women who wouldn't give up their purse to a purse snatcher, because they'd just bought a new bus pass, and got themselves killed?

Temporize. "Who the hell are you?"

"I work for the men who want their property back. But *you* know. Well, I'm bored, enough chat." He raised his gun arm casually, his voice becoming a growl. "I can go there and get you, sure. It's better for you if I didn't."

Mirabel shrank against Ashley. "Try it!"

Shut up, Mirabel.

Negotiate. "Hang on, let's talk."

"Oh, I'm fucked." This may have been a specimen of sarcasm. "I said no talk." He stepped heavily onto the plywood. It groaned and rocked under his feet. Up close, Ashley could see the blank eyes, the mouth curved downward with age and hostility. The confidence of the executioner.

His gun hand began to swing upwards. Ashley moved fast, to get inside the gun. She collided with him in the middle of the plywood. It was like trying to shove a cement pillar. He didn't even react. Her knee came up but he knew that trick and slid sideways. He grabbed her by the neck with a huge hand and began to press her down. He wasn't even breaking a sweat.

155

She slammed her fist in the direction of his groin but missed. He growled again and now brought his gun down hard. Her left hand exploded with pain and she dropped, trying to fall into it and strike a blow at his leg. It had little force. But still, he stumbled backward on the incline of the plywood with a curse. Now he was mad, and he raised his gun over Ashley's head.

He also turned slightly, and yelled to someone on land.

It was strange to see the gun spinning through the air and dropping down into the space between the boat and the quay. The thug seemed to think so too, although he was more distracted by the effect of the boathook that had just come down on his arm. Mirabel was holding it with two hands and raising it once more. Ashley fell to the ground and tried to do something unfriendly to the man's ankles. Mirabel struck again.

The Bortnik goon went over the side without a word. It was touch and go, but Ashley just managed to save herself from following.

A dull thud as the man hit the ice. They gaped as he moved down there, perhaps searching for the gun. The pale surface tilted in leisurely fashion under him. A black pool opened up and casually swallowed half his body. Two mesmerizing seconds later, the rest of him followed, with a gurgling sound that could have been his or the hungry river's. The white surface bobbed languorously upright again.

They continued to stare. Nothing happened.

"Jesus Christ. We have to do something!"

"Are you crazy, Ashley? He was going to kill us! Look, there's the gun, maybe we could get the gun."

"Are *you* crazy?"

"I think we could use a gun right now."

"Yes, but—*no*. Is there a pole? Go and look!"

"I don't want to look! What would we do with a pole? Anyway, he's gone."

They stared into the yawning gap some more, as the houseboat moved slightly, perhaps coming into contact with something under its hull.

"Ashley, we need to leave."

A guttural cry from the top of the escarpment. A firecracker pop and an insect whine.

Ashley suddenly agreed with Mirabel. "Jesus, we're being shot at, run!"

They flung themselves across the gangplank, which reared up in final protest and disappeared into the gap between la Capricieuse and the river. They were in front of a flight of stairs. Ashley looked up. At the top, she saw movement. "This way!"

Running hard, they took off eastward along the cinder path, staying in the shelter of the retaining wall. Ashley cradled her left hand as she ran. It hurt like hell. Mirabel seemed to be keeping up without trouble. They came at length to an access path. It would take them up to a complicated traffic intersection near the pont d'Austerlitz.

They stopped. It didn't seem like they were being followed. Ashley pointed. "What's up there?"

Mirabel squinted. "Well, the bridge. Also a viaduct. There'd be people." She was holding her knees, the way an athlete does after a major effort. She looked quite unlike herself. Not that Ashley had recognized the Mirabel of the boathook episode, either.

From somewhere behind them, a repetitive sound reached their ears. The crunching of footsteps on gravel.

They headed up the ramp. The traffic at road level was heavy. On their left, very near, loomed the pont d'Austerlitz. Just beyond, a train was racketing across the viaduct. They were at a red light, with cars racing by in both directions.

"There's a Métro station on the right bank, but I'm not sure exactly where," Mirabel was saying.

Ashley scanned behind them. Far down the access ramp, a human form was bobbing along at a dogged pace. There were no other pedestrians in view anywhere. "Shit! We're still being followed. What's that over there?" She pointed to a monumental edifice with a columned front, off to the right.

"The gare d'Austerlitz."

"Let's go! There'll be security."

The light changed and they launched across six empty lanes.

"Wait!" On the far pavement Mirabel stopped to adjust her backpack strap. "I can't believe we're still being chased!" She sounded peeved. "I left them the keys, you know."

Ashley gaped. "What?"

"I threw them on the deck. I mean, what was the point? The Bortniks will know where everything is now. Even if the first man who tried to jump us doesn't ... surface, this one knows."

A head on thick shoulders was now approaching the intersection on the other side. Ashley pulled Mirabel into a run once more. "Then why are we still being chased?"

"Maybe he hasn't realized yet. Ashley, how should I know? I can't explain the thinking of hoodlums."

They slowed to a fast walk as they zigzagged through a busy parking lot. The mid-size hall or ticket lobby they entered was chaotic due to construction. Although it was late, people still milled about. They came to a halt under a clock. Ashley looked around. "You don't seem winded but I can't run anymore. Also, I need ice for my hand. Let's find a coffee shop. Are there other levels?"

"Oh, your hand! Yes, this is just the original entrance. A new concourse has been completed. I know the way."

They entered the human flood.

"Ashley ... do you think ..." Mirabel frowned, a blonde angel having a trying day. "The man we pushed into the water ... I wonder if ..."

We pushed? Had anybody pushed him? Ashley had been on all

fours, and hadn't seen everything. Maybe she had toppled him. Or maybe it had been Mirabel's second swing of the boathook. She said nothing.

Mirabel tucked her hand into Ashley's arm as they hurried along. "We didn't do anything wrong. We were attacked. Anyway, who knows what happened? It was dark. He could have come up on the other side of the boat." Mirabel's eyes as she leaned over were the tender blue of a lake on a summer day. "For all we know."

They were now in the new concourse, all modern architecture, soaring glass ceilings and echoing announcements. There were shops, newsstands, food outlets. The crowds here were bigger.

"This is the main ticket hall. There's an old-style *café de la gare* down at the end. We'll go there."

The restaurant was half full and they were quickly seated at a table overlooking the concourse through incongruous half-curtains and frosted glass. Mirabel happily surveyed their surroundings.

"I've never eaten here, it's new. They made it look like something out of a Colette novel." She heaved a sigh. "That was very dramatic."

Ashley fixed her gaze on her companion. "I didn't know you were so—athletic." *What, in the boathook swing category?* She specified: "I mean, you're a strong runner."

"At my college in Lausanne, I was on the cross-country team and I played competitive badminton," Mirabel said with modest pride. She pulled out her phone, scrolled. "Two missed calls from Charles. Oh well. Isa texted me. She says she's probably not coming to Paris." She cast a furtive glance in Ashley's direction. "That's better, isn't it, Ashley?"

Ashley's nod was inattentive. She was still desperately trying to process what had just happened.

Mirabel, on the other hand, appeared to have moved on. "Isa and I are very close. That's the thing you should know. There were so many years when she and I were out of touch. We didn't know if we would ever see each other again. Now, we don't like to be apart. I wonder why they do that to children?"

Irritated, Ashley just shrugged.

"It could have been worse," Mirabel was saying, vaguely. "At least they were kind to us in our adopted families. Not like some …" Her eyes met Ashley's briefly, too briefly for Ashley to be sure whether she had imagined the cold blue flash.

No one said anything, until Ashley felt the need to return to the topic at hand. "So that's that. Let's go home as soon as possible."

Mirabel put away her phone and examined a pressed glass tumbler minutely. "All right."

This was unexpected. Ashley said: "We might be able to fly out tomorrow. How fast can you pack?"

"The day after sounds reasonable."

Could this be success at last? "I'll book our flights."

Mirabel's smile was pleasantly addled. "All right."

A *serveuse* in a half-heartedly old-fashioned uniform handed them menus, along with a litre of mineral water.

"Can we have ice cubes?" Mirabel asked her. She turned to Ashley. "Oof—I'm thirsty but, do you know, I didn't eat much and now I'm hungry too. Are you?"

Ashley wasn't sure how this could be, but she was. Badly in need of food. They ordered two *croque-madames béchamel* with the *frites maison*—because they needed, said Mirabel, to keep their strength up. "I'm sure there are desserts too," she said, pointing to a glass case. "I wonder what their signature dessert is."

"*Gâteau opéra, Madame*," the server said.

Mirabel looked interested. She seemed to have forgotten what had just happened to them. It was as dangerous a situation as Ashley had ever been in, even with luck on their side. Or was it Mirabel's quick thinking, rather than luck, that had saved them? Everything had happened so fast. When it came down to it, though, she owed Mirabel.

Mirabel improvised an ice compress with a napkin and wrapped it around Ashley's swollen hand, which had begun to go from red to mauve. "Are you sure there's not something broken?"

"I've had enough injuries playing lacrosse to know the difference between a bruise, a sprain and a break."

The food was a welcome if temporary distraction and they tucked in. But the *gâteau opéra* was not to be. Ashley saw Mirabel's face change in mid-chew.

"That looks like—Ashley, I think it's the man who—" She dropped her head beneath the level of the curtain as if searching the floor. She was already throwing euros on the table, with a speed that was commendable.

Ashley had ducked too, but was still able to see a heavyset individual through the curtain. He was close. He wasn't looking their way, but she recognized the hulking shoulders, the cauliflower ears, the Bluetooth. Instead of continuing on his way, the man was hovering in the vicinity, while people flowed by on either side. He had that restless look of someone who would turn around in a moment.

He did. But by then they were out of the booth and lurking behind a giant aspidistra in the entrance.

"We're cornered here," Ashley whispered. "Is there another way out of this concourse? He's blocking the way we came."

The man was moving now, but at a snail's pace. There was nothing about his behaviour that conveyed an intention of leaving the vicinity. Had he seen them coming up the escalator? It wasn't looking good.

"There are down escalators at the other end, but I don't know where they lead."

They saw him go to a *Paradis du Fruit* juice counter. When he began to rummage in his pockets, presumably for change, they took their chance and sprinted towards the end of the concourse. There was a bank of giant escalators there and they jumped onto the one with fewest passengers and leap-frogged down. As long as he didn't turn and see their bobbing heads, especially Mirabel's fair one.

They stepped off into a broad passenger tunnel, with lots of confusing signage but only one way to go. There weren't too many people and they ran flat out. The tunnel sloped downward and forked, one side to the Métro, the other to trains.

"Métro?" Ashley said.

"The train platform would be safer."

They ran that way, down another sloping tunnel and around a corner. Suddenly they were in another glass-ceilinged hall, this one at platform level. Personnel and travellers scurried here and there, a bedlam of voices competed with announcements, and passenger trains stretched as far as the eye could see.

Ashley stopped. "But how do we get out?"

She turned, but Mirabel wasn't there anymore. She looked around wildly. She finally spied Mirabel twenty feet away, engaged in what appeared to be earnest discourse with someone at a customer service booth. As two young boys carrying assault weapons wandered by—Ashley couldn't get used to this customary sight of heavily-armed soldiers in Paris's public places—she hurried over.

The ticket agent, with a flustered air, was shaking her head.

"I'm trying to see how we can reserve and buy two tickets at track level," Mirabel explained, as if this were the most natural thing.

"Why would we buy train tickets?"

Mirabel dropped her voice. "Because, Ashley, it's the only way out of here except the way we came. We could go back and take the tunnel to the Métro, but what if the man saw us? We'd meet him in the tunnel! This is actually a good way to get out of the station, you know ..."

Ashley opened her mouth to object.

"I have an idea!" Mirabel turned to the agent once more. "If I buy two tickets right now on my phone, can you then issue us what we need down here?"

"Yes, certainly, Madame. You will have to step aside, however, and let me serve the other customers who are here to pick up tickets." She gestured to the long line forming behind them. But Mirabel was having none of it.

"I will be so fast. Look, I'm doing it right now." People started to babble around her but she wouldn't budge. She tapped away busily at her phone. "*Trains de nuits* ... Here we are. Paris-Nice is leaving in ten minutes ... Get out my credit card, will you, Ashley? I really should remember my credit card number, considering how often I use it." The babble around her augmented. As she handed Mirabel her card, Ashley hoped the outraged voices weren't reaching the ears of the youths with the assault rifles. The agent in the booth was on the phone to someone—security, at a guess. Mirabel just continued to tap away, her head on one side, as if she was on her sofa at home, buying something nice from Brooks Brothers.

"There," she said at last, directing a dazzling smile at the agent. "I can give you the reservation number now, if you're ready?"

The agent hung up with a martyred air and busied herself on her computer. In two minutes they had paper in their hands, and were out of the line.

"That went well, I think." Mirabel turned to Ashley.

"Why Nice?"

Mirabel adopted a patient tone. "There are other stops, Ashley. I just thought we should get out of the station as soon as possible. But this will be fun! Now let's find our train."

12

LADIES ON A TRAIN

"**D**OWN HERE, ASHLEY."

Mirabel pointed to a black and dingy silver beast breathing heavily on the track. She straightened her jacket and gave Ashley the once over. "Put your bad hand in your pocket. We want to look like regular passengers, not two people who were in a fight."

Ashley supposed that, in their backpacks and utilitarian gear, they could pass for a pair of long-distance train passengers who travelled light.

Mirabel led them down the platform. "Where are the *couchette* cars? Here." They boarded. She turned to Ashley in the coach vestibule. "I got us adjoining *couchette* cabins, one for each of us. 'De luxe, tout pour votre confort,' it said. I for one could use a wash and a rest."

"As long as we don't go to Nice."

"I'm sure we can get off anywhere we want, like I said."

A uniformed attendant ushered them down the window-side corridor, which was quiet, carpeted, dim. He opened each cabin door for them with a dip of the head and a practised flourish—perhaps mistaking them for big-tipping hipster children of oligarchs, Ashley thought, when she saw the roomy two-bed cabin that was to be hers alone. His name was Kurt, he said with a smile. They only had to ring the bell if they needed him.

Instead of something reminiscent of the Orient Express as depicted in a British mini-series, the cabin was all muted and sleek blue-grey surfaces. Two generous built-in beds, done up in immaculate linen, faced each other, and there was an abundance of shelving and ropework overhead bins. A lamp over a small window table shed its soothing glow on a bowl of individually wrapped Lotus cookies. There was an adjoining area next door, closed off by a frosted partition, in which Ashley discovered a combined sink, mirror and cabinet job, more shelves with snowy towels and a discreet affair she supposed turned into a toilet.

Mirabel erupted through the door behind her. "This is very nice, isn't it? Do you want me to show you something? Which bed will you sleep in?"

Ashley pointed, and Mirabel used a strap to lift up the other bed in one easy gesture, transforming it into a comfortable-looking leather seat.

She poked her head around the partition. "Yes, you have Le Labo toiletries too, santal 33 and my favourite, rose 31. Come and smell." She uncorked a small brown glass bottle and waved it invitingly. Ashley couldn't quite integrate this gesture with the one involving the boathook. An exquisite scent of roses assailed her already much abused rational faculties.

"We don't have our own shower, but we have a bathrobe each," Mirabel said, pointing to a thick towelling robe on a hook. "And there's a shower down the corridor, according to Kurt. Ashley—you don't very look good."

Ashley was groping her way to her seat. She was suddenly lightheaded, and needed to sit down in a hurry. The blow to her hand must be catching up with her. The swelling had stopped but the colours were something to look at, and the pain was awful. She also felt confused. What had just happened? And why was she on the

Paris-Nice Intercité de Nuit, discussing toiletries with Mirabel? This was all some kind of mistake.

With a small shudder, the train began to move.

"Don't get up!" Mirabel disappeared in search of Kurt.

Wine came to the rescue, and Ashley's hand was repacked in ice. It might have been the Pino Rosso, or the Tylenol 3 that Mirabel said would work equally well for pain and stress. It might have been the speeding train—the flying darkness through the window, the lulling motion, the repetitive song of iron wheels on rails. Anyhow, it wasn't long before Ashley was being wafted to a better place.

"All right?" Mirabel looked relieved as she tucked a fleece throw around Ashley's knees. "Oh, here's Kurt with more snacks."

The wine went well with the bread, the foil squares of cheese, the chocolate, the strawberries and tangerines. Ashley's hand still hurt, but the pain had wandered off somewhere into the distance, and she was enveloped in many soothing sensations and pleasantly slow thoughts.

"What is our ultimate destination?" Her words came out a little thick.

Mirabel looked surprised. "Oh, well—I wouldn't have thought it was the time exactly for philosophy."

Ashley found this funny, then so did Mirabel.

"I just meant, where should we get off?"

They scrutinized Google Maps together, trying to sort this out. The only problem with getting off before Nice, they quickly realized, was that the train would be depositing them in a regional train station in the middle of the night. On the other hand, it would pull into Nice's Gare Thiers at a civilized, if bright and early, hour tomorrow morning. They imbibed some more wine while letting this sink in.

"It's still a good question, the ultimate destination, I mean," Mirabel said seriously, rearranging her own throw.

"Thug One found out tonight," Ashley said. "Basically, we killed that man."

Mirabel turned pale, but her voice was collected. "What a co-incidence. That's the way I think of them as well. Thug One and Thug Two. And I'm not sure I could tell them apart. Maybe they were brothers. Maybe that's why Thug Two was mad."

"Well, he should have stayed and helped then." Or they should have.

"Let's not think too much about it. It just happened." She selected a Michel Cluizel chocolate, a small perfect strawberry. "Honestly, Ashley, I'd put that episode behind you if I were you. Especially now that the Bortnik brothers got their truck back. The adventure is over."

Ashley's mind ranged over the "adventure." It was better than dwelling on bullets and rivers that cared for no man.

"Mireille ... Raymond ... the Bortniks ... what a mess." She shuddered. "At least I'm getting you back to Montreal, as per my instructions from Monsieur Saint Cyr. Of course, via Nice ..."

Mirabel was amused. "I promise! You see, that part worked out. You did the job you were paid for." She refilled Ashley's glass. "Things are usually a mess. You shouldn't bother too much."

Ashley frowned over this possibly existential statement. There were so many lurid stages to the so-called adventures, in none of which she had shone. She couldn't help putting them in review. "You and Mireille didn't pull off that crazy scheme. And the Bortnik's thugs outsmarted us. " She waved her good hand in a finger count. "Raymond showed up, and then disappeared again, who knows where. Charles—and honestly Mira, I do *not* understand your relationship with him—Charles and you are, what, getting back together again, but what that actually means I have no idea. What else? We're off to Nice, because why not. I'm running out of fingers ..."

Mirabel looked impressed with this description. "You have such a rational mind, Ashley. But why be negative? You saw Paris for the first time and had many interesting experiences of the city, from the Goutte-d'Or to the snowstorm. We met Mireille and I found out Raymond was two-timing me, which made me sad"—she didn't look it—"but at least now I know. I liked Mireille, didn't you?"

Ashley nodded in spite of herself. "Maybe a little crazy though? I wonder why she was so hepped up on that *Barthélemy et fils* scenario."

"The creative temperament. Raymond explained the role of detail to me. Also, you went to *les Puces*, we had that night with Mireille's gang, at the *Bal de la Buanderie*, unforgettable. You made a *lot* of money." Mirabel's face fell here. "I didn't make any money like I hoped, but there ..."

"*Carnaval* was unforgettable, I suppose." Ashley remembered the mask beneath the mask, at the café window. "It turned the city mad." Had it turned her a little mad too?

Mirabel seemed to read her mind. "You are the least nutty person I know, so don't worry," she said. "You never hooked up with Yanis, though. He was very handsome."

He had been. Also a good kisser. Ashley banished the thought. "I'm not like you, Mira. I don't know how you manage. With Charles and Raymond back there, in the apartment. Entrance stage left, exit stage right."

Mirabel smothered a smile. "Ashley, wait. This was the first time ever I cheated on Charles. These things are common. Of course men are still the big cheaters, but they say women are catching up with them. If Charles hadn't come to Paris against my express wishes, there wouldn't have been all *that* at rue des Arabes. You just happened to have a front-row seat." She stared into the darkness. "All men have their purposes, Ashley, and I don't say that flippantly. It's not easy being married to Charles, but you shouldn't worry about me. I knew what I was doing when I married him."

A moving row of bleak sodium lights and a deserted platform now appeared. "Is this Toulon?" she said. "I really don't want to get out here, do you? Look at the time. Why don't we have a nap now

—this would be my suggestion—and we wake up when we wake up? If it's Nice, it's Nice."

Ashley let it go. She was incredibly sleepy, for a start. Also, there was something insidiously and deeply comforting about being on this train. It felt safe to be hurtling through the dark countryside in the opposite direction from what had just happened in Paris, and a part of her didn't want the journey to end.

Hardly ten minutes passed before she tumbled, under a pile of crisp bedding and the weight of so much philosophy, into the abyss of sleep. She woke to the sound of Kurt knocking at her door to present steaming cappuccino and a brioche, and to tell her in a suitably modulated morning voice that the train would be arriving at central Nice in thirty minutes, where the day was already a sunny fourteen degrees.

* * *

Ashley and Mirabel's train pulled into a grey and rain-sodden Paris just before seven that evening. They could have been there earlier. But a stroll along Nice's *promenade des Anglais* to stretch their legs turned into a whirlwind visit they could hardly drag themselves away from. With a sufficiency of Tylenol 3s, Ashley's hand was hardly noticeable. And when would they ever be in Nice again? They could spare a few hours. This was of course Mirabel's reasoning.

Spring had come to the Côte d'Azur with a vengeance. Beneath the hard blue of the Mediterranean sky, old Nice's twisting lanes and stairs were at their most seductive. Flowers bloomed everywhere, flaunting their primary colours under the swaying palms along promenades. They went to Chez Palmyre for lunch, and when they got to the end of the beach had gelato and dipped their toes into the still frigid sea. They caught the last express of the day with a minute to spare.

Mirabel had been on the phone to Charles. He wanted to take

Mirabel and Ashley to one last gala dinner at the Hôtel de Crillon, she reported to Ashley. Was this to reward her for helping shoehorn Mirabel back where she belonged? Or was it simply that Charles wanted to dine with Mirabel and she'd insisted on taking Ashley along?

The restaurant, a former ballroom in the Baroque style, was all it was reputed to be. The chandelier directly above their table, had it dropped, would have killed them. But nothing like that happened, and Ashley enjoyed a few courses of showy food for an even more dazzling price. She wore the black cocktail creation Mirabel had given her, having thought as she put it on that at least she was getting another wear out of it. A thought worthy of her mother, or, in fact, her grandmother. She was already stowing the dress away in the back of a mental closet.

Still, the dinner was enjoyable. Mirabel was less subdued around her husband than usual and Charles exerted himself to be pleasant. The dynamics among the three of them had shifted. The old narrative of employer, employee and wayward wife no longer applied, apparently. Now Charles was dining in a spirit of masculine indulgence with two charming young women just back from a feminine escapade—the details of which he would have found much less charming.

As long as this didn't affect Charles's willingness to pay her, Ashley thought with what she hoped was a suitable simper. But the money had been deposited with heartwarming regularity into her account all through this strange job. So she had little reason to worry now, she decided, as she picked at an *éclair* that, while good, wasn't a match for the mystery dessert in the Goutte-d'Or.

Charles had reserved plane tickets for himself and Mirabel for the next day. Anything Mirabel didn't have time to pack, Béatrice would arrange to ship. Mirabel had wanted Ashley to fly back with them, but she refused. She would stay for another day or two, at her old hotel. The two women spent their last night together at the rue des Arabes apartment, from where Mirabel left a brief and pre-varicative message on Mireille Borel's phone.

At dawn the next day, before Mirabel had even woken up, Ashley took a taxi to the quai de la Rapée, where la Capricieuse had been docked. The barge was, of course, gone. She was glad. She wanted it to have disappeared. There was already less ice on the river, and for all she knew it could have been driven away complete with its load—upriver, for instance, to some densely wooded area along the Marne tributary where it would have been easy as pie to unload it without attracting attention.

There was nothing on this peaceful morning to indicate their encounter with the Bortniks' bruisers. But what had she been expecting? Police tape? A small riverside shrine to the missing thug, whose probable death had been as squalid as his life?

When she returned to the apartment, Mirabel was frantically stuffing things into a suitcase and giving contradictory orders to Béatrice. Madame Caron came by to tell them Monsieur Saint Cyr was waiting in an airport limousine downstairs and wanted to know how much longer Madame Saint Cyr was going to be. Mirabel was anxious about the antiques that would be shipped at fabulous cost to Montreal. Ashley promised she would take care of any last minute jobs Mirabel didn't have time for.

Their goodbyes were rushed. They would, of course, meet again in Montreal. Ashley doubted this.

And then Mirabel was gone, and Ashley sipped coffee with Béatrice, two hirelings contemplating the conclusion of a job. Soon she packed her own things and hoofed her spinner along the bumpy sidewalks back to the Hôtel Beauséjour. The Beauséjour, although anything but a dump, now looked drab after the luxurious surroundings of rue des Arabes. Her room was fine but overlooked an alley. She was becoming aware, once more, of the ordinary inconveniences and discomforts of the real world—well, of her real world—as the sweetness, the narcotic empty calories associated with Saint Cyr money receded from her life. But, she could reasonably hope, there would be fewer bullets.

The next day, Ashley paid an overdue visit to the legendary Number 36, quai des Orfèvres.

* * *

Although most of the *police judiciaire* had moved north to a gleaming complex near the *Périphérique,* the unit in which Claude Jaubert and Pierre Bourque worked was still located on the river Seine. Ashley was suitably impressed by the edifice's exterior, in the grandiose neo-Classical style. Inside, however, it was a working building, and the warren of offices to which she was accompanied on the third floor, after the usual stringent security screening, were poky and dull, if curious with their dusky hallways of random cabinetry displaying crime mementos.

She was feeling tense. This was always a tricky part of her job, ensuring no blowback to a well-connected employer. Complicated, in the present case, by an instinct to shield Mirabel that surprised her by its strength. She'd dressed carefully, in a jacket and a Liberty print shirt. She wanted to come across as business-like, but unthreatening. When she was sitting across from Bourque at his desk—Inspector Jaubert, looking even more like Putin, nearby in an armchair, and the light from a window strong in her face, she realized she might as well not have bothered.

She'd mulled over her strategy and memorized notes over breakfast, so that her story would stand up to questioning. She had facts to share with them, she began by saying. Some of which her client, now back in Montreal with his wife, was unaware of. Jaubert's left eyebrow rose. Well, they could draw their own conclusions.

"Madame Saint Cyr's contact information." She placed a sheet of paper in front of Bourque. After a delay, they leaned forward infinitesimally.

Unbuttoning and then buttoning up her jacket, because if you were going to betray nervousness you might as well make a show of it, Ashley launched into a judiciously modified account of the events of the last few weeks.

She began with the way they'd thought they were under surveillance: their sightings of the Mercedes G-Class, the way it popped up in unexpected places. Although, she qualified, they might have been imagining everything, which is why they didn't go to the police. She stared them down when she said this.

Now for Raymond and the Bortniks.

Raymond Boissier had shown up briefly at the rue des Arabes flat. He confirmed he was on the run, from the Bortniks. He borrowed money from Mirabel and left, urging her not to contact him except via a burner phone number. Ashley put another piece of paper on the desk. "That's his new number, or was."

The two men looked the French civil servant version of daggers at Ashley.

"You might have told us, Mademoiselle, that the missing person was no longer missing." This from Jaubert.

"He's still missing."

The next thing that happened, she said, was the appearance of a very angry Mireille Borel at rue des Arabes. She could tell this was a piquant fact for her two listeners. French men being all about eternal triangles, she supposed.

"After consuming a lot of wine, they decided to try and find Boissier themselves." How else to capture that strange evening? "They managed to get in touch with him on his burner phone and the three agreed to meet at les Halles. He never showed up." None of them, said Ashley, had had contact with Raymond since.

The *flics* were mighty interested now. Ashley took a careful breath. Here the ice—an unfortunate metaphor—would be thinner still.

That evening when Mireille visited, she continued, she'd overheard from the kitchen part of a conversation about the possibility of a truckload of designer goods, possibly hidden away in some unknown location. Fragments. It sounded like speculation. Hidden by Raymond? Mirabel must have thought so because, soon after, she wanted to search Raymond's *péniche*. Its keys were among some things he'd left at the apartment. Ashley tried unavailingly to dissuade Mirabel. Ashley thought she had no choice but to go with her.

"Why didn't you inform the police at this point?" Jaubert asked.

"If we'd imagined all that about being followed, then this would lead nowhere too."

The dirty look progressed to foul.

"Two days after that big storm, we went along the Seine after dark. We found the *péniche* moored at the quai de la Rapée. We boarded it. The hold was full of high-end fashion goods. We locked up, and came on deck. This was when we saw a man waiting at the foot of the gangplank, holding a gun."

Bourque pushed his glasses up in a taut gesture. Jaubert muttered an inaudible curse.

The struggle on the gangplank and its grisly aftermath were conveyed with few and carefully-chosen words, of which "boat-hook" wasn't one. She now finally showed them her bruised hand. "Then someone above the boat shot at us."

"*Putain de merde.*"

"Of course, we ran." She told of their arrival at the gare d'Austerlitz, how they ended up on a train.

"You—ah—took a train to Nice?"

"Yes." Again, no explanation seemed best. "The next day the Saint Cyrs left for Canada, and I went back to where la Capricieuse had been docked. It was gone. And that's it. That's all I know."

She added carefully, after a moment: "I don't see how the first man could have survived. I also think the people who were after Raymond took the boat. I don't see who else could have." Raymond himself, but she wasn't going to say that.

She relaxed her tense body carefully and met their gaze. Never had she been stared at in quite this way, as the seconds ticked by.

"One other thing. I took pictures on the *péniche*. Would you like to see them?"

***

The sun was setting over Paris by the time Ashley finally left the quai des Orfèvres.

After her initial statement, they'd all moved to an interrogation room. Bourque and Jaubert came and went; there were new faces. The questioning took hours. Everything was recorded, and then she was asked to go over it all again. The police wanted details. The details of their experience of being followed, of their various interactions with Raymond Boissier and Mireille Borel, and of the night itself when they found la Capricieuse. Then, out of left field, a line of questions about Charles Saint Cyr. Before he arrived in Paris, after he arrived, whether he'd had any interactions with Raymond, his "bitter jealousy" of the latter.

"Uh—what?" Ashley frowned. "I saw some jealousy, I wouldn't call it bitter." Had she missed the obvious?

Her questioners were courteous enough. It was, of course, awful in its way. But it got less awful with time. By mid-afternoon, after her second coffee and sandwiches, Ashley sensed that the police mostly, if not entirely, believed her account.

She thought she understood how they saw the thing. Flighty and spoiled Madame Saint Cyr had fallen in with a wrong number, and might well have tried to play detective on his behalf. But she hadn't pulled it off. She was unlikely, as the wife of a very wealthy man, to have wanted the goods herself. (Ashley was glad in connection with this that the Saint Cyrs were rich.) And of course Mirabel could have had nothing to do with the body of Langelier they'd pulled from the river. They'd seen this kind of thing before. The things women would do for men beggared the imagination. Only slightly less so than the things women would do to men.

Such was life.

As for Ashley, she'd been hired by a rich and prominent man to bring his recalcitrant wife to heel, and had no doubt been under pressure to sweep everything under the rug. Under the circumstances, she'd offered up quite a bit. Raymond Boissier would remain on their radar, but whether he ever reappeared was anybody's guess. They'd search the river evidently, although the Seine delivered up its secrets in its own time.

The two *Canadiennes* had been sorely lacking in judgement for not informing the police about any of this sooner. More importantly, an international incident had been averted. Who wanted the song and dance that would involve, the heavy-handed interest of other police departments, the exhausting and exhaustive feeding of information about Canadian visitors and so forth to the politicos' handlers, for their endless and self-serving briefing notes, diplomatic correspondence and media releases?

In a sea of predictable malfeasance and paperwork, it had been a gripping story, filled with recognizable human elements. Even police get bored.

A young female cop in jeans and a muscle T-shirt asked Ashley about her preferred martial arts techniques and suggested she should have her hand seen by a French doctor.

Jaubert said she was free to fly home the next day, although she might be contacted in Montreal.

She had one more thing to do before she returned to her hotel. She found a cab and asked the driver to take her to the corner of rue des Capucins and rue de la Charette. The ride was longer than she expected, and a deep twilight had settled over the quartier des Quinze-Vingts by the time she arrived.

The mood in this secluded neighbourhood was as she remembered it. The same faint mist, surely from the nearby basin, threaded through the narrow streets and blurred the edges of everything. Without difficulty she found the building with the Art Deco doors and the jade green tile front. After taking a cellphone picture of the facade, she stepped into a neutral lobby with a row of ivory doorbells, a different sort of arrangement than your typical Parisian building. There were names beside the buzzers. Ashley read down the list but nothing jumped out. She was about to press the buzzer beside "*Concierge*" when a young couple came through the inner doors. They were Asian, and smiled carefully in her direction.

Ashley was inspired to ask: "Would you be able to help? I'm looking for my friend who's just moved in, her name isn't on the list yet. Do you know which apartment is occupied by a Madame Saint Cyr?"

The young couple shook their heads and said, in passable French, that they were visitors to Paris and weren't acquainted with the other residents. They held an apartment through Airbnb. In fact, they added after a pause, they thought quite a few of the apartments were rented out in this way.

Ashley thanked them profusely, said she'd of course ring the concierge, and slight bows were exchanged. The concierge appeared quickly, as if his quarters were just off the inner lobby. He was a frazzled thirty-something, holding a fretful infant in his arms. Ashley went through her routine again, but sounding scatty this time. The man shook his head. No one had moved in here as a tenant in the last three months. They had Airbnb guests, of course, but Mademoiselle wasn't referring to them, was she? Anyway, he didn't know their names.

Ashley contrived to look even more confused. "Oh, well—I'm not sure, now that you mention it ..." She fiddled with her phone and showed the man a double-selfie she'd taken of Mirabel and herself by the sea in Nice.

"My very good friend," she said.

The man peered, while the infant arched its back to the accompaniment of irate cries. "I have seen her, I'm fairly sure. But she wasn't a long-term resident. I haven't seen her for several days. She could have been someone's guest, or an Airbnb visitor, but she's gone now, at a guess." Despite the struggling infant, he was now looking interested.

"You know something, I'll call her this minute." Ashley slipped away with an apologetic smile, the phone to her ear.

At the corner, she stopped to stow her phone. Her thoughts were all over the place. She looked behind her, undecided. A pedestrian was gliding towards her, eerie in the mist. Perhaps he was rubber-shoed, there were no accompanying footsteps. Yet the street seemed filled with sound, a low monotonous susurration that reached out to Ashley from nowhere and everywhere. Surely voices from a nearby building—or the grate beneath her feet. As the muttering whispers amplified, she bolted towards the closest Métro stop, that of the mournful yellow M.

By the time she got back to the Beauséjour, she was bone tired. She drew the curtains to hide the alley, turned on lamps and took a bath. The room service tray arrived in due course and she tucked into dinner with a sense of a feast well-earned. The television news, fashionably late like everything else in this city, was on in the background, and the announcers were talking about a security issue somewhere. For a moment Ashley thought they were referring to Montreal. But it didn't seem anything like a crisis, and anyway she was too tired to concentrate. Then the news programme broke, and she was sucked into the fifteen minute commercial slot that marked every last quarter of the French television hour.

Time passed. Sleep beckoned. She was, she knew, stalling about turning off the lights. She emptied the wine carafe into her glass. Here she was again, just like that first evening in Paris—how many weeks ago had it been, three, four? She took a swallow of wine. Not just like, no. She hadn't slept well for the last two nights. Shots fired and cracking splintering gangplanks had dominated her dreams. This phase would pass, she knew from experience. As a PI, she might get close to the action, but the thing was still happening to other people. And soon, an ocean away.

The faint possibility that the dead Russian wasn't dead always surfaced at this point in her ruminations. Its faintness, if she was being honest with herself, was a relief. She wanted Thug One dead as a doornail, and Thug Two counting his blessings in the spirit of healthy letting go. Sooner or later, in every dream, she found herself in the same situation. She was hurrying along an empty street, while through the darkness heavy feet pursued her. She would wake in a fright, and tell herself it was just a dream. The real nightmare was the waking thought that sooner or later footsteps might really come for her.

The next day Ashley and her spinner, both slightly battered, caught the afternoon flight to Montreal.

13

SHOW ME A SIGN

ASHLEY SMEETON WASN'T an experienced traveller. She was unprepared for the feelings that accompanied her return from Paris. The city looked wrong—the streets, the buildings, the storefronts. The pedestrians themselves, in their frowsy winter layers. The food, especially the bread and the coffee, tasted all wrong. Her nice flat on rue de Paris wasn't so much wrong as desperately in need of a cleaning. What slob lived here before, she was inclined to ask, as she hunted down her mop and broom. Then she remembered she'd thrown out her old Swiffer, and had to borrow Chantale Barry's. These post-trip feelings lasted the predictable three days. And by then Ashley was swamped with work anyway.

Winter was another matter. She'd landed back in Montreal on the last day of February. There was no reason to think winter was over. The city had much still to endure, those inevitable April snowstorms, for instance. But after Paris's soft and rainy airs—at the very end of her stay, anyway—and, above all, Nice's electric spring, the hard lockdown of winter over the city was a grievous shock.

Only according to the calendar were they at the end of winter in Montreal. After an unusually cold and snowy February, the city was now in its endless winter phase. The days were bright but bitter, the sun set red and hard, dreary and long were the blue evenings

180

and the black nights. As for the congealed snow, charmless with dirt, it was going nowhere.

The outdoorsy types were still taking to pond, rink, trail and slope, but many more people had just quietly given up and were staying indoors, waiting for a sign. This was a luxury Ashley couldn't afford. As she drove around in the course of her work, she had ample opportunity to dwell on the dirty snowbanks and the rutted black ice. Then her car heater went on the blink. When she finally found time to have it fixed, she bought herself a heated car seat, and threw in a leather steering wheel cover with four heat settings.

She could afford them, that was for sure. Never had her bank account looked so good. She'd resisted a spree, but had allowed herself to toss the polypropylene square that was pretending to be a living room carpet, replacing it with a thick Belgian wool rug in a rich Arts and Crafts pattern. Aram was enthusiastic when he came by for a visit on a Saturday morning soon after her return.

He asked about her trip. She told him as much as she felt she could, then a little bit more. He gushed sincerely over the handsome Oree wood keyboard, compatible, she assured him, with North American computers. It was, in its way, an extravagant present. But Ashley hadn't paid him much for filling in while she'd been away. He was carrying a full course load, and picked up work when he could at a downtown gym, but you would never have known it from the care he'd shown on what she'd left him.

"How was Montreal?" she asked, over coffee from Parisian beans.

"Montreal? Here in the Point, nothing ever happens, *bien non*. But did you hear about that kidnapping we had? It was just before you came back. A diplomat, from his Griffintown condo—close to here, so extra exciting."

"I haven't had a minute to pay attention to the news. I might have heard something about it on French television. What happened?"

181

Aram shrugged. "The guy escaped eighteen hours later. He was able to squeeze through a tiny basement window of a duplex in Rivière-des-Prairies. He was a little shrimp, they didn't plan for that. This is why you can't predict history. There's a manhunt on now."

"A kidnapped diplomat? That sounds almost passé. British?"

"Tsk. Serbian."

"Oh? The West Island, though, of all places."

"Ashley, you're confused. Rivière-des-Prairies is north-east."

That part of the island. "Serbia is ... a country nowadays? Ha. And it has a consulate here?"

"Some sort of honorary consulate, in the burbs. Could be offices over a pizza parlour for all I know. Who knows what it was all about? It just adds to the tension in the city. Gives the cops an excuse to run around in their extra-special fancy gear." He helped himself to a Whippet, contemplated it, sighed. "My history prof says the new Balkans are the old Balkans, all over again. But on a global scale this time. He was talking about political instability."

"Why here in Montreal, I wonder?"

"Serbia is an arms exporter, including to rival political factions."

"Aren't you knowledgeable?"

"What my prof says. He got all worked up, talking to us about it. The kidnapping was big news here. For a couple of days."

"I see." Not that Ashley did, really. She wondered whether her cop friend Nico Latendresse was back in town, and what he might have to say about it. She made a mental note to call him. He'd be curious about the Paris job, too.

"Are Ibrahim and Marie Ambre still engaged?"

"Oh, yes. They're at the stage of choosing names. Not for their children, their animals. But if you wanted to hear about the sentimental life of the neighbourhood, you should have asked. France went on her first real date a couple of weeks ago. What else? Chantale Barry's seeing someone. I hope he's nice."

Ashley nodded.

"Did you sweep any handsome Parisians off their feet?" he said.

"No. Are you on or off with Rachel this month?"

"Off." He looked mournful. "It was all going so well, until Valentine's Day. I don't really understand—Ashley, when it comes to Valentine's Day, could you explain—"

"No! I can't. Honestly, Aram, that you would think *I* could explain anything like that."

"True, what was I thinking?" Ashley found his patent sincerity slightly crushing.

He went home, and Ashley was left with a dull Saturday to get through. She could always work—there were new clients lined up—but it was hard to concentrate. She looked up Serbia on Wikipedia, read about its varied topography and vibrant economy, the latter partly dependent, it would seem, on its acknowledged role as supplier of arms to dodgy regimes and rival militias. From there, she read an online article about the custom of kidnapping Serbian diplomats, "not strictly for ransom." If not for money, then what? The article's wink-nudge tone puzzled her.

At least it all felt remote. Well, excepting skinny Serbians wriggling out of Rivière-des-Prairies windows. She felt a residual unease. Perhaps due to her recent adventures, the typically Canadian "it always happens elsewhere" reaction didn't feel as comforting. Villains were like ghosts: not real, and you didn't believe in them, until somebody waved a gun at you personally. And then you were a believer, for a while anyway.

When she got a call to remind her about the spring season of lacrosse, she was more than ready to sign up. And you bet she'd volunteer as an instructor for the advanced midget Lacrosse Camp.

★ ★ ★

She'd sent a short and formal email to Charles Saint Cyr to let him know that she'd had an interview with the *police judiciaire* before

she left Paris. She implied it was strictly to do with the disappearance of Raymond. Then she telephoned Mirabel and presented a
fuller account. Mirabel listened carefully, evidently understanding
the benefits of coordinated versions if and when these were needed.
She sounded like herself, and made out-of-focus comments about
getting together with Ashley as if they were now social acquaintances. Which perhaps they were.

These communications had been necessary, but they'd left
Ashley a little nervous. When she got a text later that same Saturday from someone called Antoinette Francis, her first reaction was
that the Paris police were on to her for something or other. It took
her a second or two to connect her thoughts with the words she was
reading:

> Hi! My dad said you visited him and Mémé. He gave me
> your number. I heard about you a long time ago, when I
> was a kid. I must have forgot. I'm not as good at online
> sleuthing as I bet you are. I looked you up now though,
> cool website! Not sure where you are in Montreal. I live
> in the east end. Want to have coffee or lunch? I could go
> wherever you are, or you could come here ...

This was her cousin, her uncle Eric's youngest. Ashley hadn't given
up thinking she'd hear from her, but Paris and the pressure of work
generally had put it out of her mind. She began to text back right
away, then deleted what she'd typed. She'd play it cool, figure out
exactly what she wanted to say. She was in that pleasant state of
alert interest mixed with nerves that was her standard response to
an invitation. She did a little surfing, or, as Antoinette called it,
online sleuthing. She found an Antoinette Francis on Facebook, a
youthful brunette with about eight hundred close friends, who posted frequently about Collège Morgan stuff. There were also several
posts about the Marché Maisonneuve. It looked like Antoinette

might work there, or was supplying wild herbs and plants to a vend-
or. Ashley recognized the name Nathan Francis when she saw it
listed among Antoinette's friends, and there was a Danielle Francis
Lortie who had to be the sister. Antoinette wasn't a daily user of
Facebook, but over time she'd posted lots of pictures of herself with
friends. In these she projected a quirky liveliness, her dark eyes
alight with fun above a lop-sided grin. If she liked you, Ashley
guessed, she liked you. If not … Ashley spent the rest of the day
thinking about how she'd approach her newfound cousin, while
using the spurt of energy these thoughts gave her to take a bite out
of her stacked-up business.

Among the new inquiries, there was an insurance company
she'd worked with before that wanted her to dig into a suspect
claim—a definite yes and a top priority; a bread-and-butter background check or two; a landlord seeking a former professional tenant who seemed to owe him thousands; a crazed-sounding male
wanting the lowdown on an ex-girlfriend, biblically praying to be
shown a sign—standard refusal, delete, delete; and a woman who
sounded drunk, wondering if Ashley could find the child she'd given
away long ago. The world was a sorrowful place. Not that this
woman might even remember leaving her the message. Still, she'd
follow up.

As she scrolled, sorted, filled her notebook, Ashley was aware
of an odd feeling. As if emotional pressure was building up inside
her, like a kettle nearing the boil, causing her knee to jiggle, her foot
to tap, her fingers to fly over the keyboard. The slew of inquiries
fed it, adding to the jitter. She needed something to sink her teeth
into, to anchor her. And then she found it.

The request was from a woman who identified herself as a
paediatrician at a downtown hospital, and who wanted to talk
about the possibility of a "very discreet" inquiry into the activities
of her partner of several years. This was a personal referral, from a
friend of a friend of Marigold Dreyfus, the gift that kept on giving.

That it might not be entirely about cheating was what interested Ashley. The woman sounded a little rushed, down to earth and kindly—just like anybody's busy doctor, really. The words she used weren't so everyday: She had begun to wonder if her partner in fact had "a double life."

Ashley got through to the woman right away. No, Doctor Porttock said, she couldn't talk right this minute. But she'd love to have coffee—it had been so long since they'd got together, she was so glad Ashley was back in town. She had errands to run for a couple of hours. Where was Ashley staying, what hotel? And she suggested meeting for coffee at a downtown indie coffee shop, popular but a little out of the way. *So that's how it is,* Ashley thought.

Sarah Porttock looked like she sounded, right down to the threads of grey running through her brown hair—something, Ashley realized, you didn't often see in women anymore. The only thing that she hadn't banked on was the low-key loveliness of the woman, disguised behind owlish glasses and dull clothes.

"I've never had a conversation like this before. I'm not sure where you'd like me to begin." Her smile was strained, but an irony-tinged warmth lurked somewhere.

The coffee shop was quiet, experiencing a weekend lull.

"Give me an overview of your situation and what you're looking for. We can then discuss terms. But first, how long can you safely stay?"

"An hour."

"All right, shoot." One day, soon, Ashley must stop using that expression.

Sarah Porttock thought for a moment, began. "I've been with Kevin for sixteen years. We have no children. He's—he was—a freelance graphic artist. His income has gone up and down over the years. I've been the main breadwinner. I bought our apartment outright, eleven years ago." She mentioned a block of mansion flats in lower Westmount where Ashley knew for a fact the units commanded a top-drawer price. "I've been all right with this arrangement. Kevin has made other contributions. He had some health problems. He always, I thought, did what he could. I thought we were happy."

Her eyes were bright with that unfortunate innocence Ashley often saw. Now they dimmed, as if cloud shadows were passing over an inner landscape.

"It would be hard for me to put my finger on when I thought things began to change. Not recently, if I look back now. At first, though, the changes were so subtle I missed them or thought I was imagining things. Anyhow, it's been building for a while."

"What's been building?"

"It's Kevin. I would go from thinking that his feelings for me were just ... gone, to thinking he was under the weather, or we were becoming middle-aged and what did I expect. Then there were times when I thought he might be deliberately faking affection. He often went out, to do with his contracts, but then he began to travel a lot. He spends far more time away from home than you would think he'd need to. He says he has contracts in Toronto and Quebec City. I mean, maybe he does ..." A shrug. "Money. I should be talking about money. For the last couple of years, three, he's asked to do the tax returns, to take care of them entirely. I'm a staff doctor, I'm on a salary, so my tax situation is simple. There was no reason for me to say no. He said he wanted to take one more thing off my shoulders.

"Last month, I was out on Jarry East, way out, getting my driver's licence renewed at that one location where the employees weren't picketing"—a passing smile—"and I ran into an old friend of his, of ours really, going back to when we were all at university together. It was one of those spring days in winter, you know. The sun was shining. We talked a long time, right there on the sidewalk. Serge congratulated me, in a half-joking way, about Kevin finally hitting the big time, and how I no longer had to pay all the bills. I had no idea what he was talking about, but I played along. What I learned was that Serge and he are now both at a big design firm. In fact they're both vice-presidents. For instance, Serge mentioned a VP bonus that Kevin got last year. He was describing a situation I knew nothing about. And as for rolling in it, I thought Kevin's income had gone down if anything in the last few years."

She rearranged the cup in front of her. "Around the same time, because I started to look in his pockets and through his things when he was out, I found another cell phone. One of those prepaid disposable phones? I'd just have asked him about it, five years ago. But —I've begun to be afraid of him."

Ashley frowned. Five years. A long time during which not to feel safe.

"He has a Mac and an iPhone but they're always on him or locked down tight. We also share a desktop computer at home. I've gone on that. I found nothing. But it did make me realize how little of a footprint there was for me to find. Bills are mostly in my name, but I pay them all regardless. His Facebook profile is really just his photography experiments. There was almost nothing for me to find ..."

"What about his email?"

"That's just the thing. He's got the one email account I know of. I know the password." A pause. "I went on that too. There's nothing on it. Lots of ads. Emails to and from a sister in Vancouver, but not many. He's not close to her. His parents are dead. Not enough work-related stuff to make me think he uses that email for anything important. I went through his paper files too. Everything seemed, you know, sanitized."

"If not family, what about friends?"

She looked a little awkward. "He has a few, from a long time ago. We don't really socialize together much, like with other couples. I'm—I'm just too busy to have personal friends. Justine from work is the closest to that. She's that cousin of Marigold Dreyfus."

"Banking?"

"I can't get into anything beyond our joint chequing account." She brightened up here. "But yes, it's his banking information I want. I'm sure he has a secret bank account. He must. I want to find out everything he's been keeping from me. I bet he has a secret email too, maybe even secret social media accounts, I want his tax information, credit card information. I want everything." She looked earnestly at Ashley, oblivious to the potential dodginess of half of what she was asking for.

"Are you and Kevin legally married?" Ashley thought suddenly to ask.

Sarah looked a little surprised. "No, but we're common-law spouses of long standing, so what does that matter?"

Oh, the criminal innocence. "Is there—do you think there's another woman in the picture?"

Sarah's eyes widened slightly, before her gaze swivelled away from Ashley. "I don't know. There might be. I've never seen a positive sign. Like a blonde hair, lipstick. Isn't that what you're supposed to see?"

Ashley said nothing. *What about sex?* Some people were too innocent to live.

As if reading her mind, Sarah said: "Ours had become more of what they call a companionate relationship. It was what he wanted. Well, I wanted it too. I mean, we still *had* a sex life ... There's more to life than sex ..." Sarah was blushing like an unhappy girl, and Ashley's heart went out to her.

The conversation went on like this for a little longer. Yes, Kevin had been at home, for once, when Ashley called earlier—thus the subterfuge. Communication would occur henceforth through Sarah's office. Sarah found Ashley's rates satisfactory. She'd find a picture or two of Kevin.

Was there a way to separate Kevin from his laptop or cellphone? And for how long? Sarah twiddled with a greying lock while her eyes became enigmatic. "He's careful, but sometimes a little absent-minded." Her smile this time was real, animated. "Something could be arranged." This was the kind of attitude Ashley liked to see.

There would be paperwork, Sarah was issued a little homework in the stratagems and ruses department, and Ashley would get back to her ASAP with a package of what she *could* find out for her, legally and practically.

Sarah put out her hand to Ashley on the sidewalk. "If I thought Kevin was just lazy, or didn't love me anymore but felt he was onto a good thing with a partner with money ... well, that would be one thing. But this seems to be more. If he's making as much money as Serge says he's making, he could just leave me, couldn't he? He's gone to enormous effort to keep things from me. Why does anyone do that? That's what I need to understand."

Ashley just gave the offered hand a quick squeeze, and they parted. As she was making her way back to the parking garage on rue Saint Paul, she put in a call to Aram.

"I could use your help with a case. A guy has a secret life, and I'm being paid to expose it. I need to know all the hows, and then I'll need technical help with the hows. You can leave the legalities to me." And the grey zones. "I'm not sure whether the woman isn't in danger, too, so it's one of *those* priorities. Are you up for it?" A rhetorical question if ever there was one.

When she got home, she broke open a new package of Whippets—dark chocolate—and despatched a breezy little message to Antoinette Francis. Antoinette got back to her quickly. A little information was shared; enthusiasm was expressed. Ashley agreed that lunch with Antoinette and her dad, who was coming to Montreal the following weekend, sounded wonderful.

Then she got on the computer to find out whatever she could about Kevin Black.

14

BEAU DOMMAGE

T HE PACE OF work turned Ashley's week into a blur. March
continued to be the cruellest month, despite claims to the
contrary. It conjured cigarette butts out of the dead land.
Roots slept on bewitched beneath the snow, which didn't melt so
much as shrink and congeal. She found solace in a novel by Esmerelda
LaFlamme from her local second-hand book store. It was a snappy
crime melodrama set in the mean streets of Montreal, with a well-
calculated sufficiency of ersatz culture to appeal to the worldwide
Francophonie without offending such as Ashley. It transformed
Montreal into a forgivably unrecognizable and golden-edged setting
for sexy soap opera evil, complete with evocative description and
interludes of the cozy. Reading it reminded Ashley of the surreal Bal
de la Buanderie, of Mireille and her LaFlamme-reading gang, transforming her memories in a similarly golden-edged way; so that she
now felt the second stage of traveller's anomie, the creeping dullness
of everyday life.

It didn't help that there was worrying news from home. Her
mother's blood pressure was too high. This she heard from Roy,
because it wasn't the kind of thing Marlene would volunteer. That
was all right, she and Roy anxiously agreed, since it meant their
mother could take the medication she needed. More troubling to

Ashley was Roy's news that he and Lucie were going through what he called a bad patch. In fact, Lucie had more or less moved out of their duplex in Fabienville, and was back with her family in Félicien —temporarily, Roy hoped. Lilou was there with her, he added, although he was seeing the child from time to time. He sounded defensive and miserable.

Roy and Lucie had been accidental teenage parents, children themselves when they got together. On one level, they had done well. Roy was a certified auto mechanic, and now Lucie had snagged a local teaching job, a pearl of luck with the surplus of teachers. It was Lucie who had changed the most, with her teaching degree. Roy had tried in his own fashion to keep up with her. But he had no way to dim the bright stars of the young men she now met. To Ashley he was vague to the point of evasive on whether there was another man in the picture. He wouldn't hear any criticism of Lucie from Ashley, but sounded sulky when he quoted her as saying that Lilou needed a father who did more than tinker with his motorbike collection during his spare moments.

"I've few spare moments and three motorbikes isn't a collection," he said.

Well, it kind of was, Ashley thought. "Is that it? Is it about motorbikes?"

Ashley was taking Roy's call in her office, her feet on her desk. As they talked she stared absently at a picture that Marie Ambre had drawn for her, of an owl family lined up on a branch.

"Well, yes and no. She says Fabienville is a dump. She talks like she wants to move. She has her new job, plus my job at the garage is good, so why? She says I should spend more time with Lilou. I should do more around the house. She finds it hard to handle all that, she says, with her teaching. She complains a lot."

He heaved a sigh. "I don't think she likes the dirt under my fingernails."

Now he sounded like he was striking an attitude. Whatever Roy was, this honest son of the soil pose wasn't it.

"You could make an effort to do more." Ashley tried to expunge the judgement from her voice. This was Roy, her little brother.

"I work *hard*. I put Lucie through college. I feel that's not being appreciated." There was a silence on the phone that Ashley didn't feel like filling. "The thing is, Ashley, I miss them. I'm trying not to overreact, or push this to a point where we can't recover. I want it to be a trial separation, nothing more."

But what does Lucie want?

"I don't even get to see Lilou as much as I should." A spike of resentment, and then his voice broke in a wave of lament. "She's my kid too."

Ashley continued to stare at Marie Ambre's drawing. A big mother owl dominated the picture, with three babies clustered alongside her. At the far end of the branch, a smaller father owl crouched. He looked like he had a bad case of moult. Now, as she gazed, his owlish eyes revealed a deeper and deeper sadness, until they seemed to hold all the sadness of imperfect fathers everywhere, of boys who hadn't quite made it to manhood and were paying the price.

"Want me to come and see you on Saturday? I've got things to do on Sunday, so I can't stay for the weekend. Okay, it's a plan. I got you hand-hemmed handkerchiefs from Paris, I'll bring them."

Roy was at a critical crossroads. He had the chance to step up, or he could carry on down a well-worn road. Ashley could do little or nothing. But she could spend a few hours with him. Bring him fancy Parisian hankies to cry into.

Ashley had picked up Esmerelda LaFlamme's book in a distracted moment, and was at the part where her hero Ambroise was trying out some old-fashioned tough guy stuff on someone called Tallulah, when there was a brisk rat tat tat at the door.

It was Chantale Barry, cigarettes in one hand and an apple pie in the other, a social smile on her face. There was something devilish about appearing at the three pm blood sugar dip hour, with this thing that invaded the room with its wanton fumes of sugar and spice.

"I figured you needed a break, Ashley. Also, I'm not sure if you had a chance to get groceries yet."

Ashley's pantry was often half bare, although what did that have to do with pie? Soon they were at her kitchen table with the pie and two steaming cups of the French beans in front of them.

"Aram said you got the most beautiful dress in Paris." Chantale sighed. "You're so lucky to go to Paris." When she'd borrowed the Swiffer, Ashley had given Chantale a version of her visit, expunging a good deal including the Bortniks.

Chantale's fingers inched towards her cigarettes. She never tried to smoke right away. She bided her time until she figured Ashley would break down.

"Here, have some more coffee," Ashley hastily said.

It wasn't a social call, as it turned out. Ashley got ready to hear the next chapter in the Dominique Taillon saga. But it was Marie Ambre's father Chantale wanted to talk about.

In a nutshell, Jacques wanted to spend more time with Marie Ambre, a lot more time. They'd always had a loose arrangement before. He'd been minimally involved, paid child support intermittently. But Jacques had recently married. Now he was making noises about custodial arrangements. Using expressions like "stable family unit" and "what's really best for Marie Ambre."

"I think he doesn't want to pay child support anymore, Ashley. His wife might have put him up to it. Or he might be worried his child support will go up, because he has a new job. It's not really about Marie Ambre at all. Do you know how often he cancelled outings with her in the past?"

There was no bitterness. Chantale sounded merely resigned. "But I'll have to agree to talk, I know. And I know I need a lawyer, so you don't have to tell me that."

"What do you want from me?"

Marie Ambre pushed away her slice of pie, half eaten. She looked thinner. She had that restless sparkle that you sometimes see in women after they begin a new relationship but before reality hits.

"It's all that talk about 'best interests.' He even uses expressions like 'most appropriate caregiver.' I wonder if he has something up his sleeve. I wonder, really, who would look best between us, on paper. I mean, from the perspective of a family court."

Ashley's eyebrows went up. There was something deeply rational about these thoughts that she wouldn't have expected of Chantale. "And?"

"And I'd like to find out more about him, more than I know now. Everything."

"You want me to dig into Jacques's past?"

"Jacques? Oh, sorry, no Ashley. I'm really expressing myself badly. I want you to look into Michel's past. I didn't mention Michel. That was silly. Michel is my new boyfriend. We've been seeing each other for a couple of months. I'd like to know all about him. I have the feeling what I don't know about Michel could come out in a custody hearing. I really like Michel. But, you know ... it pays to be careful."

Ashley was temporarily robbed of speech.

"His name is Michel Desrosiers. He's a little bit older than me. He works at an oil change place, but just since July of last year. Honestly, I don't know much about what he did before. He doesn't talk a lot, so it isn't like I could just ask him a question or two and get the full picture." She made a slight face. "Sometimes he says things like, 'Aren't we going to Kmart this afternoon?'"

"I'm not following you."

"He means Walmart. But when did we last have a Kmart in Montreal, Ashley? It's so dated. Like, it makes me think: Where was he for the last ten years? Like, you know, was he out of commission somewhere, for a while—a long while?"

"Geez, Chantale."

"I could be way off base. But then I thought: Why don't I get Ashley to do a background check? It's not like we're going to live together any time soon, but he often visits the house. Also, Jacques met him accidentally last week when we were at the Alexis Nihon mall. I could see Jacques looking him over, the wheels turning. He was paying attention to the name." She smiled brightly at Ashley. "That is the kind of work you take on, isn't it?"

"I do. Can you—what sort of guy is he anyway?"

"Just a regular guy. Look, I have a photograph." She pulled out her phone and began to scroll busily. She held up a picture.

Ah, the ineluctable charm of the worthless man, Ashley thought to herself. She couldn't of course tell from looking at the picture whether Michel was worthless. But of discernable charm there was little. He was more than slightly older than Chantale, in his forties or looked it. His thin hair was combed into his skull, like hair was a frill, and there was a nobody's home look about the eyes. Tough. Not without a sort of appeal, everything being relative.

"Michel smokes, like me. Would Jacques bring that up? But it's the stuff I don't know that I'm wondering about." Chantale extracted a scrap of paper from her cigarette pack. "Here's his full name, his driver's licence and his social insurance number. Are they helpful?"

The surprises just kept coming. "A great place to start." Ashley named a sum. "For that, I could give you work history, education, a non-work reference check, credit rating—and of course a criminal record check."

Chantale looked at her admiringly. "That would be wonderful. I can pay as much as you want up front." And she lit a cigarette with her usual excellent sense of timing.

Marie Ambre and Ibrahim now appeared at the door, a strange child in tow. They all wanted pie, and the conversation went elsewhere. Ashley watched them, Chantale and Marie Ambre in particular. Chantale's thin arms encircled the child. She turned her head away from Marie Ambre when she exhaled smoke. Marie Ambre cleaved to Chantale in that way of leaves to branches, branches to trees, trees to roots. Ibrahim looked on with spousal complacency. Little Réal, who informed Ashley he was the grandson of the Plourdes downstairs, was in it for the pie.

Ashley thought wryly that if insurance fraud ever dried up she could turn her whole business over to separating the goats from the sheep for women. It would keep her fully occupied.

She managed to get rid of the four of them eventually, closing the door with difficulty against a mean-spirited wind that was blowing a sudden snow squall down rue de Paris. March really was the cruellest month.

*＊＊

She left early on Saturday for Fabienville. Endless winter took its own form in the Eastern Townships, the temperature several degrees colder than Montreal, the snow drifts deep and hard. Roy was without Lilou and he and Ashley tagged around Fabienville together—coffee, bookstore, a walk, the proverbial run to Home Hardware where they bought Duray socks. They took a pizza back to the empty duplex. The place already had a frowsy air—things dumped everywhere, a little dusty. A little sad. As for Roy, as she observed him Ashley was gnawed with worry.

Her brother had that look of carrying a stony mass in his gut. She suspected she was looking at that most terrible of human conditions, unrequited love. She'd always suspected that Roy's feelings for Lucie had hardly changed since the arrow struck at sixteen. And then there was Lilou.

"How is Lilou taking things? I mean, being away from her home—and you."

The question seemed to drag Roy back from a great distance. "She's having nightmares, Lucie admits. She's old to have those separation nightmares, supposedly. Kids have terrible nightmares though, I wonder why."

Ashley was surprised. She remembered Roy's haunted childhood, even if he didn't. And she didn't wonder why kids had nightmares. According to some, childhood was a happy state, from which the future beckoned like the pleasant garden next door. But that happiness could shatter like glass in a single stroke.

"I'm surprised they don't have nightmares all the time. Listen Roy... if you want Lucie and Lilou back, you have to do whatever —*whatever*—it takes." She couldn't help blurting out the words, although she'd told herself she wouldn't offer advice.

But the conversation went nowhere. Roy sank slowly into a morose and silent state, looking into the middle distance without reaction, beginning sentences and not finishing them. He didn't seem to be taking anything on board. Ashley felt rage. Not at Roy, but at love. Her brother, huddled at a cold hearth where love had once warmed him, was a pitiful sight. Love seemingly swept you up and made you feel like this was living at last; but it made you half a person, incomplete without your better half. So that when it disappeared, abandoned you, you were a half person. Breached, empty.

She headed back to Montreal as darkness fell, having exacted a promise from him to visit her with Lilou very soon. She was going to talk to Lucie too, but she didn't tell him this. Oh, meddlesome sisterhood. She pondered how she could get her mother in on the act too.

That evening she rang Nicolas Latendresse, who was back in town with Madeleine and the twins. The terrorism course in DC had been well worth it, he told her, if depressing. People the world over seemed determined to believe that hate was the answer, either directly or vicariously, through the election of hate-stoking demagogues. Canada was not exempt. Ashley asked Nico about the kidnapped Serbian diplomat.

"Oh, that's simple enough. Serbia's economy depends on arms sales. They make deals with anyone although officially denying this. They're sometimes under pressure, mainly international, to clean up their act. The rival factions, the rogue regimes, they depend on the source. Sometimes these groups like to exercise counter pressure."

"So why Montreal?"

"Oh, exactly, Ashley, exactly."

He wanted to hear all about Paris. She gave him the least expurgated account she'd given anyone since her return. He was alarmed, laughed, swore occasionally, said he was glad she was back in Montreal. They exchanged family news. He and Madeleine would ask Ashley over to eat soon, because why should they be the only ones to suffer through a family dinner with Felix and Frederick.

Before she went to bed she put the finishing touches on a strategy for investigating Kevin Black. There was so much you could do with spyware, with key stroke recognition software, these days. Aram was still looking into technical issues and much was going to be down to the enterprise of Sarah Porttock. But Ashley had a sense that this gentle soul would come through.

She slept heavily that night, dreaming that she and Jon Perez were back together again. But this time love had bloomed between them, and in the dream she sat with him speechless on an old velour settee, in that narcotized dream-love state that encompassed all meaning and in which nothing more needed to be done or said. The meaning quickly evaporated, along with the point of the plush settee, when she woke.

It was a still and sunny morning as she headed east to Hochelaga-Maisonneuve. She got off the Métro a couple of stops before she needed to, and found herself enjoying the walk through a neighbourhood where she'd never previously set foot.

The place, she felt, was one of those semi-clandestine gem-like districts that hadn't yet emerged into full-on trendiness, despite its share of cute shops and restaurants. She passed tree-lined residential streets of duplexes and triplexes, many dating back to the time of long skirts and derby hats. As elsewhere in the city, old factories had been turned into loft condos. Here there had been less of the sprawling heavy industry of downtown: The mid-size brick buildings still bore in faded paint their origins, as biscuit and shoe factories, garment mills, tool and utensil works. The local business scene mixed it up: a hand car wash, beside a Tunisian restaurant with a row of turquoise resin tables in front of it, beside a Dairy Queen.

It was the corner stores, the *dépanneurs,* she fell for. Her neighbourhood had its share, but these were quainter. Anything but gentrified, deeply grafted onto their corners, they promised within their dingy aisles every obscure brand, not to mention *loto-vin-bière.* She began to take pictures of them with her smart phone.

The sun was struggling to shine, and there was the faintest hint, amid these pleasant streets, of spring. When she passed a locally owned *biscuiterie* that proclaimed its mecca-like role to the street, she dropped in on an impulse and bought a bag of jaw breakers for herself and a tin of the store's handmade chocolate chip cookies for Antoinette and Eric.

Chez Eve was the kind of place Ashley suspected had been more common in the city a generation or two back. It was pure Montreal, channelling elements of bistro and brasserie and a seasoning of the legendary vegetarian co-op, the Commensal. It apparently turned into a jazz café after dark. It was big, and on this Sunday just before noon it was busy, many of the well-worn blonde wood tables already occupied. Ashley hovered, and then saw a wave from across the room. She made her way across, to be enveloped in a hug by Antoinette and, after a slight hesitation, by her father.

"I recognized you right away. I said: 'Dad, is that her, that tall woman over there!'"

Antoinette's smile was even more infectious in person. She was clearly one of those bubbly extroverts. Ashley hoped this would help with the inevitable awkwardness of the occasion.

"How could you recognize me?" Because of her work, Ashley's social media footprint was carefully small.

"You look like Leo! I mean, it's like nowhere and everywhere in you. I only saw pictures of him, of course. But I see my aunties in you too, the ones that passed. Doesn't she, Dad?"

Eric was as Ashley remembered him, a tall serious man with a lot on his mind, his Blackberry never far from his hand. In the presence of Antoinette, however, he was like a door that had opened to let the sun shine through. Seeing this, Ashley felt something sharp inside her for a nano-second, as the universe whispered to her that alien word, *father*.

"We don't drink much, but this is a celebration! Look, it's now one minute past twelve. So will you join us, Ashley?" A server was bringing two frosted mugs of beer to their table. Ashley nodded as she reached for her wallet. "No, put that away, my dad says it's his treat today!"

After they'd ordered lunch, Antoinette sat back with an eager and appraising smile. "Nathan and Danielle will be so jealous I met you!" Was there no end to this young woman's charm? "And what an exciting job. Doesn't she have an exciting job, Dad? How did you pick a job like that, with your degree in social work?"

Ashley wasn't asked this question often. "There's more crossover than you might suppose. Of course, I pay my bills with the corporate work. But if I do my job, there's some looking after people in it. Looking after people and their problems."

"But what if you hate a client?"

A picture sprang suddenly to Ashley's mind, of Charles Saint Cyr at his worst. The misleading way he presented himself to the world, the way he talked to his wife. Not that she'd hated him, not really. But someone could.

"Well—there have been times when I've disliked clients, for sure. One way or another though, there's usually someone that needs taking care of."

Eric and Antoinette were now looking engrossed. There was no avoiding telling them about some of her cases.

"But you," she said eventually, "you're studying engineering. That sounds exciting."

Antoinette rolled her eyes. "It's tough. It's pre-engineering, at Collège Morgan. But the engineering degree will be shorter when I transition. Dad really wants me to get that degree. I also co-own a booth at the Maisonneuve Market, traditional herbs and plants, that keeps me busy too."

"Her and four other people." Eric smiled.

"I love it! I share a duplex with some other students and I use the back room as a mini greenhouse. We also have two community plots in summer."

She was like her pictures, a good-looking young woman with bright dark eyes and untidily chic asymmetrical hair. She tossed this around as she spoke and used her hands to emphasize everything.

Plates piled high with food arrived.

"How is Odette?" Ashley inquired politely of Eric.

"She's well enough." His eyes grew a little thoughtful. "Her heart, it's not good. But she gets good care. She's very alert." A pause. "She's wondering when you'll come and visit her again."

The words made Ashley glad. "Soon, I hope."

Eric asked after Marlene, and Ashley spoke about her mother, her brother and Lilou, passing over Roy's recent family difficulties. Antoinette insisted on seeing pictures of her other cousins, as she called them. The smile dropped briefly from her face as she mentioned her own mother, who had died six years previously.

They reordered beer, agreed the food was good, but were sure they would still have room for dessert. Ashley belatedly handed over the tin of cookies to Antoinette, who said: "Oscar's! Look,

Dad, Ashley already has discovered one of the treasures of the neighbourhood. The Maisonneuve Market is another one. Maybe if the sun is still shining after lunch we can take a walk there. It's such a nice day."

And when the server placed a jolly little posy of red, white and blue flowers on their table, spring came without warning. *I could have done this years ago,* Ashley thought to herself, feeling giddy with beer and newly discovered extended family.

The side trip to Maisonneuve Market was not to be. Chez Eve was a bustling place. People were table hopping as they greeted one another or snagged window tables. This was perhaps why Ashley didn't immediately notice the three women who'd moved to the table next to theirs. She was in the middle of a sentence when she looked up and recognized, first, Isabel Jadois's multi-coloured locks and, then, the exquisite profile of Mirabel Saint Cyr. The sisters were in the company of an older woman.

Ashley's abrupt pause and open-mouthed stare made Antoinette turn and look. And so it came about that they both spoke at the same time: Ashley to say, with slight hesitation: "Mirabel?" And Antoinette to call out an unrestrained: *"Voyons donc, Madge!"*

And then everyone was looking at everyone else in mild astonishment.

***

It turned into one of those afternoons that Ashley, who liked to think of herself as an interested window shopper on social life, looked back on with various wonder-spiked emotions.

Mirabel was effusive with delight at encountering Ashley. Isabel was in her talkative *Montréalaise* mode. By one of those Montreal coincidences, Antoinette knew the third woman, Madge—knew her well, in fact. Madge had been Antoinette's instructor at Collège Morgan, and was clearly something of a friend as well. It was even the case that Antoinette the student and Isabel the instructor knew each other by sight. How amusing, they agreed under the influence of a couple of fresh pitchers, was this tangled skein of connections. Eric was bemused but agreeable when someone suggested they pull their tables together. This made theirs one of the most festive tables at Chez Eve, in the face of some competition on that sunny Sunday afternoon.

Mirabel came around the table to sit beside Ashley to swap news. Without a beat, she picked up conversationally where they'd left off in Paris, although Paris had become Bortnik-less in memory. The antiques had arrived. She was thankful for Ashley's help there. Charles was "rejoicing" at being reunited with his wife. (Odd, Ashley felt, that way Mirabel had of speaking of herself simultaneously as both subject and object.) She was still exploring opportunities at Holopherne.

Mirabel, soignée in head-to-toe black, her fair hair neatly smoothed back from her flawless face, drew glances as always from the room. But she seemed oblivious, more like an enthusiastic child faced with an unexpected treat. She was so glad they had run into each other, because she had been planning on reaching out to Ashley anyway. Her cousin was *chouette* and her uncle was so nice—and handsome too. Spring was around the corner. There was so much to celebrate!

The surprise of the table, and the secret thrill of Ashley, was the discovery that Marguerite (Madge) Stewart, a woman of around sixty with untidy grey hair, was not only a well-known Quebec poet of difficult free verse of the sovereigntist persuasion, but the pseudonymous author of the Esmerelda LaFlamme books. This was news to everyone except Isabel—even Antoinette hadn't apparently known this. When Ashley triumphantly pulled the battered paperback of *The River Runs Deep* out of her bag and requested an autograph, their meeting at Chez Eve took on the aura of a thing foretold in the legends. The story of the *Bal de la Buanderie* and Mireille's LaFlamme-reading friends was inevitable, demanded, given.

Eric happened to be seated next to Madge Stewart. Ashley wasn't too far away to notice that, as the afternoon wore on, they seemed to be getting along awfully well in their quiet way.

"That's the old song, *Harmonie du soir à Châteauguay,* isn't it?" she overheard Madge say suddenly to Eric.

Ashley could hear in the background a folksy harmony, something about a man and a woman, a summer evening by the river. Melodious, gently charming. And now, Ashley intuited, on a winter day decades later, nostalgic, perhaps even sad.

"Beau Dommage." Eric looked over at Madge. "A while since we listened to that."

Under the influence of the song, or something, he put away his Blackberry. And Madge's cheeks grew pink, as her hazel eyes widened with more than myopia. She was, Ashley realized for the first time, nice-looking. Her untidy hair, for instance, had after all a soft *decoiffé* charm. Also, Mirabel was right: Ashley's uncle was handsome.

The man and the woman listened together, and much was left unsaid. Embarrassed to watch any longer, Ashley refreshed everyone's beer glass whether they needed it or not. Time passed, and they were all always about to walk out into the sunshine, to take a stroll—around the nearby market with its fine hundred-year-old pavilion or up the hill to the Château Dufresne grounds. Yet they never did.

But very firmly Ashley and Antoinette were invited to a costume party the following week at Madge's house in Cité Jardin. Partly Isabel's party, but Madge was kindly offering up her house for what promised to be the event of the late winter season, as far as Isabel was concerned anyway. A costume, she warned, was not optional! Eric would come too, of course? *Désolé,* Eric would be back at work in the Eastern Townships. But he often—a glance in Madge's direction—came to Montreal.

Ashley wasn't in the mood to work that evening but she did a little anyway, as a wet snow began to fall gently. She received a call from Sarah Porttock, who told her things were looking good for temporarily getting hold of Kevin's phone, if not his laptop. Ashley said a smart phone was a great place to start, and could give them most of what they were looking for.

She cleared her throat. Just to be clear ... Ashley didn't do this kind of thing herself. It would be off the books. The associate was highly trustworthy. If Sarah was agreeable to this level of informality, they would need the device for an hour. She then spoke in general terms of what hacking could do, about the cracking of passwords, the installation of keystroke software. Borderline? Perhaps, in the sense of the usefulness of the results in court. Despite this, she assumed Dr. Porttock still saw the benefits of knowing?

Dr. Porttock sounded quite effervescent about the whole thing. She had a plan, she said. It was a good one.

Ashley was glad, in fact, that this case was moving along. She didn't want to bring this up yet, but things were beginning to look pretty hinky with Kevin Black. A little light surveillance on her part, for instance, had already revealed that, when Kevin had told Sarah he was going to Toronto, he'd in fact been heading east on the green line, in the opposite direction from the airport.

15

DIVERSIONS

ASHLEY HAD NEVER been one of those work hard-play hard people. More of an all work, (almost) no play person, unless sitting around thinking about things was considered a form of play. So this weekend was completely out of character for her, she thought before her mirror, as she put the finishing touches on what she called her John Dillinger costume.

This evening, Friday, the party was at Madge's house. Tomorrow evening, there'd be another costume party, although no doubt of a very different order, at the Saint Cyr abode high up on the summit.

When she'd texted Isabel to get the Cité Jardin particulars for party one, Isabel, after providing these, had added that the gathering was as much a cosplay event as a costume party, and did Ashley know about those? Of course, Ashley lied enthusiastically, and went online to find out. Cosplay, she concluded after surfing the net, was a coming together, under some pretext, of people who took their costumes very very seriously. It wasn't about wearing the costume; it was about being the costume.

When she'd been over to see Nicolas Latendresse and his family, Madeleine had thrown herself passionately into finding the right costume for Ashley, sweeping Ashley along in her wake. Ignoring Nico's half-hearted protests, she'd plundered his wardrobe for an old forties-style suit with exaggerated lapels and a pinched waist. It even had a matching waistcoat. It was high time anyway, Madeleine said, that Nico got rid of his forties revival wear. He never threw anything away. It made no sense. Ashley had trouble remembering a forties revival and, even more, picturing Nico as youthfully enslaved to fashion excess. The suit, however, looked pretty authentic. There was more, and Madeleine seemed eager to unload it all: a belted overcoat, that slouched in the appropriate gangsterish style, a fedora, even black wash-leather gloves, the better to grip your Thompson gun, Ashley supposed. Over spaghetti and meatballs and above the noise of Frederick and Felix, Ashley had idly commented that she wanted to go as a forties gumshoe. Kitted up this way, Ashley would look more like a gangster, everyone agreed, and thus John Dillinger was reborn.

"Feel free to alter whatever you like, like around the waist," Madeleine said. "We don't need it back." The only thing Mad couldn't produce was the automatic weapon. A resigned Nico told Ashley she could get all the weaponry she needed at any well-stocked dollar store. This proved, unnervingly, to be true. The specialized portable cannon she chose was three dollars of white plastic but it transformed well under a spray of black matte paint in the back yard. She practiced carrying it around in that relaxed one-handed James Bond way of suited gunmen everywhere, until her admiring audience of small children grew too big.

Undisturbed now in front of her mirror, Ashley took a few swaggering turns, the hem of her coat flapping and coiling suggestively around the gun. The fedora had found a happy home tilted forward, with her hair tucked out of the way in a low knotted braid. She tried out her red lipstick from Paris, and then wiped it off. Dillinger wasn't a lipstick kind of guy.

Cité Jardin, in Rosemont, where she arrived at dusk, was a surprise. She'd heard about the place, of course, a forties cooperative social experiment whose purpose had been to create a kinder, gentler suburb for the *classe ouvrière* on the eastern borderline between the city and pristine countryside. Now it had been enveloped by big city on all sides, but that's what made its small houses, towering trees, internal network of footpaths and small parks all the more unexpected. Long-term residents had tried to beat back a tendency for *parvenus* to tear down the modest houses and build McMansions. But unless you'd bought your house a long time ago, Cité Jardin, so unique and charming, so close to the main Métro line, was well beyond the reach of most purchasers nowadays. Madge Stewart's house was a compact brick one-and-a-half storey, painted white, encircled by lofty pines. She had probably been there for a long time.

Glowing a little like the mini-lights in the shrubbery around the porch, Madge greeted Ashley at the door. Behind her the house already hummed with music and voices. Ashley was surprised to see her uncle hovering in the archway to the living room, given what he'd said at Chez Eve. Eric Francis was outfitted as a late stage Elvis, and looked remarkably good in costume. Maybe he was partly responsible for Madge's glow. Ashley was immediately surrounded by several people in the hall. Everyone marvelled at her costume, including some strangers. Somebody put a champagne flute in her hand, and the party, hers at least, was off to the races.

***

Ashley could tell almost immediately this would be one of those parties that was going to suck her into its maw. Looking around the packed main floor, she felt an unfamiliar pleasure on the threshold of fear. She'd been invited with the first wave of guests, and there was a splendid buffet. The look of everything, the wild and witty costumes, the people-watching groups, the animated gossip and laughter, they made the food oddly tasteless. She said this to Mirabel, as they balanced plates together. Mirabel was dressed for war as

Joan of Arc, with dull silver armour, her fair hair in a charming short cut suitable for the busy woman on the battlefield.

Mirabel speared a juicy jumbo shrimp with her fork. "I used to feel that way, but of course now I'm married," she said. Charles, Ashley had ascertained, was at a company gala dinner.

Someone was dimming the lights as people continued to arrive in droves. Someone else turned up the music against the surging voices.

Mirabel considered Ashley's gun. "Oh Ashley, you're always on the job," she said with an ambiguous smile. "Still, your costume is the best in the room." The compliment wasn't as welcome as Ashley would have expected.

Mirabel produced a magnum. "You might as well have a little more champagne—although it's really *spumante,* but on a night like this all cats will look the same."

Ashley took a reckless swallow and felt herself falling backwards into her teenage years. She said to herself: *If that tall guy over there turns around and looks at me now, what Mirabel says is true.* The tall guy spoke into the ear of the woman beside him as he squeezed her buttock. Ashley decided the *spumante* wasn't very good.

A petite woman dressed in a Cupid costume, beautifully turned out but with a disgruntled expression, waved a cruel-looking dart gun in Ashley's direction as she passed.

"Keep up with me," her lips seemed to say.

***

Ashley, three glasses later, now felt completely in control—confident, eloquent, kindly disposed towards all. Right at home. She said to Antoinette, whom she'd met in the crowded kitchen passage: "How are you enjoying the party?"

Antoinette just said, above the noise of the music: "Did you come alone?"

Ashley didn't feel this was the most diplomatic of questions, but it hardly made a dint in her cheer. She nodded.

"I wish I had!" Antoinette was dressed as a pirate, which would have been boring had she not pulled it off so well. She held a teacup and took a swig of something almost certainly not Red Rose.

"I brought my *p'tit chum*, or anyway that's the way I've been thinking of him. But now I'm not thinking of him that way. Ashley —you're a detective. Tell me! Have I misread the signs, the *clues?*" Antoinette pointed sloppily to a threesome framed in the doorway to the back. Ashley wondered just how long Antoinette has been sipping from her teacup. The bearded *p'tit chum*, who was neither *petit* nor young, was holding forth to two exceptionally pretty girls.

"Is he—er—your prof?" Ashley asked.

"He *was*. But last summer, for a course I took last summer." As if this explained, or mitigated, or ensured against, the abject facts. Not that the abjectness was in any way apparent to Ashley. She gazed with all the compassion in the world at her cousin. How such a perfect creature could be anything less than deliriously happy at an event such as this was a mystery.

Antoinette dully watched her father go by with Madge, carrying a platter for her. Madge, dressed as what might or might not have been a Game of Thrones character, looked youthfully happy as she turned to say something to Eric. Eric said something back, and smiles were suppressed on both sides.

"I'll *show* him!" But Antoinette's piratical defiance wasn't up to much. "You know, when my dad is having more fun than me— and he's fifty-nine ..." This seemed abominably wrong to Ashley too. She opened her mouth to concur but a group pushed boisterously between them. When they'd passed Antoinette had been swept along, leaving Ashley talking into the air.

* * *

The living room was dangerously candlelit, and the throbbing heart of the party now.

A tall guy—was it the same tall guy she'd wished on?—made his way purposefully towards Ashley. He reminded her of Yanis from the night of *Carnaval*—was it the lips? A Québécois version. He clutched two glasses, and offered Ashley one.

"I've been watching you all night," he said—or seemed to say. The noise around them was frightful. "I love women with guns. If there was dancing, I'd dance with you."

"If there was dancing, I'd dance with you too." Ashley felt safe in saying this, although when it came to dancing she belonged to the lost generation.

Now he gave her that sudden thoughtful look, basic, male, a little surprised. Ashley, for her part, had no idea what she had in mind. The milling crowd pushed the tall guy up against her. He smelled of sandalwood, salt, other things.

"I'm Pierre," the man said—or it might have been "Gilbert."

"And if there was kissing …" Dark eyes held hers, before travelling over her surfaces.

Her heart jerked. Ashley knew what *baiser* really meant. She didn't feel anywhere near as in control as before. But three times the confidence came to her aid. She smiled. *She,* unlike Antoinette, was capable of reading all the signs, the *clues.*

"My wife—Charlotte—she dumped me at Christmas, you know," Pierre or Gilbert said, right on cue, with the requisite sigh. As he slid a hand along her upper arm, a female voice just behind him made him turn slightly. His eyes flickered, before long lashes dropped down. With proficient speed, he moved a centimetre or two away from her.

Someone had thrown open the French windows and a blue-black sting of cold caressed Ashley's neck, where he'd have been kissing her, perhaps, by now. The human crush flowed and they moved with it, away from each other, Ashley thinking she heard someone calling her name. She looked around, but all she saw were strangers. She consoled herself with the thought that Pierre/Gilbert would drop the other woman like a hot potato if Charlotte ever came back.

* * *

Madge was turning her attic into a kind of rec room. Its only furniture so far was a long couch on which five people were squeezed. One of them was Ashley. She'd left her fedora somewhere and her coiled braid had come undone. She was now holding a half-empty cocktail glass. Barely outlined against the dormer window, a couple kissed on the window seat, two anonymous cats. The music from downstairs was causing the plank floor to vibrate slightly. It was much later.

"So *this* is where you ended up," Isabel Jadois said, looking even more of a wandering fortune teller than usual. She made it sound like Ashley had sought refuge on the bordello level. "You're missing all the cosplay downstairs."

"So are you," Ashley replied, nudging the hand of someone called Laurence away from her knee.

"*Voyons donc, Laurence, fiche le camp,*" Isabel said, and sat down beside Ashley. "He was my student last year."

"We meet again," Ashley said.

Isabel laughed, like there was a joke there somewhere. "And the theme isn't Mirabel." She lit a cigarette, her face appearing briefly in the flare of the match. Friendly, in spite of the dry laugh. "But I should tell you she found you a great help in Paris."

"I should confess that I wasn't. It wasn't, you know, one of my regular jobs."

"People don't always help the way they think they help."

Other things were happening along the couch, people changing places, but these two sat on together. Ashley sipped her diluted

213

drink with a sense that the evening was coming to an end. A tall man sat down on the far side of Isabel. Ashley couldn't see him in the light from the stairs, but with a hollow sensation she recognized the voice: Pierre/Gilbert, although apparently his name was actually Robert.

She could hear his sexy witticisms, hardly the worse for a night's wear, in Isabel's other ear. Had Ashley really thought them even slightly worth listening to? She sat there for five more minutes, give or take, each minute like a reckoning. It *had* been that kind of party. All the inglorious phases had been lived through, in tiny cartoon form: from worm-like expectation, to helpless hope, to dull waiting, to betrayal.

Ashley, barely nicked by the roving dart gun of love, picked up the pieces and went home.

***

She slept well and felt good the next morning. It was another changeable March day, with the promise of a warm front moving in later. Never mind that it was Saturday, and she was going to the Saint Cyr party that evening, work was uppermost in Ashley's mind. Sarah Porttock had earmarked this day as auspicious for extraction of Kevin Black's smart phone. Ashley was driving Aram to the rendezvous so he could work on the smart phone right then and there.

In the middle of the afternoon they headed out in her Crown Victoria to Sarah's swanky Westmount apartment. They waited at the rear service entrance, in an area of brick walls and shrubbery. Aram got a text and stepped out of the car. Ashley watched as Sarah—looking shockingly unlike herself, in a slinky purple dress and her hair carefully styled—appeared at the door and handed Aram something in a little paper bag.

"What a seriously hot woman." Aram was enthusiastic as he

climbed into the back seat where his two laptops were waiting. "If her husband is cheating on her, all I can say is some men are crazy."

"Sarah—hot?"

"She smelled really nice too. Man."

"All right, stop." Ashley was suddenly aware of how Sarah was planning to distract Kevin for the next hour. They'd been together sixteen years, and yet … Ashley didn't want to consider what this meant, either about men or love.

She drove the car down the lane into a small dead-end area, while Aram got down to business. He was relaxed as he worked, chatting occasionally. It hardly took him any time at all.

"See—I'm not diving deep. We'll get you those couple of things you wanted. But the trick will be afterwards."

Ashley passed him a sour gummy worm. She had a bag from Aliments en Vrac. He'd said these helped him concentrate.

"Afterwards—let's see—it's the spyware that'll do the work. If he uses his phone to log into his bank account, for instance, then you will have the information in real time. His emails too, everything. Everything he uses his cell phone for, basically, password protected or not."

They didn't need the hour. In the time left over, Aram was able to show Ashley a few things. There was plenty to suggest that Sarah Porttock's instincts had been well-founded. Kevin's emails, from an unsuspected Yahoo account, made it pretty clear that he was, at the very least, having an affair. With a woman called Ghislaine LeMay. Messages sent during the time when he'd told Sarah he was in Toronto had content that suggested otherwise. So far, so predictable.

But there were other things that made Ashley think they were only skimming the surface. Why would Kevin text Ghislaine that he couldn't make it across town to let the decorators into the house, and could she? Why would he talk about his deposit cheque for them, which he'd left on the hall table under the Lalique vase? Ashley was now picturing Ghislaine as some sort of *demi-mondaine* kept

woman, all expenses paid right down to the Lalique. Was Kevin that rich? There was more to this, somehow, than met the eye. And what there was stank.

When Sarah came down to collect the phone, Ashley got an even better look at her. Her hair was tumbled and she was pink-cheeked. She looked feverish—in love, or almost. What was it about desire that made it increase with duplicity, suspicion, frustration? Remembering Pierre/Gilbert from last night, Ashley shuddered slightly. She gunned the motor to get out of this shady grove of two-faced love and back onto sunny Sherbrooke Street, among the everyday out-of-love types with whom she felt safe and, better than safe, lucky.

"Honestly, Aram, I really do not understand men."

Aram looked taken aback. "Well, as you know, I don't understand women."

"How's Rachel?"

"She might be a little less mad at me."

"How did you swing that?"

"If I knew, I'd tell you. Are you sure you can't give me any advice? Your work makes you so experienced."

"If I didn't like you, I'd be resentful of that comment."

Ashley gave him a look. Aram's expression was a little bemused, a little forlorn, but at least he didn't have that skewered and heartbroken air she'd seen in Roy. She did like Aram. "Okay, here's some advice. A man's gotta do what a man's gotta do."

"I've heard that before."

She handed him the bag of gummy worms. "You can keep these—a bonus. But I wasn't finished."

Aram helped himself. "All right, finish then."

"A man's gotta do what a man's gotta do, and then a man's gotta do more."

***

Mirabel Saint Cyr phoned Ashley while she was getting dressed. "I hope you're coming to the party," she said.

"I'm getting ready now."

"It was so nice to see you last Sunday. And last night too, but I didn't get a chance to talk to you like I wanted."

Ashley wasn't sure how to read this. "It was one of *those* parties, I guess."

"Let's try to find a quiet corner somewhere in the house and talk tonight. There's something I'd like to tell you." A pause. "You know how I've come to rely on you, Ash*lee*." Faintly alarmed, Ashley rang off.

She shoved her black cocktail dress back into the closet. She'd been rejecting outfits for the last fifteen minutes. Mirabel had told her that some of the guests would be wearing costumes but others would not and Ashley could wear whatever she liked. She was dithering uncharacteristically. When she'd first been invited by Mirabel, she'd been on the point of refusing. Then she thought, why not.

It was getting warmer tonight, in one of those sudden March about-faces. A rising wind shook the tree by her balcony, banging its branches against the railing. A moment ago, Ashley had opened the balcony door, to be caught off guard by a lungful of damp spring air. That air of early spring, forgotten at other times, with its overwhelming bouquet of decay, growth, memory and promise.

It was the wind, she thought, that was giving her this odd restless feeling again tonight—almost breathless, her brain asimmer, her gestures faster than her thoughts. Surely, for a night like this, she had something better to wear? Her hand fell on a thing her sister-in-law had made her, a casual summer-night-out sort of item, she'd explained. Lucie had a unique approach to sewing, bringing back remnants, trash and treasure, from the lost corners of the sewing world. Ashley hadn't asked for this item, and had never worn it. Because a sleeveless ankle-length coarsely woven dress, in a pattern of writhing crimson vines on a dark rose ground, gathered at the waist with a V-shaped belt, all metal links and leather, wouldn't ever have been Ashley's first choice, or any choice, in the what-to-wear department.

In a spirit of derision she tried it on. It fit well, but—absurd. She wove her black waves into a loose braid, letting it fall heavily down her back. Well, maybe in summer, with a pair of sandals. She remembered she had flat booties somewhere, with wraparound ties. She laced them on. With their pointy toes they made the whole outfit look medieval. Marie Ambre had left a metal hairband behind on her last visit. Ashley arranged it like a circlet on her forehead, tucking the ends into the braided hair at the back.

She considered her firm strong arms. She supposed medieval warrior queens didn't go around bare-armed. Or maybe they did—all the better to bring down wild boar with their lethal full-size bow and arrows. Of which she had a set, left over from archery club at university, stashed in her closet. It was the usual beginner equipment, but at least she'd opted for plain brown and black rather than neon turquoise. She tied a couple of arrows to the bow and slung the whole thing across her back.

Who was she, anyway? She waited while it came to her. Some Saxon noble's imperious wife, or his wayward eldest daughter perhaps, the doomed and radiantly tall product of feral in-breeding, having one last fling in the chantry-like recesses of the forest primeval, before being arrested by the Norman overlords, *apparaylled yn a lewde rayment* or such, for obscure *abhomynacion unto the worlde*. Ashley decided to go in costume after all.

* * *

The summit home of the Saint Cyrs took on a whole new look at night, sandwiched between the starry sky above and the radiant city below. Belgrave Heights was busy, cars pulling in at a brisk pace and dropping off their passengers like so many coaches at a Regency ball. The door swung open for her before she had time to ring, and a woman in a maid's uniform with short green hair ushered her into the hall. Ashley realized belatedly this was an actual maid, just with a certain taste in hair. Someone else received her coat and the ticket Mirabel had given her, as she took in the brilliant assembly. The double doors at the far side of the hall had been thrown open and she was able to see down a vista of capacious rooms leading into other capacious rooms. The crowd was in glittering fancy dress that could have been high society formal wear, or formal wear that could have been fancy dress. Music came from a live chamber orchestra somewhere, over the drone of voices.

Ashley didn't recognize a soul. But that, she told herself, was all right. She adjusted her bow and arrows in a big nearby mirror—the outfit had survived the taxi nicely—and had a good look around. She saw that she was under a massive oil painting of a woman in red, an arresting thing that drew the eyes. The picture could have been painted by the Beaver Hall Group, except for its emotive excess. The woman's expression was nothing short of melodramatic: Ashley thought she saw Pietà-like sorrow, but the longer she looked the less she understood the face.

She supposed she was amid the Québécoise *haute bourgeoisie*, and their hangers-on, all assembled in one place. Or at least those who made their money from fashion. And how they liked their clothes, these people. No one had come as a zombie bride or a Crayola crayon. Ashley remembered the photographs she'd seen online of Charles Saint Cyr at tony fundraisers. Whatever tonight's purpose, whether charity or business alliances, it was that kind of event. She was attending a Beaux Arts ball. Time, Ashley told herself, to circulate.

* * *

Mirabel and Charles seemed glad to see her, greeting her, almost, like a friend. Charles, impeccable in formal wear, didn't linger. Smiling but preoccupied, he left the two women to catch up. They were at the back of the house, one level down on the mountainside, in a beautiful conservatory where spring had come early. A few people came and went, as Mirabel pulled Ashley behind a bank of narcissus and violets.

"Our voices will be drowned out by that tasteless water feature."

Mirabel surveyed Ashley closely. "Ashley, you look … remarkable." There was genuine wonder in her voice. "Last night's was very good, but this …"

Mirabel's words embarrassed Ashley, or made her nervous anyway. She took a gulp of her highball. After all that cheap champagne of the night before, she was going to stick to rye and ginger.

Mirabel stretched like a cat, a cat got up as Marie Antoinette. "It's so nice to take a break. For Charles, tonight is all about business. It's where the next two to four years for Holopherne first take shape, where the deals of the future are dreamed up. And where rivals are identified. I have to play my part."

This didn't mean a heck of a lot to Ashley. She *had* been wondering about the sheer numbers, the security logistics of bringing so many people into a beautiful house like this one. How did Charles trust the place to so many people, not all of whom could be vouched for?

When she asked, Mirabel laughed. "Half the people you're looking at are security. As for the other half, well, the business leaders won't be pocketing any knick knacks, I suppose. As for the others"—she gestured towards a trio who looked like bit players in a crime thriller, although dressed to the nines—"that's why there's so much security."

The topic seemed to bore her. She picked at her dress. "Did you see how Charles and I are getting along now? I feel *quite* different about him."

Ashley smiled noncommittally. Was she supposed to be responsible for this too? She figured Mirabel was wending her way slowly to the point.

Isabel erupted suddenly into view. She had come to the party as a Grace Kelly knock-off, and the costume increased the resemblance between her and her sister. The maturity of Isabel's face and her swagger set them apart. She squeezed onto the bench with them, so that Ashley was in the middle.

"I think I'm still being followed," Mirabel said in a pleasant tone.

"*Bon Dieu,* did you have to come out with it just like that?" Isabel said. "Ashley will think you're imagining things!"

Mirabel sounded a little hurt. "Well, I believe it's true, Isa, and so do you. I mean, you saw the man ..."

"I *thought* I saw a guy, and *you said* he was like the guy that chased you and Ashley into the train station in Paris."

"Well, there you are," Mirabel said. Isabel snorted.

Ashley swallowed, held up a hand. "Wait. Just wait."

"You know what a close look we got at him from the restaurant, Ashley. There's nothing wrong, at least, with my eyesight. People are always doubting me, even you, Isa."

"Could you just tell Ashley what you saw?" Isabel emptied her glass. "Stick to the facts."

"I was going to. Five days ago, I thought I saw the man, you know who I mean. Isa and I were on Saint Catherine at lunchtime and there were crowds, so it was hard to be completely sure. Then, two days later, I had just parked my Fiat, a nice little 500 litre, up at Saint Joseph's Oratory—I like to go there sometimes, just to be alone, to think—and I saw him again, getting out of a car at the end of the lot, behind the pilgrim information centre. There was a van between us, but I swear it was him, and he dodged when he saw me looking."

Ashley hadn't been to the gigantic Oratory on the northwestern slope of the mountain since she was six, when she'd been taken by her Anglican grandmother Smeeton for some reason. She could still picture the raw spring afternoon—the scudding cloud, the harsh light and black racing shadows. And she could still remember the sense she'd had of being overwhelmed. To small Ashley, the place had been too broodingly big, too exposed, too battered by wind. Insert Mirabel Saint Cyr, solitary and thinking, into the picture, throw in a popemobile Fiat, and the whole was haunted by the ghost of Hitchcock.

"That would be very problematic—if it was true," she said at last.

"That's what I thought," Mirabel said. Her mood as she spoke was predictably odd. Where, for instance, was the fear? "Also, Isabel really does believe me. She just doesn't want you to think I'm crazy. Isn't that right, Isa?"

Isabel sighed, nodded briefly. "I guess. Anyway, I'm afraid." And she looked afraid. Uncomfortable, uneasy, with fear behind these.

Ashley was trying to form a coherent perspective. "Why, though? The Bortniks can't think you have the loot, Mirabel. Besides, we thought the Bortniks were the ones who made off with the barge."

Mirabel nodded. "We thought that. But what if—just for instance—while we were being chased at the railway station and before the Bortnik reinforcements arrived, Raymond took the barge upriver? Did you ever think of that? He had his own keys. The ice would probably have allowed him. They might think I know things."

"Has Raymond been in touch with you since you left Paris? Or, I don't know, that woman Mireille?"

"No! The French policeman—Bourque?—called once. That was it. Cross my heart, Ashley."

As always, Ashley didn't know what to make of the little girl act. "Well, no one's been following *me*," she said. With everything going on, with so much work, would she have noticed?

Isabel got out her pack of cigarettes. "Can I smoke here?"

"No, Isa, stop. Charles would be very angry."

"That man. All right. Get to the point, I need a smoke." She turned to Ashley impatiently. "The *point* Mirabel is trying to make is she would like to hire you again."

The thought that Bortnik thugs were wandering around Montreal had been a jolt to Ashley. But all she felt at the idea of working for the Saint Cyrs again was a clutching weariness.

She was opening her mouth to suggest the police, when Isabel said: "Don't say no right away. Please—think about it, all right? No tough guy stuff, just finding out who, if anyone, is following my sister. Then Mirabel would actually have something to take to the police, which she doesn't now."

"And when Isa says I would like to hire you, she means Charles would like to hire you. I've already spoken to him about this, told him everything." Mirabel assumed a matrimonially virtuous air, like sharing everything with her husband was a given. "If you want to talk to him, you should. Charles told me he would be happy to talk to you. So you see ... Oh, he's there." Charles Saint Cyr was signalling to his wife from the other end of the conservatory.

"I have to go, Ashley. There'll be someone Charles wants to introduce me to, so I can deploy my charm for some business objective." She checked her lipstick in a mirror. "Do I look charming enough? I won't be absolutely crushed if you refuse. We can talk about it some more, though, I could go down to your office. I'd like to do that. Did I mention it would be at the same rate? You'll at least think about it for now?" And she hurried away, in a sway of pannier crinolines.

Isabel slid down carelessly on the bench, her skirt hiking up to reveal long legs. Ashley was pretty sure the princess of Monaco had never sat like this. Her smile was wry.

"I'm sick of the whole Paris-Mirabel shebang. Let's not think about it any more tonight." She pointed to the black wall of glass in front of them. "Look at those treetops! The radio forecast a windstorm. We should go out onto the terrace later, see if we get blown away. But now we both need fresh drinks. Also, do you want me to introduce you to some actual fun people here, Ashley? Come on—I'll take you to the real party."

* * *

It was, she remembered afterwards, when she and Isabel were threading their way through the big central foyer, towards the west wing where the alleged fun people were, that Ashley came upon Jon Perez.

She remembered the spot because, just before she saw him, she'd looked at the Woman in Red again and thought she'd been way off in her interpretation of the expression. In the rigid planes of the woman's face she now saw, or thought she saw, mortal anger. She'd had just enough rye to postulate the theory that extreme emotions in humans tended to fuse and merge, becoming increasingly indistinguishable, and wanted to blurt this revelation to Isabel, when she recognized the mellow brown eyes resting on her.

She might not have recognized him. He looked very different. How did a couple of years do that to a man? The summer she'd worked at Columbine Lodge, he'd been nothing more to her than the maid Silvia's little brother, with a frisky way about him and a complicated relationship to the immigration authorities. And there'd been that couple of bedroom episodes, evidently.

Jon had cut off his pony tail, there was that. Gone also were the low-slung cargo pants and the shirts open to the waist. And instead of the almost fixed expression of flirtatiousness that she remembered, she was looking at a contained, even reserved, face. This was a discreetly dressed man, whose steady gaze asserted itself gravely before the world. In his elegant suit, good-looking, too. Just as good-looking as ever.

It was the second look at him that confirmed it for Ashley. And she wouldn't have glanced a second time but for the shock on his face. They somehow wafted into each other's orbit, converged. She got close enough to hear his low words very well: "Is that really you? Ashley?"

Isabel measured the situation with a long glance, decided her role for now was over. She melted away.

"I was asking myself the same."

His gaze went all over Ashley, still shocked, but now also—what the hell *was* the look—stricken? "You're so different. But you aren't, no. You're just the same. But I can't believe—I can't believe it's really you." The dark eyes settled on hers, warm, intent. "I've thought a lot about you, Ashley."

They moved off together, Jon sending quick glances her way only to look rapidly away again when she turned to him. Ashley tossed her braid slightly, secretly gloating as every shockwave registered. "Why don't we find somewhere quiet and catch up," she said.

There was no swelling music, like in the movies. But it was, at last, just as Isabel had promised and what no doubt she'd been looking for herself: the real party.

* * *

Time passed, but no one was keeping track.

Ashley and Jon wandered into an old-fashioned pantry where they found a large stash of candy. Jon shared Baci with her, one bite for her, the rest for him. His manner was so meticulous he might have been illuminating a manuscript. He wasn't doing the aching-calculating thing with his eyes anymore. He was well past that. They were well past that.

Later, they slipped past security and wandered down a felted corridor in a part of the house where they were completely alone. They came to a wing of bedrooms. Each half-open door revealed tall curtained windows, high beds, luxurious stillness and space. Each time Jon paused, looked at her, and they went on.

They did speak, from time to time. For example, they swapped facts. His sister Silvia was doing well, now that her accountant credentials had been recognized in Quebec. Jon had gone back to Colombia for a while. He'd returned to Montreal last year. Scant detail was offered, just that he was now in the fashion business—freelancing. The greyness of this washed imperviously over Ashley. She told him she'd moved.

"Oh, so *that's* what happened to you," he said, as if she'd assumed a new identity in Siberia.

Back in the conservatory, they lingered amid the lush greenery, the scent of flowers and peat moss. "Nature is formidable," Jon said, squeezing her hand.

They were practically alone, the call to a sumptuous midnight supper having emptied the place. Jon slid an arm around Ashley settling his hand firmly on her hip as they watched the branches on the mountainside thrashing in the wind.

"I know how to get out to the terrace without meeting anyone," he said. "I know the secret way."

He produced a Saint Cyr umbrella from somewhere. Outside, it was all they could do to hold it against the wild night. Here above the city, the wind roared and flung volleys of warm ozone-laden rain in their faces. The treed slope beneath them was alive with restless movement. The smells were overpowering—resinous catkins, sap, fresh mud, putrefaction.

Ashley was without a coat, but indifferent—it was extraordinarily mild for a March night. The wind picked up her long skirt and tossed it out before her like a flag. She felt airborne, raised her arms. She was the flag—or a sailboat running before a gale. Jon held her against the raging wind, a pleasant conceit of lovers in a storm. Playing along, Ashley, a solid five feet ten, said: "It's like that old rhyme we used to sing: *The wind, the wind, the wind blows high, it blows Ashley through the sky …*"

It had been a while since she'd left her bow and arrows behind.

Then the wind wrenched the umbrella from Jon and tossed it upward like a broken kite into the void of the sky. They watched it go, a scrap of deeper blackness against the boiling sky and the rocking trees below. Jon plucked the damp tendrils of hair from Ashley's face and lips and kissed her, carefully at first, as if she might say something hostile. Something like: "I wasn't in Siberia, you know." When she responded, he took her head in his hands and kissed her thoroughly.

Much later—but it was still night and the warm humid wind still roared outside—they were in her apartment on rue de Paris, which Jon eventually recognized as the place he'd casually inspected a couple of years ago. "I can't believe you live here, it would have been a great place for lying low," he murmured. Ashley took this in the romantic sense. They were in the doorway of the back bedroom, and he was looking at Ashley's wide mattress on an artful arrangement of tatami mats she'd bought at a futon place over on Saint Denis.

"I needed a bigger place for my business, with a better layout," was all she said. Although hardly this room.

They kissed again, his fingers working the buttons on her dress. Lucie had done something complicated involving loops and this required all his attention. Ashley laughed. She felt heavy with desire yet light as air. It was going to be all like this, she told herself, hope fusing with certainty. Then he stopped his fumbling and looked at her, and she looked back into his deepest core, finding there knowledge, understanding—and marvelling admiration. And in a click of time something sprang to life inside her, like a weird seismic twinge in some sensitive area, small but signalling more to come. The next kiss went on and on, their eyelashes quivering against each other's skin, their lips barely moving.

The question afterwards, for her anyway, was what had hooked and landed her. Not thinking about Jon Perez day to day hadn't meant very much after all. Two summers ago, apparently, she'd paid a visit to a strange bank in an unfamiliar part of the city, and there made an unremembered and sizeable deposit. Her high school teachers had been right. Compound interest really did add up.

She was an Ashley transformed. An Ashley perhaps only ever previously encountered in dreams or under the influence of Percocet combined with Percodan after a violent wisdom tooth extraction. Ashley under completely new and reckless management. Tall, dark and romantic in her own original way, winged huntress of the forest primeval with her bow and arrows, the becoming gown, despite it being a little hard to get out of, a pleasant finishing detail. And indistinguishable from the hapless herd, love finding the hidden weaknesses and so easily breaching her defences.

They settled on the bed, half undressed, with glasses of a cheap red she'd dug out of the pantry. The weed tree outside the window was putting on a nice show for them, moaning and whispering in the wind.

"Is the place like you imagined it?" she said.

But Jon was done with idle chat. He got rid of their two glasses, and even more quickly dealt with the rest of their clothes. He was still the same proficient lover, truthfully even more proficient thanks to who knew what during two years of absence. But for Ashley it wasn't a purely physical experience anymore. Emotion confused, made her awkward—made them both a little desperate, almost panicky with want.

The second time, following a lull during which they watched the sky turn a deep indigo, was better. And the third was shortest, after which they slept.

16

HARBINGER

THERE WAS PROBABLY a dubious world out there of articles and blogs discussing love/work, love/children/work, love/love, love/hate and love/sex, but Ashley, technically admissible at last, was too busy to read them. Her preoccupation necessarily remained love/criminality. She did spend a little time on makeover websites, a feminine example of the theory of rising expectations, but since Jon seemed deliriously satisfied with what she already had she soon grew tired of these.

They spent all the time they could together. Which wasn't a lot. Ashley was swamped with work as usual and Jon professed that he was too. They snatched hours and enjoyed talking about all the things they would do together in that glorious vague future when everything would be more settled.

They were already spending a few nights a week at each other's places before Ashley heard from Isabel and Mirabel again. Then she heard from them both in one day. Isabel rang up in the morning. Ashley took the call at her local coffee shop, having left Jon asleep at rue de Paris.

"Are you still thinking about that job Mirabel talked to you about?" Isabel asked.

"Thinking," Ashley said. "But no one's been in touch with me since." After the night of the Westmount party, she'd begun to pay attention and was confident no one was shadowing her at least.

"Well, that's about to change. Mirabel's not doing well. She's under a lot of stress with this new trouble. Charles will pay top dollar, as we said."

Ashley made a noncommittal sound, while finding herself thinking about what another ride on the Saint Cyr gravy train would give her and Jon—a trip, in particular, to somewhere warm and glamorously exotic. Where she would show herself off showing off Jon.

"My sister's not crazy. I mean—you know. I believe she's being followed. As for Charles, I think he thinks Mirabel is just suffering from delayed shock or something. She could be, I suppose. It would explain some things ... But Charles thinks if you do the required digging it will ease her worried mind, as the song says."

"There *are* a lot of songs about easing worried minds."

Isabel laughed. "Also ease his worried mind. I think he's trying to be a Better Husband too. Can you hear my capitals?"

Ashley said awkwardly, "Mirabel did say the two of them were getting along better ..."

Isabel's laughter changed in character. "Well, maybe Raymond is history, but Mirabel's been very restless since she returned home. The thrill of those antiques lasted about a week. She's spending a lot of time away from home, and not just up at the Oratory meditating, I promise you. There's a new crowd that she hangs with. Arty, entrepreneurial—wild, even by my standards. Look, you'd find this out sooner or later so I'll tell you. She has another boyfriend. Well, a very close friend is how she describes him, but please."

"I'm glad I wasn't hired as a marriage counsellor then." This, if true, was a bit much. Why couldn't the woman just find one tall-dark-handsome significant other, say like Jon, and commit? Then Ashley couldn't help wonder if Jon really was her significant other in the full sense. Feelings were one thing, understandings another.

"Are you still there, Ashley?"

"Yes, of course," she said. "When will I hear, and from whom?"

"Mirabel's going to visit you today." A pause. "Oh, by the way, that was an interesting guy you connected with at the party. Jon Perez? Sounds like you knew him from before."

"I met him a while ago on the job. What about him?"

While fishing, Isabel didn't hold back. "He was hot. Are you two an official number?"

"A number?"

"Ashley. An item."

But Ashley was having none of it. "We're friends," she said.

Isabel sounded amused once more. "If you say so."

* * *

Mirabel, a harbinger of spring in a lilac belted wool coat, pale suede gloves and a matching envelope clutch, peered around the office with an interested air. They were seated across Ashley's desk from one another, and Mirabel had just removed one glove so as to place Charles's generous retainer cheque on the desk. The zeros were just as visible to Ashley upside down. This and the charming picture that Mirabel always presented helped improve the cold and overcast day.

"So this is where you work? I like it. I like the neighbourhood too. I like everything about it."

Madame Saint Cyr was as exquisite as ever, Ashley could not deny. But she didn't look the same. She looked, to use Isabel's word, stressed. The blue-grey gaze with its lights and shadows still reminded Ashley of a changeable sky, but a tension in Mirabel's regard was new. Ashley couldn't read it. Was it the fixity of fear? There was resolution in there somewhere. But what did Mirabel have to be resolute about? The new beau?

"He's followed me twice more since, and I am sure, Ash*lee,* that this man is the same one we ran from in Paris. Thug Two, as we called him. Do you remember? Paris ..." Mirabel looked about to relinquish the thread, in a trip down memory lane.

"How close did you get to him?" Ashley said.

"Close. Fifteen feet, under twenty anyway ..." Mirabel seemed very confident. They discussed it all. Identifying features, the man's demeanour, the make of the car, times of day. It was a strange story, when baldly laid out. Thug Two had, apparently, hopped the pond along with his Bluetooth and was shadowing Mirabel around the city, at random times of the day. Not approaching, and not trying to skulk unseen either, if Mirabel's account was to be relied upon. And, Ashley remembered, Mirabel was on the whole an acute observer.

Senseless, almost. Senseless, unless there was a whole part of what had happened in Paris that Ashley was missing by a mile. She mused momentarily about this. For a start, *Bortnik frères* ... Although she could picture the brothers in her imagination, down to the last unappealing detail, she'd only ever seen their emissaries. However, the police had corroborated their existence. But what did Ashley really know about the Bortniks?

But she'd already decided to take the job. She was going to accept this payment and a few more. They discussed how you shadow a shadower, and what Ashley wanted Mirabel to do.

Mirabel agreed with alacrity, but added: "If you have the time, though, it would mean a lot to me if you could sometimes accompany me? I'm often with my friends, often with Léandre. Charles wants that too, if you can manage it. I would feel so much safer. I know how busy you are, but when you have time."

So there would be a security aspect. Shades of Paris returning. But Ashley thought once more about the money to be made, and knew she could make the time. Aram had been hinting about more jobs just yesterday. It didn't take a math genius to calculate how very far ahead the magnanimous Saint Cyr rate, with Aram's pay subtracted, would still leave her. She'd been reading about the Leeward Islands.

Mirabel had begged for a coffee, which Ashley figured was just an excuse to hang around longer, and they now both moved into the kitchen while she made it. Mirabel was thrilled by everything there as well. They took their coffee into the living room, where the knock-off William Morris wallpaper and handsome rug were duly commented on.

It had become quite dark during this time. Ashley was reaching to turn on a lamp when Mirabel, standing at the window over-looking the street, said: "Don't do that, Ashley."

"Okay. Why?"

Mirabel just continued to stare unresponsive through the window. Ashley could hardly hear her words: "How could he have ..."

Ashley stood up abruptly. "What's going on, Mirabel?"

Mirabel took a rapid step backwards, sloshing her coffee, while at the same moment the sound of slow heavy footsteps ascending the iron stairs reverberated through the room.

"It's him, the man who's been following me, Ashley." Mirabel's voice held shock. Ashley moved rapidly to the window, but Mirabel grabbed her arm and pulled her back. "He's looking up, he'll see us!" she hissed.

The footsteps were coming up to the front door, that looked directly into the office as well as the passage to the back. The door had half glazing and, due to the darkness of the day, the blind was raised. The steps kept coming. If they went into the passage now, they'd be just in time to see their heavy-footed visitor framed in the glass—peering, no doubt, right at them.

The night of the confrontation at the barge was now in front of Ashley again, a sudden sickness of the memory: the thug's empty eyes, the ham fist casually holding the big gun, the blooming vio-lence. Her mind raced, she fought panic.

Mirabel was still gripping her arm. "We could hide in that cupboard," she whispered, pointing to the little wallpapered door in the corner.

Which gave Ashley her solution. "Out the back," she whispered, drawing Mirabel with her.

The little door was rarely used and stuck for a horrible moment. But Ashley got it open and they stepped directly into the kitchen, tripping over the vacuum cleaner and Chantale's unreturned Swiffer. Through the kitchen they darted into the hall, where Ashley grabbed their things off a peg, and into the bedroom. The balcony door stuck too—it wasn't square to the frame and there'd been frost overnight—but Ashley got them out onto the balcony at last where they were able to scramble down the spiral stairs to her car. Her heart still thudding; she took the lane at speed; and they joined a cross street farther down. They were away.

As she drove, second thoughts surfaced about their dash to safety. "I should have just faced him off. What was he going to do? Shoot us in the office?"

"I didn't see a gun, but I'm glad we ran."

And later: "Did you get a good view of him, Mira? You're sure it was the guy from Paris?"

Mirabel was calmer now too, and replied: "Yes, Ashley, I'm sure."

They drove around, finally stopping on Centre Street for a coffee that neither of them needed.

"Your car's back there," Ashley said. "You'll have to go back."

"Actually, I parked at that Impark lot up on Wellington. I wasn't sure you had street parking."

Ashley now decided she wanted eyes on the street. She called Aram on the off chance he was home. He was. "Listen, I need you to do something. By the way, I'm going to have some more work for you soon." Enthusiastic noises. "But now I need you to look around outside my place, the front *and* the back, and see if there's a man lurking around. Biggish, tough-looking, a kind of thuggy Slavic look, if you know what I mean." Aram did. "He'd have driven to rue de Paris, so look out for a car, something big at a guess. He may have followed a client to my office, and I want to know if he's still around."

A few minutes later, Aram called back. He'd checked the front, checked the back, up and down the street, the laneway end to end, looked through Ashley's windows. There was no sign of anyone. In an attack of initiative he'd even checked Ashley's mailbox. There was a small Canpar package with a return address from Librairie Raffin, but that was all. He said he'd wait outside until Ashley came home, but she told him not to bother.

Ashley dropped Mirabel off at her popemobile, and drove home thoughtfully. If Thug Two was going to take this direct approach, she was going to have to rethink her strategy. Maybe he just wanted to talk? That sounded improbable. However, his boldness wasn't necessarily a bad thing. If he wasn't taking the trouble to hide, he'd be easier to investigate. If only, she thought, she'd gotten a glimpse of him. Tomorrow she'd go over to see Charles Saint Cyr, finalize the paperwork, have a little talk with him, reinforce some basics about his wife's safety.

After that experience, it was time to head to the kitchen to make much-needed pasta for supper. Not that she'd distinguished herself today, of course, but discretion *was* the better part of valour. Anyway, who could have predicted Thug Two would just walk up to her door? She tried to stoke up enthusiasm. But she couldn't rid herself of the nagging worry that this whole Bortnik plot had simply dragged on too long, and that this in itself meant something. She just couldn't figure out what.

The Canpar parcel was nothing more than the latest Esmerelda LaFlamme. After dinner she tucked into it on the couch, back to her normal self except perhaps for the amount of time she spent checking doors and windows and making sure the window coverings showed no gaps.

This one, which Ashley had elected to try in French after Madge had expressed dissatisfaction with some of the translations, was called *Les jeunes veuves,* a racily Victorianesque title although the book seemed to be about the usual urban crime and corruption, heavily seasoned with domestic mayhem. The story featured a number of unhappily married young women. No young widows yet, but presumably an untimely death or two would produce those. The hero was called Léandre, like Mirabel's special friend. He'd just come across, and become combustibly re-involved with, an old flame, which made her think of her own situation.

Distracting thoughts of Jon followed—how well they were getting on, how in sync they were, in bed, out of bed, every damn place—which was a pity since he wasn't going to be able to spend the night with her. When Roy called and they arranged for him and Lilou to visit her the following weekend, Ashley was glad, for her own sake as well as for her brother's.

* * *

Roy and Lilou were a welcome distraction. On the principle that everyone needed distraction, she had Jon, Aram, Ibrahim, Chantale and Marie Ambre over for a sit-around-the-floor supper on Saturday evening. To her considerable surprise, Chantale brought Michel Desrosiers. Up close, he didn't contradict Ashley's worst suspicions. What she hadn't seen in the photo was the low-slung simian way he moved. His face looked deprived; his soul looked deprived. But in his body there was a contained animal life, although the containment might have been due simply to weariness from long hours on a creeper under cars. Ashley couldn't fault his manners, however. Although he seemed half involved with his surroundings, and keen on his outdoor smoke breaks, he used his pleases and thank yous when addressed directly with simple questions like: "Will you have a beer?" She'd better get a move on with his reference check, she reminded herself. It had slipped down the queue, in part because of the urgency of other cases and in part because she'd given Chantale a very preferential rate.

She'd invited Antoinette as well, who'd refused with what appeared to be genuine regret, citing a conflict. Now that her relationship with her cousin was off to a good start, Ashley found herself a little at a loss regarding how to proceed. Eric was always going to be aloof. It was his personality apart from anything else. Antoinette was different. Still, how did you develop a relationship with a first cousin you'd met for the first time in your twenties? What, if anything, was going to cement the bond between them?

Lilou was clingy with Roy at first, something Ashley had never seen before. But the presence of the other children brought her out of her shell. Roy, still looking hollowed out, supervised with anxious pride. Ashley watched him watch over his daughter. If he couldn't make it up with Lucie, Lilou would be all he had. She could read this thought in every line of his face, every weary gesture. She wanted to yell at him: "You'll always be her father. Nothing will change that." But she suspected this was the last thing a person believed in a situation like his. There was horror in all this: first, the loss of your other half, and then the fear you would lose the child of that love as well. It would be enough to drive anyone crazy.

Jon spread his charm around the room, but didn't stay over because of the out-of-town guests. One of the many nice aspects of Jon was how flexible he was. He wanted to spend as much time with Ashley as she wanted to spend with him, but, if something came up, he was philosophical. After the meal, he washed the dishes and said goodbye. His hand sliding down her back promised they'd make it up another time. "Everyone," he said, "needs family time." Ashley herself had been thinking more about the thinness of the walls.

Roy and Lilou left on Sunday afternoon, and Ashley buried herself in work for the rest of the day. She was about to present her report to Sarah Porttock, and it wasn't pretty. It was also very weird.

* * *

"I have my work cut out for me," Sarah Porttock acknowledged. By which she meant her lawyers would have their work cut out for them.

It was the end of what must have been for her a long workday. She still wore her work clothes. Her coffee remained untouched before her. She was very pale. Otherwise, remarkably calm, considering she'd just discovered that her partner of sixteen years led a double life. The deception wasn't just about his job and the money he earned. Kevin Black had a second long-term relationship, and lived with the woman in a second home.

"This information will give you the chance to plan an exit strategy that will protect your interests." Ashley hoped she didn't sound glib. What else did you say to a woman in such circumstances?

Far away at the other end of Montreal, well beyond Antoinette's stomping ground, somewhere in the unknown eastern, northeastern really, reaches of the island, amid places with alien names like Bellerive, Longue-Pointe and Bout-de-l'Ile, Kevin Black, for the last three years, had lived in connubial bliss in a co-owned condo with Ghislaine LeMay.

Once the computer and bank accounts had been hacked, the rest was easy. And the things you could find! For instance, Ashley was able to take a virtual tour of the love nest of Kevin and Ghislaine, from a leftover realtor.ca advertisement still floating in cyberspace. The condo was a modern thing of creamy surfaces, mirror glass and flashy architectural detail, that Ashley personally found tacky. It was trying too hard—not in a class at all with a mansion flat in Westmount. To get to it, you drove east for quite a long time, or took a farther bus or train from the terminus of the green line. This, Ashley supposed, must have satisfied Kevin's need for separation. As for his job, as Sarah herself had learned, he was a VP and joint owner of his firm, and he was absolutely rolling in money, although his expenses seemed equally lavish.

For her part, Ghislaine was a successful real estate agent, a polished woman with a glossy website. She also had a Facebook account with privacy settings it had been easy to bypass. There were several pictures of Kevin among her photos, on holidays and at social gatherings, for all to see. It was all there, waiting to be found once you were through the door—any door.

Did Ghislaine LeMay know? Ashley had to ask herself. Or rather, what did Ghislaine know, amid the distortions, red herrings and partial truths that Kevin may have fed her?

Another question, of course, was why. Ashley had had a chance to brood on this but the answers didn't come readily. At first Sarah seemed no better able to explain things. But when she mentioned, almost apologetically, that the Westmount apartment—on the sunny top floor of the building, the penthouse really, to the extent that those old buildings had penthouses—was now worth about five million, Ashley thought she saw the light at last.

"Is the apartment in both your names?" she asked.

Sarah frowned, like she wasn't sure. "No," she said after a moment. "Kevin, he'd mention the ownership thing from time to time. He'd wonder why he wasn't co-owner. Drop hints. I had no reason not to put the place in both our names. I just somehow never got around to it. Since we were common law, I supposed it would make no difference ..." Her voice trailed away. She looked embarrassed. "I see I have no idea what the status of ownership in law is ..."

"And that," said Ashley, "is what you need to talk to a lawyer about pronto. Although any claim he made is going to look pretty questionable now in the light of his betrayal, his double life."

At least, Ashley hoped this was true. She also hoped that Sarah Porttock would run, not walk, to see her lawyers. She hesitated to be too explicit, but if Kevin's motive was acquisition of the Westmount apartment, or any other assets of Sarah's, she could well be in danger. People killed routinely for a fraction of five million dollars. The flat not being in both their names wouldn't necessarily protect her. Married to neither woman, Kevin would have a very good chance of keeping the second relationship under the legal radar in order to facilitate a claim on her estate.

"I'm glad I was able to assist, if this information will help you protect yourself," Ashley said, when they were on the sidewalk in front of the coffee shop. "Contacting a lawyer should be your top priority now." She added: "I am sorry." Sarah Porttock smiled, like someone who'd forgotten the meaning of smiles.

Ashley was going to meet Jon for dinner at a fancy restaurant. His treat. She would be just the right amount of tantalizingly late. Her step was measured and buoyant on the pavement, and she caught people taking a second look at her, in her Parisian coat open over her rustling black cocktail dress. The April air was mild in the purple dusk. She could smell a trace of her own perfume, the one that made Jon crazy, mingling with rush hour exhaust fumes. She couldn't help it. In spite of the meeting she'd just had, her heart lifted up, giddily, and she seemed to hear in the dull roar of the city the whispered news of long-awaited happiness just around the corner.

***

Charles Saint Cyr, when Ashley met him the next day in an office wing of a Holopherne distribution centre in a South Shore exurb, was all too eager to sign her on for another stint. Not that he conveyed that he thought Mirabel was in real danger. Or, if he believed in the reality of the danger, he believed it was equally likely she was imagining the whole thing, triggered by post-Paris nerves. If Mirabel was really as—what?—childishly credulous, kooky, as he thought, why on earth was he so keen to reproduce with her? Ashley couldn't help but wonder. Was it her physical attributes? Were men really that simple? She also wondered what if anything he knew about Léandre. When Ashley told Charles about the footsteps on the stairs, his eyes darkened. Clearly, he didn't know how to react. But the solution would be the same. Ashley was to devote a good chunk of her time—not all her time, as in Paris—to watching over Mirabel, while she tried to get a lead on the man who was haunting her.

She sat for a few minutes in her car, in the charmless wasteland of Holopherne's parking lot, thinking over what she'd just signed on for. Was she ready for another Mirabel immersion experience? Not really. But the sunny south beckoned. Meanwhile she'd dumped a few jobs on Aram's plate. He was thrilled to be learning the ropes, and Ashley knew he was imagining himself as her associate. In the back of her mind she thought she could do much worse than Aram.

Being with Mirabel, especially when she was determined to go out in the evening, did cut into Ashley's time with Jon. They made it up, somehow. When they could both manage it, he would drop by Ashley's place for an hour during the day. There were distinct advantages to working from your home. A lot could be accomplished in an hour. Ashley had continued to cherish a mental picture of the two of them, in her back bedroom, making love in dim golden light filtered through autumn leaves. If the time of year was wrong, she found that an ochre-coloured Indian bedspread tacked up before the door and window was a satisfactory substitute.

***

Mirabel, along with her new group which included Léandre, often went to clubs in the evening. These didn't seem to be your typical Montreal clubs, not that Ashley had much knowledge of the Montreal club scene. The locations were unusual: a partly demolished warehouse tucked into the centre of a spaghetti junction of overpasses; a hangar on a derelict road behind railyards. Unlike the Parisian *buanderie,* these places did in fact seem like legitimate venues once you were in them, although the half-finished look and edgy mood suggested they might have been legitimized five minutes ago and who knew what the next five minutes would bring. When Ashley remarked that she was finding identical patterns of cigarette burns on the tables, Mirabel made a vague comment about a thirty-day grey zone between permitting and final inspection. Was Léandre, or someone, moving stuff from venue to venue, flipping clubs in other words? And how did that pay?

The live music was fabulous; the vibe was cool and casual. Her jeans and motorcycle boots worked fine, with more makeup than she usually wore. *Ashley Arabella Smeeton experiencing life to the utmost,* she would say to herself, while wondering what exactly had been in that shot besides vodka. She limited herself to a drink per evening, feeling however that she needed one to blend in.

Léandre Bergeron was surprisingly unlike either Charles or Raymond Boissier. He made money, somehow, off art. He had a clever understated manner, was less handsome than fundamentally attractive, and was no more than a couple of inches taller than Mirabel. At first she couldn't put her finger on it, and then she recognized the resemblance: He was like a bohemianized version of French president Emmanuel Macron. It was in the eyes especially. You could see in Léandre's gaze the quiet force of the man, how he meant business.

Watching him interacting with Mirabel gave few clues to the exact nature of their relationship. He was quietly attentive to her. But wasn't he intelligently attentive, quietly dashing, with all the other women in the group? They were a charming lot, these women, the whole crowd being in fact hatefully attractive. If Léandre showed any preference for Mirabel, from what Ashley could observe, it may have been a quasi-gallant deference to the explicit signals she was sending him. They almost certainly had a sexual relationship. But Ashley also suspected Léandre of sleeping with half the women in the group. Later, Ashley had other thoughts. Mirabel had apparently met this group through her husband's work as patron of the arts. Had Saint Cyr money paved the way for Mirabel's entry into the group, and was there accordingly a certain conscious cordiality in the way they dealt with Madame Saint Cyr, Léandre not excepted?

As for Mirabel, Ashley soon found herself theorizing that in Léandre Bergeron she might have met her match. Mirabel continued to convey that she was under a strain. Was Léandre partly responsible for this? Was Mirabel, so apparently capable of having relationships that seemed ninety-nine percent sex in a pink cloud of more sex, finally and at last in love?

If so, why pick Léandre? Ashley wondered, as she watched him across the room of Le Loup Garou, bending confidentially over a brunette of barely legal age, while Mirabel beside her stirred her cocktail with a dreamy and unreadable look. But you didn't choose the one you fell in love with, Ashley reminded herself, as a mental picture from an evening a few days ago surfaced, of Jon's warm brown eyes looking into hers as they got it on. God, now *she* was quoting Stendhal. Mirabel, as if reading her thoughts, sighed and pushed back her chair.

Much later, Ashley in her own car followed Mirabel to Léandre's Old Montreal condo, where she was apparently spending the night. What explanation of her night away would be provided to Charles, Ashley could only imagine. But setting aside that part of Mirabel's eternally complicated Venn diagram of love, Ashley was at least sure that, where Léandre was concerned, for this night at least, it was Mirabel one, youthful brunette zero.

The next day Mirabel said she was staying home, and Ashley decided to watch the Belgrave Heights house. This was time consuming but she took her laptop and was able to accomplish quite a lot while sitting in her car. However, despite one false alarm that led her on a chase to Verdun, she saw nothing suspicious. And this was equally true on other days when she attempted surveillance on the suddenly very shy Bortnik thug. Mirabel, on those occasional

17

DARK UNFAMILIAR STREETS

S PRING WAS ON its way, in that one step forward, two steps backward fashion familiar to Montrealers. There was a paralysis, a deadness, to the days. But there was also one evening, after a cold day of rain, when Ashley took a walk through her local park, and noticed the sheen of lemon-coloured light on puddles, and in the rinsed atmosphere the rich sharp smell of poplar catkins cast down by wind. When she got back to rue de Paris in the gloaming, there were children still playing on the street, or rather hanging out in a cluster under a streetlamp. A voice called her name, and she waved. Even Ashley, a solitary child, had done her share of this. She supposed children would gravitate to neighbourhood street lamps until the end of time. Anyway, it was nice to think so.

Her mood was shattered as soon as she stepped through the door. Charles Saint Cyr was on the phone. She'd never heard him so emotional. Mirabel had been driven off the road. Deliberately, apparently.

By the time Ashley arrived at the house on the summit he had got hold of himself but he was pacing the hand-waxed floorboards of the drawing room. Mirabel, wide-eyed, was hunched on the couch. The green-haired maid was pouring out what looked like camomile tea.

"I told him, Ashley, it had nothing to do with you. I went out on a whim, to see a friend. You can't always accompany me, I know that. Besides, I didn't even ask you."

"What do you mean, friend?" Charles interrupted his pacing to glare.

"I *told* you—Léandre Bergeron. You know him. He's from my arts community work. And he's just a friend." There'd clearly been previous rounds of this.

It was after ten at night. With the pace of her life recently, Ashley felt tired and not at all equal to this. "Why don't you just tell me what happened?" she said to Mirabel.

It was simple enough. She'd decided to take a drive to Léandre's place, at Bout-de-l'Ile.

"I thought he lived in Old Montreal?"

"That's his *pied-à-terre*. He has a house in Bout-de-l'Ile, over-looking the river. It's far, so he's got the apartment too." Charles looked about to emit smoke at the ears. The green-haired girl hovered protectively.

"So what happened?"

"I don't always like to take the Metropolitan, so I follow, you know, Hochelaga, Notre Dame." Ashley didn't know, but she was aware these major streets stretched eastward practically forever, transforming in character with the miles.

"I was on that industrial stretch, not by the refineries, before that. There was no one around although it wasn't dark yet. I was hit from behind. I didn't see the vehicle coming. A big SUV, darkened windows, just like in France. But I don't know if it was the same make, so don't ask me. After I was bumped, the SUV pulled back, and then came alongside me and sideswiped me." Mirabel's face lost colour as she revisited the details.

"I went off the road. I missed a pole by inches, and went into a waste area, with nothing in it, just garbage and old snow. I ended up hitting a chain link fence. It was half falling down and I think that's what saved me. I kind of bounced into it. When I got out of the car, the SUV was gone. There was no traffic but then, of all things, I was able to wave down a tow truck. That was lucky, wasn't it, Ashley? He couldn't take my car, but he was able to call another truck, so the car was towed and I even got a lift."

"Did you call the police?"

"No, she didn't." Charles looked irate. "But I have a highly-placed friend in the Montreal Police Force and I intend to call him tomorrow, I promise you."

"He was gone, Ashley, what was the use? Also"—Mirabel's gaze wavered—"I'd left my wallet at home so there would have been that ..."

"Can I see the car?"

Mirabel looked startled. "If you want to. It's at a garage. It's got some damage, I don't know how much. The tow truck driver said those Fiats are sturdy, so it might just be body damage." She scribbled down the location, while Charles muttered that he'd personally lock Mirabel up unless she promised to stay indoors from now on. Always the *mot juste*.

Ashley sorted her thoughts for a moment. "It wouldn't hurt to call your police friend tomorrow, Monsieur Saint Cyr," she said. "But the police won't investigate this. It's too minor and Mirabel has no leads. I'd like to take a look at the Fiat myself." She didn't say why. "More immediately"—she gestured towards Mirabel, ashen on the couch—"I'd suggest a doctor have a look at your wife. She's had a bad shock." She restrained herself from adding: *If you have a highly-placed friend in the medical field.* She pulled on her coat. "I'll call you after I visit the garage."

The garage was inconveniently out in Anjou but she went there right away. The place was big, and still open. A young guy was willing to show her the towed Fiat. Under lights, the damage was clear. Ashley examined the car closely. Not that she was an expert, but she wanted to see whether the damage lined up with Mirabel's frankly far-fetched story. To her dismay, it did. The back fender was badly crushed and the denting of the body on the driver side was significant. Ashley took pictures with her phone. It was a cute vehicle and it was sad to see its shiny dark green curves battered in this way.

"Why didn't the air bag deploy?" she asked the youth.

"The driver disabled the air bag."

She wasn't in a position to object to that. "Do you think there's engine or frame damage?"

"Hard to say." He warmed to his specialty. "Obviously we'll check. Could just be external damage. These mid-size Fiats are rugged. Probably to deal with what Italian drivers dish out." He grinned. "I'm Italian, so I can say that. If so, we can have her looking as good as new in a few days." Ashley knew this would cost Mirabel a bundle, and that neither she nor Charles would care.

There was an eeriness to the long drive back through dark unfamiliar streets, with their endless undistinguished apartment buildings, car dealerships and strip malls, strangely interrupted once in a while by a steep-roofed *habitant* house that looked like it had been teleported from a *roman du terroir*.

The drive gave her plenty of time to reflect. In spite of Mirabel's evident shock, Ashley had been deeply suspicious of her story. It was almost ludicrous to think of the events on the foggy A28 at Alençon happening all over again in Montreal. Now that she'd seen the car, however, she would have to take this seriously. The unsettling thought surfaced once again: What if the target had never been Raymond Boissier? But how did that make sense? All she could surmise was that there was some unfinished business in France, and someone thought Mirabel involved.

But what could Mirabel have done? Her fear had been genuine, that much was certain.

***

Deciding she could take a page out of Charles Saint Cyr's book, Ashley called Nicolas Latendresse the following day. After they'd caught up—Ashley set aside for later why she didn't mention Jon Perez to him—they talked about Mirabel's accident.

"You took pictures. That was the right thing to do," he said. "And they should file a police report. Don't expect the police to make it a priority, however. Your client wasn't hurt. In that area, I can tell you from direct experience there's little or no electronic surveillance. There's no evidence she was deliberately hit. *She* might have been the one at fault. No, I know, but they'd think that. With road accidents, police get told all kinds of wild stories."

"You're forgetting France."

"I'm not forgetting France. It just won't have a lot of weight with Montreal *flics*. This isn't exactly an Interpol-level incident. No one was even hurt."

It all made sense to Ashley. "Okay, just checking. How's work?"

"Crazy. All security-related too. And before you jump to conclusions, the crazy part comes from dealing with the feds. I'd take a nice reasonable terrorist over a member of CSIS any day. And you didn't hear me say that."

Ashley laughed. "Makes you wish for the good old days of retrieving stolen designer purses. Or saving innocent orphans."

"Saving orphans anyway," Nico said. "Just like a cop in the movies."

***

"One of my earliest memories, when my parents were still alive, was my mother bringing me and Isabel up here for lunch. I was so excited to have a processed cheese sandwich, because she wouldn't let us eat that kind of thing at home. She had a streak of hippy."

Mirabel poked gently at her rubber cheese sandwich on Wonder bread. "Up here" was the cafeteria at the Saint Joseph's Oratory shrine, where Mirabel had suggested they have lunch. Ashley didn't probe into the exact reason why—more Hitchcockian meditation? —but it worked because Ashley's job that morning had taken her to Queen Mary Road.

After lunch they were going together to Holopherne on the South Shore. Wonder of wonders, Charles, or someone under him, had at last found a job for Mirabel. It was for one day a week, to start. She'd be doing a little of everything: assisting in production, design, sales and public relations. It sounded like something you'd give an intern. Mirabel said it was just to start, and she'd be focusing more on one area later.

Ashley took a bite of her own rubber cheese sandwich. "I came here once with my Gran too, for lunch. The food's good, in a timewarp way. You can ruin a process cheese sandwich if you're not careful." She looked around. "The cafeteria is the same, like it hasn't been renovated since."

Mirabel considered. "Maybe the chairs?"

"All right, the chairs." It was your typical mid-century cafeteria, the colour scheme a sedative blend of soft greens and beiges, with a long wall of windows overlooking a hillside garden. Ashley remembered a vista of budding green trees.

Mirabel was trying her best to act normal, Ashley could see. She'd gotten over the worst of yesterday evening's shock, but she hadn't really recovered, Ashley decided. That new look of strained determination was stronger than ever, a flood gate under pressure.

"I can picture my mother very well from that day," Mirabel said, as if to herself. "When you lose a parent at six, the memories can be hit or miss. She was wearing a turquoise blue *imperméable*, a strong colour—you know what the nineties were like—but with her pale blonde hair it was perfect on her. Angélique Rivière. Isn't that a beautiful name? My mother was beautiful, you know. Everyone thought so."

Ashley said nothing. She was surprised to hear Mirabel talk

about her past. She'd been good at winkling childhood memories out of Ashley but shown little interest in dredging up her own life history.

"Isa remembers more than me, of course," she said. She took a sip from her cardboard cup. "You don't know this, Ash*lee,* but my mother, she once worked for Charles."

That made Ashley sit up. "She did?"

"She was his secretary. They would call it executive assistant now because she had so many responsibilities. Back when he was starting out in the business. He was a very young man and his father had just died and suddenly the whole Holopherne enterprise dropped onto his shoulders. He relied on my mother for a lot at first. That's how I met him later."

Mirabel seemed to take a deliberate pleasure in telling Ashley all this. "First, though, Isa ran into him. I mean, we knew of him, because the people who adopted us had a business relationship with him. Anyway, Isa met him first. That must have been about three years ago, maybe four. And then I did." She smiled enigmatically. "Isa dated him first, something else I'm sure you didn't know. You look surprised."

Ashley stared. "I am. She doesn't strike me as his type."

"Oh, well ... Charles is very intellectual in his way. He was working towards a PhD at the University of Montreal when his father died and he had to abandon it. Also, people change. Take me. When I was younger I was definitely the wilder of the two of us, from what Isa describes of her life. The Duvals, the people who adopted me, were very rich. They sent me to convent schools to control me. They had other children and they thought I was a bad influence. It was one convent school after the other, and then Catholic finishing school in Lausanne. Oh, but I have no complaints!" An empty smile. "Isa's adoptive parents were different. The Jadois. They lived in the country, past Sept-Iles, overlooking the Gulf. Wild country. She had a different life. The Jadois had lots of land. They bred horses—one of them won the Belmont Stakes. They hunted. Their house was full of guns. In some ways, I wish Isa and I had been switched. In some ways, I wish ..." Her voice dropped. "It was Charles, you see ..."

"What do you mean?"

"Oh nothing. Anyway, Isa and I found each other when I was nineteen."

"How?"

"Through Facebook."

Ashley was finding all this fascinating. "Everything you're telling me surprises me." She thought a bit. "Excuse my nosiness, but how come Charles switched from Isabel to you? Did Isabel grow tired of him? Did he grow tired of her?"

Mirabel studied the table demurely. "It's not nosy, I'm telling you freely. Isa and Charles clicked at first. Later, that changed." She was choosing her words carefully. "I stood down when they were going out together, although sometimes I was included, like at social events. When Isa vacated the field, Charles asked me out."

Clear as mud. Either Charles had found the forthright Isabel incompatible or Mirabel had muscled in on her sister. It was also possible that Isabel's interest had waned, but the latter struck Ashley as an exceptionally pragmatic woman and she didn't see her walking away from all that money. Still, as romantic triangles went, this was a murky one. One man, two sisters who *seemed* close, and a mountain of cash: straight out of Esmerelda LaFlamme. Or was it three women? Could the young and suddenly bereaved CEO have found in his beautiful older executive secretary, the solace blah blah etcetera ... Yes, straight out of Esmerelda LaFlamme.

"You shoved your sister to the curb," Ashley stated.

Mirabel didn't seem put out by these words. "When it comes to true love ..."

Ashley's face must have registered scepticism, because Mirabel said with a grave look: "A lot of things can happen over time, Ashley." Ashley thought of Jon Perez, and felt a small chill.

She played an oblique move. "Maybe it's time you stopped thinking about Léandre Bergeron."

Now it was Mirabel's turn to look defensive. "In case my free spirit sister decides to steal Charles back?"

"I wasn't thinking of that. You have a lot of stress in your life. Why add more? Anyway, Léandre seems like the type who plays the field."

"We're just good friends."

The old lie. But Ashley's words had manifestly struck Mirabel in a vulnerable spot and her expression withered. What she said next struck Ashley dumb.

"Sometimes, I'm not sure how I can go on."

There was a strained silence. When Mirabel spoke again, her tone had shifted abruptly. "I'm very well aware that Léandre and the others all think I've bought their friendship, or Charles's money has bought their friendship. We look like friends, we act like friends, but we're not friends, not really. Léandre, he's attracted to me. Most men are. He's willing to go to bed with me. He's a man."

Ashley felt bad. "Are you in love with him?"

Mirabel shrugged. "In a way. But not like Charles," she said.

More of *that*, Ashley thought. You could never get down to the level of Mirabel's feelings with any truth.

This conversation had gone on way too long. "We'll get through this," she said with fake heartiness. "Look at the time. You don't want to be late for your first day on the job. Let's go."

The thing that really gnawed at Ashley was that this whole conversation of theirs, so confidential, so friendly-like, had also been purchased with Saint Cyr money. Whatever Mirabel imagined, there was no "we." And if there were subterranean rivalries between her and Isabel, the sister found a few years ago on the internet, then that would mean Mirabel Saint Cyr was without a single friend in the world.

* * *

Despite Mirabel's new job, and any passing threats from Charles, the hard partying continued. There was a weakness, Ashley now began to see, in the man, at least where Mirabel was concerned. Behind the verbal bullying, the belief that he ruled the relationship, there was a lot of nothing. If Mirabel often did what he wanted her to do, just as often she did whatever she felt like. And if he thought Mirabel neurotic, it might be equally true that she thought of him this way as well. Against all this, their intimacy continued. One of the myriad strange faces of love.

Thug Two, if it had been him, remained elusive. There were no more road incidents. Mirabel's artfully patched up popemobile continued to take her to Montreal's underground hotspots where she met her new friends, and Ashley continued to follow her—a mini convoy of the babysat and the babysitter. She managed to snag one free weekend and she spent it with Jon in Quebec City, but the trip was too rushed for real enjoyment.

Mirabel's fatal fascination—was that the right characterization? —with Léandre Bergeron continued, even intensified. There was a scene of sorts, one night at a bar. It was the strangest place yet among those visited by Ashley. They were somewhere in the heart of the Montreal portlands, where she'd never been before. To get there she'd driven along a wide gravel road in the darkness, between miles of container yards on one side and old brick buildings on the other. The club could have been in an empty grain elevator for all Ashley could tell: The pulsing light made everything bizarre, unrecognizable. It was hard to stick to Mirabel in the noise and crowd.

After the scene, which involved gesticulations and a spilled drink but whose verbal histrionics Ashley, no more than anyone else, could hear, Mirabel's drinking became systematic. Ashley soon realized she couldn't let her get behind the wheel. It was well after midnight before Ashley was able to persuade Mirabel to call it a night. *This isn't a job,* was her silent sentiment as she gathered their things and followed the stumbling Mirabel into the diesel-tinged air. Mirabel, dishevelled although still fetching in her velour jacket and denim mini, looked around for her car.

"Mira, *no,*" Ashley said. "You can't drive home tonight."

Mirabel didn't seem to hear her, and continued to twirl in a vague circle. "Where are we, Ashley?"

A good question. There was a radiance to the southwest indicating the downtown, but here it was so dark you could barely see your surroundings. Old buildings with lots of space between them loomed against the orange sky, and Ashley could see the outlines of an expressway and a bridge. Lonely streetlights illuminated signs: The Mystical Trading Company, for instance, and, directly across from the club, a painted Popeye above an illuminated lobby with someone hunched over a desk.

A cheap motel, here? Were they as near the ships as this? Did sailors actually come here? Or was this also some kind of trendy venue in disguise? Sandwiched between the Mystical Trading Company on the left and a blank wall on the right, it looked like a flophouse, but that didn't mean anything. They'd just been partying in a dilapidated grain elevator.

"I'll drive you," Ashley said. "Where did you park your car? This isn't the best place to leave a vehicle overnight."

Mirabel pointed to the gravel strip in front of Popeye the Sailor Man. "There—it will be fine, there's a desk clerk," she said, with the large confidence of the very drunk.

Ashley knew this was crap, but if they were going to sacrifice one car to this surreal neighbourhood it wouldn't be her Crown Victoria Interceptor.

"Also, it will be easy to remember where I parked it. Right in

front of The Stag House, Rooms by the Week, the Day, the Hour."
If Mirabel hadn't been so drunk, Ashley would have suspected her
of joking.

By the time Ashley delivered the half-asleep Mirabel to Belgrave
Heights and made it back to the Point, dawn was approaching. Still
a few hours to sleep, but it would be a short night. She was surprised to find Jon, who had a key, waiting for her in the flat. Still
awake, or pretending to be. Surprised and appreciative.

"You look all in, Ashley," he said, his warm brown eyes alive
with concern.

"I am." She clung tightly to him, feeling weirdly emotional.

He lifted her chin, frowned. "That job! *Enough* with those
Saint Cyrs."

"Soon," she muttered. "But Saint Kitts awaits us ..."

He smiled. "Tell me what I can do ..."

"Right now?" She slid her hands inside his hoodie.

The night ended up being shorter still.

* * *

Sometimes the body just took over. Her bedside clock said 10:57
when Ashley woke the next morning. Jon had gone, leaving a tender
little note tucked beneath it. She used the last of her special Parisian
beans to make herself coffee. Aram came by and they discussed
cases, and a little of everything else. She found it difficult to hurry
on this sunny morning, as if sleep had reduced the levels of compen-
satory adrenaline in her system.

She was dealing with paperwork when Mirabel called after
lunch. She was staying in today, she said, so she didn't need Ashley
right away. She would send a house staffer to pick up the Fiat, so that
would be taken care of too. But she wanted to know whether Ashley
would be available after dinner to take a drive out to Bout-de-l'Ile.

She had thought about things long and hard and she wanted to have a confrontation—a *reasonable* confrontation—with Léandre at his home. A once and for all discussion. It would, she said—well, she hoped it would—settle things. Would Ashley be able to come with her? Not too early. Charles was having a business dinner at the house and she had to play her part. Ashley repressed a sigh and agreed.

It was dark by the time she rang the doorbell at Belgrave Heights. Mirabel was waiting at the door, her coat open over a stylish dinner dress. Looking tense, she said a little breathlessly that her Fiat was still where she'd left it. Then something about how she'd forgotten to ask Judith—the green-haired girl—to pick it up and now Judith was at a movie. But never fear, she sometimes drove Charles's new Audi and she would drive that.

"We can go together," she said. "Bout-de-l'Ile is far."

As soon as they were off and driving, Charles called. The car had a hands-free device and Ashley got to hear every word of the conjugal *bagarre*. *Why* had Mirabel taken his car? Didn't she remember he needed it this evening? No, Mirabel was sorry, she had temporarily forgotten. Well, he would take her car, where had she left the spare keys? Of course—oh, but her car was still parked outside a club. Couldn't Charles take a cab? Mirabel *knew* how much he hated cabs. Well, could Isabel drive him? That was a ridiculous suggestion. She was *only* trying to help. She could call her sister right away. It was ten minutes from Atwater to Westmount. No, and she should stop making absurd suggestions, and just tell him where the keys were. He'd get another staffer to drop him. Anyway, why hadn't Mirabel asked Madame Stang? Because Madame Stang, she was sure, didn't like her.

Mirabel seemed upset for all of fifteen seconds after she disconnected. "I'll call Isa. He'll still be there fuming by the time she makes it up the mountain."

Isabel picked up right away. She seemed unsurprised to hear

that Mirabel wanted her to give Charles a lift. But she laughed outright at the suggestion. "*Criss,* he has servants enough!" she said, and hung up.

"Well, I tried," Mirabel said. "You know, Ashley, this wouldn't happen if Charles agreed to each of us having more than one car. As for me, I'm happy with the Fiat. Just the right size, four doors, a hatchback, great for kids or pets." Since Mirabel had neither, Ashley didn't know what to make of this comment. Mirabel shook her head. "It's him I'm thinking about. I like to drive the Audi though. It's the biggest and most powerful model on the market."

Ashley examined the elaborate instrument panel, as she stretched her full length in the luxurious tobacco leather seat. She knew little about Audis, but this midnight blue monster of beauty and power was like nothing she'd ever driven in. She could understand its appeal for Mirabel. It fairly leapt under Mirabel's competent handling.

Bout-de-l'Ile. She'd finally see the easternmost tip of the island of Montreal. Was it really as pointy as it looked on a map, as if you could crouch down and dip your hands ceremonially in the north and south shore waters at once? Although Bergeron might live nowhere near the pointy bit.

"You know, I think we'll take the Metropolitan Expressway," Mirabel said dreamily.

Her voice became unreadable.

"Let's open her up, and see what she can do."

18

THE NIGHT IN QUESTION

D IFFERENT NAMES TO the exits, different apartment blocks and dealerships, different malls. But at night the eastern Metropolitan, eight lanes if you counted the service roads, was very like its western counterpart. It was the Audi that elevated the drive into something else. The vehicle was like a moving beast beneath them, devouring the miles with ease, showing only a small part of what it could do. The sodium street lights in their hypnotic succession were like a pathway into a dream.

"Everyone thinks of this as the east end." Mirabel broke the silence as they passed a billboard advertising cheap online spectacles. "But they're *wrong*. The island curves and by now we're driving practically north. Did you know?" She delivered these observations like she was revealing the mystery of the ages.

"Well, enough of that," she said after several exits. "We'll go back to Hochelaga and Notre Dame now. I want to show you where I was hit."

In the darkness, the place was as bleak and semi-deserted as Mirabel's description had conveyed. The malefactor had chosen his location well.

The refineries of Montreal East, which they passed through next, were a half-seen nightmare landscape of tank farms, railyards, vast factory-like sheds and miles of elevated pipeline network, some of which they drove under. There was contaminated wasteland too, since at least one refinery was being decommissioned. "I read somewhere that rare wild flowers are coming back to these open areas." Mirabel gestured. "Although it will be a toxic zone for hundreds of years."

And yet as she looked to the horizon, Ashley could see, far away beyond the railyards and waste areas, orderly streets of small old-fashioned houses. Diminutive and mysterious in the distance, in their setting of glowing street lamps and sheltering trees they were oddly endearing. Places, even if enveloped in the fumes of refineries, where people unknown to her had lived their lives for generations and would continue to do so. Unknown but not hidden, except to those who'd never taken the trouble to go there, to look and see.

"Where did you live when you were a kid?" she asked Mirabel.

"Not Westmount. The Duvals had a small private island on the north shore, and a house in Outremont. I was mostly on that island. Well, I was *mostly* at those convent schools. You?"

"See that dystopian Canadian Tire Christmas village? In a neighbourhood like that, in Waverley. My mother rented a post-war box."

Mirabel peered at the horizon, causing the car to swerve slightly. "Oh, it looks like a real home. That's all you need, a little place that's yours, and with the people who truly know you." Ridiculous, really, how Mirabel could say this and not sound unbearably condescending. No mention of where she lived when her biological parents had been alive, Ashley realized after a moment.

On they drove, and Ashley began to see old-growth trees, an improbable windmill, a mesmerizing blackness that was the river. Bout-de-l'Ile, with its fifties fourplexes and wide silent streets, was like a suburb she might once have visited in a duplicate life. Then more trees, a looming sense of finish—and Mirabel pulled into a playground feebly lit by one streetlamp.

"We can't go farther without a boat," she said. "Let's look at the tip of the island."

The pointy bit at last. "You read my mind." The long drive had made Ashley drowsy, but now she was awake and interested.

The park was small, held a swing set and monkey bars. Prosaic, for a place of myth. They followed a path to a narrow sloping verge —"watch the rocks here"—to where the remains of an orange snow fence lay in shreds. "We're here."

And Ashley could see ... nothing at all. Darkness to her left, darkness to her right, lights twinkling on two distant shores. But she could, at least, hear: the different sounds that two wide rivers made, singing in different registers, as their currents converged—embraced would be too strong a word—in a deep whispering roar.

They went right down to where the water lapped against the sand. Ashley, who wanted the immersion experience, put a hand in each stream.

"Well, we came all this way, let's get the visit to Léandre over with." For someone about to initiate a romantic reckoning, Mirabel sounded surprisingly laid back.

Bergeron's house was an old clapboard two-storey surrounded by shrubbery. The porch light was on and there was no car in the driveway. They rang the doorbell. Ashley already knew no one was home.

"That's funny. He told me he'd be here. He's working to some big deadline." Mirabel sighed. "I was sure ..."

After a while they crossed the road to a grassy area overlooking the dark Saint Lawrence. Out here, the odours of an early spring night were countrified, watery notes mingling with earth smells.

Mirabel thoughtfully pulled out a tube of Mentos as they sat down at a picnic table. "Why would you call fruit candies Mentos?"

"I couldn't say." Trying to see her watch in the dark, Ashley had to suppress a tone.

"What about taking the south shore back?" Mirabel touched

Ashley on her sleeve. Her voice was coaxing. "Would you like to drive the Audi?"

It was a compensation of sorts. And the city skyline across the channel, multi-coloured, dazzling to the eye, was spectacular. On a deserted service road, they got out to admire the panorama. As they were leaning against the Audi's warm flank, Mirabel's phone rang. It was still in speaker mode and Ashley could hear.

A man asked to speak to Madame Saint Cyr.

"*Oui, c'est Madame Saint Cyr, c'est moi.*"

The man identified himself as a Lieutenant Pascal Langlois from the Montreal police. He said: "I'm afraid I have some bad news, Madame Saint Cyr."

Ashley, listening, felt a small vibration in the air, a slight tilting of the world.

"Are you sitting down?" the man said. "I don't want you to be driving."

"I'm not driving, no," Mirabel said, faintly.

"It's about your husband. I'm sorry to tell you that Charles Saint Cyr died this evening. He was shot, in front of a place called The Stag House. We'd like to speak with you as soon as possible, Madame. Where are you now?"

Mirabel just continued to hold the phone in her hand, staring at it, saying nothing. Ashley grabbed it from her.

"My name is Ashley Smeeton, I'm with Madame Saint Cyr. We're on the south shore, just coming into Montreal. I'll drive. Where should we go?"

They arranged to meet at the house in upper Westmount.

"Where is he? Where is Charles?" Mirabel leaned over Ashley to speak.

Either Langlois didn't hear or didn't choose to say the word "morgue." "Belgrave Heights, we wait for you there. *Madame Saint Cyr, mes condoléances.*"

It took a little fiddling with awkward fingers before Ashley found the off button. When she turned to hand the phone back, the sight of Mirabel, silently sliding down against the car to crouch on the ground, struck her with fear.

"Get up, Mirabel, we have to go," Ashley said, taking her arm. She was using her most encouraging voice, but it sounded false, alien.

Mirabel looked up at her, her face parchment-coloured under the streetlight, her eyes concealed in a bar of deep shadow. She didn't take the phone. "Call Isa for me, Ashley, I have to have Isa," she said. "Tell her to meet me at Belgrave Heights." Then, to herself: "That was meant for me. Don't they see? That was meant for me."

* * *

Ashley was wanted for questioning, and stayed for hours at the house in Westmount. Most of the time she sat around, watching police come and go and the staff flit about hollow-eyed, first in dressing gowns, then in hastily pulled on clothes after the realization hit they weren't going to bed. Isabel arrived in a cloud of alarm and big-sister aggression, wearing camouflage pants and a "Nous vaincrons" T-shirt. If she'd hoped to annoy les flics, it didn't seem to work.

Mirabel's questioning took a while, and then Ashley had to corroborate many aspects of her statement. Their improbable adventures in Paris had to come out and did—how glad Ashley was that she'd gone to the police there before she left—and there was considerable interest in Mirabel's contention that she'd been followed and driven off the road. Langlois, a squarely-built individual with a calculating gaze, seemed equally divided between curiosity and scepticism, but Ashley knew they'd follow up, including with the French police. Charles Saint Cyr was a Quebec aristocrat, and no stone would be left unturned. They were also interested in the pop-up nightclub in the granaryesque structure, almost as much as in The Stag House across the way.

Ashley was finally allowed to go home, with the promise that she would remain available for further questioning. On the front steps she ran into Isabel having a lonely smoke.

"How's Mirabel holding up?" Ashley asked, for something to say.

Isabel looked almost as stunned as Mirabel. But if her eyes were haggard, suddenly old, her chin was resolute. "I'm sticking with her through all this. She'll need a lawyer. Not the Saint Cyr family lawyer either. I'm taking care of her."

An answer but not an answer. "Mirabel seems convinced the bullets were meant for her." Charles had been shot twice, once through the head. He would have died within minutes. There'd been an alley running alongside The Stag House. Ashley pictured it, a perfect possible escape route. Apparently Léandre's club had once again moved on, and the area would have been empty, with scant visibility.

Isabel nodded, exhaled smoke. "You know he needed the Fiat for the evening since Mirabel had taken the Audi." A bleak little smile. "He got the housekeeper to drop him off, and she left. He was alongside the driver's side of the car when he was shot. It's possible the shooter didn't see more than a dark outline. He was found on the ground by a drunken sailor."

"A what?"

"Like the song. Sorry, I should have said an inebriated guest of the establishment."

"Do the police have any ideas?"

"None they shared with me. They're going to put Mirabel through the wringer, I can already tell. My sister inherits everything, all the private assets, plus there's an interest in the company. Did you know?" Ashley said nothing.

"She's terrified, of course. She's as scared as she was when our parents died. She's more scared than shocked, and more shocked than sad. But don't think she's not grieving." Ashley had caught glimpses of Mirabel from time to time in the house, sometimes with the police, sometimes shepherded by the green-haired girl. She'd even managed to exchange a few words with her, although the police were keeping people apart. She thought Isabel's words summarized well the expressions she'd seen on Mirabel's colourless face.

"She and Charles always had an interesting relationship. I prefer my relationships a whole lot simpler, if you know what I mean."

Thinking of Jon, Ashley said: "I know what you mean."

"Because she thinks Charles was just in the wrong place at the wrong time, she feels guilty too."

"What do you think?"

"What do I think? I should ask what you think." Isabel's voice held a challenge. "You're the one who's shared some of those weird adventures with her. Also you're a pro. Tell me what *you* think."

Ashley could only shake her head. "It could be something leftover from France. But it could be unconnected. Something to do with Holopherne? Or a random attack. Was his wallet taken?"

"Like a mugging, you mean? A mugging gone wrong? Or a mugging gone right. Could it be that simple? Mirabel doesn't seem to think so, but who knows."

"Well ... let me know if there's anything I can do," Ashley said, feeling inadequate.

"Mirabel asked me to ask you—Charles probably owes you money still? Just tell us how much." Isabel's tone was final. "We'll see that you're paid." As she descended the steps, Ashley realized she'd just been dismissed.

At home, she was unable to sleep. Her mind was raising hell while her body felt like lead, aching in every muscle. She hadn't especially liked Charles Saint Cyr, but his death was a shock. Where, she wondered wearily, would this latest chapter in the endless Saint Cyr melodrama take her? Whatever people thought about PI work, close encounters with suspicious death weren't for her a common occurrence.

Although it was after four am, she called Jon. He didn't pick up and Ashley supposed his phone was turned off. She made herself a rye and ginger ale, with the intention of knocking herself out. There was an almost full bottle of Caribou Crossing in the house, brought over by Jon.

As she sipped she thought about her passionate swain. This bottle represented the new Jon Perez, his taste in whisky complementing his taste in suits, in all the good things in life. And then, a thought she hadn't meant to entertain intruded: how his work, importing and exporting "luxury lifestyle goods," to use his words, took him so often to the airport—he said the airport—at random hours. Under the influence of three fingers, she faced up to the fact that she had little idea what Jon did for a living. And, as the whisky continued to excavate, she resolved that she would, one of these days, find out.

* * *

Ashley ended up telling the whole story to Aram the next day. It was already in the news, a short and cryptic version, but with a big glossy picture of Saint Cyr looking his richest and a few of lovely Mirabel trying to avoid the camera. Aram was a sympathetic and intelligent listener.

"I'm worried about Mirabel," Ashley said. "She has an alibi, so not that, but how she's going to handle it all. And in case she's still in danger."

"You could do a little investigating on your own," Aram suggested.

"My contract is over."

Which was odd, considering Mirabel should want to get to the bottom of things even more now. She and Isabel must think the police were finally taking her seriously.

"Well, if there's anything I can do."

Ashley had good reason to be worried about Mirabel, after all.

She and Jon were working their way through an extra cheese thin-crust at a pizza parlour near his place, an underfurnished bachelor off Decarie where he never cooked, when she fielded a call from Isabel. About the last person she expected to hear from again, so soon. She took the call out on the sidewalk.

Isabel sounded worked up. "Sorry to bug you, but something's happened and I'm freaking out. The police have been talking to witnesses, well, a witness, and this guy, the night clerk at The Stag House, says he rented a room to a woman answering Mirabel's description on the night Charles was shot."

"What? That's not even possible. When you say night, what do you mean?"

"A little before the time of the shooting."

"But that's just—malicious."

"That's what I was thinking! They had those pictures of her everywhere on social media and I think the clerk just wanted the attention."

Ashley thought. "She was at a business dinner until I picked her up. I spent hours with her afterwards, until the police called. I presume there are lots of Charles's associates who can vouch for her, and then I can vouch for her for the rest of the time. The police can't be taking this seriously."

"They're taking everything seriously. That business dinner was only three other guys, from a rival company. What if there was some business conspiracy, like a hostile takeover, and say Mirabel was in league with one of them."

"Mirabel and I were driving east when she had that conversation with Charles about you taking him to the Fiat. After which she called you ..."

"Oh, right, that."

"Besides, what you just described sounds farfetched."

Isabel laughed. "All right! But I know nothing about big business. I teach lit. Spelling and grammar, but I call it lit."

"Mirabel will be all right. She's covered." Ashley hoped she didn't sound dismissive. Her pizza would be getting cold.

"I hope so. But they're going to fingerprint her. *Mirabel,* yes! This woman the clerk said he saw, he was so sure. He gave her a room at the end, where there's an exit onto the alley. She paid cash, and then he says he never saw her again. Mirabel told me all this"—a sucking noise as Isabel inhaled—"from what the police told her. Housekeeping doesn't seem to be a big priority at The Stag House and there was a treasure trove of trace evidence. Best not to think about *that* too much. But lots of fingerprints, and they're going to fingerprint my sister."

"That's … thorough."

"Tell me we'll be okay."

"The police will find no fingerprint match. They'll probably go over the times again with me, and then that will be that."

Ashley's pizza was cold by the time she rejoined Jon. He insisted on ordering her a fresh one. A delightful proof of love, but when it came she found her appetite had lost its edge. The Stag House clerk must be one of those ever more common weirdoes who would do anything for attention. Otherwise the story was just too bizarre. For a stray moment Ashley asked herself: *What if the clerk was misremembering the time? What if Mirabel had previously taken the room?* Why, though? Sex with Léandre? She wasn't sure how long his club had been in that location, or what they might have done under the influence of who knew what. Unlikely, however—she hoped.

* * *

The following morning, a Saturday, the sun shone in a bright blue sky. It was this sky that people remembered, afterwards. This sky, as Montrealers heard the news on their car radios, or looked to the northeast and saw in the distance the tower of black smoke staining the horizon.

The kind of explosive device used would take some investigation, but its blast force and incendiary capability had left no doubt. The blast site, the Cottage Grove Mall's busiest entrance, had been chosen for impact. The death toll mounted as the day wore on. By the time the fire was under control, the casualties were being reported as thirty-eight injured, several of these critically, and twenty-four dead. There'd been some kind of live show for children in the mall's main atrium, and, of the total dead, eleven were children under the age of twelve. People couldn't even admit to themselves that the deaths of a pet shop full of animals, where a well-attended cat adopt-a-thon had been in full swing, was the absolute and final straw.

All day the bombing was what Montrealers thought about, and talked about. The casualty numbers, of course, and all the other questions: who, how, why. That evening, the police announced there was a credible claim of accountability, by an underground faction with links to Serbian arms dealers and Middle Eastern militias. Most disturbing, had people known it, was the emerging police theory that the bombing had been ingeniously devised by a home-grown Quebec coalition intent on expanding black market interests at the expense of business rivals. Money had been at least as important as hate. Meanwhile, politicians rushed to comfort the population by vowing hard-line justice against the usual visible targets, the ones known to all through Twitter and tabloid columnists.

As for why the target was the Cottage Grove Mall, a busy shopping centre in the northeast of the city, the likely reasons were simple: It was handily near the 40 east, and on a Saturday morning in April it was full of people.

While the politicians inflated their sound bites with lofty outrage, federal, provincial and city police dropped everything to focus on the massive investigation. Fire and paramedic services soul-searched every aspect of their response. And the city's forensic mortuary resources were stretched to absolute capacity. All eyes turned towards the aftermath. All hands were needed.

"It still hasn't really sunk in," Aram said to Ashley a day later, speaking the thoughts of a few million Montrealers. "Montreal has always felt so safe. First you say to yourself: 'It can't be real, nothing this dramatic would even happen here.' And then when you get over that you start to wonder about everything."

"Everything?"

"Like how you could have missed the signs. And how many more you're missing right now, through ignorance. It's hard to explain. It's like you lose faith. And confidence."

This was a little abstract for Ashley. "It's true that lots of us aren't going to feel safe for a while."

"You say to yourself: 'Anything can happen.' But instead of this being an optimistic thought, it's the opposite. The world is inherently unpredictable and we face a chaotic future, whether we realize it or not."

"Aram—geez, will you stop it! Also, if you feel powerless go and donate blood."

"As it happens, I already did." He smiled at Ashley. "Keeping busy's a good idea too. Er—did you have any more work for me? I feel I'm getting awfully good at sussing out cheating partners."

"Soon, probably, yes. If you shut up about the chaotic universe, I'll even think about hiring you permanently."

* * *

Ashley didn't hear from either Mirabel or Isabel for a while. Then Mirabel telephoned to give her the latest. The investigation of Charles's death was slowly progressing, subject to the bombing aftermath, the new priorities. She'd passed her fingerprint test with flying colours—that was how she actually put it. Other than that, there was little to report. There was no sign of either the weapon or the mystery woman. The police, she said, were increasingly sceptical of the motel clerk's account. Apparently the guy whiled away the wretched hours of his job with a hip flask and a bag of weed.

"Did they do a line-up?"

"They said something about it, but nothing happened so they must have changed their minds. They think he probably just saw a dressed-up blonde wearing makeup, and his mind made the leap to those pictures of me on the internet. Lots of, um, ladies of the evening check in and out of The Stag House. I'm not sure how I feel about being mistaken for a lady of the evening."

"There isn't a woman in this city who hasn't been taken for a lady of the evening, I'm guessing. Men, you know."

Mirabel laughed faintly. She was, Ashley realized, sounding better. Better than the night in question, anyway. They moved on from the murder: talked of Mirabel's efforts to come to grips with assets and effects, agreed that the city didn't feel the same in the aftermath of Cottage Grove. Mirabel said she was seriously thinking of leaving Montreal, and so was Isabel.

Ashley got out the Whippets while she thought about their conversation. Mirabel hadn't mentioned being followed. Ashley assumed this was because she hadn't been. Had the following finally stopped? Was a dead husband part of the reason? Although how? Also, why did Mirabel and Isabel really want to leave Montreal? The big fat mystery of it all blocked Ashley's thinking at every turn, no matter how many Whippets she ate.

Work in its more mundane aspects began once again to fill Ashley's days. But even the daily grind wasn't the same, with Jon in the picture. Roy came into the city, this time without Lilou, and he and Ashley, with Jon, Antoinette and Aram, along with the elusive Rachel, had a cathartic night on the town. Aram and Antoinette were funny, Jon deployed his charm, and the others fell in with the mood.

For Ashley, in a world that held Jon, there was a rich and ever-present luminosity in ordinary things. A remote and theoretical part of her brain informed her that it was regrettable and possibly even hateful that a man could make so much difference to the way a woman felt about her life. But on another level, where love songs on the radio had hitherto unimagined depths and emotion was all, she simply lived her new life.

Time enough to ask him about his job.

* * *

One chilly grey afternoon, Ashley was in what she believed was the neighbourhood, and felt the impulse to pay a daylight visit to the scene of Saint Cyr's shooting. It took some finding, as The Stag House popped up on Google Maps as The Love Shack. But then she was able to find a listing for the "corporate head office" of the Mystical Trading Company, and after a drive through increasingly seedy streets, she came upon the place at last. Despite the buildings which were occupied after a fashion, and the rumble of traffic from the expressway, she felt she was in a kind of lunar badland. Which didn't at all go with the area's hundred-year-old name, Chickentown. The legendary community of squatters and their scrap-built cottages had long ago disappeared, she learned from Wikipedia. The granary where she'd attended the pop-up rave clearly wasn't one, but its actual former purpose was far from clear. The other buildings, of age-stained brick, were more ordinary. Tall dead weeds in the vacant lots and unpaved streets added a rural touch, and somehow conjured the small vanished homesteads of Chickentown. It was a place that had once been something, was on its way, although in no hurry whatsoever, to becoming something else, and was for now a mysterious third place in between. It held a certain appeal for Ashley.

The Stag House was as lively as Chickentown got. Ashley could see another clerk, a woman, through the glass, and there were three or four cars parked outside. The lighting in the lobby consisted of fluorescent strips, detracting from atmosphere but making it up in visibility. The night clerk would have gotten a good look at Mirabel's alleged double.

Ashley wandered to the mouth of the alley that ran alongside. A side door with a red exit sign opened conveniently here. The alley didn't look too forbidding and she followed it to the end. A narrow path revealed itself between two other buildings. She followed this path and came out onto a street one block over, just as lunar, and with direct access to the expressway service road. A perfect escape route.

With preoccupied thoughts, Ashley made her way back to her car. She almost missed the movement in the gloom, a stirring in a pile of rubble. She had to look twice before she saw it again, as well as the gleam of eyes. A rat, a big one! She stepped back in a hurry. But no, not a rat. Cautiously, she crouched down. She was able to make out a tiny triangular face, with crusted eyes beneath big ears. A cat. A kitten, maybe a couple of months old, filthy from what she could see. Old enough to be on its own, but not old enough to survive for long.

It was an axiom of Chantale Barry's that you never moved through the city without a pocket full of various scraps, nuts and seeds. Because you never knew when you would be called upon. Ashley didn't subscribe to this admirable code of living, but the thought came to her nevertheless that she had a deli bag on the passenger seat containing a half-eaten chicken sandwich and a carton of milk. Why her mind followed this path would be anybody's guess; perhaps it had to do with the memory of the dead cats at the Cottage Grove pet shop. Now if she could just grab hold of the little bastard.

This proved to be heartbreakingly easy. The kitten wasn't going anywhere, it was well past the stage of putting up a struggle. Ashley undid her pashmina and swaddled it. She made her way back to the car, uttering what she hoped were soothing sounds. In the car she fed it with scraps of chicken and gave it milk from a makeshift saucer fashioned from the bottom of the carton.

She watched it try to chew shreds of chicken with its tiny teeth. What the hell was she going to do with it? Chantale. She put in a call. Chantale picked up, said it was Ashley's lucky day because there happened to be no strays at her place just now—she was thinking of contagion—and Ashley should bring the little thing over. Ashley floored the gas and was there in no time.

In Chantale's cluttered kitchen, on an Arborite table covered with the remains of lunch and a little of everything else, Chantale unwrapped the bundle. With the finesse of a pro she looked over the kitten. A male, orange stripes dingy beneath the dirt. Three months old, give or take. Thin and hungry, but his condition could be worse. Someone had once taken good care of the little guy.

"Someone?"

"His mother. Ashley, he's not in terrible shape. Eye drops, his shots right away, lots of good food, he'd probably be okay. His biggest problem is he's undernourished." She put a scoop of wet catfood in a saucer and the kitten practically dived in.

Chantale looked at Ashley: a new Chantale, authoritative, appraising. "I can get him cleaned up, de-wormed, de-flead and get him his shots for almost nothing, because I have connections. But the question is what *you* want. Do you want a kitten? Do you want to take care of him?"

Ashley opened and shut her mouth. "I don't know."

Chantale stroked the small head. "If you're not sure, you could look after him for now, until you find a permanent home. You could foster him."

Ashley liked the sound of that word. Responsible, yet without strings. "Okay, sure, I do work from home often enough. I could foster him."

The kitten had climbed into the saucer and Ashley gently rearranged him in front of his food. Her hands, as she picked him up, experienced the lightness of the tiny body as a tactile shock that travelled through her core. He looked up at her and let out a piercing squeak, his first sound.

"He thinks you're his mother already. You fed him, so why not?"

Ashley was too busy doting on his fluffy stump of a tail and missed the shrewd gleam of accomplishment in Chantale's eye.

19

THE CHILDREN OF LUCIFER

IT WAS MIRABEL Saint Cyr on the phone. "Ashley, I would like to take you to lunch, to thank you for all your help, all you've done for me."

All she'd done? Ashley couldn't put a finger on what that was.

It was a brilliantly sunny day, although still very cool. Light streamed in through the windows of Café Dido, half way up the mountainside. Their table was well back from and facing the windows. It was a little like looking out of the wide mouth of a cave, at the vague glittering panorama of sky and river.

Mirabel, dressed in black, which might or might not have been mourning, looked much better than the last time Ashley had seen her. The night of Charles's murder, so hardly surprising. Her mood was different too, although Ashley was at pains to characterize it. Mirabel said she was getting used to life on her own, although it would be a long road. She spoke without constraint about the police investigation, its progress or lack thereof. They were, she said, assuring her that in the chaotic politics of post-Cottage Grove they were still working her husband's case. "It's nice of them to say it, I suppose."

She suspected they believed she'd made up the whole being followed thing, although they didn't come right out and say so.

276

"Langlois says things like: 'Madame, your experiences in Paris were difficult, and no doubt they've left their mark.' I don't really like him, do you?"

"A cop's cop, I guess."

"I know they're not neglecting the case. I asked him about a police line-up, just so we could deal with the hotel clerk's identification, but he said there were so many pictures of me in the public realm now it would affect the results and wouldn't be worth it." Mirabel looked faintly amused. "I was almost looking forward to being in a line-up. It would have been something to talk about at business dinners." Her brow clouded. "What business dinners? That was silly."

As well as gathering fingerprints, she said, the police had done DNA swabs. "Not of my DNA, although that would have been interesting too. I've been excluded with my fingerprints. Hotel room DNA trace evidence, so they'll have it in their databank. They think it was a random shooting, or a case of mistaken identity—or something to do with Holopherne. Especially that one, I think. Who knew the clothing trade was so cutthroat? Well, we did, after Paris." She shovelled a piece of rare steak into her mouth and chewed daintily.

"What will you do now?" Ashley asked.

"Sell the Westmount house. I was never happy there. Isabel and I are going to look for somewhere outside the city to live. Her teaching contract isn't being renewed, so we might as well. I'm going to divest myself of everything to do with Holopherne, I'm done with the company. *We're* done with the company. I told you, didn't I, my mother worked there, before she died? We Rivières have been involved with Holopherne for a long time ... too long. But that chapter is over."

"Sorry, ah—Rivières?"

"My real name, remember, Ashley? Before I was a Duval. Or a Saint Cyr."

"Oh, right." Ashley was finding this conversation as unexpected as Mirabel's mood. Well, not really the conversation, but something in Mirabel's tone.

"On the plus side"—a faint smile—"I'm very rich." She hesitated. "Ash*lee*—could I give ... I feel you deserve a bonus. Could I give you a bonus?"

"God no!" Having just received the last bloated Saint Cyr payment, Ashley felt the idea practically bordered on offensive.

Mirabel looked crestfallen. "No, of course not. That wasn't a good idea. It's not you at all."

"Loads of business on the go, no need for that," Ashley said, to make light of it. "I've never been busier, what with work and social life."

Mirabel lifted a brow. "You're hinting at something, aren't you?"

Ashley realized she was. "I'm seeing someone. I mean not just dating but going steady, if anyone says that anymore." It felt good to share this, she'd told so few people. "Someone I met at your big party, although I knew him from before. A guy called Jon, Jon Perez? You might not know all the guests ...?"

Across the table from her, Mirabel showed absolutely no reaction. As the moment stretched, it got weird.

"Jon Perez?"

Ashley's skin prickled. "Yes. Do you know him?"

"No, I don't, at least I didn't. Is he ... from Colombia?"

"Yes."

Slowly, slowly, Ashley felt herself detaching from the conversation.

The look on Mirabel's face was both conscious and very serious now. She seemed to search for words. When she found them, she had to drag them out of herself. "It's just that Jon Perez ... well, if it's the same Jon Perez, and it must be ... Ashley, I'm pretty sure, no, I *know,* my sister's got a thing going with Jon Perez, the Jon

Perez from the party. A physical thing." Her eyes were overbright, as she watched Ashley. "Isa asked you if you and he were together —and you told her you were just friends?"

Ashley waited for the world to recalibrate before she replied. This took a little while. Or it might have taken only seconds, but they felt like an eternity.

"I think I did tell Isabel that, because I thought she was being nosy. When you say a thing ..."

"With Isa it's just a friend with benefits situation, that's all!" Mirabel rushed to say, her face falling immediately as she realized how awful the words sounded. Not better, worse. "If she'd known, Ashley, I don't think ..."

"I get it."

"You know my sister. She's a free spirit, she ..."

"I know your sister."

It was, apparently, Jon Perez she didn't know.

But when Ashley was driving home, listening to Simon and Garfunkel on the radio warbling "hello darkness, my old friend," she felt in her bones the familiarity of the news, and couldn't honestly says she was surprised. She'd seen the mask beneath the mask. Known Jon Perez, and known this.

* * *

A few hours later, as she sat at her desk pretending to work and wondering about the dead weight of loss on the human body, she got a call from Antoinette Francis. It was to tell her that her grandmother—their grandmother, Odette Francis—had died quietly the day before.

The funeral would be in two days. Eric and she both hoped Ashley could come. Also, er, was Ashley driving to Fabienville, and if so could Antoinette snag a ride? Soon after, her mother telephoned her as well with the news. And then Roy.

Before that news, though, she'd had a brief phone conversation with Jon. She wouldn't have called him, except that she'd thought about Mirabel's friends with benefits comment, and had begun to imagine that she might have overreacted to the revelation. Begun to hope. Hope being such a strange substance, with the power to creep back, like gas through the cracks, after you thought you'd buried it in a deep pit and stomped on its grave.

The conversation hadn't gone well. When he'd suggested they meet for coffee so he could "explain," she agreed, just to stand him up. The petty revenge of the dumped.

The thing that Ashley always remembered afterwards, about that April day on Paris Street, was how bright the sun was, how coldly blue the sky. And then, when Chantale came over later with the kitten to effect its formal transfer to Ashley's foster care, how Ashley's whole soul cravenly revolted against taking on the particular task, this one small task like the countless others her neighbour took upon herself every day.

Chantale, her unfortunate purple leggings showing too much hipbone and a cigarette dangling from her lips, dumped on the kitchen floor a blue Ikea bag filled with miscellaneous cat equipment. She said she hoped Ashley would it find useful. "Here are his vet's papers and some instructions. But come by anytime or just call. There's enough kitten chow in the bag for a week. He looks better, doesn't he?"

The kitten—a committee of children had chosen the name Hubert, Huey for short—looked as rat-like as ever, but cleaner, fluffier and with a distended stomach. He looked as if he'd been overeating steadily and his skin could barely keep up with him.

Ashley wanted to say: *I don't want to look after this kitten. Any kitten.* Instead, she said: "You do a great job, Chantale."

Chantale shrugged. "I can't resist strays."

"I mean, in general."

Chantale seemed surprised, and then beamed. "How's the

background check? I wanted to ask. Because you know, Jacques is being a problem."

Oh that. "Michel, you mean?"

"Well yes, but Marie Ambre's dad is being the problem. I'm sure he's up to something." A bleakness stole over her features.

"A couple more days. Sorry for the delay."

Chantale sat back, waved an unlit cigarette. "Did I leave my ashtray here?"

Humbly, Ashley put the kettle on.

***

The way things fell out on the day of the funeral, Ashley and Antoinette found themselves on a rackety old train together.

There'd been wet snow and freezing rain overnight in the Eastern Townships, and one of those thirty-car pileups on the main highway had made that route impassable. They'd debated taking back roads. But if the autoroute was a disaster scene, the back roads would be worse. Casting around for an alternative, Antoinette saw that a train was leaving Central Station in forty minutes. It was a milk run, and it would stop in Waverley. Ashley's mother could collect them and take them to the Fabienville church on time.

"Take me to the church on time. That's a love song, isn't it?" Antoinette said.

Ashley, staring out the window at the passing countryside, a study in slush and earth tones, didn't want to know. She still listened to love songs on the radio, noticing now that many of them, about broken hearts and such, were deep in another way. She'd also had time to observe that dull endurance was just that, and didn't make you feel better.

Antoinette seemed moderately down about Odette's death, in part because she knew how much her father was feeling it, she said. She'd been closest to her maternal grandmother, she confessed. It was just the way things fell out sometimes. She fussed with her lipstick, asking Ashley whether it was too bright for a funeral.

In a black coat and some discreet beaded jewellery she told Ashley she'd made herself, she looked charming, dignified and clear-eyed. Reading her demeanour, Ashley thought her cousin had recovered from her romantic setback of the night of Madge Stewart's party. The prof, anyway, had either come to heel or been effectively banished. Some other day, Ashley decided, she'd ask Antoinette for tips.

The funeral was to be in Fabienville's big old Catholic basilica, because the little church on the reserve was too small for the expected attendance. When Ashley walked into the church she was taken aback. It was packed, a scene of spectacle and glittering candlelight. Soaring organ riffs indicated the funeral mass was about to begin.

People still hoping to be seated were being held back by ushers. Antoinette presented herself to one of them and he motioned her through. At the last minute, she turned to Ashley and beckoned her forward. Ashley shook her head, but Marlene, right behind her, gave her a push. Thus Ashley found herself walking side by side with Antoinette to the reserved pews at the front of the church, an interminable yet somehow ceremonious procession up the central aisle, watched on both sides by the crowd. Everyone scrunched over a little to let Ashley fit in beside her cousin. Eric came out of the pew ahead of them to shake Ashley's hand gravely. Ashley recognized in front of her Madge Stewart, who nodded a greeting.

The funeral was formal, and very long. There was a high mass, with scads of priests and small attendants, and four speakers in addition to the eulogist. The tapers smoked, the organ intoned, incense hovered like a cloud. Communion alone must have taken twenty minutes. Odette had been an important person in her community. An elder. Ashley hadn't fully realized what that meant. At one point Antoinette whispered to her that she'd never really figured out whether Odette was a wholehearted Catholic, or even a remote-ly orthodox one. But Mémé would have liked a send-off like this just the same, Antoinette was sure.

Most people were heading back after the funeral to the community centre on the reserve, and Ashley said goodbye on the steps of the church. Antoinette hugged her tight, after a brief hesitation Eric gave her a modest hug too, and then a few people from the reserve, to whom she'd been quickly introduced and who may or may not have been Abenaki relatives, gave her hugs as well. In Marlene's car on the highway, Ashley continued to feel the ghostly pressure of these arms around her.

She was in the front seat beside her mother. Much to her surprise, Roy and Lucie, with Lilou between them, were in the back. Marlene had invited them all to a late lunch at her house. There was something about someone's car being out of commission that required a deeper understanding of the current Roy-Lucie situation for Ashley fully to decode. It wasn't until after lunch that she was able to corner Roy and get the goods.

"Are you and Lucie back together?" she asked. It had seemed like it during the meal.

"Oh, well, yes. It seemed like the best thing. We—I—have a lot of work to do." He said this like he was intoning the Possum Lodge Man's Prayer: *I'm a man, but I can change, if I have to—I guess.* He cleared his throat. "Under the circumstances." He looked happy, but was not without a hangdog air.

"Circumstances? What do you mean?"

Roy's expression grew more hangdog. "I might as well tell you, because you'll find out. Lucie ... she's, uh, expecting."

Ashley stared, and Roy helpfully added: "Pregnant."

"Yes, I know what expecting means. Jesus, Roy. That's big news. Is it yours?"

"Ashley! That's an awful thing to say!"

"Well?"

"I'm sure it's mine."

"You were living apart, and yet you were—"

"Will you stop it, Ash? We never stopped being friends. Apart from anything else, there was always Lilou. Plus I think Lucie found full-time work and single mothering hard. But, I mean, we also never stopped, you know ..."

Ashley's big sister stare finally resolved itself into a weary smile. "Yes, I do know." She hugged Roy. "I guess I should say congratulations. Does Ma know?"

"Yes."

"Huh. When were you planning on telling me?"

Roy looked apologetic. "Soon. It's just that you seemed so busy and happy with Jon Perez and my love life is so inept. I thought you might laugh. Which you should really—laugh. Anyway, I don't care. I've got them back. I don't care *how* I got them back. And we're having another kid. You'll be an auntie again."

They were on the back porch together, looking out at the sleeping wet garden. Ashley had taken Roy's arm, now she let go. "Jon Perez. Well, there's a story there."

When she'd finished telling it, Roy just said: "Can I now admit that I always hated his guts?"

* * *

Michel Desrosiers was in the backyard affixing new super-duper windshield wipers to Ashley's Crown Victoria.

"Why pay for that, Michel can do it," Chantale had enthusiastically volunteered.

It was the first of May, and, while all the buds on the trees were still closed tight, one optimistic dandelion was blooming in a crack in the asphalt.

Michel had many skills, Chantale confided to Ashley. He was also, the reference check had revealed, a largely blameless individual.

He'd spent his adult life performing underpaid tasks around cars, with brief intervals of unemployment. But they'd been brief. He'd dropped out of school at sixteen. There might have been a learning disability in the picture but his rural school hadn't risen to it. He'd looked after a widowed mother in that same small town until she died of cancer, by which time he was middle-aged. He was well-liked at the oil change place. When he was a boy he used to repair the local kids' bicycles for twenty-five cents. After a while he'd upped his price to fifty cents. When he stole some copper wire from a local recycling yard at the age of seventeen, this was brought forward by more than one character witness at his trial, to show that, whatever he'd done and whatever he was, Michel Desrosiers wasn't greedy.

It made you philosophical, Ashley had to admit. As any good detective knows, appearances can be deceiving. Where Jon Perez was concerned, she'd airbrushed out what she hadn't wanted to see, and then filled in the spaces with paint-by-number illusion. Whereas with Michel Desrosiers, it seemed to be a case of the opposite. He was what few people, and no gem traders, recognized: a diamond in the rough.

Ashley had to demonstrate the new windshield wipers to a small admiring crowd. Then someone asked how Huey was keeping, and she couldn't prevent everyone from trooping indoors, or eating her Whippet Brownie Sticks, some hinting they were better than those globulous marshmallow things, while she made tea, feeling like a spectator.

* * *

Still Ashley's treacherous heart whispered, mourned.

When she met Nicolas Latendresse for a beer one evening, she was glad she'd never told him at least about Jon Perez. Nico was looking exhausted. He said he was involved in the Cottage Grove investigation, and it was relentless. Yes, the international arms trade and its rivalries was involved, and that was all he was saying. Ashley hadn't asked for more. Shocking, perhaps, but the Cottage Grove bombing hardly resonated for her any more.

"You look tired yourself," he commented, giving her one of his long stares.

She nodded, said something about cases, poured them more beer, and reflected to herself that sadness must sit on the human face like tiredness.

"Mad doesn't want any of that costume party stuff back in the house, so don't tell her I'm asking, but I'd really like my fedora back. I can do without the rest, but that fedora, it's important to me."

"Men and their hats. Okay, I'll bring it around."

Which meant she'd have to pay Madge Stewart a visit, because she'd left it there by mistake on the night of the party, along with a couple of other things according to Madge. Ashley had been putting off collecting them. The party in Cité Jardin had been on the fateful weekend when Jon Perez had come back into her life, and she shied away from anything that reminded her of that. Best get it over with.

"Take care of yourself," Nico said to her when they exchanged goodbyes. "Get some sleep." He gave her a perfunctory hug, something he rarely did, and his arm around her shoulders stayed there for a moment or two. She hadn't really fooled him, she supposed.

***

A few weeks passed before Ashley got around to visiting Madge Stewart. She'd become excessively busy again. This was in part because of an unfortunate quarrel with Aram. When he'd found out that she and Jon Perez were history, he'd expressed robust if ill-advised pleasure. It turned out that Aram, on his own and under the influence of Ashley's training, had done a little quiet digging into Jon Perez. When Mirabel dropped the bomb, he'd been about to tell Ashley about the guy's visits to Isabel Jadois's apartment, and show her an awful selfie he'd dug up online of Jon fanning himself urbanely with a bunch of hundred dollar bills. The fan of bills was bad enough, the closest she'd ever come to getting a handle on the dodginess of Jon's business dealings, but it was the sense that everyone had seen through him except her that pushed her over the edge. Humiliated, she picked a stupid quarrel with Aram. She needed him, as a friend as well as a colleague, but couldn't bring herself to reach out.

Cité Jardin was transformed in the late May sunshine. It was lilac time, and there were massive banks of them blooming everywhere, every shade of pink and mauve mingling with deep magenta and creamy white. The day was still and the air was saturated with their aphrodisiac scent. Ashley was dimly aware that this moment, had it been fused with happiness, would have been unforgettable. Also that her outfit, an unravelling shaker sweater and jeans, was an affront to nature's display.

Madge had the kettle on and sandwiches and cupcakes awaited them in the small conservatory overlooking the green backyard. Ashley learned that her uncle and Madge were still an item. Love is always on the go, k.d. lang was singing on Madge's radio. But not quite yet, for Madge and Eric.

Over tea Madge delivered the surprising news that Mirabel and Isabel had already left the city. The house in Westmount was on the market for the requisite fabulous sum but they'd jumped the gun and acquired an old farmhouse with some land attached, on Ile d'Orléans. It was minutes from the bridge and had a view of Quebec City's Cap Diamant in the distance. Yes, Madge agreed, it was sudden. But they'd found a place they loved, with the pastoral solitude they craved, and the location allowed them to be close enough to the city. And to hospitals.

Isabel and Madge, Ashley knew, were personal friends. But these remarks tapped against her tired brain on a couple of levels.

"I always thought of them as city slickers." She selected a cucumber sandwich triangle from the plate. "But what do you mean, near hospitals?"

Madge looked serious. "You weren't aware, then, that Isabel is ill? Very ill."

"No."

"She has lung cancer. She's being treated at the Hôtel-Dieu de Québec. She was holding her own for a while but she's had a relapse and it's progressing rapidly. It's no secret. I'm surprised Mirabel didn't tell you."

Major news. "I'm surprised too."

But Mirabel's look of strain now took on a new meaning for Ashley. Not to mention Isabel's hoarseness that Ashley had attributed to smoking or winter viruses. Everyone had more on their plate than you knew, she reminded herself, grudgingly. Being crossed in love made you self-absorbed, she'd begun to realize, so she made an effort. "I'm sorry. I did see changes in her, in both of them, recently. Isabel had begun to look old, I thought. I guess substitute sick for that. I'm learning that I miss a lot."

Madge's look of surprise told Ashley that she'd sounded more mournful than she'd intended. "It's true, illness aged Isabel. She'd begun to look much older than her sister."

"Well, she is the older sister."

"By twenty minutes, I understand."

"I'm not following you."

Madge smiled now. "You didn't know they're twins? It's true they don't look all that alike at a quick glance. That's the illness, partly, and how different their styles are. Pink and blue hair, septum piercings, all that. Isabel is myopic and she wears those coloured contact lenses. But yes, they're identical twins."

Ashley continued to stare with her mouth open and Madge laughed outright.

"Don't worry, Ashley, you're not the only one. Almost no one knows that. Apart from their different styles, they don't move in the same circles, so it tends not to come out. I think probably just me and Charles. Well, Charles *did*."

Ashley felt like a huge door had swung open in front of her. But the light shining through made it too bright to see anything. "Charles ..." She groped for something. "He has—had—an unusual relationship to the two of them, didn't he?"

Madge looked a little quizzical now. "Do you mean their mother?"

Ashley shook her head. Although she would get to that. "No, I mean the romantic triangle. Charles first dates Isabel, and then dumps her for the identical twin sister. It's like a plot in one of your novels."

"Yes, as a matter of fact, *Les Roys de Rosemont*," Madge said demurely. "But that situation ended in someone jumping off a cliff for love. Unless they were pushed, the novel leaves it uncertain." She refilled teacups. "Isabel, however, had no such strong feelings for Charles, I'm sure. Isabel just met him first, they dated for a while, she introduced Charles to Mirabel, and that was, supposedly, the *coup de foudre*. Isabel told me all this herself."

The conversation was making them both hungry and the little cakes were disappearing fast.

"There were no hard feelings?"

"None that I could see." Madge appeared torn between silence and saying more.

"Why did you mention their mother?"

Madge tucked a flyaway wisp of grey hair behind her ears while looking out over the lawn, where a robin was engaged in the business of tugging a juicy worm out of the ground.

"I don't think this is a secret," she said slowly, "or I wouldn't tell you. Also, you've done a lot for the Rivières. They've both told me so, and I think you deserve to know, to understand."

Ashley nodded encouragingly. She didn't say a word, sensing even juicier revelations still in the balance.

"It's not even important, in a way. It's just odd. It points to how truth can be stranger than fiction. According to Isabel, their mother had an affair with Charles. It was one of those long-term but very secret relationships that sometimes occur between a boss and an employee. She was beautiful, older. He was young, didn't even want to lead Holopherne. She helped him through the transition after his father's death. She was very capable although not especially well-educated, and he gave her that promotion in return. They were lovers for a long time, until she and her husband died in that car crash."

Ashley kept her tone deliberately casual. "Mirabel hinted at this, it seemed more than possible." More than possible in her lurid imaginings, but she wanted to spur Madge on to more admissions. First the revelation of twinship, now this, which seemed uniquely significant on its own.

Madge hardly needed encouragement. If her political poetry took no prisoners, she was also Esmerelda LaFlamme, whose natural element was melodrama. Ashley watched her waver and nod, unable to help herself. "Neither sister made a secret of it. After they became orphans, Charles was also helpful in preventing them from being sucked into the child welfare system. Few people want six-year-olds, and even fewer want to take two children at once. Charles used his contacts and position to find good homes for them." The expression grated on Ashley, made her think briefly of strays, like little Hubert.

"It was unfortunate they had to be separated. Very unfortunate. But the outcome could have been so much worse."

"Yes, I knew that too. But how did Isabel even meet Charles? Montreal's a big city."

"She tracked him down," Madge said. "When she came back from Laval, after getting her PhD, she approached him at some sort of social function. They became friendly, with the connection already there, and then dated. Charles, it must have struck you, wasn't without his quirks. His work had become his life, and he was one of those men not really made for the modern world. Out of touch. Of course various women threw themselves at him and he could take his pick."

How she loved her trite *tournures de phrase,* Ashley thought. And how Ashley loved them too since they appeared to grease the confession's wheels.

"It was probably the desire for an heir that finally caused him to marry. Plus, let's be honest, Mirabel isn't what you would call a modern woman."

Ashley thought furiously. Sex with the bold Isabel, procreation with her submissive twin. Yes, that worked with the Saint Cyr she'd known. Abandoning the pretense of discretion, she leapt to the connection of more dots. "Funny, in a way, since they weren't going to have any kids. One of the things you learn about another person when you share accommodation with them is whether they're on the birth control pill."

A tidbit, but at last she'd scored a hit with Madge. The other looked mildly interested and thoughtful. "I'm not surprised if Mirabel didn't share everything with her husband. There was a great age gap, and he could be overbearing. She was restless, burdened by the wifely role. A Saint Cyr heir would have been an additional burden. No wonder she ran away to Paris. She was bound to have her secrets."

Did Esmerelda LaFlamme's plots have the last word for every human situation then? Madge's faint smile was like the Mona Lisa's, a Mona Lisa working out details for her next potboiler. "Men are good at pretending—what if women were even better?"

The thing that struck Ashley most of all was the total absence of judgement in the other's voice. Another question occurred to her. "How on earth did Isabel and Mirabel know about their mother's affair with Charles? They were so young when she died."

"Charles told Mirabel. He apparently said he thought it wasn't a secret he could keep from her."

"God! I would have kept it." Ashley swigged the last of her tea. Suddenly, she had to get out of there.

Madge brought a shopping bag to Ashley at the door. "There's the fedora, and your magnificent semi-automatic weapon." Madge peered into the bag. "Your gloves, you won't need those for a while. That pink burner phone of yours … I'm surprised you didn't need that but in my books PIs always have lots of burners so I assumed you didn't have an immediate need for it. I've kept it charged." She looked up innocently at Ashley.

"That's—that's right," Ashley said, with what she hoped was a sincere smile.

She'd forgotten all about the pink phone she'd last seen Mirabel use in Paris. She'd been so suspicious at the time, so curious. Back in Montreal, she'd forgotten about it. A thing of Paris that had stayed in Paris.

But now, the impulse was instantaneous. Ashley had learned much today and the pink phone would help her learn more. And after the Kevin Black case she knew exactly who could reveal its secrets. So an excuse to make it up with Aram on top of everything. Oblivious to the great clustering lilacs, she congratulated herself as she hurried down the road.

As if that made it any less disreputable—but she was out of that zone and in another. Enquiring minds wanted to know.

* * *

She thought about the revelation that Mirabel and Isabel were twins as she drove home, without coming to any particular conclusion. She was sure there was more to unpack, but for now the mystery of the phone's contents called like a siren. Aram came over right away. They exchanged a few awkward words and bygones became bygones. Aram fiddled with the phone, said he wanted to take it back to his place and try a few things. Could he come back after supper?

Ashley put more effort into her own supper than she'd done in a while, and ate it on the back balcony, in the loveliness of the evening. Late May weather could still be brisk in Montreal, but this was an evening of milky mildness and bird song. Even the drab lane view was transformed through a veil of half-opened leaves on the weed tree. When she went in, she threw open all the windows and put on a sweater as freshness stole through the house.

Aram came just before dark. He had a funny look on his face. "I got in all right. Under the oh-so-cute Hello Kitty case is a reliable disposable android smart phone. It's not Mirabel's though. It's her sister's—Isabel? She used it exclusively to communicate with Mirabel. Mirabel probably had her own. That's my guess." He scrolled through what he'd found, showing Ashley as he went. "There's a record of calls. They texted each other too, and I was able to get into a gmail account, Isabel's, but not in her name. Again, emails are exchanged exclusively with Mirabel, who also had a gmail account that wasn't in her name. The content identifies them."

He was making a deliberate effort to be business-like. The funny look, it dawned on Ashley, was unease. She had a flash of intuition. "Is it about Paris?" Aram knew a great deal about their Parisian adventures by now.

"Yes. And afterwards."

"Whatever's there has to stay between us." She hoped it wasn't too late with this warning. She hadn't told him why she wanted to know the contents of the phone.

"Of course!" Aram looked almost relieved. "I mean, it seems to have been all some kind of game anyway. At least, that's what *they* call it ..."

"A game?"

"With a capital G. I didn't read everything, so you might understand it better. I know you didn't tell me to review the content. It was just that I had to read some to figure out who was who ..." Aram's voice trailed away.

Ashley's heartbeat was quick but she spoke calmly. "Sure. I'll look at everything myself. Summarize for me what you found."

"I went back to February. Tell me if I'm remembering this wrong, but Isabel never went to Paris as far as you're concerned, did she?"

"What? Oh, she said she was coming, but no."

"Well, she went. She was in Paris, at least for some of the time. You can't tell why. Just, the Game. But she talks about you seeing her one day on the street, far from Mirabel's *appart*. She freaks out about this, calls it a *putain de coïncidence,* which is very Parisian honestly. Then Mirabel freaks out. Then they both seem to make light of it."

Ashley remembered with a heavy shock her sighting of the woman in red, with the lace disguise painted over her face. Even the small mannerisms of the woman had looked familiar, conjured Mirabel. Was that because even the twins' gestures bore an uncanny resemblance?

"But why?"

"That's the thing, Ashley, there doesn't seem to be a reason. She mentions a *Carnaval* event, also a meeting with a French academic colleague, but there's no reason provided for the secrecy of Isabel's visit. Read it yourself, you'll see."

Ashley just said: "I will. Go on."

"Okay, fast forward to Montreal ... This is Mirabel now texting her sister." He scrolled, pointed.

"We saw" Thug Two at Ashley's place today.

"But I never saw him."

"'We saw' is in quotation marks. Anyway, it goes on." He scrolled, pointed again.

Remember when you talked about hearing steps that weren't there? Well, there happened to be heavy steps just then on the stairs! Isa, I told you—we trust to luck. She and I escaped out a convenient back way.

"She wouldn't let me look! It was that fat postman!"

"Fat postman?"

"Never mind. Go on."

"The next one freaked me out completely. You know that time that Mirabel says she was rammed and driven off the road, in eastern Montreal? Well, that was staged, from what I could tell."

Ashley stared. "Staged? How in hell can you stage so much car damage?"

"Well, it probably didn't feel staged for the other driver. Listen, you should look at what they say and see if you come to a different conclusion. I don't want to put ideas in your head." Under the light of the desk lamp the beaded moisture on Aram's forehead was visible. "What it looks like to me ... is Mirabel deliberately collided with a car and then deliberately drove off the road and hit a fence."

Stunned, Ashley shook her head. "You—you have to be mistaken, Aram. Mirabel would have been taking her life in her own hands." She thought. "Plus, the other driver would have reported her."

Aram shrugged helplessly. "They talk about that. Mirabel says she's okay with the risk. And they both say things like: 'Let's see if anyone reports it.'" He pointed once more. "They don't seem to care! They're very casual about the whole thing. They're *curious*."

Ashley seized the phone from him. She read. Aram was right. There were occasional references to the Game, one absurd comment from Mirabel along the lines of what did Isabel think Joan of Arc would have done.

Ashley sat back in her chair and rubbed her face. Aram finally broke in on her thoughts to say he was going home if she didn't need him anymore. "It's kind of amazing, isn't it?" He spoke ruefully. "How much people will put in writing. We all do it, too."

Ashley just nodded speechlessly. There were another few weeks of texting to read, and she already feared what she was going to find out.

When Aram was gone she did a little quick research into identical twins, DNA and fingerprints. It was as she surmised. She began to read the texts.

She'd been half right.

On the night of the death of Charles Saint Cyr, Isabel and Mirabel had only phoned each other, not texted. Ashley herself remembered them talking while she was in the Audi with Mirabel, driving out to Alibi Land on the eastern shore. But during that afternoon the sisters had exchanged several texts.

Isabel wanted to know when she should head out for The Stag House, and Mirabel, sounding very much in charge, had told her she could check in whenever was convenient, but a little darkness would be good. Then Isabel asked how Mirabel was arranging the time. Mirabel replied that the Fiat was still in front of The Stag House, and that Charles, with his taxi phobia, would want a member of the staff to drive him over to collect it after dinner, when he found out she'd taken the Audi. When that happened, she'd call Isabel on some pretext. It would be the signal to get ready, that he was on his way. She'd timed the drive. Twenty-five minutes in average traffic. After it was over, all Isabel had to do was leave quickly, and wait. Once Mirabel got the call from the police, Isabel would next hear from her. There were general allusions to the Game, and philosophical comments by Mirabel, that would have been grandiose had they not been so bizarre, about the power of luck.

But Mirabel was not without an eye for detail. She wrote:

I should still be with Ashley when the police call, since the drive is such a long one. I might even ask her to call you. After all, I'll be terrified the bullets were meant for me. Plus I'll be a sorrowing young widow by then. It would be the right note to strike, wouldn't it?

The sisters were agreed. It was the right note to strike. It was even, they concurred, the right thing to do.

20

IF THEY SAY I NEVER LOVED YOU

TIME PASSED AND Ashley spoke to no one about her ideas. More than ideas. She was sure.

She'd found out that identical twins shared DNA but not fingerprints. The police had dusted The Stag House for fingerprints and taken DNA. Mirabel's DNA might have been highly revealing. But they'd only ever taken her fingerprints.

Ashley had ruminated long and hard. A call to the police, even just to her cop pal Nico. Isabel's prints or a DNA swab from Mirabel ... Charles's murder solved? But still she did nothing.

The thought that she was possibly impeding a criminal investigation came and went. The texts were suspicious, but were they suspicious enough? It was far from clear whether they provided the police with grounds for a warrant to fingerprint or take a DNA swab. Approaching the police at this point, she told herself, would be premature.

What really bugged her, if she was being honest, was not knowing why. Any reason she could come up with seemed incomplete. Why would two sisters, one of them terminally ill, conspire to kill the husband of one of them? Money had to be part of the answer. But only money? There was a vexed history between the Rivières and the Saint Cyrs. Enough to explain homicide? The sisters had had difficult lives, maybe much more than Ashley knew. When you ratted someone out to the police, it was better to know nothing at all about them or everything. Stuck in the middle, you just worried about consequences. Unintended harm. It was paralysing. Ashley therefore preserved a troubled silence, as May gave way to glorious June.

She had other things to think about, during the long June days. Roy and Lucie and Lilou were back together again. Roy wore a left-over valley of the shadow look but seemed deeply thankful. Lucie, mutedly happy with the turn of events, had begun to show, and Ashley was ruining expensive yarn trying to knit baby clothes for the antici-pated bundle of joy. Chantale had promised to come over and help her unpick everything so she could start over with a simpler pattern.

Michel, she told Ashley, was talking about them all moving in together, but she for one was in no hurry. She liked her life right now, in her home in the Point with Marie Ambre and all her friends and neighbours. "Love isn't always what you think it is, and it sure isn't what other people tell you it is," she informed Ashley. Ashley nodded, feeling sheepish.

She rarely thought of Jon Perez these days, except to wonder at the mystery of it all. The meaning, the mood, even the hurt that had followed—all just melted into thin air. She would deliberately sum-mon to mind the heady days of March and April, the delicious rush, all the firsts between them, to see if she could recapture any of it. But Jon might as well have been a distant acquaintance, for all the impact his memory now had on her.

She'd become aware of her new indifference around the time the lightbulb had come on regarding Charles's death. The association between these in her mind was unclear. In the general lifting of masks, had it been easier to let go of the mask of Ashley-in-love? Whatever the reason, these old selves, the old Jon and the old Ashley, had van-ished, like stray thoughts and trivial dreams abandoned with hardly a second thought.

You could mope and stew endlessly over the mystery of love. Its psychology, its anatomy, its myriad forms—although Ashley felt that Nature gave no fucks whatsoever for these distinctions, true love and shallow infatuation being all one to her. But still in its sheer power it baffled. A labyrinth within the labyrinth of her life.

"I fell for him like a ton of bricks and now I can't feel a thing," she told her brother on the phone one day.

"These things happen."

"Not to you."

"You should forget about it. Flushed down the toilet of experience."

"Thanks for the image."

"It's going to be a boy, Ashley. We saw it on the ultrasound." Roy was jubilant.

Her brother's advice was good, though. Knitting another garter stitch row of her modest baby blanket, Ashley reflected afterwards that, in view of the overpopulation of the planet, there was surprising consolation in people being born all the time.

***

If Ashley thought less about Jon Perez, she thought more about the Rivière sisters. In the end all she could conclude was that Mirabel had wanted the money for herself and her dying sister, and hadn't loved her husband anyway. The latter being glaringly obvious, when you thought about it. And, of course, she, Ashley, had been monumentally used. Also glaringly obvious. But why this thing called the Game? Why call it that? Perhaps thinking that way reduced the women's feelings of guilt. Or gave them courage to plot.

Madge Stewart and her uncle Eric were still an item, according to an enthusiastic Antoinette, and the thought crossed Ashley's mind to do a little more digging about the Saint Cyrs via Madge.

But in the end she didn't. She didn't want to be responsible for what she might find out.

On the whole though, people were easy to kill.

***

In the middle of a mundane midsummer workday, an old-fashioned postcard arrived for Ashley. It was one of those vintage sepia post-cards displaying an old photograph of daily life in the city. In this case, a French city that might have been Paris. It was postmarked Paris, at any rate.

On a tree-lined street with Second Empire houses in the back-ground, a young man with a peaked cloth cap and a mover's apron, hardly more than a boy, stood in front of an old-fashioned moving truck with spoked wheels. Ashley flipped the postcard idly. The message was a scrawl. She turned the postcard over again. Her stomach performed a bungee jump. On the side of the truck was written *Paris et Europe,* and underneath, in big bold lettering, *Déménagements Barthélemy et fils.*

Ashley was sure she was remembering correctly. *Déménagements Barthélemy et fils* was the name Mireille Borel had given, in a flight of fancy, to the imaginary getaway truck that would take her along with Raymond Boissier's stolen loot to the south of France.

What the hell was this? She stared at the postcard again. Was it really even a postcard, or was it a photograph made to look like a postcard? There was no fine print that might offer a clue. She studied the human figure closely. A strippling, willowy, the face partly in shadow due to the big cloth cap, so it was hard to say whether the face was dark-skinned. It might have been.

Ashley looked at the scrawl again. The signature contained a capital M, perhaps a capital B: but, really, it could have been any-thing. The message seemed equally indecipherable. But as she stared, words emerged. She saw *masque* and *je* something *finirai pas* ... It took her a minute of Googling to find the words, from a quotation from someone called Claude Cahun: *Sous ce masque un visage. Je n'en finirai pas de soulever tous ces visages.* And then, simply, *Adieu, mes chères amies!*

Whether this was a case of life imitating postcard art, or its opposite, the message was abundantly clear.

Ashley had thought at first that the Bortnik brothers must have taken back what was theirs, according at least to the gangster code. Then she'd wondered whether Raymond Boissier hadn't somehow gotten in ahead of them on that eventful night by the Seine. Just recently, the French investigating magistrate had called her in relation to her statement, and during their discussion had told her that Raymond was still missing, leading the police to think that he'd met the same fate as his accomplice. Ashley had been guiltily relieved. A happy-ever-after ending for the Bortniks would be safer all round. She'd never given a passing thought to Mireille Borel. Unless the postcard was an elaborate and pointless joke, Mireille must have gotten away with her bold scheme after all.

Memories of those evenings of wine and snacks in the rue des Arabes *appart,* and their phantasmagorical night out on the town during *Carnaval,* came flooding back. Ashley felt a sudden visceral urge to speak with Mirabel, to ask her whether she'd received a mysterious postcard as well, to speculate, assess. But that, evidently, was impossible—and Ashley felt inside herself the pinch of regret.

She looked up Claude Cahun instead. A non-gender conforming artist and photographer, a rebel during WW2, imprisoned by the Nazis. Cahun's health had been affected by this and the artist had died relatively young. Cahun's photographs explored the mysteries of identity, and were joylessly bold—visionary at the expense of happiness. Ashley found herself wondering whether Mireille was happy now, and this thought led her to wonder about Mirabel's happiness. But there she could not go, even as the pinprick of this thing resembling regret probed her secret places.

At 3:47 am, Ashley woke to thudding consciousness. She thought: *What if Mireille had gone even further?* She pictured the péniche held fast in the ice, its priceless contraband sending a signal through the dark. That night on the quai de la Rapée had been the first fine night after the storm. Could Raymond and Mireille have been around? It was probable the Bortniks had sent reinforcements. Before the sun rose, had Mireille, with or without the help of her *Marseillais* brothers, contrived to offer the Bortniks the consolation prize of Raymond? Ashley remembered Mireille on the rue des Arabes rooftop, baring her teeth as she faced down the snowstorm. The two Miras side by side, a pair of *jeunes veuves* out of Esmerelda LaFlamme, already anticipating their inheritances.

* * *

The three of them were sitting at Ashley's kitchen table. It was a rainy day in late August and Ashley had the lights on.

"I talked to Aram about this, now that he's your associate," Chantale Barry was saying. Stirring her coffee, Ashley let the alleged promotion pass. "He said I should bring this to you."

Aram Idris nodded seriously. Honestly, she might as well make him her associate. Recently graduated, he was practically a full-time employee with her these days. From job to job, he'd grown in leaps and bounds. He even had the look of a pro, restrained, a little dry.

Ashley pushed the milk carton across the table. "All right. I assume it's either about Michel or Jacques."

"Oh—no," Chantale said. She lifted Huey's claws out of her shirt and placed him gently on the table surface. He promptly rappelled up her sleeve again. "It's about Dominique. Remember Dominique Taillon? She was at my holiday party?"

The lively heavyset woman with brilliant eyes. "Oh, that Dominique. Sure. What about her?"

"She's disappeared. She's been missing for almost a month. I

302

told the cops. They didn't seem that interested. Seems like she owed some back rent at her apartment and they thought she'd just decided to disappear. A civil matter, they said. They said there was no indication of foul play. But I'm worried."

Ashley suppressed a sigh. "What's worrying you?"

"I think someone killed her."

"Jesus, Chantale, what makes you say that?"

"Dominique was—is—actually a very shy person."

Ashley thought of the swaggering woman with the unnaturally green eyes. She nodded noncommittally.

"I told her she should get out more. She knew how I'd met Michel. I told her she should take a chance on life, like me."

What had happened to the breach between the two women? This made it sound like ancient history. She suppressed a gesture of impatience. "But why do you think she's been *killed?*"

"She put a lonely hearts ad on some websites." Chantale frowned. "The free ones. I don't think it was Craiglist or Kijiji, but like them ..."

Aram spoke up. "She was contacted by a man and they began to email each other. She created a dedicated email for this, so it's not as dangerous as it sounds. I read the emails—Chantale showed me. They had lots to say to each other. The guy seemed fabulous. Show her the picture, Chantale."

Chantale fiddled, held up her phone. The man looked like an Iranian film star of the seventies.

"He gave his name as Ahmed Ben Hassan."

"*Toujours les Musulmans,*" Chantale muttered vaguely to herself, with spectacular obliviousness. She hadn't been able to wrap her mind around Serbian arms deals at all, and had her favourite scapegoats, like half the city.

Aram cleared his throat, looking pained. "*Any*way. Since that's the name of the sheik in that old Rudolf Valentino silent movie from the 1920s, there's a good chance it's made up. The emails carry on, and then they agree to meet. They make arrangements to meet in a coffee shop in the Quartier des spectacles, one evening. And then the emails just end."

Chantale resumed. "I called her a couple of days later to find out how her date went, and the phone went to voicemail. I haven't been able to reach her since. I've tried email, phone, texting. After a while, I went to Maisonneuve, the Viauville end, to her place, and got an earful from her landlord, who lives downstairs. He said she skipped out. But I don't think she did. I think Ahmed Ben Hassan lured her somewhere. I think she'd dead."

Ashley looked at Aram, who shrugged slightly and said: "It doesn't look good."

It didn't.

"Did you let the police know about this aspect of the case?" Ashley asked Chantale.

"I tried. They just kept saying they were *very busy* just now."

Ashley doodled on her yellow pad.

"It was always the two of us against the world," Chantale said, triggering a distant memory in Ashley of these words. "For her to leave like that without a trace, never even get in touch with me ..." Chantale scrutinized the table, avoiding Ashley's gaze. "She wouldn't do that."

Ashley with deliberation flipped the yellow pad to a fresh sheet. The truth was out there, as someone or other had said. "I need to understand more about this."

She gave Chantale her best private investigator stare. "Tell me your story all over again. And this time, Chantale—are you listening to me?—for the love of Mike don't leave out the parts you left out the first time."

EPILOGUE

IT WAS ANOTHER cold and cloudy fall afternoon, more than a year later. As Ashley drove along Ile d'Orléans's winding rural roads, she could sense the huge presence of the river—in the blurred edges of things, the vaulting sense of emptiness beyond the yellow treeline. Church bells rang out on the misty air. Église Sainte-Jeanne-d'Arc, she noticed as she drove by the old stone building. A fitting place for such a church, dedicated to the little maid of Orleans.

Ashley had left Montreal before dawn and now she was tired from the long drive. She hoped Mirabel Saint Cyr would offer her coffee. If it came to that, she was ravenous too. She hadn't realized just how big the island was. She caught glimpses on the horizon of the grey sea-like Saint Lawrence as she drove, but the island was its own complete world of peaceful hills and dales, winding roads, unspoiled woodland and absurdly picturesque villages. Also lots of small churches and big gas stations.

The "cottage" for which Mirabel had given her directions was anything but. It was built on a slope above encircling woodland, a grand sprawl of clapboard wings, with a wide veranda looking back to Cap Diamant and the clustered buildings of Quebec City, matchstick stubs in the distance. Besides the Audi and the Fiat, there were a few cars parked nearby and Ashley supposed that Mirabel, as always, couldn't live without staff. Towering pines framed the rear and sides of the house and gave it an air of seclusion. Under the heavily overcast autumn sky, there was a darkness to the scene.

Ashley had messaged Mirabel once she'd crossed the bridge, so she'd be expected.

Mirabel's completely unexpected text, the previous week, had been simple: *Ashley, I often think of you. We're still on Ile d'Orléans. Madge told us you took Isabel's pink phone. But there's more to tell, if you want to hear it. Would you visit us?*

Life, like a fast-flowing river, had moved on for Ashley since the death of Charles Saint Cyr, and she'd even considered refusing. If she acquired more information, for a start, she'd have to decide what she would do with it. But curiosity got the better of her, and here she was. She rang the doorbell.

It was a shock to see Isabel Jadois at the door, but an Isabel transformed, restored apparently to health, the years fallen away from her. It was an even greater shock when the woman spoke, saying: "C'est moi, Ashley, c'est Mirabel."

Mirabel seemed to know that Ashley would mistake her for her twin. Her hair was longer, had some coloured streaks in it, and she wore an Isabel-themed South American pullover over a long blue linen skirt with ankle boots. Her face was neither hers nor Isabel's. The vagueness was all gone; the gaze was calm but alert, perhaps ironic. Mirabel's startling beauty, unspoiled by tobacco and illness, remained.

"Isabel is in the palliative ward at the *Hôtel-Dieu*," she explained. "The end is near now. The doctors can't explain why she even lived so long. But they say now that she has days to live. You'll forgive me when I tell you that our meeting today has to be short. I will have to go back to the hospital."

They were now in a big living room with the same view as the veranda. It was a spectacular space, but its white distemper walls, aged pine floor and comfortably shabby furnishings gave it an air of simplicity.

Mirabel turned to Ashley. "It's good to see you, Ashley. I didn't think you'd agree to come." For a moment Ashley caught a glimpse of the old Mirabel, the wavering eyes seeking escape or disguise, not sure of her worth in this or any other world.

"We have a condo in the old city and I'm often there these days, because of Isabel. But I wanted to meet you here today."

A woman looked in at the door, a small boy at her side.

Mirabel's smile lit up her face, as she said: "This is Daniel. *Dis bonjours à la madame, Dany.*" And then, turning to the woman: "*Le café, s'il te plaît, Solange.*"

"Short and to the point is good." Ashley sat down.

Solange returned almost immediately with a tray which held a coffee service and some food. Ashley tucked in with relief. She sensed she'd need sustenance for what she was about to hear. Mirabel sat back in her armchair and was silent for a moment.

"I know you have your ideas," she said at last. "You don't have to tell me what they are but, with the exchanges you must have seen on Isa's phone, you would have connected the dots. We waited, Isa and I, waited to see what you'd do. When it seemed to us you'd do nothing, we were grateful. I wanted to wait longer, until after Isa is gone, before I contacted you. But Isa wanted me to offer you an explanation, before she died. She—prayed about it and said it was the right thing to do."

Those words again. Also, did murderers pray? The thought shocked, but Ashley couldn't see why not.

"This isn't a confession. We don't want to make any admissions." Mirabel's tone, as she uttered these bald statements, was gentle, reasonable. "Anyway, none of that is necessary. Not to us, anyway. We just wanted you to meet Daniel, really. You always struck us as the kind of person who wanted to understand things. Dany is the why."

Perhaps just to hear her own voice, Ashley said: "Your son or Isabel's?"

"Mine." Mirabel savoured the word. "He was our brother's son, but he's mine now. Gilles. You never knew about Gilles. He died. We're now looking after Daniel. I should say I am." She offered a croissant to Ashley and selected one herself.

"Have another. I can tell you're hungry. So am I. For a change —there's been so much anxiety with Isa. I'll tell you two things. One is the story of what happened to my family. The other is what Isa and I thought about it and what we decided to do. Or let's say the outcome we wanted." She smoothed her soft blue skirt, a thoughtful madonna. "I know you won't waste time with recriminations, because there isn't time to waste anyway."

Ashley took a gulp of coffee. "Okay. Just to pick up on that, I know about identical twins, DNA and fingerprints."

Mirabel nodded eagerly. "Of course, you do." She hesitated, frowned. "I'm hesitating because I want to get the dates right for you. My parents died in 1992. We didn't have any close relatives, at least no one who wanted to look after twin girls and a boy of barely two. I never understood at first why Charles got so involved in helping find homes for us, until he told me that he'd had a long-standing affair with our mother and felt responsible for us." Mirabel pursed her lips. "Charles and his megalomania. He must always place himself at the centre of everything and play the saviour to what he's already destroyed."

Ashley didn't correct her use of the present tense.

"That pretty much describes my marriage to him, but never mind that. He personally arranged adoptions. I got the Duvals, Isa got the Jadois, at the other end of the province. Where she became expert with guns. And Gilles, adopted by a family called d'Entremont, was supposed to have gotten the prize because they were ultra-rich and had no children of their own. Rex D'Entremont was one of Charles's close business associates, a man Charles had some risky arrangements with. These plans were, however, going to transform Holopherne from a multi-million dollar enterprise to a billion dollar one. Isa and I think that's the reason Charles didn't say anything when he found out about the abuse Gilles was suffering at the hands of the d'Entremonts. From the man himself, who was a paedophile, but the wife was in it too."

"How do you know this? I mean, how do you know that it happened and how do you know Charles knew?"

"Gilles told us. His life, until he ran away from home at the age of fifteen, was one long waking nightmare. He told Charles, he said, more than once, when he was a little boy. Maybe Charles didn't believe him, but Isa and I are pretty sure he would have. We believe he kept silent to protect his business interests." A pause. "And of course to save face." Another pause. "And perhaps even to avoid prosecution himself, since who knows how long he knew the true state of things, of Rex's nature. It's a crime, you know, not to report child abuse."

Ashley put down her half eaten croissant. The room no longer felt as pleasant as before.

"I was nineteen when I began to look for my twin. Don't ask me why it took so long. We were so helpless when we were young. Psychologically lost. And remember that was 2005. Social media wasn't so advanced then. I was still in Europe and Isa was a student here, and we didn't even get to meet right away." Mirabel's face assumed a blankness Ashley had often seen. "I'll leave it to you to imagine what it was like to be reunited with a twin sister after fourteen years. Once I was back in Montreal we decided we'd try and find Gilles. We had terrible luck. He'd run away from the d'Entremonts by then."

Mirabel cast a quick look at her watch. "I want to keep track of the time. We didn't find him until five years later. He was by then an addict. He committed suicide a year after that. He left behind a newborn son." Mirabel's voice had become flatter and flatter with these statements. "I'll just focus on the facts here. Gilles had told us about his life. We were fascinated that Charles Saint Cyr was still swanning around Montreal, one of the city's leading citizens, an admired patron of the arts—all that ..."

Ashley jumped in. "I can understand why you blamed him." She was careful with her words. "But why not blame d'Entremont?"

"Charles was the one who was ultimately responsible. He could have done something. And then d'Entremont died anyway. We tried to maintain a relationship with Gilles's girlfriend, which wasn't that successful. She was an addict too. She kept thinking we had money, wanted to exchange contact with Daniel for money. But neither of us had any money at all! Isa had her student loans to exist on and I was back living with the Duvals, although they wanted me gone, you could tell."

A brief silence, another look at the watch. "I told you about Isa meeting up with Charles, and then me. He and I married a year later."

Ashley couldn't refrain from blurting out: "Are you going to tell me why you married him?"

"It was a good way to be closer to him." Without irony, she added: "He had no problems switching. He was able to call us both Belle."

"Convenient." It was dawning on Ashley how much she'd always disliked Saint Cyr. Not that you could condone Mirabel. "And just as he loved you in his own way, you loved him in your own way."

"In a way." The ambiguous *moue* Ashley remembered. "You always seem worried about that aspect of things, Ashley. I'll explain as well as I can. I did fall in love with Charles at first, for about a month or two. Which was a great surprise to me, actually. I knew what he'd done to Gilles, but it didn't seem to matter. He's rich, good-looking in that tormented saint way. He wooed me with poetry. He's easy to fall in love with. And then my feelings just died, or changed, entered a second phase. You *could* say two months is too short for real love. That's one opinion. But how often is marriage ever based on love? Most often it's two lonely people, frightened of being alone, who enter into something half way between a friendship and a business relationship. There's nothing wrong with that, but if one of them betrays the other, it would disintegrate into enmity just as quickly as any *grande passion*. My second phase was sex. There's nothing wrong with that either."

Ashley now identified what was buried in the ambiguity of the other's regard: a veiled superiority. And that Mirabel had always looked like that. She thought about Raymond and Léandre. All that desire witnessed up close had gone straight to her head, but it dawned on her they'd been of no importance to Mirabel.

"The following year Daniel's mother overdosed and our little nephew went into foster care. We had to do something." Her tone remained mild. "It was all just an act of imagination at first. For a long long time, really. We did think of other things, alternatives … even, for example, getting Charles to adopt Dany."

"Did you ask him?"

"He'd have refused. He only wanted biological heirs; he told me this. Isa and I also talked about Isa adopting him, but by then she'd been diagnosed with cancer."

"This act of imagination? Was it what you called the Game?"

"Yes. You understand so much. But France changed everything. It began with Raymond. When Raymond went missing, we thought: What if the police think Charles, the jealous husband, killed him? But that fizzled … Really, we had the most terrible ideas. They were all ridiculous. We were like a couple of six-year-olds trying to plan something."

Mirabel's childishly light-hearted smile disturbed Ashley deeply. They *were* like a couple of six-year-olds, she thought. Something had stopped growing inside them when life tore them apart. Something very fundamental had been arrested. It must be that.

"What exactly did you hope to get out of your plan?"

"Money. We needed money. I needed my inheritance and freedom. I wasn't wrong either. I've adopted Dany now. It's what I've been busy with all this time. It took a lot of work. Since last month, I'm officially Daniel's mother. Isa and I are both so happy this happened before she died. We've waited so long."

Solange appeared in the doorway. The little boy ran in, clung to Mirabel. He was fair like his aunts, a little peaked, underdeveloped for his age. He seemed a nervous kid, and no wonder, Ashley thought.

"The hospital called, Madame," Solange murmured. "I'll get Antoine to bring round the car."

Mirabel stood up abruptly, the child still clutching her blue skirts with small frantic white hands. "I have to go, Ashley."

Ashley's mind now desperately circled the remaining details, as if these were of the utmost importance. "Why the pink phones?"

"Privacy."

"What was Isabel doing in Paris?"

"That was pure coincidence that you ran into her. She came because I wanted her. After having been separated for so long, we—don't do well apart."

"But why not just tell me it was her?"

"Because, Ashley, it gave us *the idea*."

The idea ... To use the drama of Raymond's disappearance and its aftermath as a deliberate distraction back in Montreal, and substitute one sister for another, so that the likely suspect, Mirabel, would have a cast-iron alibi. To use Ashley herself, to furnish the alibi.

"That," Ashley said, "is just the dumbest plan!" She couldn't help herself. "How could you possibly think it would succeed? It's as full of holes as Swiss cheese. The police could have decided to take DNA swabs of everyone. They didn't even believe your story of Bortniks transplanted. You couldn't have counted on the Cottage

Grove bombing to distract them. Your sister left her incriminating phone where it could be found. You had to know a private investigator would be suspicious!"

"You summarize things so well, Ashley. No, I agree, all our ideas were terrible. And don't even give us credit for all that about twins sharing DNA but not fingerprints. We didn't know any of that until later."

They were now standing at the front door, Dany in Mirabel's arms. He was playing with his mother's coloured locks, not understanding any of this English conversation.

"You know what a game is like." Mirabel spoke quietly. "It's a game, so you say: We'll see what happens. We could have stepped back at any time, too, but clearly luck was on our side. We did succeed in the end."

The Audi was pulling up. Ashley couldn't let go. "You got what you wanted, like that Russian oligarch's wife, without paying full price." She hadn't meant to sound so accusatory.

Mirabel's regard became fixed, glassy. Beneath the fringe of lashes her pupils appeared dilated so that the blue hardly showed. "You've been fully paid."

Ashley thought about this last exchange, as she headed towards the bridge back to the mainland, while curtains of cold rain moved across the landscape. Mirabel's parents, brother and husband were dead. Her sister was about to follow. In Dany, Mirabel had, with reckless disregard but surgical precision, salvaged all that was left. Success? It was hard to imagine their future. Although families were so strange. Not just because of the hurt and lies they harboured, but also for their ability to seal off the parts destroyed, force their way into other channels and flow free.

Ashley could hear the bells of the little church dedicated to Saint Joan ring out mournfully. Despite the bad driving conditions, she increased her speed. She wanted to get home as soon as possible. Home to the now strapping Hubert, home to her new associate

Aram who was holding the fort with an urgent case. Home to Roy and his family, augmented by a son, who were coming to Montreal on the weekend. She wanted to swap silly childhood memories with Antoinette. She wanted to drive to Waverley with Huey in his carrier, swing by the Abenaki reserve to say hi to anyone claiming to be a relative. And then she wanted to spend a weekend with her mother, and tell her, sharing chips on the couch, all about what had happened—well, some of what had happened. As much as she could.

The figure of Mirabel Rivière Duval Saint Cyr, standing with wordless dignity in the doorway with Dany in her arms, kept coming back to Ashley. A woman stripped to the bone. Unless of course she had just witnessed Mirabel's best role yet. If so, it hardly seemed to matter. The image of woman and child turned in Ashley's heart like a sword. The rain was practically a torrent now, the road awash, as if the river had broken its bounds and was obliterating the land. She slid her hands down so they were on opposite sides of the Interceptor's wheel. If she was to set aside the question of success, so must she lay down the question of paying, of retribution. It wasn't going away, in any case. The question would always be there for her to think about. Some things were irretrievably lost in the one-way flow of the river of time. But Ashley figured she'd face that bloody question again and again.

ACKNOWLEDGEMENTS

T HANK YOU TO the various people (you know who you are) who encouraged me to write. And thank you to the wonderful folks at Guernica. I couldn't be happier that April on Paris Street has found a home with you.

ABOUT THE AUTHOR

ANNA DOWDALL WAS born in Montreal and eventually moved back there, which surprised no one but her. She's been a reporter, a college lecturer and a horticultural advisor, as well as other things best forgotten. Her well-received domestic mysteries, *After the Winter* and *The Au Pair*, feature evocative settings and uninhibited female revenge, with a seasoning of moral ambiguity and noir(e).